Author's Note:

On May 15, 1940, just five days after Hitler's forces invaded Holland, Belgium, and Luxembourg, the Battle of Sedan, in France, ended. The German army was across the Meuse and into France, with a clear, virtually unopposed path to Paris. General Gamelin, the man in charge of the French forces and, therefore, the defense of France itself, had said that the Germans couldn't possibly reach Sedan before the 19th. They reached it on the 12th, and Sedan fell just three days later. The people in Paris began to evacuate, fleeing the capital. Surely the Germans would go straight to Paris. Yet they did not. They turned west to begin a race to the Channel, determined to cut the Allied forces in half and trap the bulk of the divisions in Belgium and northern France.

While the roads south from Paris grew increasingly crowded with refugees, slowing down Allied reinforcements on their way north, German Panzer divisions tore across France to the coast. Blitzkrieg raged, stunning France, and the world. By May 20th, the German army had reached the northern coast of France. With the British Expeditionary Force trapped in Belgium and northern France, England's entire trained army was at risk of being captured…or worse.

France was in chaos, and with it, so were her people. The German Blitzkrieg had triumphed, exceeding even the German High Command's own expectations. While there were many French divisions that fought heroically until the end, the battle had already been lost the moment the German Panzers entered the "impenetrable" Ardennes. France would fall.

And England would be the last to stand against the power and might of Nazi Germany.

Into the Iron Shadows

"It is not mere territorial conquest the enemy is seeking. It is the overthrow, complete and final, of the Empire and of everything for which it stands, and after that the conquest of the world."
~ *King George VI, May 24, 1940 Empire Day Speech*

Prologue

Berlin, Germany

Obersturmbannführer Hans Voss stood in the corridor with his hat under his arm, his eyes fixed pensively on the portrait of the Führer that hung on the wall opposite. He had been called back to Berlin from France abruptly, and he was fully aware of the reason for the summons. His lips tightened and his eyes narrowed as a wave of displeasure went through him.

He had failed.

Without warning, a door opened a few feet away and a short man in uniform came into the corridor, nodding to Voss.

"Standartenführer Dreschler is ready, Obersturmbannführer Voss," he announced soberly.

Hans turned and followed him through the door and into an outer room with two desks. A young woman was seated behind one, typing away, her eyes on the notes beside the machine. She didn't look up as they entered, keeping her attention on her work as the two men strode through the small room towards the office door a few feet away. A moment later, Hans was being ushered into the large, uncluttered office of his superior officer.

"Heil Hitler!"

He saluted smartly as Standartenführer Dreschler turned from a filing cabinet, a folder in his hand.

"Heil Hitler."

The older man walked over to his desk as the door closed softly, leaving the two men alone. Hans stood to attention before the large, heavy wood desk, his eyes fixed on the wall behind it. Standartenführer Dreschler sat in his chair and studied him in silence for a moment. Finally, after a long, heavy pause, he waved a hand.

"Sit down, Voss," he said tiredly. "I didn't call you back to discipline you, although you certainly deserve it."

Hans looked at him, startled, but recovered quickly. "Thank you, Standartenführer," he murmured, seating himself in one of the two chairs placed before the desk.

"I read your report this morning before you arrived in Berlin. Would you care to tell me in your own words what the hell went wrong? It seemed simple enough. The courier was in Belgium and you were in pursuit, were you not?"

"Yes, Standartenführer."

"Then why are you not presenting me with the packet of confidential and classified plans that were stolen in Stuttgart?"

"In all honesty, Standartenführer, because the Führer chose that precise moment to invade Belgium," Hans replied bluntly.

Dreschler sat back in his chair. "You're blaming the Führer and the advance of our troops for your failure?"

"No. I'm blaming the timing of the advance. If I had one extra day, just one, I would have not only the plans, but the courier as well. However, as it stands, the courier had fled Brussels before I even arrived. I followed, but never caught up. Not really."

"Yet your report says that you did." Dreschler sat forward and flipped open the folder on his desk, scanning the pages inside. "In Marle," he added after a moment.

"The report states that I believe I caught up with the courier in Marle, but I have no definite proof that it was the same courier. I did make that clear, I thought, in my summation."

The hint of a smile crossed Dreschler's face before being sternly repressed. "So you did. How careless of me to have overlooked it."

"I don't believe it was carelessness, Standartenführer."

"You're correct. I've spoken to Mueller in the Abwehr in Hamburg. He assures me that Eisenjager made every attempt to assist you. They, at least, believe it was the courier in Marle. Why don't you?"

"Without having been able to detain and question her, I cannot say that it was definitely the same woman who took the packet from the Dutch agent in Antwerp. I think it was, but I won't swear to it."

Dreschler studied him for a long time in silence, then sighed. "I've known you long enough to trust your judgement, but I also know that you pride yourself on providing proof. What about the man?"

"He was a Belgian that Eisenjager was looking for," Hans said with a shrug. "He was of no interest to me."

"And now they are both gone." Dreschler glanced down at the open folder before him. "At least the famous Eisenjager failed as well, eh? It would appear the whole operation was doomed from the start."

Hans was silent, not trusting himself to comment. The anger he felt towards the Abwehr assassin was still very sharp. When he'd embarked on his trek through Belgium and into France, hoping to retrieve a packet of stolen plans containing blueprints of the new underground bunkers at the munitions plants in Stuttgart, he had realized the odds of getting them back were reduced drastically with each passing mile. Yet he had almost succeeded; would have succeeded if it weren't for the presence of Eisenjager in Marle. If the assassin hadn't spooked the couple as they left the house, Hans would not only have got the packet back but would also have finally caught the elusive British agent known as Jian. Operation Nightshade would have been a success without him even trying! He had recognized the courier as the British agent as soon as he saw her, but that information had not been included in his report. Dreschler could never know that Jian had slipped through their fingers yet again.

"As I'm sure you're aware, the offensive into France is going well," Dreschler said, pulling Voss' attention back to the present. "The Generals expect to be in Paris within the month."

"Yes, I've heard."

"When that happens, I'm assigning you to Paris, Obersturmbannführer Voss."

Hans stared at him. "Standartenführer?"

Dreschler looked up with a grin. "There's no need to look so surprised, Voss. This latest setback notwithstanding, you are my best officer. You have done well in the past year, and I'd already made the decision to reward you. That decision stands. Once we are in control of Paris, you will be in charge of our operations there. It will be an extended posting, so I suggest that you use the next few weeks to make any arrangements here that will need to be made. You will be assigned quarters once you arrive. I trust you have no objections?"

"No, Standartenführer!" Hans exclaimed. "I thank you!"

"Good." Dreschler picked up a pen and unscrewed the top, preparing to sign the order on the desk. "As I said, this current loss notwithstanding, I need someone I can rely upon in Paris. You will be expected to identify and apprehend all Allied agents in the area, as well as all other enemies of the Reich." He glanced up suddenly, his gaze sharp. "Of course, I will expect no more incidents like Marle."

"Of course, Standartenführer."

"Good." He signed his name and replaced the cap on the pen, standing up. "Congratulations, Obersturmbannführer Voss. Paris is a coveted assignment, and you've earned the right to enjoy it. Perhaps it will also help get you closer to your elusive British agent."

Hans stood and clicked his heels together, bowing slightly. "Thank you for the opportunity to try, Standartenführer."

Chapter One

Paris, France
May 14, 1940

Evelyn Ainsworth sipped her coffee and gazed out over the early morning streets of Paris. Despite the uneasiness pervading the city, business continued as usual, and Parisians hurried along the pavement below on their morning errands. The sun shone brightly over the busy Rue de Grenelle, doing its part to add to the illusion that everything would be fine. Life would continue as normal until it no longer could, and then the citizens of Paris would adapt and readjust. It was how it had always been and, God-willing, was how it always would be.

Raising her eyes, Evelyn turned her attention to the horizon just visible between two buildings opposite. Beyond them flowed the Seine, and across the river lay the 8th Arrondissement where her uncle's Paris house was located. Were they still there? Or had Tante Adele and Uncle Claude taken their household to the château in the south where they would be assured some degree of safety for the time being? There was no way for Evelyn to know, and she daren't risk going to the house. They had no idea she was in Paris, nor could they, ever. As far as her family was concerned, she was safely tucked away on RAF Northolt, just outside of London.

"Marie! You've had a message back from London."

Evelyn turned to watch as a man with curly red hair came into the spacious sitting room, a piece of paper in his hand.

"It just came through," he continued, holding out the paper. "I hope it's good news."

Evelyn moved forward and took the paper. Jens Bernard only knew her by one name: Marie Fournier. When she had met him in Brussels a scant week earlier, it was the name she had been using, and she saw no reason to correct it now.

"Thank you."

Jens nodded and went over to the wireless, switching it on while she sat down at a small writing table near the window.

Into the Iron Shadows

"I'm going to see if there is any news yet from the border," he said, tuning the dial. He glanced over at her. "This won't disturb you?"

"Not at all."

Evelyn turned her attention to the coded message in her hand. They had arrived in Paris early yesterday morning after fleeing Marle ahead of two German agents, and yesterday evening, Jens had relayed a message to her handler in London with his radio. The response last night had been for her to await further instructions, but she hadn't expected those instructions to come quite so quickly.

Picking up a pencil, she set about decoding the message, her brow furrowed in concentration. She hadn't mentioned the possibility of bringing a Belgian radio operator back with her in her message, but if these instructions were for her to go home, she would have to give Bill fair warning. While she was anxious to get back to England, Evelyn was also equally as anxious not to leave Jens to his fate in a city that was strange to him. If it transpired that it was impossible for Jens to accompany her back to England, then she would be staying in France for the time being. Jens had helped her escape Belgium ahead of the full might of the German army. She wasn't about to abandon him now.

Pausing in her decoding, Evelyn looked up and stared out of the window, her brows creasing as a wave of anxiety washed over her. If she remained in Paris and the German army pushed further into France, she would have to find somewhere for her and Jens to go. They were safe in this apartment for the moment, but any day now Jean-Pierre, or Marcel, as Jens knew him, would arrive, and they couldn't expect to stay here then. They could go to a hotel, but if things got really bad and they had to leave Paris, then what?

Shaking her head, she turned her attention back to the message. There was absolutely no point in getting ahead of herself. She and Jens might be in England in a couple of days, and then she would have wasted time and energy worrying over nothing.

A few moments later she finished decoding the message and sat back, staring down at it in consternation.

RENDEZVOUS IN MORNING AT AIRFIELD OUTSIDE PARIS - EIGHT O'CLOCK. PLANE WILL TAKE YOU TO BERN. TELEGRAPH ONCE ERRAND COMPLETED TO ARRANGE FOR RETURN. MUST HURRY. CANNOT GUARANTEE RETURN FLIGHT DUE TO CURRENT EVENTS. ACKNOWLEDGE RECEIPT.

Bill was sending a plane to take her to Switzerland? Evelyn pinched the bridge of her nose, exhaling. She had asked him to arrange for her to go when she returned to England, but she was surprised that he was sending her now. She would have thought that the rapid advance of the German army, along with the smuggled packet of blueprints in the lining of her coat, would have taken priority over the clue her father had left in a Chinese puzzle box.

"I can't find anything new from Belgium," Jens said disgustedly, drawing her attention as he switched off the radio impatiently. "It's all what we heard last night."

"Perhaps that's a good thing," she said, turning to look at him sympathetically.

"Do you really believe that?" he countered, meeting her gaze squarely.

Evelyn held his gaze for a moment, then sighed and shook her head. "No."

"Nor do I." He ran a hand through his curly hair and took an impatient turn around the room. "I simply want to know if my parents are safe. The rest, well, what will happen will happen."

"Where are they?"

"They are in Linter, between Liège and Brussels." Jens sighed and dropped onto the sofa, shaking his head. "I suppose it will be weeks before I can get word to them. I did send them a message when we left Brussels, so at least they know I am safe for now."

"Try not to worry. I know it's hard, but it really won't do any good, you know."

He nodded and looked up. "And you? Is the message good news?"

Evelyn glanced at the paper on the desk. "Yes, and no. I'm to go to Calais, and then on to England," she lied.

"That's good, no?"

"Not if I can't bring you with me. I don't want to leave you here alone."

"Have you asked them?"

"Not yet." She looked at him with a small smile. "I will. I have to send a reply and I'll see what can be done."

Before Jens could respond, the sound of a key in the lock at the door made them both stand up quickly. Evelyn slid the paper on the desk towards her, picking it up and folding it quickly so the message couldn't be seen, her heart in her throat.

"Who's there?" Jens called, starting towards the door.

"No need to be alarmed," a male voice said as the door opened. "It's only me."

A tall, slender man with light brown hair and gray eyes stepped into the apartment. He carried a suitcase in one hand and had a newspaper rolled up under his arm. Evelyn exhaled in relief upon seeing him, her face breaking out into a welcoming smile.

"Marcel!" she exclaimed. "You're here already? I didn't think to see you for another few days!"

Jean-Pierre closed the door behind him and set the suitcase down on the floor.

"I didn't think to be here this soon either," he admitted, taking off his hat and dropping it onto the table inside the door. "I'll tell you about it once I've freshened up. Did you encounter any difficulties getting here?"

"None at all," Jens said, holding out his hand with a grin. "We drove as if the Devil himself was chasing us and arrived early yesterday morning."

"The Devil wouldn't have been as dangerous," Jean-Pierre said, shaking his hand. "I'm glad you didn't have any trouble."

"Have you eaten?" Evelyn asked, crossing the room. "We stopped at a market yesterday. There isn't much, but I can make you toast and coffee."

"That would be wonderful." He smiled at her. "I left at dawn and drove straight here."

Evelyn nodded and turned to go towards the kitchen down the hallway. "I'll get it started."

Jens followed her into the kitchen as Jean-Pierre carried his suitcase down the hallway to the bedroom.

"I can help you," he offered. "Shall I make the toast?"

"If it's a bother, I'm quite happy with bread and cheese," Jean-Pierre called from down the hallway. "You did buy cheese?"

"Of course!" Evelyn called back with a laugh. "And fruit as well!"

"That's perfect!"

Jens went into the small pantry to gather the food while Evelyn emptied the coffee pot and rinsed it to make a fresh one.

"What will you tell your people in London?" he asked in a low voice, emerging with a selection of cheeses and a bowl of fruit.

"That I've acquired a new friend," she replied with a shrug. "I'll tell them that I think you would be very useful. I can't imagine there will be a problem."

"Then why are you worried?" Jens asked. "I have not known you long, Marie, but I am beginning to learn when you're worried."

Evelyn looked at him sheepishly and nodded. "I am worried," she admitted, filling the coffee pot with fresh water and setting it on the stove burner. "It's the timing, you see. I must go to Calais, but I'm

15

afraid the passage is only for one. I'll have to come back for you, or make arrangements for you to travel separately."

"I'm quite capable of traveling on my own," Jens said humorously.

"Yes, of course." Evelyn scooped ground coffee into the percolator basket and closed the lid, bending to light the burner. "I'm thinking more of what happens if the German army makes it well into France before we can get you out."

"Get who out?" Jean-Pierre asked, striding into the kitchen. He'd discarded his jacket and rolled up his shirt-sleeves, and he looked completely relaxed.

"Jens." Evelyn said, turning to lean against the counter. "He's coming back with me."

"To England?" Jean-Pierre raised an eyebrow and glanced from one to the other. "Whatever for?"

"Well, I can't go back to Brussels," Jens said with a shrug, "and I don't know anyone in France."

"You know me," Jean-Pierre pointed out, sitting down at the small table and reaching for a knife to cut the bread. "And you know Luc and Josephine. I would think you would want to stay here and help fight."

"Yes, but how? I thought I was doing my part, but it turns out that all I was doing was sending information right back to the Nazis." Jens seated himself at the table and reached for a strawberry. "If I go to England, at least they can put me to work."

Jean-Pierre spread a freshly sliced piece of bread with cheese and glanced up at Evelyn. "And your boss is agreeable?"

She had the grace to look sheepish. "I don't know yet."

He nodded briskly and bit into his bread, chewing thoughtfully while he considered Jens.

"If you'd rather remain here, I can set you up and give you work," he said after a moment. "There is much to be done, and if France falls, we will need all the help we can get. Someone with your training and skill with radios will be invaluable."

"If France falls, surely, so will the networks?" Evelyn asked. "You can't continue if France is occupied by the Nazis."

"If the roles were reversed, and it was England we were discussing, would you stop?" Jean-Pierre countered, his gray eyes meeting hers across the kitchen.

"No." Evelyn pursed her lips for a moment. "But if France falls, you will have to stop at least for a short time. It will be too dangerous. The Nazis will be looking for anyone who opposes them."

Into the Iron Shadows

"We will have no choice," he said grimly. "Luc is aware of this, as is Josephine. If that happens, we will be forced to go underground, but we will still continue. The trouble will be getting the information to people who can actually use it."

"The English." Jens said, reaching for another strawberry. "You'll need radios."

Jean-Pierre smiled. "Precisely."

Jens glanced at Evelyn. "That is why you said you thought I would be valuable to your people."

She nodded. "Yes. They would train you and then send you back here, or to Belgium."

"We can do that here," Jean-Pierre said, slicing off another piece of bread. "I'll arrange for a new identity, a place to live, and a job. While you're living the life of a respectable citizen, we'll train you."

Jens stared at him. "You can do all that?" he stammered. "Who *are* you?"

Something like a smile twisted Jean-Pierre's lips briefly before he turned his attention back to spreading cheese on his bread. "Don't worry about that. I'm in a position to do what I said, and I'll do it gladly if it means that you can transmit the information we gather."

Evelyn pressed her lips together, studying him from her place near the stove and echoing Jens' question in her mind. Who *was* he? She had already determined that he worked in Paris in the government in some capacity, but how? How would he have the ability to create a whole new life for a perfect stranger? Was he a ranking official in the Deuxième Bureau de l'État-major général? If so, he was more at risk than people like Josephine. If France fell, he would be one of the first to be arrested.

He glanced up and caught her gaze, his gray eyes sober. He smiled faintly.

"You're trying to decide what my occupation is," he said in amusement. "You could simply ask."

Evelyn nodded. "Very well. What is it that you do here in Paris?"

"I work in the Ministry of Foreign Affairs. I'm an assistant to what you would call the undersecretary. I work daily with the army and the Deuxième Bureau, and have made several very good friends in both. So you see, Monsieur Bernard will be in perfectly capable hands."

"That was never in question," she murmured, turning to pour the coffee into a cup. "What will you do if France falls?"

"I'll remain in the government for as long as possible. Then," he shrugged, accepting the cup of coffee from her with a nod of thanks, "I shall do what I must. My family has a business that will no doubt continue to thrive regardless of what happens, and that is where I will go if there is no other alternative."

"What kind of business?" Jens asked curiously.

"Shipping." Jean-Pierre sipped his coffee appreciatively. "We have offices in America, Spain, Canada, and Barbados, to name a few that are so far unaffected by the war."

"What on earth are you doing in Paris, then?"

"Trying to save my country."

"You say it's your family's business?" Evelyn asked, raising an eyebrow. "You don't have anything to do with it?"

"No. I'm a shareholder and am briefed on the quarterly accounts, but the daily running of the business I leave to my father and brother. They are far more interested and skilled than myself. I went into government instead of shipping, to their everlasting confusion."

Evelyn smiled faintly at that. "Are they still in France?"

"No. My father is in New York, and my brother runs the office in Spain." He looked from one to the other. "But that is quite enough about me. We need to discuss the two men who were chasing you in Marle. They left the village before I could find out very much about them."

"What is there to find out?" Jens asked. "I thought we'd already established that they were German agents."

"Yes, but who? And which one of you were they after?"

Evelyn raised her eyebrows. "I thought they were after the packet I carried from Antwerp."

"So did I, until I went to Asp's house yesterday morning before the police got there. I arrived before anyone knew anything was amiss. I'm the one who called the police." Jean-Pierre wiped his mouth with a napkin and set it down. "I've taken care of the body, by the way. I removed the blanket and the pistol. Did you know you'd left it on the floor?"

"Pistol?" Jens repeated. "I'd completely forgotten about it!"

"I'm afraid that's my fault," Evelyn said. "I wasn't thinking very clearly."

"Well, I took it so that the police wouldn't think there was anyone else there. The way he fell, it could have been an accident. That's what the police think, anyway. It turns out that no one actually saw you go to the house that night, so they are treating it as an unfortunate accident."

"Well that's a good thing, isn't it?" Jens asked.

"It is." He nodded. "The less people who know you were even in the village, the better it is for all of us."

"Why do you question who it is the German agents were after?" Evelyn asked. "What happened to make you think it wasn't me after all?"

"I found a letter that Asp must have been in the process of writing when you arrived. It was addressed only to "My dear," so the intended recipient is a mystery, but he said he'd received a visit from a very unexpected person. He went on to say that his visitor knew about the man from Brussels and was waiting for him to come."

Evelyn stared at him before slowly turning to look at Jens. His face had paled considerably and he was staring at Marcel with wide eyes.

"Who was the visitor?" he whispered.

"That, my friend, is also a mystery. There was no hint of his identity in the letter, but there can be no doubt that 'the man from Brussels' is you. And so I must ask you, Mssr. Bernard, why would German agents be looking for you?"

Chapter Two

Evelyn looked up as Jean-Pierre walked into the living room. She was seated at the small writing table near the window, composing a short message for Jens to transmit to Bill acknowledging the new instructions.

"Jens is having a bath," he said, walking over to the sideboard and opening a cigarette box. "He's considering staying here with me. He'll decide while he's washing so you will know how to respond to your superior."

"Will you really train him and provide a whole new identity?" she asked, turning in her chair to look across the room at him.

"Yes, of course."

"Why?"

"Because I can use a skilled radio operator, and if France *does* fall, he will be invaluable."

"Despite the fact that the Germans are obviously aware of his existence and presence here in France?" she asked, standing and crossing the room to accept a proffered cigarette.

"Tell me, how do you think they became aware of his location?" he asked, lighting her cigarette for her before turning the match to his own.

"I haven't the faintest idea. I'm still trying to wrap my head around the fact that they are. I was certain they had been following me."

"And they may well have been. We can't dismiss that possibility." Jean-Pierre blew smoke up towards the ceiling and turned to go over to the sofa, seating himself. "There were too many reports of an SS agent on the trail of the courier to simply ignore them. Do you want to know what I think?"

"What?" Evelyn crossed over to stand near the window, glancing out into the late morning sun.

"I think there were two agents in Marle, but I don't think they were necessarily together. If they were, they both would have been seen, and yet only one was noticed by the villagers."

"The SS officer?"

Into the Iron Shadows

"Precisely. I had a description from the butcher, and it was different from the man who came to my house looking for the two of you." He crossed his legs and looked across the room at her. "As bizarre as it sounds, I think the agent was on your trail and the mysterious man who came to my door was looking for our friend Jens."

Something close to a chill went through Evelyn and she lifted her cigarette to her lips.

"And if that was the case, who was the mystery man?"

"That's the big question, isn't it?" Jean-Pierre tapped ash into the glass tray on the table at his elbow. "Whoever they were, they're both gone now. They've undoubtedly gone back to Germany now that they lost your trail."

Evelyn turned her attention out the window, her lips tightening. Who was the tall man who had chased them down the alley beside Ash's house? If he wasn't part of the SS then who was he? Another chill went through her and her mind went back to a cold and snowy mountainside in Norway. She had been huddled behind a bush in the darkness the first time she heard the name of the assassin who tracked her through the mountains on her way to Namsos.

Eisenjager.

Almost as soon as the thought came into her head, she frowned and dismissed it. What interest could the infamous German assassin possibly have in Jens Bernard? If everything she'd learned about the Iron Hunter was true, he was only sent after high value targets. Targets like herself, although why they thought she was high value was also a mystery.

"What if they haven't?" Evelyn turned to walk over to the sofa. "What if they're still in France?"

"Then the sooner you get back to England, the better." He watched as she sat beside him. "You are going back, are you not?"

"Yes. I'm leaving in the morning." Evelyn glanced at him. "And Jens?"

"If he decides to stay and work with us, I'll see to his safety," he assured her. "And even if he doesn't, I'll make sure he's kept hidden until you can get him to England."

"How? With the German armies advancing so quickly…"

"Let me worry about that." He stubbed out his cigarette and shot her a small smile. "You just concern yourself with getting that packet you're carrying safely to London, or everything that we did in Marle will be for nothing."

15th May, 1940

Dear Evelyn,

How are you? It feels like an age since I've seen you, even though it's only been a few weeks. We've been busy here, up flying every day, and I still haven't seen hide nor hair of a Jerry. A couple of the chaps saw some action on Monday, lucky blighters. They bagged themselves a Junkers, if you can believe that. Your brother dearest and yours truly were up over a different location at the time and had no such luck. But at least we know they're out there, and any day I'll get my chance. I don't mind telling you, because I know you'll understand, that I can't wait to finally see some real fighting. I feel as though I'm just coasting through this war while our BEF is left holding the bag.

When you next hear from me, I shall be writing from a new station. I can't tell you where, but I'll say that it will put me further away from you. We'll be joined by another squadron of Spits, 19 Squadron. I'll miss this place. The CO says that we're going to a new station, with brand new buildings and the like. It's meant to be for the bombers, but we'll be staying there for a bit. I think they're going to move us somewhere again, but the CO is keeping mum about it. Why else stick us on a bomber station that was just finished if it isn't temporary?

All of this means, of course, that our stolen hours in London or in pubs between our stations will become more difficult. We'll have to wait for a proper leave and, with the way Hitler is moving through the Low Countries, time off will be harder to come by. I'll miss seeing you somewhat regularly. Will you miss me?

Rob was trying to get hold of you earlier to tell you the news, but he wasn't able to get through. Are you off on one of your training stints again? If so, you barely had time to get your bag unpacked from the last one. I hope that's not the case, for your sake.

Well, I'm for my bed. I have an early flight tomorrow. Another patrol. Will tomorrow be the day I finally catch sight of some Jerries? One can only hope.

Always yours,

Into the Iron Shadows

FO Miles Lacey

Paris
May 15

Evelyn set her case down near the door and turned to hold her hands out to Jens.

"You promise me that you will take care of yourself," she said, grasping his hands. "We didn't make it all the way from Brussels just so that you could go getting yourself caught here in France."

Jens grinned and leaned down to accept a kiss on each cheek from her. "I can't promise that I won't ever get caught, but I do promise to take care of myself." He straightened up and smiled down at her, his eyes warm. "You understand, don't you? Why I've decided to remain here and not go to England?"

She smiled and squeezed his hands before releasing them. "Of course I do. I'm glad you'll be in good hands." She turned to hold her hand out to Jean-Pierre, meeting his gray eyes. "Thank you."

"There's nothing to thank," he replied with an easy smile, grasping her hand. "I'm happy to have him, and it was a pleasure to work with you, even if it was briefly. Josephine thinks highly of you, and that's quite a recommendation, I assure you. She doesn't like anyone, or so I'm told. How will you go to Calais?"

"I'm taking the train." Evelyn released his hand and bent to pick up her suitcase. "Or at least, I will if I don't miss it."

"You'll reach the station with time to spare."

She nodded and turned for the door, then hesitated. Turning back, she looked at Jens.

"You'll let me know where you are?" she asked suddenly. "Once you're settled?"

"Yes, if you like."

She nodded. "I would, thank you." She hesitated again, then looked at him squarely. "If you ever change your mind, you know you can contact me and I'll do what I can to get you to England. I owe you that much for getting me out of Belgium."

Jens nodded and smiled at her. "I know. I'll be fine, though. I did give it quite a bit of thought, and this is where I belong. You just worry about getting to England safely. I'll send a message once I'm

23

settled somewhere."

"Thank you." Evelyn looked at Jean-Pierre and smiled. "Take care of yourselves, both of you."

"We will. Now go, or you *will* be in danger of missing your train!" Jean-Pierre said with a laugh, reaching around her to open the door. "May God go with you, my friend."

"And with you," she said, meeting his eyes one last time. "Good-bye."

Evelyn went through the door and walked towards the marble staircase leading down to the foyer. Reaching the top of the stairs, she glanced back over her shoulder to find Jean-Pierre watching from the door of his apartment. Seeing her look, he smiled and lifted his hand in farewell. Evelyn smiled back and started down the stairs with a heavy heart. She had only known Jens for a little over a week, and Jean-Pierre only a few hours, really, yet she felt as if she was leaving dear friends behind. The heavy feeling of sadness was compounded by the knowledge that she had lied to both of them. She wasn't going to Calais, but to an airfield, and then to Switzerland. She was continuing her search for answers to a riddle her father had left behind, while they were going to stay and face the grim reality of a war that none of them wanted.

And she was very much afraid that she might not see either of them again.

Maubeuge, France

The sun was shining brightly over the countryside and a soft breeze blew across the field, brushing against the woman's face as she stood at a fence and stared out over the expanse of farmland. It was hard to imagine that such a perfect day wasn't as tranquil and perfect just over the border in Belgium. The same breeze that carried the fresh, clean scent of earth and flowers to her carried the acrid stench of smoke and death to others.

The sobering thought brought a crease to Josephine Rousseau's forehead and she turned away from the fence and started back towards the farmhouse. Marc should have some news by now on what progress was being made by the French and English armies, if any. He had been busy on his wireless radio all morning, checking in with others along the borders with Belgium and Germany. She shook her head as she walked through the small kitchen garden to the back door. That radio had turned out to be their best source of information over the past few days. With the chaos across the border, they had been unable to get intelligence from their usual sources, instead relying on what they could decipher from the jumbled and chaotic transmissions Marc was sent from other agents throughout France. Their entire system was rapidly breaking down, and Josephine was very much afraid that in a few more days, they would be deaf and blind, cut off from the intelligence they were trying to get to Paris. If that were to happen, they would be helpless and forced to reevaluate their position. Their superiors wanted them to stay and gather what information they could, but remaining in the face of an invasion without the benefit of gaining actionable intelligence would be the height of foolishness. Better to withdraw, reevaluate, and live to see another day.

Josephine opened the back door and went into the kitchen, pulling her hat off her head and tossing it onto the old table where the remains of their breakfast still lay. She would clear it up, then go find Marc and see what he'd learned. As she began to gather the empty plates and coffee cups, a shiver of dread went through her, bringing a scowl to her face. In the two years that she'd been gathering intelligence for the Deuxième Bureau, she had never been this uneasy. There had been a couple of tight spots, once in Strasbourg and another in Metz, but even they hadn't left her with this constant feeling of disquiet. It was as if she was waiting for something terrible to happen, and she was powerless to prevent it. All she could do was wait, knowing it would happen, and pretend that everything was normal.

Carrying the dishes over to the large sink, she piled them in and turned on the tap. Waiting for the water to heat up, she gazed out of the window, her eyes straying to the woods in the distance. Mathieu and André should have returned days ago. They had crossed the border into Belgium almost a week ago to see what news they could gather on the position and strength of the German armies there. While they were doing that, they were also planning on trying to convince one of their contacts to come back to France with them. The entire trip should have taken no more than two or three days, but they had been gone five now with no word from either of them.

Josephine pursed her lips and dropped her gaze to the steaming water in the sink, reaching for the soap. When they had first suggested they go, she had readily agreed. None of them had considered the possibility that the Nazis would move so quickly through Belgium and Holland. The day Mathieu and André left was the day after Hitler launched his attack on the Low Countries. Shaking her head, she filled a dishpan in the sink with soapy water, reaching for a cup. The possibility of being threatened by enemy troops at the border this soon had seemed laughable, yet here they were, just over the Belgian border, with the German army already at Sedan, and Brussels and Antwerp under constant bombardment. Hitler's Blitzkrieg was proving to be just that: a lightning war that was sweeping through Belgium and Holland as if their defenses were nothing. Luxembourg had fallen that first day, and the next the Germans had breached the mighty Ardennes. The unthinkable was happening. France was on the verge of falling to the Nazi war machine, just like Poland and Norway.

And Mathieu and André were caught right in the middle.

As Josephine washed the breakfast dishes, her mind wandered to the contact they were trying to locate and bring back. He'd been feeding them a steady stream of information for a few weeks now, all of it good. Although he was a fairly new recruit, he was quickly proving his worth. She shouldn't be surprised, really. He was one of Bill's finds.

Her lips curved faintly. She really didn't know how he did it. William Buckley had a knack for discovering the most unassuming people imaginable, that no one would consider remotely suited to this kind of work, and then turning them into invaluable sources of intelligence. Evelyn was a perfect example. When Josephine met her in Strasbourg before the war began, she'd been struck by the intelligent young woman. Young, pretty, and clearly from a social background higher than most, she was everything that other agents were not. And yet she had quickly become one of Bill's most prized and effective agents.

Another smile curved Josephine's lips. She hadn't been surprised to hear snippets of a new English agent's successes over the past two years. While she'd only spent a few hours with the woman in Strasbourg, it had been enough to convince her that Evelyn was made for this life. And she hadn't been wrong.

Now Mathieu and André were trying to bring back another one of Bill's recruits. It was at his request, and Josephine had been surprised by the message. It was unlike Bill to enlist their aid. MI6 tended to keep to themselves these days, especially after Venlo. There were too many spies abroad now, and it was getting too dangerous to be as open and free as they once were. In fact, she thought with a scowl, it was getting so bad that soon they would have to conceal their work altogether, even from citizens of their own country, or risk being exposed and hunted down. Not everyone agreed with what they did, or with what their government was doing. There were many who would welcome a change, and that made what Josephine and the others did even more dangerous. The fact that Bill had been willing to take the risk to bring the new recruit out of Belgium said something. Not for the first time, Josephine wondered what to expect from the raw agent, and what made him so valuable to MI6.

Movement outside the window caught her attention and she looked up, her hands growing still in the sink. Relief surged through her and she let out a soft gasp at the sight of three figures moving out of the trees behind the garden. Grabbing a towel, she dried off her hands as she rushed to the back door, throwing it open.

"Marc! Luc! They're here! They've returned!" she shouted over her shoulder before running outside.

At the sight of her rushing through the garden, one of the men raised a hand in greeting. Josephine felt a suspicious lump in her throat as she threw open the garden gate and ran towards the trio.

"My God, I never thought you two would look so good to me!" she cried, meeting them halfway and throwing her arms around the tallest one. "Thank God you're all right!"

"I've been thanking Him since we crossed the border," the man replied dryly, closing his arms around her in a bear hug. "We almost didn't make it back."

Josephine pulled away and looked up into his tired and drawn face. She turned to the man next to him and hugged him tightly.

"André!" she murmured. "You look half dead!"

"I feel half dead," he replied gruffly, pulling away and smiling at her. "I'm better now that I see your face."

A soft flush tinged her cheeks and she smiled back before turning to the third man. He looked just as exhausted as the other two. A hat was pulled low over his brow and he carried a battered suitcase that looked as if it had seen much better days.

"You must be Monsieur Maes," she said, holding out her hand. "I'm Josephine. Welcome to France."

"Please call me Finn," he replied, grasping her hand. "Thank you."

Josephine nodded briskly and turned to link her arm through André's.

"Come and have something to eat. I'm just cleaning up from breakfast. I'll make you something. You can have hot coffee while you wait."

"Has Marc had any news from Sedan?" Mathieu asked as they walked towards the house.

"He's been on the radio all morning. I'm sure he's learned something. The last we heard was that the German army had broken through the Ardennes and reached Sedan."

"I was afraid of that," Mathieu muttered disgustedly. "They're advancing everywhere. I'd never have believed it if I hadn't seen it with my own eyes. They're breaking through every front as if it wasn't even there."

"Completely unopposed as far as we could tell," André added. "It seems like the only place they're meeting resistance is in the west, towards Antwerp, and in Holland."

"Yes, well that was obviously the plan, wasn't it?" she asked. "Lure the armies into Belgium and Holland and then come through the Ardennes."

"It worked. They'll be in France in a matter of days."

Josephine's face paled and she stopped in the kitchen garden to stare up at André. "Days?" she repeated, her heart pounding.

He nodded grimly, releasing her arm. "That's only if the air force can hold them off that long. I don't see any hope for a stand at the border. Not with the force of their Luftwaffe. Holland won't hold out much longer, either. They're being bombarded."

Josephine swallowed painfully, but before she could answer, a man appeared in the open kitchen door.

"Luc! André says that Holland won't hold out much longer, and the German armies will be in France in days!"

Luc nodded grimly, holding his hand out in greeting to Mathieu as the small group reached the house.

"I agree," he said. "Marc just heard that Rotterdam was bombed yesterday. The entire city is gone, flattened."

Josephine gasped and a hand went to her mouth involuntarily. "What?!"

"The whole city?" Mathieu demanded, his jaw tightening.

"That's what we're hearing. Holland won't resist any longer. They'll want to preserve the rest of their country."

"And a death toll?" Finn asked, his face pale.

Luc looked at him soberly. "Fires are still burning out of control. They don't know yet, but it must be in the thousands." He held out his hand. "My name is Luc. You must be Finn. I'm sorry to greet you this way. I wish I had better news."

Finn shook his hand, shaking his head tiredly. "It is the way of it," he said with a shrug. "This is war."

"And the Dutch government?" André asked as they filed through the kitchen door.

"Expected to surrender today. The Germans have threatened to do the same to Utrecht if they don't capitulate."

Into the Iron Shadows

"Destroying an entire city of innocent civilians!" Josephine exclaimed, picking up the cold coffee pot and carrying it over to the counter to make fresh coffee. "Monsters!"

"And those monsters will be here in France in a few days, at most."

Chapter Three

Bellevue Palace Hotel
Bern, Switzerland

Evelyn finished signing the registration book and looked up with a smile, setting the pen down.

"Merci, Mademoiselle Dufour." The man behind the desk smiled back. "I hope you enjoy your stay with us."

"I'm sure I will," she said, accepting her room key. "Thank you. Is the restaurant open for lunch yet?"

"Yes it is. Shall I have a porter take your case up to your room for you?"

"Thank you very much."

Evelyn nodded and turned away from the desk as a porter materialized beside her, bending to pick up her suitcase. He nodded to her politely before accepting an extra key from the man behind the desk. Evelyn watched him go towards the stairs before crossing the large, elegant lobby towards the restaurant on the other side. There was nothing of importance in the case. The secret packet wrapped in oilskin was secured in the lining of her coat, nestled comfortably against her ribs. In the extremely unlikely case that the porter got curious, all he would find were clothes and a notebook with random thoughts jotted down regarding her travels.

She moved across the marble tiled floor, secure in the knowledge that the most important thing she carried was safely hidden away. The second most important thing she carried was in her purse, clasped securely in her left hand. She no longer noticed the weight of either the packet in her coat, or the pistol in her purse. They had both become part of her wardrobe almost as much as her stockings or shoes.

A gentleman passed her, nodding in polite greeting, and Evelyn inclined her head slightly, taking in his sensible woolen suit and freshly polished shoes. A businessman, she decided before she realized what she was doing. A well-to-do one, but a businessman just the same, and Italian by the looks of the suit. A faint smile touched her lips and she resisted the urge to sigh. Noticing everyone around her was fast becoming second nature, and she wasn't sure just how she felt about that.

Evelyn glanced at her pearl and gold watch. She would have to wait until this evening before she could make contact with the night manager, Philip Moreau. That was a meeting that Bill had no knowledge of, and she was surprised to find that she was glad of it. When she was in Brussels to meet with Vladimir Lyakhov last week, just before the Germans had begun their invasion, it had been for the purpose of setting up direct communication with the Soviet agent. Neither Bill nor herself had been happy with the arrangement, but Vladimir had insisted. After meeting with him in the church, Evelyn could admit that she felt much more comfortable now. She still didn't trust the man, but at least now she felt more at ease about communicating with him directly. However, it had necessitated a trip to this hotel to set up the arrangements with his contact here. It was just plain luck that Bill had arranged a flight for her so quickly.

He wanted her to follow the clue left behind by her father, and she would do that tomorrow. Tonight she would arrange for secure communication between herself and Vladimir, arrangements that Bill would know nothing about. It was one thing for Lyakhov to contact her when he had something. It was quite another for her to contact him, and Evelyn suspected that MI6 would gladly take advantage of that avenue of communication if given the chance. No. It was best for them to know nothing about the reciprocal arrangement she and Lyakhov had come to, at least for now.

As she walked towards the doors to the restaurant, Evelyn saw a small crowd clustered around a tall, stand-up radio placed to the side of a small seating area. They had been talking in low voices a moment before, but now they fell silent and one of the men reached out to turn a knob on the radio. Curious, Evelyn changed direction to join them.

"Here is the news from Amsterdam. This morning, shortly after ten o'clock, in the nearby town of Rijsoord, the commander of the Dutch forces, General Winkelman, signed the surrender of Holland to the German army. Following yesterday's brutal bombardment of Rotterdam by the Luftwaffe, which destroyed the city and led to the deaths of thousands of civilians, the Dutch have surrendered to Germany. Holland has surrendered all territories, with the exception of Zeeland and the overseas colonies. I repeat: Holland has surrendered to Germany. Queen Wilhelmina and the government fled The Hague amidst the invasion and ensuing fighting, and arrived in England two days ago. The Queen has vowed resistance, and the government is expected to continue in exile, assisting the Allies in every way possible."

Evelyn listened in silence, her heart sinking. It was happening. Holland had surrendered, and it would only be a matter of time before Belgium would also be forced to capitulate. France would then be the only country standing between Hitler and England.

"In France, the German army is expected to break through at Sedan by nightfall, leaving an open path to Paris. In Paris, citizens are already beginning to flee the city and move south, away from the expected path of the advancing armies."

Evelyn turned away, her vision suddenly clouded by a sheen of tears. If the Germans did break through at Sedan, they would be in Paris within the week. If that happened, France was lost, and her beloved Paris would fall under the dark shadow of the Nazi regime. A vision of thousands of troops pouring into France, as she had witnessed them pouring into Norway from a mountainside, filled her head. She swallowed painfully, holding back the wave of intense sorrow that washed over her with a deep gulp of air. It was hopeless. Hitler had been allowed to run amok for too long, and now all of Europe was paying the price for the failed policy of appeasement perpetuated by her government, along with that of France and the rest of Europe. The German forces were too strong to hold back, and soon they would set their sights on England.

What then? Who would come to England's aid?

Despair rolled over her in waves and Evelyn reached out to steady herself with a gloved hand on the back of a leather armchair. The German armies would have to approach England differently. Their Blitzkrieg wouldn't work as effectively as it did on the expanse of land in Europe. They would send their Luftwaffe over first, but their armies would still have to cross the Channel. It would be an air battle first. They would have to have complete control of the skies before they could commit their armies to the crossing. Miles, and Robbie, and the rest of the young RAF fliers would be the first line of defense, trying to stem the tide of the Luftwaffe. If they failed, England would suffer the same fate as the rest of Western Europe.

Evelyn realized with a shock that her entire body was shaking from the effort to contain the rush of emotions vying for attention within her. Straightening up, she took a long, deep breath, forcing herself to focus on the doors of the restaurant.

It was no good thinking of what could happen when it hadn't happened yet. No useful purpose would be served by worrying about tomorrow. Today was where her focus needed to be. Regardless of what the future had in store for any of them, she had a job to do today. She had to meet with the night manager and set up a system of communication between herself and Vladimir, and then she had to find the easiest and most expeditious way to get to the address in Blasenflue that her father had left behind. Beyond that, her movements would be determined by what she found there. That had to be her priority.

Taking another deep breath, Evelyn straightened her shoulders and lifted her head again. Pressing her trembling lips together, she continued towards the restaurant. She would eat lunch, have a strong drink alongside it, and then go up to her room to compose a telegram to send to Bill. She must continue, and let the fate of France take care of itself.

London, England

William Buckley looked up when a light knock fell on his office door, calling the command to enter. He glanced at the clock and sat back with a yawn, stretching. It was past the time when he should have left the office to go home for dinner, but Marguerite was attending the theatre with friends this evening, and he still had several reports to go over.

"Still here, Buckley?" Jasper Montclair demanded, coming into the office and closing the door behind him. "I thought we agreed you would begin cutting back."

"So we did, sir," Bill said, standing and coming around his desk to wring his superior's hand. "How was Paris?"

"About what we expected," the older man said with a shrug. "There's not much more that can be done. Hitler's commanders have out-planned, out-strategized, and just plain out-maneuvered us in every way possible. Did you hear about Holland?"

"Yes, this morning." Bill waited until Jasper seated himself before going back to his chair behind the desk. "Not surprising, given the beating Rotterdam took yesterday."

"No." Jasper rubbed his face and looked across the desk at Bill, crossing his legs comfortably. "They're saying the Germans have taken control of all the bridges across the Meuse. Sedan is lost. They'll be in Paris within the week."

"Yes."

"Is that why you're here late tonight?" Jasper asked. "Trying to warn all your agents?"

"I doubt they need any warning from me. They're well aware of what's happening, probably more so than us."

"Have you heard anything from your agent that was exposed by that damned letter?"

Bill shook his head, his expression grim. "Nothing. I contacted a member of the French network and asked for two of their agents to go across the border into Belgium to try to find him. I haven't heard anything yet."

"When was this?"

"Almost a week ago now."

Jasper frowned. "You should have heard something by now. Of the other three names, we've only heard from one. Carson believes his agent is dead, and I've been informed that the other one was in Rotterdam and, well, we know what just happened there."

"I'm still holding out hope," Bill said slowly. "The fact that I haven't heard anything could be a good thing."

"No news is good news?" Jasper grunted. "Not in this business, Bill. You know that."

"That's not what I meant. If anything had happened to the agents, Josephine would have told me. I don't think they've returned yet."

Jasper perked up at that. "Josephine? Isn't that Henri's girl?"

Bill smiled faintly and nodded. "Yes."

"And she's still active?"

"Very much so. She's positioned at Maubeuge, just over the border from Belgium."

"Hmm."

Jasper was quiet for a moment, but just as he opened his mouth to speak, another knock fell on the office door. He raised his eyebrows.

"Are all of your people working late?" he demanded.

"Well, there *is* a war on, you know. Come in!"

The door opened once more and his assistant Wesley rushed in with a sealed message in his hand.

"I think we've finally heard something, sir! This just came— oh!" He drew up short at the sight of Jasper. "I'm sorry, sir."

"Don't be." Jasper waved his hand with a smile. "This is an informal visit. Continue."

Wesley nodded and turned his attention back to Bill.

"This just came in from France," he said, crossing to the desk and holding out the message. "Maubeuge."

Into the Iron Shadows

Bill took it and quickly ripped it open, scanning the contents. When he finally raised his eyes, he couldn't stop the grin of relief that spread across his face.

"He's safe!" he announced, jumping out of his chair. "They've arrived back from Belgium and Oscar is with them!"

"That's good news, sir!" Wesley exclaimed, grinning from ear to ear.

"Yes it is. Bloody good news! It's about time we got some." Bill rounded the desk and strode to a map on the far wall. After studying it for a minute, he glanced over his shoulder. "Wesley, take down this return message."

"Yes, sir." The assistant went around the desk to pull a sheet of paper out of a cubby and reached for a pen. "Go ahead."

"Proceed immediately to Calais, stop. Take room at inn on Rue de Vic as Mason Berne, stop. Wait for instructions, stop."

"Calais?" Jasper queried. "Is that wise? If France is overrun, the port towns will be the focus of the Luftwaffe."

"I want him in position to be able to get to England as soon as Jian can rendezvous with him."

"Jian? I thought she was already on her way home."

"No. She's in Switzerland at the moment."

"Switzerland!" Jasper exclaimed, turning in his chair to stare at Bill. "What on earth for? She's carrying a highly sensitive packet with her. She can't be gallivanting all over Europe!"

Bill suppressed a smile and turned from the map to nod to Wesley. "Have that message sent immediately and wait for acknowledgement."

"Yes, sir." Wesley nodded and headed for the door.

"Once we have it, bring it to me and then go home, Wesley," Bill added as he reached the door. "It's late."

"I'm all right, sir."

"I'm sure you are, but you won't be if you keep this up. I've no doubt that there will plenty of nights when we have no choice, but this isn't one of them."

Wesley nodded and opened the door. "Yes, sir."

The door closed behind him and Bill looked at Jasper. "She's not gallivanting all over Europe," he said in amusement. "She's in Switzerland to follow up a lead on Robert Ainsworth's treasure hunt, if you must know. Then she's coming straight back to England, hopefully with Oscar in tow."

"Ainsworth! When did we get another crack at that?" Jasper furrowed his brows. "I thought we'd all decided that whatever he'd discovered was lost."

"So we did, and I firmly believed that until last autumn." Bill walked over to a tall wooden cabinet along the wall and unlocked it, opening the doors to reveal two bottles and a few glasses on the top shelf. "Scotch?"

"Yes, thank you. What do you mean until last autumn? What happened to change your mind?"

"Ainsworth Manor was broken into and the study and library were thoroughly searched, or so we believe." Bill poured two fingers of golden liquid into two glasses and turned to carry one over to Jasper. "Nothing was taken and the intruder went through pains to make it appear as if he'd never been there."

"How do we know that he was?"

"The lock on the study window was broken. Thomas was woken by a light. He got up to turn it off and found the broken lock the next morning. He thinks he disturbed the intruder, and he's positive the light was off when he retired for the evening."

"Thomas?"

"The butler."

Jasper nodded and exhaled before sipping his drink. "And the police? What did they say?"

"That it was probably some young local youths on a lark." Bill shook his head and sat down, sipping his drink. "There were no other incidents in the county, though, so it seems unlikely."

"Does Evelyn know?"

"She's the one who told me about it." Bill looked at him sheepishly. "I didn't see any point in telling you until we knew we had something."

"And now you do?"

"Yes. After the break-in, I sent one of our men up there to keep an eye on things. It turns out that Robert left a puzzle box with Evelyn just before that last trip. She's been working on getting it open. We decided to leave it at Ainsworth Manor for safety rather than have it sitting on an RAF station unprotected. She finally succeeded in opening it right before she went to Belgium."

Jasper leaned forward. "What was in it?"

"An address in Switzerland."

"An address? Nothing else?"

"No. Just an address. And that is why she's in Switzerland."

Into the Iron Shadows

Jasper shook his head and sat back in his chair, raising his glass to his lips. "It could be anything," he said after a moment. "We don't even know for sure that this has anything to do with the information he said he'd obtained in Vienna."

"I think it's very likely that it does. There was another break-in at Ainsworth Manor last week. This time our man saw him."

"What?!"

Bill nodded. "The dogs alerted him as the intruder was leaving and he saw him disappear into the woods. Someone is definitely looking for it, and they're convinced it's in that house."

"Good Lord." Jasper stared at him. "Then we have to get to it before they do. Do we have any clue or indication what the information is?"

"No. We're still just as much in the dark as when we received that fragmented message from Robert when he was in Warsaw."

"And that wasn't much at all. It mentioned national security, didn't it?"

"Yes, and nothing else. The rest of the message was illegible."

"And he died before he could tell us more." Jasper exhaled again and sipped his scotch. "Now you think we have a lead. Where in Switzerland is she?"

"I received a message from Bern today, but she's leaving tomorrow. She'll contact me when she's finished and ready to depart."

"You don't know where she is?!"

Bill shrugged. "Not the faintest. The plane flew her into the airfield just outside Bern, but where she's going is anyone's guess. She didn't tell me."

"When she's finished, how will you get her out? It won't be safe to fly over France soon."

"I know. I've warned her that I can't guarantee a flight out."

Jasper nodded. "And Oscar?"

"I'll have him wait in Calais. When Jian's finished in Switzerland, no matter how she gets out, she'll have to go back through France and pick up Oscar."

"And if she can't?"

"Then I'll contact Josephine and ask her to set him up somewhere out of the way until we can get him out."

Jasper grunted. "If the Germans continue the way they're going, we may not be able to get him out."

"Well then, that will be another problem I'll face when it happens."

Jasper shot him a keen look. "If I know you, you've already thought that problem through."

Bill grinned. "So I have, but let's hope it doesn't come to that."

Chapter Four

Bellevue Palace Hotel

Evelyn watched as the night manager crossed the lobby towards the front desk. She had been watching him for the past hour from her place in an armchair near the wireless radio. The radio that had brought the news of the Dutch surrender earlier was silent now, and she had the evening paper open in her hands. Every time Philip Moreau moved, blue eyes watched from behind the newspaper, noting how he walked upright and spoke with quiet authority to the porters and the clerk behind the counter. One and all treated him with deference, and appeared to genuinely enjoy working with him if their smiles were anything to go by. The man himself was very unassuming, standing at an average height with a slim build and brown hair cut fairly short. His brown mustache was neat and precise, as was his suit and tie. He was the type of man that seemed pleasant and friendly enough, but whom one would be hard-pressed to recall if asked to describe him.

Lowering her eyes back to the paper in front of her, Evelyn pressed her lips together thoughtfully. How on earth was she going to approach him? Vladimir had given no instructions, no secret password, and really no advice at all except to say that she would have to make arrangements with the night manager. How did one go about arranging clandestine messages and communications with a spy through a manager in a hotel? She certainly had no idea.

While she sat there, staring blindly at the typed French words on the page before her, she suddenly remembered something Vladimir had said in the church. He and her father had an arrangement, and that arrangement had been through this hotel as well. Evelyn lifted her eyes again to glance across the massive lobby to the front desk where the manager had his head bent over a thick ledger. Had Philip Moreau been her father's go-between as well? If he was then he would already be familiar with Lyakhov's codename, as that had remained unchanged from her father to her. Perhaps that would be her opening.

Folding the paper, she placed it back on the table with the selection of other complimentary newspapers and rose to her feet. Regardless of how she did it, it had to be done, and it had to be done tonight. Time was not on her side, especially after the news this evening that the German armies had, indeed, broken through at Sedan. If she wanted to have any hope of making it to Calais and across the Channel to England before Paris fell, she would have to move quickly, and move now.

Crossing the lobby, she took a deep breath to calm her nerves. As she approached the front desk, the manager looked up from his ledger and smiled at her.

"Good evening, Mademoiselle," he greeted her. "I trust you're enjoying the evening?"

"Good evening. Yes, thank you. I've just been reading the newspapers. It's appalling, isn't it?"

"There certainly doesn't seem to be anything good in them these days," he agreed. "It's very unnerving."

"It is, indeed." Evelyn smiled at him. "Forgive me, but I wonder if I might ask you to procure something for me?"

"Of course, Mademoiselle..."

"Dufour. Geneviève Dufour. I'm staying in—"

"The Rose rooms," the manager finished smoothly with a smile. "Yes, of course. How can I be of assistance?"

"It's rather a strange request. Would you be able to procure a bottle of Shustov vodka? Friends of mine stayed here a few months ago and said that they had the most wonderful cocktails and the waiter said they were made with the Russian vodka."

As she spoke, Evelyn watched a flash of surprise light his eyes before being effectively hidden. He nodded slowly and closed the ledger.

"I do believe I can lay my hands on a bottle. I recall seeing a few left in the backroom. If you'd like to follow me, I'm sure we can find something to your liking."

Evelyn smiled brightly. "Thank you!"

Philip Moreau motioned to a clerk a few feet away, asking him to mind the desk for a few minutes. The clerk nodded and Philip stepped out from behind the wooden counter, smiling at Evelyn.

"This way, please. We had a nice unexpected shipment over the winter, which is no doubt when your friends were with us."

He led the way to a narrow corridor a few feet away and they went down a few steps to emerge into a very plain and serviceable hallway with doors leading off on either side.

Into the Iron Shadows

"Not many realize what a treasure Shustov is outside of the Soviet Union."

"So I'm told," Evelyn said wryly, looking around the hallway as they moved towards a closed door at the end. "I must admit to being skeptical myself, but I'm willing to take a chance, as it were."

A flash of amusement crossed his face and he glanced at her, remaining silent. A moment later, Philip stopped before the door and unlocked it with a key from an overcrowded key ring.

"Let's hope that we can set your mind at ease," he murmured, opening the door and standing aside so she could enter.

Evelyn stepped into a surprisingly spacious office equipped with a dark wood desk and two armchairs. A double-glazed window overlooked the night and what was, no doubt, a stunning view during the day. Philip closed the door behind them and motioned her to one of the chairs with a slight nod of deference. She sank into the offered chair gracefully and began to pull off her gloves.

"I understand you are the man to speak to about setting up an arrangement whereby I might contact Shustov."

"And who gave you this information?" he asked, walking over to pick up a box from the corner of the desk. He opened the lid to reveal a selection of cigarettes, offering her one.

"Shustov," Evelyn said, shaking her head to the offer.

"Ah. I see. Do you mind if I smoke?"

"Not at all."

He selected a cigarette and went around the side of the desk to seat himself, pulling a lighter out of his pocket.

"I suppose I should introduce myself properly," he murmured, lighting his cigarette. "Philip Moreau, at your service."

Evelyn inclined her head and watched as he lit his cigarette and laid the lighter on the desk, sitting back in his chair. Hazel eyes considered her thoughtfully for a moment, then he raised his face to blow smoke towards the ceiling.

"Before we begin, by what name shall I know you?"

"It will vary, of course," she answered calmly, "but would you suggest that we use a single name between us?"

"I would." Philip nodded decisively. "Preferably one that no one else will know. I'm sure Shustov assured you of my discretion. I maintain it through an overabundance of caution. I really must insist on a unique codename. It will protect us both, you see. When I see it, I will know it is truly you, and vice versa, of course."

Evelyn nodded, thinking. "Yes, I can see your point. Very well." She was quiet for a moment, then she raised her eyes to his. "I think perhaps Elena."

He nodded. "Very sensible. It is quite a common name in Switzerland, and one that would hardly arouse suspicion."

"This is the first time I've arranged anything like this, I'm afraid," she confessed with a small smile. "I'm not quite sure what to do."

Philip smiled. "You don't have to do a thing, Mademoiselle. I shall arrange everything. Shustov explained how it will work, I presume?"

"The basics, yes, but not the details. I understand that he will send you a message and you will forward it to me, and then await instructions from me. Is that correct?"

"That's the basic gist of it, yes. I guarantee to pass the messages to all interested parties within five hours of receipt. If there are to be any changes to the procedure or where the messages are sent, those must be made in person here for everyone's security." He paused and leaned forward to tap his cigarette into the ashtray on his desk. "I do, of course, charge a small fee for the service."

"Of course." Evelyn smiled faintly. "That is not a problem."

He nodded. "Good. Then all that is to be done is for you to tell me where to send the messages."

Evelyn opened her purse and pulled out a piece of paper. "I've written it down," she said, getting up and passing him the paper. "What if you're not on duty when a message comes in?"

"All of my telegrams are brought to me immediately."

"Even on your days off?" she asked, surprised.

The chuckle Philip gave was genuine.

"Even on my days off. When I am not in the hotel, I am in my private home not far from here. You may rest assured that any messages will be processed in a timely manner."

He opened the folded piece of paper and glanced at it, nodding after a moment. "Very well. And you will have someone on the other end to receive it?"

"Yes." She sat down again and tilted her head, studying him. "Why do you do it?"

His eyes met hers and he leaned forward to stub out his cigarette.

"Would you believe me if I told you it was out of a sense of patriotism?"

Into the Iron Shadows

She raised an eyebrow skeptically. "Patriotism? To two different countries?"

"Oh, more than that," he said lightly with a laugh. "You and Shustov are not my only clients. The fact is that I'm not loyal to any country. Instead, my patriotism is to the human race, and I find that it is being threatened without compassion and without empathy by most countries."

"How does this help?"

"You'd be very surprised to hear, and I'd be a fool to tell you." He got up and went over to a large safe against the wall and bent down to open it. "Suffice it to say that my services are making more of a difference than I ever imagined."

"Well, they'll certainly make a difference to me," Evelyn said after a moment. "What about your fee?"

"It is fifty francs per month. You can arrange a monthly wire at your convenience," he said over his shoulder. "I'll give you a bank account before you leave. It is not much, but enough to cover my risk and expenses."

"Very well." She watched as he pulled a small book out of the safe before locking it again. "What if something should happen to you?"

"I have a contingency in place. You will be notified to cease all communication, and then of course, you and Shustov will have to come to another arrangement." Philip walked over to hand her the small book. "This is a codebook. It's of my own invention, and rather simple, but quite effective. We will use this for all messages. Each page is a disposable code. We will start with the first page for the first message. Once that message is complete, destroy the page and move on to the next one for the next message. Understand?"

"Yes, of course." Evelyn opened the book and glanced at the pages, then closed it and slipped it into her purse. "I must say this is all very well organized. How long have you been at this?"

"Since '36. It has developed into a more effective system since then, of course." He leaned on the desk and crossed his arms over his chest, looking down at her. "You remind me forcibly of someone and I cannot, for the life of me, think who it might be. That's unusual for me. Have you been to the hotel before?"

"No. This is my first time in Bern."

"Hm. I suppose it will come to me. In the meantime, is there anything else I can assist you with?"

"Actually, there is one thing," Evelyn said, looking up at him. "I'd like to go out tomorrow. I have an address, but I have no idea how far away it is or how to get there."

"Of course. Where is it?"

"Blasenflue."

He nodded. "It's not far from here. Perhaps half an hour by car. It's a mountain peak with fantastic views. Shall I arrange for a car?"

"I'd actually prefer not to have a car. I'd rather not draw attention to myself."

Philip was thoughtful for a moment. "It's too far to walk, but you could cycle. I can arrange for a bicycle to be at your disposal. It will take about two hours to cycle, I should think. If you decide to do that, I'd suggest leaving quite early."

"Would it be shocking to wear trousers? How are the local residents?"

"Goodness no! Not if you're on a bicycle. We aren't that old-fashioned here." He uncrossed his arms and went around the desk to pick up a pen. "I would suggest taking something to eat. I'll arrange for a picnic lunch for you. What time would you like to leave?"

"Shall we say eight o'clock?"

"I'll make sure the head porter takes care of you." He bent over to write on a clean sheet of paper for a few moments. When he finally looked up, he smiled. "I've written out directions for you. It's very straight-forward. You shouldn't have any trouble at all."

"That's wonderful. Thank you!"

He blotted the paper and folded it, handing it to her. "There is nothing to thank. It's my pleasure."

Evelyn tucked the paper into her purse and pulled on her gloves, standing up. "Nevertheless, I thank you just the same. You've been nothing but helpful, and I do appreciate that."

Philip inclined his head in acknowledgement, then followed her to the door.

"If you'll wait in the corridor, I'll just go into the cellar and find a bottle of vodka for you to take with you," he said. "Appearances, you see."

Evelyn nodded and stepped into the hallway, looking around. It was empty and she watched as Philip went to an open door, disappearing down a flight of stairs. He was efficient and obviously attentive to details, both of which set her mind at ease with this strange arrangement between herself and Lyakhov. It had been much easier to arrange than she'd imagined, sitting there in the lobby behind her French newspaper, and she was very glad that it was done.

Into the Iron Shadows

Now she could focus on Blasenflue and then get home to England before France was overrun.

London

The man sipped his drink and loosened his tie, crossing the room to a large, heavy desk gleaming with wood polish. The sun had disappeared and the heavy curtains were drawn across the windows, closing out the night. Soft light glowed from a few lamps, casting shadows over the leather-bound volumes on the shelves lining the walls. He sighed in contentment, rounding the corner of the desk and sinking into the leather chair. It was good to be home.

He took a moment to savor the superior scotch in his glass, leaning his head back on the chair and staring up at the ceiling. It had been a busy few days. When Hitler decided to move into the Low Countries at last, his entire building had been thrown into a tizzy. It wasn't that they hadn't known it was coming. Quite the contrary. They had been expecting it in January, and then again in March. April brought the surprise of Norway, yet still no move towards France. No. All of the government had known it was coming. The invasion of Belgium and Holland hadn't been the shock. The shock had been the Ardennes.

His lips twisted briefly. Everyone said it couldn't be done. The French were so sure and confident that Hitler would come through Belgium that they committed all their best troops, and England's too for that matter, to that avenue of defense, leaving the Ardennes completely unprotected. And the Germans had taken unabashed and full advantage of that tactical error.

And *that* was what was causing the ruckus.

No one could believe that Sedan had fallen. France's General Gamelin swore that it would take at least five days for the German armies to cross the Meuse, yet General von Rundstedt had done it in three. The news had come through this evening. The German Army Group A was through Sedan and now had a clear path to Paris. In response, all the troops not tied up in Belgium were being redirected east to protect the capital. Unfortunately, it was far too little and entirely too late. Gamelin had severely miscalculated, and was on the verge of losing France because of it.

Henry sipped his drink and lowered his eyes to the blotting pad on the desk before him. There was talk of Prime Minister Reynaud removing Gamelin from command and installing Weygand in his stead, and Henry wouldn't be surprised to see that happen. Although, to what purpose was anyone's guess. France was finished. The German Blitzkrieg was too much for them to handle. It was only a matter of time.

Sitting forward, he set his drink down and pulled his keys from his pocket, unlocking the bottom drawer to his right. Soon the German armies would converge on France, and the French forces would be forced to capitulate. When that happened, there would only be England left.

Churchill was being obstinate, as always, when pressed about the possibility of peace talks with Hitler. Lord Halifax and Lord Chamberlain both were supportive of mediation with the Führer, but Winston wouldn't even hear of it. Not yet.

Henry opened the drawer and pulled out a large square case, hefting its weight up onto the desk. He was sure the new prime minister would rethink his position in the next week or so when he lost the entire BEF in Belgium and France; he would have no choice. England could not fight without an army, after all.

He unlocked the case with another small key and glanced at the closed door before lifting the lid. He'd told his man that he didn't want to be disturbed, and he had every confidence his wish would be respected, but he was keenly aware of the risk of sending messages directly from the library in his London home. Not that he believed for one moment that he would be caught. The very idea was absurd. He was above suspicion, at least for the moment, and he intended to keep it that way.

Once the wireless radio was set and ready to go, Henry turned to lift his briefcase from where his man had set it next to the desk. He opened it and removed the stack of reports from inside, lifting a false bottom to pull out a folded sheaf of papers. Setting the case aside, he unfolded the papers and scanned them before setting them next to the machine on the desk. He reached back into the case for the codebook and pulled a piece of paper towards him on the blotter.

A few weeks ago, his handler in Berlin had instructed him to discover the names of any known Allied agents in France. He had gladly accepted the task, relieved that they had dropped the little matter of Robert Ainsworth and his missing package for the time being. However, he was very much aware that he had to provide solid and outstanding results this time or his usefulness to the Germans would begin to be questioned, and that was something he couldn't have happen. Not now.

It had been tricky, but not impossible. Despite the fact that MI6 was treating everyone as a potential spy these days, there were still several ways to find the information one needed. One just had to know where to look, and whose good graces to get into. A bit of luck never hurt either, and Henry seemed to have his fair share of that as well. As a result, he had a list of twelve names to pass on to Berlin, all agents of the Deuxième Bureau or MI6. Once France fell, the agents would be picked up before they could recover and rebuild a network or, worse, begin a resistance movement.

Henry opened the codebook and began composing the message he would send to Berlin. He had a suspicion that it was the threat of an underground resistance network that concerned the Nazis more than any organized governmental intelligence network. After all, once France fell, it would be nearly impossible for England to get agents in, let alone get them out again. He paused in his writing to lift his head and stare thoughtfully across the room. In point of fact, once France fell, MI6 would be both blind and deaf on the continent. They had waited too long to begin to build a network in France and Belgium, and then when they finally did realize that it might be needed, the Venlo Affair put paid to most of it. If only Jasper Montclair and William Buckley had been able to convince the rest of the upper-echelons that ungentlemanly warfare was both necessary and crucial to the nation's security, perhaps things would be different. Unfortunately for England, their arguments had fallen on the ears of old men who still believed that wars must be fought on a battlefield according to a certain code of conduct.

Henry's lips twisted and he lowered his gaze to the paper again. Their stupidity and lack of foresight was all to his advantage. It was strange, really, how things worked out in the end. If someone had told him just five years ago that he would betray his country and throw his hat in with the Nazis, he would have been horribly and terribly offended and told them where to get off. Yet circumstances changed. People changed. More importantly, the entire fabric of the world was changing, and the very strong English tendency to cling to traditions and the past had forced him to look long and hard at what he believed the future held, and who would have a place in the rapidly changing societies. The Führer had secured his place in the halls of leaders with resounding confidence, and unfortunately the British government had not. It was that simple. Henry wanted to be on the winning side when this was all over, and it was very clear which side that would be.

He finished writing and closed the codebook. Picking up the

headphones, he settled them on his head and tuned the dial on the radio, glancing up at the clock on the mantel. He was right on time. Someone would be standing by to receive his message.

EVIDENCE OF SEVERAL AGENTS IN FRANCE. STANDBY FOR LIST OF 12 NAMES. ALL AGENTS OF FRENCH AND BRITISH INTELLIGENCE. ALL CURRENTLY ACTIVE IN FRANCE. WILL CONTINUE TO SEARCH FOR OTHERS. - HENRY

He sent the message, then reached for the folded papers from his briefcase. He scanned them once more before setting them where he could easily see them while transmitting the names. After taking a fortifying sip of scotch, he began. A few minutes later, he sat back, finished. Then, with a frown, he looked at the sheets again. He had only transmitted eleven names. Yet he was sure there had been twelve. The frown turned to a scowl and he turned back to the briefcase, going back into the false bottom. There, pushed against the back corner, was another sheet of paper that had become separated from the rest. With a shake of his head, he pulled it out and composed a third message.

ADDITIONAL TRANSMISSION TO PROVIDE MISSING NAME. ADD THE FOLLOWING TO PREVIOUS LIST: JOSEPHINE ROUSSEAU.

Chapter Five

Blasenflue, Switzerland
May 15

Evelyn pedaled along the country road that wound its way in a constant incline up the side of a mountain. She had the optimism and energy of youth, and was in fairly good nick, but even she admitted that the constant uphill climb, no matter how gradual, was becoming tiring. Her breath was coming steady, but fast, and she was covered in a fine sheen of sweat that had developed over an hour ago. At this rate, she would be a sopping mess before she ever reached her destination, and that would never do. Ladies simply didn't sweat.

Despite her discomfort, a wry smile of amusement settled on her face. She could almost hear her mother's admonishment when she was much younger and they were living in Hong Kong. She had just come in from a particularly energetic game of cricket with Stephen Mansbridge. Cricket was a man's sport, not a lady's, her mother had informed her. Ladies didn't sweat. They sat in a dress on the sidelines and looked pretty.

The wry smile turned into a grin. Evelyn had never had much patience for sitting on the sidelines, something that had followed her through her teenage years and well beyond, much to the dismay of her mother. Thankfully, her father had run interference on her behalf, understanding this burning need for movement and action. The grin faded. Now she knew why. He had suffered the same emotions, and they had led him into the same service that she had later joined. It seemed that this need for action inevitably led to patriotic duty, and was something that he had passed on to his daughter.

And his son, she reminded herself as she lifted her hand to wipe moisture off her forehead before it dripped into her eyes. Robbie was every bit as reckless as she was herself. The difference was that it was acceptable in the son of the house, whereas it was *not* in the daughter. And so, while Robbie flew his Spitfire at speeds upwards of 350 miles per hour, she was pedaling up a mountainside in Switzerland on what could very well end up being a wild goose chase. The wry

49

smile emerged once again. She wasn't sure which of them was in more danger, he in his fighter plane, or she with all her narrow escapes from invading Germans. Perhaps it was a draw.

Thinking of Robbie inevitably brought Miles to mind, and Evelyn wondered if he was up in the air right this minute. Was he still flying endless patrols over the North Sea? Or was he flying over France now? Surely his squadron would soon be sent as air support over France, and then what? Would he finally get the taste of the action that he'd been yearning for since she'd first met him? The smile faded and she brushed a rogue lock of hair out of her eyes. It was inevitable that all the pilots would finally meet the enemy. All she could do was hope and pray that he and Robbie proved a match for the more experienced Luftwaffe pilots. A heavy feeling of anxiety settled over her, as it always did when she allowed herself to consider the weeks and months ahead. The thought of her fun-loving, reckless brother fighting fiercely in the skies against a faster and more experienced enemy left her cold and shuddering. Men like Robbie and Miles were all that stood between Hitler and England, and they were on the older end of the spectrum. Robbie had written in his last letter that the pilots coming in were barely eighteen. If Hitler turned his eyes to Britain, the very young RAF pilots had to succeed. If they didn't, there was no hope for any of them.

Shaking off the thought, Evelyn went around a curve in the road. Ahead of her, a man was leading a flock of sheep across the road to the field on the other side. When she came around the corner, he glanced up and touched his hat respectfully as she slowed down. She nodded in return, watching as the sheep moved into the road, blocking the way.

"Good morning," she said, getting off her borrowed bicycle.

"Morning, miss." The man paused and looked at her. "Lovely day for a picnic."

"Pardon?"

He motioned to the basket tied onto the back of her bicycle. "Your picnic basket."

Evelyn glanced at it and laughed. "Oh yes, of course!"

"Are you heading to the point, then?"

"No. I'm…well, actually, you might help me. I'm looking for an address and I think I must be getting close, but perhaps you can direct me?"

"Where's the place you're looking for?"

She told him the address and he scratched his chin, looking at her thoughtfully.

Into the Iron Shadows

"Ay, that's not far from here. Just another few minutes up the road. That farm's stood empty for quite some time now, though. Are you sure that's the right address?"

"Yes, I believe so. I didn't realize it was empty. How long has it been since someone lived there?"

"Oh, let me think," the man said, pulling off his hat and scratching his head. "It must be going on for almost a year now. The owner died last summer. Strange business, that. I saw him the day before in town and he was right as rain. The next day he was dead. They say it was heart trouble."

A chill went through Evelyn despite her warmth. "Heart trouble?"

"Yes. Never knew him to complain of it before, but you never really know, do you?" The man settled his hat back on his head. "The old place isn't much to look at now. No one goes there anymore. You're better off continuing on to the point, where you'll have a nice view for your lunch."

Evelyn smiled. "I might do that, but I've come all this way. I might as well take a look around."

He shrugged. "Well then, you'll continue on this road until you reach an old rotted oak tree. It should have fallen down years ago, but it's hanging on, bless it. Just past it is a lane on the left. That'll take you up to the old homestead."

"Thank you very much."

The man nodded and got his sheep moving again. "Good luck to you."

Evelyn waited until the small flock had cleared the road, then got back on her bicycle and began moving again. Her head was spinning. The owner had died unexpectedly in the summer, just as her father had. More chilling was the fact that he had also died of a heart condition that no one seemed to know anything about.

Heart conditions were, unfortunately, a fact of life for some men. The family doctor had told her mother when they received news of her father's death that sometimes the first symptoms were the last. They had all thought it strange, though. He had never complained of any kind of shortness of breath or fatigue. In fact, that last weekend before leaving on his fateful trip, he'd spent the entire weekend outdoors with the horses. He seemed as full of life and energy as ever. Even so, they had accepted the findings of the doctors in Switzerland without question. As that man with the sheep had said, sometimes you just never knew.

And that would have been the end of it, and she wouldn't think anything of the same fate befalling the farmer at the address ahead, if it weren't for that one, strange sentence uttered in the church of St. Michael and Gudula in Brussels last week.

"There is too much at stake for me to take risks if you are killed as well."

Evelyn's lips tightened as she pedaled on, her breath once again becoming labored. Lyakhov had said those words while discussing her father and how similar she was to him. He had said that she was like her father, only better. What he meant by that was anyone's guess, since it had been forcibly borne in upon her that her father's death had been a severe blow to MI6. Certainly Jasper Montclair didn't seem to think she was better than her father in any way. He seemed to tolerate her with a grudging humor, looking upon her more as a young woman whom he was indulging, allowing her to play at being a spy for a short time. At least, that was the impression she'd had from him of late. Bill, on the other hand, made no bones about how valuable he found her to be. Yet even he had never indicated that she was anything other than a young agent. So why did Shustov think differently? What was it that he saw that her own handler did not?

And what had he meant by saying if she was killed *as well*?

When she'd questioned him on his choice of words, he'd shrugged and said that her father was dead and if she died, she would be dead as well. Perfectly reasonable for a man who, while he spoke English extremely well, was Russian by birth. His use of English words was bound to be questionable at times.

And yet as she spotted the rotting oak tree in the distance, Evelyn was suddenly caught wondering if perhaps Vladimir had slipped in the church, saying something that he hadn't meant to. It seemed like too much of a coincidence that another man had died unexpectedly in a similar fashion in the same summer as her father.

Especially after her father had left his address for her find.

Maubeuge, France

Josephine finished fastening the last clasp on her bag and looked around the small bedroom. There was nothing left, but she went through the empty wardrobe and single chest of drawers anyway, opening each drawer and looking inside to make sure that it was empty.

Into the Iron Shadows

She couldn't leave any trace.

They had known this might happen, but even so, it had come as a shock this morning when Marc had announced with a grim face that German forces were expected to reach Marle that day. After breaking through at Sedan, they hadn't hesitated in sweeping across the countryside. In less than twenty-four hours, they were already deep into France and on their way to Paris. He had suggested that they leave now and go south before the Germans closed that route of retreat to them. Josephine hadn't hesitated. It was clearly time to go.

Now, looking around the empty bedroom one last time, she felt an almost overwhelming sense of despair roll over her. It was really happening. The Nazis were really coming into France. She picked up her bag and turned towards the door, taking a deep breath. There was nothing to be done now except to go south and try to continue the fight there.

She went out of the room and saw Finn coming down the hallway towards her. He was in his shirtsleeves, dark brown suspenders a stark contrast to his white shirt, and his hair had fallen over his forehead in disarray.

"Marc sent me to see if you need a hand carrying anything," he said, taking her bag from her. "Is this all you have?"

"Up here, yes. I have more downstairs. Have Luc and Mathieu returned from town yet?"

"No."

Josephine glanced at him as they headed to the stairs. "And so you are on the move again. I'm sorry that you aren't as safe as we supposed."

He shrugged. "I knew when I came with André and Mathieu that the Germans were close behind. It was only a matter of time."

"Then why did you come?"

"Because I thought I would have a better chance here than in Belgium. Of course, I didn't know that I would be asked to go to Calais instead."

Josephine chuckled. "Yes, well, that's what comes from working for England." She looked over her shoulder at him as she went down the stairs. "We may be going with you to Calais if the Germans keep coming at this speed."

"I don't think you want to go to Calais. The Luftwaffe will concentrate on all the port cities as they advance. I'm not looking forward to going myself."

"Is that what they did in Belgium?"

"Yes, and still are." They reached the first floor and Finn

moved around her. "I'll put this with the others, ready to go into the truck."

"Thank you."

Josephine turned and went to the front room where Marc had been listening on his radio, trying to get as much information as he could about troop positions. If Finn was right, it would never do for him to go to Calais as Bill had ordered. He'd be at more risk there than he would with them. What was Bill thinking?

"Marc, I think we should send a message to Bill," she said as she entered the room. "I'm worried about Finn going to Calais."

"I'm more worried about us getting out of here," he muttered, looking up from the pad of paper in front of him. "The Germans will be in Marle and Dercy before we can leave here. We can't go south. They're moving too fast, and will cut off any route to Paris."

"Then we will have to go southwest." Josephine joined him at the table and laid a hand on his shoulder. "Have you heard anything from Vervins? Will your uncle stay there or leave?"

"He will stay. He has no interest in running. He has no need. The Germans will have no use for him. He is a farmer, and too old to be a worker for them." Marc stretched and looked up at her. "Why do you worry about the Belgian? He has been ordered to go to Calais and wait there."

"He said that the Luftwaffe concentrate on the port cities. If he goes to Calais now, he will be in more danger from the bombing there than he is with us."

"That's none of our concern."

"Perhaps not, but I question whether or not Bill is aware of just how quickly the Germans are moving, and how dangerous it has become here."

Marc stared at her with his dark, unfathomable eyes for a moment, then exhaled.

"I will send a message," he said grudgingly. "Although I still say it's none of our concern. What will we do? Take him with us? We don't even know where we're going yet."

"We can't just leave him to fend for himself in the middle of all of this," she said. "If Bill agrees, we can bring him with us until we can find a safe place for him to wait."

"At this rate, there will be no safe place left," he retorted, reaching for his headset again. "I'll send the message, but if we don't receive a response soon, I won't wait. We leave as soon as Luc and Mathieu return. Start going through those papers over there and feed them into the fire. Burn everything. We need to insure that when the

Nazis come, there is nothing for them to find."

Josephine nodded and went over to the two boxes stacked on a chair. She carried one of them over to the fireplace where a cheerful fire crackled away. Settling herself before the flames, she began to pull maps, directives, and addresses from the box to toss into the fire.

"The truck is ready to be loaded." André walked into the room, wiping his hands on an old rag. "I fixed the leak in the radiator, but we'll need to take water just in case. As soon as Luc and Mathieu get back, we can leave. Any idea where we're going?"

"Not yet. Josephine suggested we go southwest. Take a look at the map and see what you think," Marc replied, glancing up from the message he was composing on a piece of paper. "I'm sending this message for Josephine to London, then I'll try and find out if any troops have crossed the border to the west yet."

André nodded and went to pull a map from a stack on the desk. "I think southwest is a good idea," he said, glancing at Josephine with a nod. "The German armies are coming across from Sedan. We don't want to run into them."

"What about Amiens?" Josephine asked, looking up from the fire. "Matilde is there and perhaps can give us somewhere to stay temporarily."

"If she can't, she can send us to someone who can," André said after a moment of thought. He spread out a map and studied it for a long moment. "We could go to Amiens, and then continue south to Rouen. But if the Germans keep coming and France falls, there will be nowhere left to go."

"Then we go home," Marc said from the table, not looking up from his radio. "If France falls, we will have to go underground. It will be too dangerous."

"That's easy for you and Luc, but not so easy for me," Josephine said. "If France falls, my father will be imprisoned with the other army Generals, and our home will be taken by a German commander. I can't go home."

"She's right," André said, glancing up from the map. "She's better off heading south and trying to settle somewhere else."

Marc finally looked up from his radio and looked from one to the other.

"Then we will part ways," he said slowly, "at least for a time. It might be better that way. If Josephine sets up a command somewhere in the south, we can feed information and messages through her."

"To where?" she demanded. "If France falls, there will be no Deuxième Bureau to send them to."

"We will send them to the only place left to help: London."

"Work with the British?!" André straightened up with a scoff. "Are you out of your mind?"

"Do you have a better plan?" Marc asked. "Would you rather roll over and allow the Nazis to take everything from us without a fight?"

André was silent for a long time, staring down at the map. "How will we get information to them?" he finally asked. "Once the Germans come, that radio will be useless. You'll have to destroy it. You know what we were told."

"I know."

"Then how will we contact London? There will be no way to get the information out."

They were all silent for a moment, then Josephine exhaled.

"We have a way," she said slowly. "I don't know how it will work, but we do have a way."

André turned to look at her. "How?"

"Marie Fournier."

Marc sat back in his chair thoughtfully. "Is she still in Paris?"

"I don't know, but if you contact Marcel, you can find out," she said with a shrug. "She is a direct link to London. Bill won't lose contact with her. He rates her too highly."

"You also have me," a new voice said from the doorway.

They all turned to look at Finn, leaning against the door jam.

"How long have you been standing there?" Marc demanded.

"Long enough," he answered. "When France falls, and it will, you will have to go to ground, but I won't. Bill is trying to get me to England. And so you will also have me."

"You say France will fall. How can you be so sure?" Josephine asked, her eyes flashing.

"Because I was in Belgium when it started there. The German Panzer divisions move too quickly. If they had been stopped at the Ardennes, you would have had a chance. As it stands now, they have no resistance on the way to Paris."

"He's right." André turned back to the map. "It's only a matter of time. We must decide what shall be done once it happens."

"You can't just give up like that!" Josephine leapt to her feet. "We still have our army. We still have the English soldiers."

"They are in Belgium, not here. They've been outflanked," André said with a shrug. "Unless a miracle occurs…"

"Josephine, calm yourself and get back to those papers," Marc said, a note of steel in his voice. "We will worry about tomorrow,

tomorrow. Right now, those papers must be destroyed and then we must leave. We're running out of time."

Josephine took a deep breath and nodded, sitting before the fire again and reaching for a pile of paper. Finn crossed the room to join her, grabbing the second box on his way. Settling himself next to her, he reached out and squeezed her hand.

"It will be all right," he said gently. "Marc is right. Worry about today, and let tomorrow take care of itself."

She glanced at him. "And you? Is that what you will do in Calais?"

"It is what I have been doing for seven days now, since they invaded Belgium and Holland."

"My God, it's only been seven days," André breathed, overhearing. "Impossible!"

"Clearly not," Marc muttered, going back to his radio and putting the headset over his ears. "If nothing else, the Nazis have shown that nothing is impossible."

Chapter Six

Evelyn got off the bicycle and leaned it against a tree, looking around. She was standing in an overgrown garden of sorts before an old stone house that looked as if it had been forgotten by both man and time. One of the front windows was broken, and paint peeled away from the wood in staggered rows on the front door. Weeds had overtaken what were once flower beds, and the stone path leading to the front door had long ago been claimed by encroaching moss and rough grass. Tilting her head back, she shaded her eyes and gazed up at the first floor. The windows were bare of curtains, but seemed intact. With the exception of the state of the garden and the one broken window, the house was really in quite good condition from the outside.

Turning, Evelyn looked out over the fields to the left of the house. They were covered with grass and wildflowers, the ground uneven where it had once been plowed. A sweeping feeling of sadness went through her, making her frown. There was something about the sight of neglected farmland that never failed to depress her, no doubt the result of growing up on an estate in the country. She was used to well-tended fields and flocks of sheep, and the sight of the forgotten land sent another wave of sorrow over her.

She exhaled and turned to walk along the overgrown path to the front door. A washed-out, tired looking sign near the door proclaimed that the house and land were for sale, but it had been half-hidden by a overgrown and thorny evergreen bush. It was as if the homestead had been half-heartedly listed for sale, and then promptly forgotten. Evelyn looked around and sighed. It was a mid-sized house and sat on a good piece of land. Someone should have snapped it up long before now. The fact that it still stood empty was a telling reminder of the state of the world economy.

Reaching out, she tried the door handle and was surprised when the door swung open easily. Bending to look, she shook her head when she saw the broken lock. She wasn't the first visitor to the empty homestead. Evelyn reached into her purse and pulled out her pistol, gripping it securely as she stepped through the door. She had no idea if anyone was inside, but it was better to be safe than sorry. The P-35 was a high-powered pistol capable of hitting a target at fifty meters, and Evelyn had become very proficient at doing just that. If there was anyone inside, they would be advised to think twice before trying to cause her any harm.

She stepped into a large, open room and looked around. Sun streamed through the front windows, cutting a swath through the gloom inside and highlighting swirls of dust in the air. The house was completely empty, and the wooden floors were covered with a fine sheen of dirt and a few dead leaves. She glanced over to the broken window, noting the oak tree outside. The window had been broken since the autumn. Standing still, she listened intently to the silence. There were no signs of disturbance in the large front room and she moved across the floor, glancing at the massive fireplace on the far right wall. She imagined that a roaring fire would warm most of the front of the house quite easily. Pulling her gaze away from it, she turned her head to peer into an empty room on her left. It was smaller than the main room and had a window that overlooked the overgrown fields. Stopping in the doorway, Evelyn looked around the bare room curiously. A study, perhaps? Or a small bedroom? She turned away, that strange sense of sadness coming over her again. Whatever it had been, it was nothing but an empty room now, covered in dirt and grime, with cobwebs in the corners, and void of life or personality.

Evelyn exhaled and followed a short hallway to the back of the house and a large, square kitchen. She didn't even know what she was looking for. All she knew was that her father had thought this house was so important that he had to conceal it in a Chinese puzzle box, which he knew only she would be able to open.

The sudden realization of the enormity of that act crashed upon her as she stood in the middle of the empty kitchen, looking around helplessly. Why on earth would he think she was the best choice? Why didn't he leave it with Bill? Or Jasper? Why her? He had no idea she was working with MI6 at the time.

Evelyn sucked in her breath suddenly and her eyes widened as she stared blindly at the large metal sink under a window overlooking rolling hills in the back. He had to have known! That was the only possible explanation for him leaving the box with her. He must have realized that Bill had recruited her, despite all their efforts to keep it from him. How? How had she given herself away? Even during the three months of intensive training in Scotland, her absence had been explained by a long visit with an old school friend. That was in the spring of last year, long before war was declared, and before the

WAAFs had been resurrected to assist in the coming war effort. She had been so careful to continue to behave as she always had, and had even stopped discussing the coming war with her family in fear that she would slip and reveal that she knew more than she had any right to know in her position as a young society butterfly.

Vladimir Lyakhov shot into her mind and she lifted a hand to her forehead as more and more of the strange events over the past year began to make sense. Of course! Daddy must have told Shustov that his daughter was also working for MI6. That was why Lyakhov insisted on meeting only with her in Oslo, and again in Brussels. Why hadn't any of them realized? Why hadn't Bill realized? Or had he?

Her lips tightened and she lowered her hand, spinning around to stride over to the open pantry, glancing inside. Seeing nothing but empty shelves, she turned to leave the kitchen, her mind spinning once again. Bill hadn't seemed very surprised when she told him about the break-in at Ainsworth Manor at Christmas. In fact, he'd very quickly decided that the puzzle box held a clue to something that he knew her father had brought out of Austria. She should have realized that he had arrived at the conclusion too quickly, that he was working with more information than he was sharing. If he knew her father had left the clue for her, then he must have known that her father knew about her involvement with MI6. Had he told him? Had Dad figured it out and gone to Bill for confirmation? And why on earth didn't Bill simply tell her? Why let her believe that her father had died not knowing that his daughter would continue his work, however ineffectually?

In the hallway, Evelyn took a moment to lean against the wall, her lips trembling. This changed everything. If Dad knew she was being trained to work on the continent, he knew that she would have the access and ability to come to Switzerland, to this house. He had trusted that she would know what to do when she arrived. She choked back half a laugh and looked around the dingy hallway. She had no idea what to do, and furthermore, she had no idea if he had expected the man who used to live here to still be alive when she arrived. If it was the man who was the answer, they were out of luck. That was the game, set and match. It was over.

The silence in the house was broken suddenly by a loud bang upstairs, like a door slamming shut. Evelyn's heart surged into her throat and blood began pounding in her ears as she tightened her grip on the P-35. Listening intently, she moved along the wall to the front room, straining to hear footsteps above. There was no other sound, only silence, but she swallowed and rounded the corner to the narrow staircase. She had to go up and investigate. There was no choice.

Into the Iron Shadows

Taking a deep, calming breath, Evelyn started up the stairs, silently reminding herself that not only did she have a high-powered pistol in her hand, but she was also trained in the Chinese art of Wing Chun. Gun aside, she herself was a weapon. There was nothing to fear. But while her mind knew that, fear still snaked down her spine as she made her way up the old steps. She winced when one creaked so loudly that she was sure it could be heard all over the house. She froze, listening. After a moment of complete silence, she continued, wincing again as the step creaked once more when she removed her foot. Whoever was up there knew she was coming now. There was no sneaking up on them.

Reaching the top of the stairs, Evelyn took another deep breath and peered around the corner. The second story was not large. A hallway ran the width of the house with two doors to the left and one to the right. One of the doors on the left was closed, and she looked to the right. Pressing her lips together determinedly, she turned right and went to the open door. It led to a small bathroom with an old-fashioned claw-foot tub, and a ceramic vanity with a sink. A toilet was at the end, the lid to the tank missing and the seat up. Otherwise, the room was empty. She turned and looked down the hallway at the closed door. Swallowing once more, she moved quietly along the wall until she came to the other open door. Glancing into the small room, she found it empty with nothing but a large spiders web in the corner near a small window.

Evelyn adjusted her grip on the pistol and moved to the closed door. She paused outside, listening. No sound came from inside, but someone had to be in there; doors didn't just slam shut on their own. She reached out to touch the door handle, her heart pounding in her chest. Taking a deep breath, she slowly turned it, forcing herself to remain calm as her breath came short and fast. Feeling the latch release, she took a deep breath, sent up a quick prayer, then shoved the door open, her heart in her throat. She moved into the doorway, raising the gun and steadying it with her other hand.

A loud screech preceded a rush of movement as something launched across the room towards her. Evelyn ducked instinctively, covering her head with her arms as long talons came within inches of her face. Looking up from a crouch, she watched in wonder as a huge cream-colored bird flew around the room before landing on the ledge of what was left of the window. She stared at the barn owl for a second, then lowered her arms, panting.

"God, you frightened me!" she exclaimed, glancing around the empty room. A brisk wind blew in through the window, ruffling the bird's feathers as he fixed her with a steely brown gaze. "Don't worry. I'm not going to hurt you."

She straightened up slowly, backing out of the room as the owl stiffened and gave every indication of launching another attack. Lowering her gaze from his, she moved back into the hallway, not daring to reach out to close the door again. Barn owls, she knew, were not something one wanted to tussle with. They always came out the winner. Once she was safely in the hallway, she moved to the side of the door and leaned against the wall while she caught her breath. After a moment, a reluctant laugh bubbled up from inside her and she looked down at the gun in her hand. She slid it back into her purse and turned to go back towards the stairs. She wouldn't need the pistol for a barn owl. She was quite alone in the old house.

Evelyn was halfway down the stairs when the door slammed shut again, causing her to start despite herself. She shook her head. The wind must be coming through the window at just the right angle to catch the door. She frowned as she reached the first floor. Why had the door been open before if the wind was in the habit of blowing it closed? Her eyes went to the front door with the broken lock and she shook her head. This old abandoned homestead was probably a favorite hangout for the local children. She looked around the empty front room. At least they weren't destroying the place in their play.

She walked to the middle of the front room and turned around slowly, a frown on her face. This was impossible. She didn't know what to look for, or even if it was still here. The house was completely empty.

Think! Dad wouldn't send you all the way here for nothing. There must be something!

Evelyn pursed her lips and went over to the edge of the wall. Lifting her gloved hand, she knocked lightly on the wood, listening. It sounded solid. She began to make her way around the room, knocking as she went. After circling the entirety of the front of the house, she ended back where she started and exhaled, turning to stare helplessly around her. The walls were solid, with no hidden compartments or doors. She dropped her eyes to the floor, suddenly remembering the cubbyhole in the floor of Asp's living room in Marle.

She crossed to the front door and went outside, returning a few moments later with a long branch discovered in the trees to the right of the house. She tapped it on the wooden floor inside the door, then moved to her right, tapping as she went. Evelyn felt silly, but she had to check everything thoroughly. She had come to Switzerland at great cost to MI6, and in the midst of Hitler's invasion of France. She had to do her best to find whatever it was that her father had left for her. She would finish checking the front room, then go through the small room to the side. If there was nothing, she would have to do the same in the kitchen.

There was always the possibility that it wasn't even inside the house, but outside, she thought as she made her way methodically across the floor. If that was the case, she could spend a month of Sundays here and never find it.

Evelyn had reached the center of the room when she paused and lifted her hand to brush a thick lock of hair out of her eyes. It had slipped from under her hat and she leaned the branch against her before raising both hands to readjust the hat. As she did so, she glanced up at the chimney above the fireplace. Her hands froze and she stared at the bricks, her eyes fixed on the carving near the ceiling. It was similar to a crest, with a picture and two words beneath it. The words were a name, but the picture was what arrested her attention. It was an ornate carving of an owl, not dissimilar from the type of barn owl that graced the upstairs bedroom at the moment, with a twisted branch of greenery in his beak, the leaves of which wrapped around the bird's neck. It was an unusual carving, and one that she'd seen before.

It had been part of the design on the Chinese puzzle box her father had left her.

Evelyn moved forward, dropping her hands from her hat. The branch clattered to the floor unheeded as she went to the fireplace and laid her hands on the shallow ledge that surrounded the hearth. She finally lowered her eyes from the crest and ran them along the ledge, looking for any kind of marking that would indicate a loose brick or hidden compartment. There was nothing.

Pursing her lips together, she lowered her gaze to the gaping, empty hearth. Scanning the bricks on the floor before the fireplace, she saw nothing out of the ordinary. One was slightly discolored, but when she bent down to tap and press it, it was still firmly set with the others. Evelyn sighed, crouched before the fireplace, and looked up at the chimney. If there weren't any lose bricks in the chimney, or hidden cracks, where could something possibly be concealed? She had no doubt that it was here, in the chimney. But where?

Evelyn sucked in her breath suddenly and lowered her eyes back to the yawning hearth. Of course! Without a further thought, she moved forward and stretched her arm up inside the chimney, her gloved fingers feeling around. She wrinkled her nose and made a face when her hand knocked years-old soot down, but she continued to slowly feel around. It had to be here. It had to!

CW Browning

Her fingers brushed against something that wasn't brick or stone and she paused, then angled her shoulder slightly to reach higher. It felt like a box of some sort. Frowning in concentration, Evelyn moved her hand along the top edge of the object, trying to feel how it was attached to the bricks. Finally, as her impatience got the better of her, she closed her fingers over it and tried to pull. It didn't budge. Sweating now from holding herself at an impossibly uncomfortable angle half inside the fireplace, Evelyn bit her lip and slammed her palm up against the bottom of the box. Something gave way with a crack and the box was suddenly free, falling off the inside of the chimney. With a gasp, she fumbled, trying to catch it. After a few seconds of juggling, she finally trapped it against the side of the bricks and exhaled in relief.

Pulling the box out of the chimney, Evelyn backed out and stood up, grimacing at the black soot that covered her cream glove and jacket. Then all thoughts of ruined clothes faded as she stared down at the flat, smooth silver box in her hand. Three initials were engraved on the lid: RMA. Robert Matthew Ainsworth.

Shock warred with sorrow as she stared at the cigarette case that had been her father's. The years in the chimney had done nothing more than allow the silver to become tarnished. Certainly no fire had been lit in the fireplace since it had been placed in its hiding place. Had he put it there after the owner had died? Or had the owner put it there before he died? Evelyn looked around the empty room, trying to imagine what kind of man lived here who would have garnered the trust of her father. Had they had a drink together in this very room, before this very fireplace? Had her father been here, knowing that one day she would stand in this very room, looking for answers that he'd sent her to find?

She closed her fingers over the case, suddenly feeling short of breath. She took a ragged breath and went towards the door. She needed fresh air. The combination of still air, old soot, dust, and the realization that her father had been in this very house was making her feel ill with emotion. It was almost too much for her.

Stepping outside into the sunshine, a brisk gust of wind blew against her hot cheeks. Evelyn filled her lungs, sucking in the clean air, and stumbled over to sit on a tree stump not far from the house. She forced herself to breathe steadily until the buzzing in her ears went away and the trembling in her hands stopped. She didn't look at the cigarette case clutched in her fist, but instead stared out over the fallow field and the rolling hills beyond. Birds sang to each other in the trees and she sat for a moment, allowing the serenity of the surrounding mountains to wash over her.

Into the Iron Shadows

A few moments later, Evelyn finally lowered her eyes to the case in her hand. She turned it over in her fingers before finally pushing the clasp on the side. The lid sprang open and a key fell out into her hand. Her eyebrows soared into her forehead as she stared at the key sparkling in the sunlight. It was pristine, as if it had never been used. A card was still in the case, tucked under the bar that would have held her father's cigarettes, had he been a smoker. As it was, the only thing she'd ever seen him smoke was a pipe, and that only in the evenings. Why, then, did he even have an engraved cigarette case?

The question flitted through her mind as she slid the card out. It was a business card and the embossed crest on the corner was one she'd only seen once before, many years before on a skiing trip to Switzerland with her mother. It belonged to one of the largest banks in Zürich. She remembered going to the bank with her mother. Yes, there was the address printed on the card, with the name of a manager. Evelyn turned the card over and stared at the account number written neatly across the back in her father's hand.

Raising her eyes from the card, she stared across the overgrown garden at the stone house. This was what he wanted her to find. A key, and a bank account in Zürich. The trail continued. There would be no answers yet.

Evelyn replaced the card and key and snapped the case closed, getting to her feet. She tucked it into her purse and turned back towards the bicycle. She would leave this place and find the point that the man in the lane had spoken of to eat her lunch. Then she would go back to Bern and have Philip make arrangements for a first class ticket on the train.

She was going to Zürich.

Chapter Seven

RAF Horsham

Miles Lacey folded the letter from his mother and tucked it back into the envelope, setting it aside. He sat back in the chair before the writing desk, looking around the small room. They had flown up from Duxford early that morning with just enough time for their planes to be refueled and for them to drop off their kit before going back up to run a patrol over the coast of Belgium. Reports of run-ins with Jerries were coming in from all the stations of Eleven Group, in the south of England. They were also flying daily stints over the Channel, and they seemed to be having all the fun. So far no such luck had been forthcoming for his squadron, and today had been no different. They hadn't seen hide nor hair of the blasted buggers, and they were all getting a bit tired of it, if the truth were told.

Miles stood up and went over to the bed to undo his suitcase. At least the new station was nice. Everything was brand new, including the living quarters. The officers' quarters were much better than they had been at Duxford, but the CO had cautioned them not to get too comfortable; they wouldn't be staying. This station was meant for the bombers. They would be moved again soon enough.

He was just hanging his uniforms in the narrow closet when a knock fell on the door, followed almost immediately by Rob Ainsworth strolling in. He'd discarded his jacket, but still had a blue, striped silk scarf tied at the neck of his shirt, lending him a rakish look.

"Jolly good digs, these," he said cheerfully, looking around. "We all have our own rooms."

"So I noticed," Miles said, turning back to his case on the bed. "I didn't realize it would be such a large selling point. Chris was in here earlier saying the same thing."

"Well, it is, you know. You didn't have to share a room with Snoring Slippy," Rob said, crossing over to look out the window. "You wouldn't believe how badly that man snores! There must be something wrong. His sinuses are probably all knotted."

Miles chuckled and turned to the closet again. "I'll remember that if I'm ever paired up with him."

"Aye, see what you can do to get moved before it's too late," Rob advised with a nod, turning away from the window. "What are you doing putting your kit away? Where's your batman?"

"He's gone home on compassionate leave. His father's dying. Won't be back for a few days, so I'm on my own."

"Good Lord, how inconvenient. Still, I suppose it's worse for him if he's to lose his father." Rob watched him for a minute. "Shall I wake you in the mornings?"

"I think I can manage, thanks."

He grinned. "I don't know that I could. Peters has the devil of a time getting me up, y'know."

"I will miss my tea in the morning," Miles admitted. He glanced at Rob. "How long have you been down?"

"They scrapped my last run. I assumed they'd grounded everyone. You must have already been up." Rob plopped into the chair at the writing desk and pulled out his cigarette case. "Have you heard the latest news out of France?"

"No, but I'm sure it's not good."

"Not a bit. Do you mind?" Rob held up a cigarette.

Miles raised his eyebrow. "Of course not. Why are you asking? You never have before."

"Chris said Mother suddenly took offense to us not asking before smoking this morning at dispersal. Strange thing, that. Mother smokes like a chimney. Why does he suddenly care?"

"He suddenly cares about a lot of things since he became Flight Leader," Miles said over his shoulder as he hung the last of his clothes. "Haven't you noticed? He tried to bark orders to Slippy yesterday."

"Good Lord, what did Slippy do?"

"Told him where to get off. I had to step in before things got out of hand."

Rob's eyebrows soared into his forehead and he grinned at Miles, his cigarette forgotten for the moment.

"You? Good God. I'm surprised there weren't casualties."

"Ashmore came in," Miles replied with an answering grin. "Once Mother was outranked, it was all over."

"Funny how the CO has that effect, isn't it?" Rob lit his cigarette. "Lord, I hope I don't get like that when I'm promoted."

"I won't let you, don't worry." Miles stowed the suitcase under the bed and turned to open his leather toiletries case. "What's the latest from France?"

"The Germans have broken through Sedan."

"Yes, they did that last night."

"Well now they're sweeping across France unchecked." He scowled. "They say they'll be in Paris in the week."

Miles paused, glancing up from where he was laying his shaving kit out on top of a table with a wash basin in the center.

"They're definitely heading for Paris?"

"Well, where else would they go?"

"If I were them? To the coast."

Rob stared at him. "What on earth for? They're not on holiday, y'know."

"To cut off our British Expeditionary Force and trap them." He finished emptying his bag and turned to look at Rob. "If they go to the coast, they'll catch them in a pincer move. Our troops will have nowhere to go."

"Bloody hell," Rob breathed. "I never thought of that."

"I can assure you that Hitler's generals have." Miles felt in his pockets for his cigarette case, frowning upon finding them empty. Without missing a beat, Rob picked up the missing case from the desk and tossed it to him. "Thanks. To be honest, I'd be relieved to hear that they're going to Paris."

"When you put it that way, so would I, as much as I don't want them there. Lord, can you imagine them goose-stepping down Champs Elysée? It's horrifying to even contemplate!"

Miles lit a cigarette and crossed the room to open the window. "Might be inevitable. It's not looking good."

"No," Rob agreed with a sigh. "People are already pouring out of Paris and going south. I've been trying to reach my mother all afternoon to see if she's heard anything from our aunt and uncle. The last I heard of anything, they were going to escape to their château in the south of France if the Germans broke through, but I don't know if that happened. God, I hope they're all out of it."

"You have cousins as well, don't you?" Miles asked, turning to look at him. "Evie mentioned them once. She called them the fun ones in the family."

Rob let out a bark of laughter. "Yes. Nicolas and Gisele. She's right. A more jolly pair you've never met. They're twins, y'know. Not identical, thank God."

"Yes, so she said. Are they going with your aunt and uncle?"

"I don't know. In fact, I don't know much of anything when it comes to them. Evie would know more." He tilted his head thoughtfully. "Maybe I should be trying to get through to her. She always seems to know what's happening with Zell and Nicki."

"I wouldn't count on getting her on the line. She's in Dover at the moment. I had a letter from her today."

"Dover! She was just in Cornwall, wasn't she? You know, I think she travels more than we do!"

"To be fair, we don't travel. We fly patrols. Bit of a difference there."

"True. It'll have to be Mother, then. I'm just concerned that they won't get out in time."

"I'm sure they've already left Paris. Your uncle wouldn't want to take any risks. At least, I know I wouldn't if I were in his position."

"Oh, it's not him I'm worried about. I know he and Auntie Adele will come to England if it looks as if France will fall, and it's starting to look like that, isn't it? No. It's Gisele and Nicolas I'm worried about. They're just the types do something stupid."

"Stupid? Such as?"

"Such as stay in France." Rob stubbed his cigarette out in the ashtray on the desk and shook his head. "Along with all that good cheer and excitement comes a very strong streak of recklessness. They're hot-heads, the both of them."

Miles considered him with a faint smile of amusement on his face.

"I can't imagine anyone else in your family that might be like that," he murmured.

Rob caught the sarcasm and grinned unabashedly. "Yes, but I have the luxury of being reckless in service to my King and Country. With me, it's not recklessness. It's patriotic duty."

"And with your sister?"

"Evie?" He laughed. "Evie has spirit, I'll grant you, but she escaped the reckless card when God was passing them out. She would never do anything truly dangerous."

Miles pursed his lips thoughtfully. "I'm not too sure of that," he said slowly. "There's something about your sister that I can't quite put my finger on. I think there's a lot more to her than we know."

Rob looked at him in surprise. "She's m'sister, old man. I know all there is to know about her."

"All right, then. There's a lot more to her than *I* know," Miles said easily.

"That may be, but I can assure you that she's the most level-headed out of all of us, thank God. She's saved my bacon more than once." He looked at his watch and got up. "I'm off to try ringing the family pile again. Are you coming down to the pub for a drink with the rest of us?"

"Yes. I'll be down in a bit. I have some correspondence to see to."

"Well, don't take too long. I'll ride along with you, if you don't mind."

Miles nodded and finished his cigarette, walking over to put it out in the ashtray as Rob disappeared. He watched the door close behind him thoughtfully and sat down, pulling a sheet of paper out of the top drawer and reaching for his pen. As he prepared to write a letter to his mother, his eyes strayed to the small stack of letters he'd received today. Evelyn's was on the bottom and he smiled faintly, thinking of her. Rob thought his sister was the practical one, but Miles had a very strong suspicion that she was every bit as reckless as he was. In fact, he would be willing to wager the Jaguar on it. The good Lord hadn't passed on bestowing her with the same traits as the rest of her family. He had simply given her the skills to conceal them.

Miles wondered if he would ever see that side of her. He sincerely hoped so, for he had a strong feeling that *that* was the real Evelyn Ainsworth. The polished society lady was a facade. He was sure of it. He didn't know why, but he was determined to find out everything there was to know about the woman he was falling hopelessly in love with.

Even if it took the rest of their lives.

Bellevue Palace Hotel

Evelyn stepped out of the lift and glanced at the front desk. Philip was speaking with a heavyset woman wearing a turban around her head and dripping with jewels. One look was enough to convince her that the matron was complaining about something. She turned decidedly towards the lounge. She would wait until the woman had finished her tirade and departed before approaching the night manager.

She entered the lounge a moment later and looked around. Large comfortable chairs and settees were arranged tastefully throughout the large room, beckoning guests to sit and read a newspaper in quiet elegance. Along the wall on the far side were a few writing desks stocked with pens, paper, envelopes, and telegram papers. Evelyn headed for the nearest one and seated herself, laying her clutch purse on the surface and reaching for a telegram pad. Bill had to be alerted to her change of plans. She would send him a message, then go into the restaurant for a late dinner. Reaching into her purse, she pulled out a slim codebook and opened it, moving her purse over it discreetly. She composed her message, pausing frequently to stare unseeingly at the wall before her. She had to be careful with what she told him. Her father had left this task to her, and not to MI6, for a reason. She had no idea what that reason was, but she intended to honor his last wishes for as long as she was able. After starting and discarding a few messages, she finally lowered her head and filled in the telegram sheet.

WENT TO ADDRESS. TRIP WAS SUCCESSFUL. LEAVING FOR ZURICH IN AM. WILL CONTACT AGAIN IN 24 HOURS. IF ANY NEW INSTRUCTIONS, SEND TO BPH. WILL FORWARD TO ME IN ZURICH - JIAN

She read it over twice, her lips pressed together. If Bill had new instructions regarding her return to France, Philip could forward the telegram on to her in Zürich.

Evelyn gathered everything together and stood up, turning to leave the lounge. As she made her way to the door, her eyes flicked over the few guests in the armchairs out of habit. All of them were men and, of the four seated with newspapers, two were definitely German. However, they were dressed well and hadn't looked up when she entered, nor were they paying any attention now as she was leaving. She continued on, confident that neither of them were members of the dreaded SS, which seemed to haunt her every step these days. As she walked out of the door and into the large lobby, Evelyn reflected wryly that she was getting rather used to looking for the enemy everywhere she went. It was becoming second nature to her, and she really wasn't sure how she felt about that.

There was no sign of the heavyset woman at the desk as she crossed the lobby and, as she approached, Philip looked up and smiled in greeting.

"Good evening, mademoiselle. How was your excursion today?"

"Very nice. Thank you so much for the use of the bicycle and the lovely picnic lunch. The onion tart was delicious."

"That is a particular specialty here in Bern. I'm pleased you enjoyed it."

"Everything was wonderful. And the views! You were right. They were absolutely breathtaking!" Evelyn laughed sheepishly. "I'm afraid the ride was a bit much for me in the end, though. I'm exhausted."

"Yes, it is quite a distance, especially if you aren't used to the mountains." Philip grinned. "I imagine you were very glad to come back and coast downhill all the way."

"I was indeed."

"And what can I do you for you this evening?"

"Could you arrange a first class compartment on the train to Zürich in the morning?"

He raised his eyebrows. "Are you leaving us so soon?"

"Not entirely. I find I have to go to the city unexpectedly, but I shall return. I'd like to keep my room here if I may."

"Yes of course. How long will you be away?"

"Only one night. I can't imagine my business will go into a second day."

"If you'd like, I'll arrange for a suite at The Storchen. It is on the Limmat River, in the heart of Zürich. I think you will find it quite comfortable."

"Thank you. I do appreciate it." Evelyn glanced down at the folded telegram in her hand. "Also, would you mind sending this telegram for me as soon as possible?"

"I'll see to it personally." Philip held out his hand for the telegram. "The earliest train leaves at half past eight. Is that convenient?"

"Yes, that's perfect. Thank you."

"My pleasure, mademoiselle. I look forward to seeing you when you return."

Evelyn nodded and began to turn away, then turned back. "Oh! Just one more thing. There may be a reply to that telegram. If it arrives after I've left tomorrow, will you forward it to me at The Storchen?"

"Yes, of course. Will it wait until I come on duty, or shall I have my daytime associate send it along sooner?"

"I don't think it will be time sensitive. Tomorrow evening should be fine." Evelyn smiled at him. "I appreciate your assistance."

"Of course, mademoiselle. If you need anything else, please don't hesitate to inquire."

She turned away with a smile and started across the lobby towards the restaurant. Philip really was a gem among night managers. She was suddenly very glad that Shustov had shared his contact with her. It seemed strange, but Evelyn had the feeling that no matter the situation, Philip was one of those men who would always find a way to be efficient and effective.

And she knew that was something she would need to depend on in the months, and possibly years, to come.

Into the Iron Shadows

Paris

Henry crossed the hotel lobby, walking towards the elevators and glancing at his watch. He would just have time to refresh himself and get changed before meeting his associates for dinner. It would be a long and tedious evening, but it was necessary. Appearances had to be maintained, as did the relationships that would see him through this war.

Stepping into the lift, he nodded to the attendant and watched as the liveried man closed the gate. A second later they jolted into motion, rising towards the upper floors. Stifling a yawn, Henry watched as the arm on the dial moved towards his floor. It had been a long day in a series of endless meetings that never seemed to go anywhere. France was lost, yet no one wanted to acknowledge it. They all preferred to pretend that there was still some hope. Even Churchill had promised to send more fighters over to aid in the fight, refusing to back down from his promise to aid France in all ways possible. There were rumors in London that the new prime minister had applied to President Roosevelt for aid, requesting destroyers and aircraft in support of the defense of Britain. He had to know that France was lost, and seemed to be planning for that very eventuality, yet was still promising to send more fighters. For what? To honor an agreement with the French government? What foolishness. It was the French government's reliance on old generals married to the antiquated battle plans of the last war that had landed them in this position. They had gambled with the lives of soldiers, and lost. Churchill owed France nothing. Still, England's foolishness would be to Germany's benefit.

It would make it that much easier to invade the island when the time came.

The lift came to a stop and the attendant opened the door and then the gate, nodding to him as he stepped out into the corridor. Turning, Henry strode down the hall towards his room, pulling his key from his pocket. A moment later, he was closing his door behind him and exhaling in some relief. Away from the eyes of the hotel staff and fellow guests, he could relax for a few precious moments before getting ready to go out again and play the diplomat. What a bore it was becoming!

Henry crossed the room to the writing desk on the other side and turned on the lamp, tossing his keys onto the smooth surface. Reaching into the inside pocket of his coat, he extracted a sealed telegram before removing the coat. He laid it across a wooden valet positioned at the foot of the bed and turned to seat himself at the desk. Ripping open the telegram, he read it quickly, a sharp frown slashing across his face. It was from one of their men in Switzerland.

INFORMATION RECEIVED THAT SOMEONE VISITED THE OLD FARM IN BLASENFLUE. HOUSE STILL EMPTY. NO SIGN OF ANY FURTHER ACTIVITY. DUPLICATE MESSAGE SENT TO BERLIN.

Henry laid the message down on the desk, staring at it with his lips pressed together unpleasantly. So someone was suddenly interested in the old farm, were they? Now why would that be? The house was empty, cleaned and thoroughly searched by them last summer. There was nothing there. Yet, to be safe, they had someone who kept an eye out for anything out of the ordinary. Anything like this.

He tapped a long finger on the desk thoughtfully. Perhaps they had been too hasty in eliminating Robert Ainsworth's contact last year. At the time, he himself had argued that the man could be useful to them. Yet, when presented with the opportunity, the farmer had refused, leaving them little choice. They had searched the house that very night, and then again after Ainsworth had died and it became clear that the information he'd stolen in Austria was missing. Nothing was there. Whatever Ainsworth had done with the package, it wasn't at the farm in Blasenflue.

Could they have missed something? Or was the mysterious visitor simply a curious nobody? Henry's eyes narrowed. The house had stood empty for months with no interest from either buyers or random visitors. Why would someone go there now? It seemed like too much of a coincidence when he himself was still trying to locate that missing package. There was absolutely no reason for him to think that the two could possibly be connected, except for the fact that the farmer had been a known contact of Robert Ainsworth.

He pulled out his cigarette case and extracted one, tapping it on the desk thoughtfully. Berlin would say that it was nothing and not to waste time on it. At the moment, they were more interested in rolling up the allied network in France than in the missing information stolen a year before. That wasn't a priority for them right now, not when it was obvious that the information was still well hidden. If the English had been in possession of it, they would certainly have been made aware of it.

It wasn't a priority for them, but he was still very interested in recovering it. He had told them that he would be able to do so and, so far, had failed. That was unacceptable to him. If there was even the slightest chance this strange visitor could lead him to the missing packet, then it was worth pursuing in his mind.

Henry lit his cigarette and stared at the telegram. It was too late to search the house again. Even if there had been something there, it was certainly gone now. He had to learn more about this visitor. Who were they? Were they Swiss? French? English? Were they staying in Bern?

He was just bending his head to write an answering message asking these questions when he paused, staring across the room blindly. Were they a relative of the farmer? The thought made him frown. He seemed to remember that there had been a son that showed up after the man's untimely demise. Was that the mysterious visitor? Had he gone back to the homestead to retrieve something left behind? If so, why wait so long?

After a long moment smoking, Henry finally stubbed the cigarette out in the ashtray and reached for a pencil. He would answer the telegram and request more information on the visitor. He would also send a message to Berlin before he went to dinner, requesting any information they had on possible family members of the farmer.

It was time to make sure they hadn't missed something crucial last summer.

Chapter Eight

Somewhere Over the Belgian Coast
May 17

Miles checked his bearings and glanced to his right. Not far off his wing Chris flew in perfect formation and, as he glanced over, he saw him turning his head and looking up behind them. Smart man, the Yank. He hadn't stopped searching for enemy fighters since they crossed the North Sea.

"We're only a few miles out." Rob's voice broke over the headset and Miles looked left to where Rob and Slippy were also in formation. "I'm going down to see if I can spot any of the blighters."

"Red two and I will go a little further in," Miles said. "If you see anything, let us know."

"Righto."

Miles watched as Rob and Slippy peeled off to begin a descent towards the water. They had been sent over to patrol the coast after a reconnaissance flight spotted German ships going towards Belgium at dawn. Their orders were to attack the ships if they found them, and they were more than willing and able to do so, if they could just find them. The problem was that they hadn't seen *anything* since crossing the sea, bird or boat.

"We're right over where Control said the ships would be," Chris said a few moments later.

"Right. Let's go fishing." Miles glanced at him. "Keep a watch out for fighters. We're in their back garden."

"So they keep telling us, but I have yet to see one of the bastards. I think they're all hiding from us. Probably heard the Spits of 66 Squadron were coming," Chris retorted cheerfully.

Miles grinned and dropped the nose of his plane, moving down into a long stretch of clouds. When they exited through the mist, the waves of the North Sea were below them, glittering in the sun. He blinked and refocused, searching the water for any sign of the German navy.

"There!" Chris called suddenly at the same time that Miles

spotted three long, dark shadows in the distance.

"I see them," he said, his pulse leaping at the sight. "Let's go say hello, shall we?"

They steered for the ships, closing the distance quickly. As they grew closer, Miles recognized the shapes and swallowed. Two were battleships and one looked to be a cruiser. They were definitely the ships that were spotted earlier. He glanced at his fuel gauge.

"Watch your fuel, Red Two," he advised. "We have time for one or two passes. Make them count."

"Roger that."

Miles couldn't ignore the surge of excitement that went through him as they increased speed and began to dive towards the ships. This was it. This would be his first battle engagement. This is what he'd been waiting for for months. He was finally going to do something to help the poor blokes on the ground. The blood pumped through his veins in anticipation as he focused on one of the destroyers through his gun sight, waiting for it to come into firing range.

"Fighters!" Chris yelled at the same time that machine gunfire erupted behind them.

Miles twisted his head around, searching for them, as he broke off his attack and banked to the left. The excitement turned to fear in an instant at the sight of two Messerschmitt Me 109s in perfect position behind them.

"Where the hell did they come from?" he yelled as he pulled his stick to the right to avoid another stream of bullets from the one behind him. "On your tail, Red Two!"

"I see him!"

Chris' voice sounded breathless and Miles turned his plane again, trying to get away from the German fighter behind him. As he did, he saw Chris avoid a burst of bullets from his opponent, the sound of the machine guns from the 109 blasting through his shock. In that instant, the fear disappeared, and in its place was a strange feeling of determination mixed with focus. *This* was what they had trained for, and this was what this beautiful Spitfire was built to do. They just had to stay alive long enough to do their job.

"Two more incoming!" Chris cried a moment later.

Miles was still angling to try to get a shot at the writhing, twisting airplane before him when he saw another 109 shoot into his peripheral vision. He pulled up and rolled to the right just in time to avoid landing in the new fighters' line of fire. The Spitfire responded instantly to every nuance on the stick, and Miles had never been happier for his machines instant response than he was at this moment as he watched a burst of bullets go past his canopy.

"That was bloody close," he muttered, twisting his head around as he tried to see where the fighter had got to.

The dogfight had moved them out of sight of the ships and back up towards the clouds. Looking up and seeing the cover above, Miles was struck by sudden inspiration.

"Head for the clouds, Red Two! Use them as cover!"

He pulled back on the stick as he spoke and sped upwards, breaking into the clouds a moment later. Turning, he then dove down suddenly, catching both enemy fighters below him. Emerging from the clouds with one directly in his sight, Miles sucked in his breath. The shot would never get any better. He pressed the button on his control stick and the Browning guns mounted in his wings let loose with a stream of bullets, the vibrations going through the plane and clear through his hands and up his arms. He'd fired the guns before, multiple times, at targets, but this time was different. It was as if every nerve ending in his body was responding this time, making his palms damp and his heart race. He stared through the windshield as his bullets ripped into the back of the 109 before he banked, pulling back up towards the clouds. Looking back, he saw smoke start pouring from the airplane and it dropped into a dive towards the water.

Before he could feel anything other than relief, bullets tore past him again. Twisting his head around, he found two 109s on his tail. Stifling a curse, he wrenched back on the stick and twisted out of the range of the closest one. Glancing at his fuel gauge, he let out a curse.

"Fuel, Red Two!"

The expletive that came through the headset echoed his own and Miles swiveled around, looking for Chris. All he could see were the two German fighters on his tail. Where the hell was he?

And then there he was, shooting out of the clouds hard on the tail of the third 109. Miles saw the burst of ammunition from Chris' Spit, but they didn't seem to have any effect on the vicious little fighter before him.

"Get up above the clouds, Red Two. We'll have to outrun them. Get as high and as fast as you can!"

Miles barked the instructions as he proceeded to do just that, pulling up into the clouds then continuing to climb past twenty thousand feet. He was approaching thirty thousand when Chris joined him. He looked over and nodded, relief going through him at the Yank's cheerful thumbs up. A burst of fire from the 109s behind him made him wince and he turned his nose for home, opening the throttle. They'd been told that Me 109s were no match for a Spitfire's speed at these altitudes. It was time find out if Fighter Command had got it right.

He and Chris sped towards home, hopping in and out of cloud cover whenever possible to help them evade the enemy fire. As they did, Miles kept looking back, watching the distance between them grow.

"Goddamn, it's true!" Chris crowed a few moments later. "They can't keep up!"

"We're not out of it yet, Yank," Miles retorted. "Keep moving!"

But after another minute or two, the remaining 109s fell back and then disappeared, turning for home. With his heart pounding and sweat pouring down his face, Miles looked over at Chris flying next to him. They'd done it. They'd survived their first encounter with the Jerries, and neither of them had been hit.

As they crossed the North Sea for home, the strangest feeling of elation mixed with numbness stole over him, and Miles lifted his hand to wipe the sweat off his face. Realizing that it was shaking, he shook it, trying to stop the tremors. Not only had he survived his first air battle, but he'd actually hit one of the blighters! He had his first kill, but it didn't feel anything like what he'd expected. He didn't feel anything. He just felt numb.

And jolly happy to be alive and heading home.

Amiens, France

Josephine carried a tray laden with coffee, mugs, bread and cheese across the large garden to the old shed at the bottom. Early morning sun washed the gentle slope with bright, hopeful light and she inhaled deeply, enjoying the scent of lavender as she went. It was a new day, fresh and calm for the moment. Birds were chirping and there seemed to be no indication of the weapons and tanks of war that were tearing through northern France towards the coast.

They had arrived in Amiens late the night before, going to the only house where they knew they would be assured of a welcome. Matilde was a matronly woman, and André's second cousin by marriage. She liked to say that she was nothing but a woman trying to keep her young cousin out of trouble, but whenever any of them came through Amiens, they were always welcomed with open arms. They were housed, fed, fussed over, and then rearmed with every weapon and ammunition that they could possibly want. Matilde was much more than a housewife and cousin, and Josephine didn't think she would ever cease to be amused by the dichotomy of a very French farmer's wife handing out semi-automatic rifles as if they were ice cream cones. Where she obtained them, no one knew or dared ask. They simply took them with gratefulness, leaving what payment they could afford behind.

When they all showed up on her doorstep after ten o'clock last night, she had taken one look at the group and had her husband usher all of them out to the shed. A few moments later, she arrived with mounds of blankets, pillows, and a bottle of wine. Then, without any further ado, she'd taken Josephine firmly by the arm and led her back to the house. No single woman was sharing her shed with five men, and that was that. Josephine wasn't about to argue. A comfortable bed in Matilde's tiny extra bedroom was infinitely preferable to a stone floor.

"Let me take that for you!"

A voice called behind her, causing her to turn around, balancing the laden tray carefully in her hands. Finn was hurrying towards her from the direction of the woods that bordered the property on the left.

"Good morning!" she called with a smile. "You're up early."

"I always am," he said, joining her and reaching out to take the heavy tray. "The others should be awake now. Marc was getting up when I left."

Josephine moved ahead of him to knock on the shed door. It opened a moment later and Marc looked out, his face brightening at the sight of the tray.

"Good! Coffee!" he exclaimed, opening the door wide to allow Finn room to maneuver the large tray. "Come in and join the argument, Josephine."

"Argument?" She followed Finn into the shed, glancing at Marc quizzically. "I left you alone for six hours, and you're already arguing?"

"With good reason," Luc told her, rolling up a map that was spread out on a makeshift table put together with boards and stacked bricks. "Put that down here, Finn. It should hold it."

"What good reason?"

"Marc thinks that it's too dangerous for us to remain together," André told her from the shadows where he was leaning against the back wall, his arms crossed over his chest. "He thinks it's better for us all to go our separate ways."

Into the Iron Shadows

"That's not exactly what he said," Luc said, shooting André an exasperated look. "It's not about going our separate ways. It's about making us less of a target."

"Yes. Working separately."

"Why would we do that?" Josephine asked, looking from Luc to Marc. "We've been assigned to work as a team. Have you received new orders?"

"No, and that's the problem," Mathieu said, pouring the strong, black coffee into a mug. "We're not getting any orders at all. Everything is in chaos."

"But Paris—"

"Is also in chaos," Marc said, taking the coffee pot from Mathieu. "The German armies are rolling through France with virtually no opposition. Paris will fall. When it does, the Deuxième Bureau will cease to exist. We will have nowhere to send our intelligence. No one to give us orders."

"So you want to quit?" she demanded, aghast.

"No! Not quit." he said forcefully, turning to face her with a chunk of bread in one hand and coffee in the other. "I will never quit! But for us to stay together is suicide. When the Germans come—"

"When the Germans come!" André exclaimed, cutting him off. "You keep saying that as if it's inevitable! France still has a chance."

"What chance? No one wants us to win this war more than me, but we must face the facts. We are outmatched, with both men and artillery, and we have been outmaneuvered. Holland has surrendered, they've taken Brussels, and Antwerp will be next. Belgium will surrender soon. They will have no choice. That leaves us with only England, and all the English troops are trapped in Belgium along with our own." Luc shook his head. "We must accept that France is next, André. To refuse to do so is foolish and dangerous."

"If we fight—"

"But that's just it, isn't it?" Marc asked quietly. "We're not fighting. Our soldiers are laying down their weapons and surrendering without ever firing a shot."

"What?!" Josephine gasped, her face paling.

Luc laid a hand on her shoulder. "We weren't going to tell you," he said gently. "That's how they rolled right through Sedan. Our army isn't defending us. The ones in the weaker positions along the eastern border aren't trained. They're surrendering rather than fight."

Josephine stared at him, then looked at the somber faces of the others. "Why weren't you going to tell me?"

"Because your father is a general. We knew it would upset

you."

"Yes, and my father *is* fighting in Belgium!" Josephine rubbed her face, shaking her head. "I can't believe it. How do you know that soldiers are choosing to surrender?"

"Pierre witnessed it outside Sedan," Marc said reluctantly. "He sent a warning message to all of us to prepare for a rapid advancement of Nazi troops."

Silence fell as the men ate their breakfast, and Josephine tried to wrap her mind around this new nightmare. It didn't seem possible that the French soldiers would simply surrender, and yet she believed the report from Pierre without question. He had never been anything but blunt, sometimes embarrassingly so. If the soldiers were simply surrendering rather than run the risk of fighting, she supposed it was because they were so inexperienced. All the strong units had been sent into Belgium. If the weaker units were faced with the German Panzer divisions, they may very well be unequipped to handle it.

"If our own soldiers will not fight, then France will fall," she finally said, breaking the silence. "Marc is right. How can it not?"

"And if France falls, we cannot all be together. The Germans must never know who we are or what we can do."

"You want us to separate so that we don't all get caught," she said slowly, "but then what?"

"We continue. In secret."

"And what do we do with whatever information we collect?" André asked. "There will be no one to give it to."

"That's not necessarily true," Josephine said thoughtfully. "England will never give in, not with their new prime minister. Churchill is a bull. He will continue to fight until there is nothing left. And if they mean to continue the fight alone, they will need all the information they can get."

"And how will we get it to them?" Mathieu demanded.

"We already have a few contacts," Marc told him. "While you and André were in Belgium retrieving our friend here, I met one of them. She'll do."

"She?" Mathieu began, then caught sight of the steely look in Josephine's eyes. He grinned ruefully. "Not that women aren't capable," he said appeasingly. "But an Englishwoman? Are you serious?"

"She doesn't sound like an Englishwoman," Luc said. "In fact, I thought she was French."

"I think she is," Josephine said. "I don't know where Bill found her, but I'd swear she's from Paris."

"Or at least has spent a lot of time there," Luc agreed.

"All right. So we have a possible outlet for any information we manage to gather," André said with a shrug. "But how will we communicate? You're the only one with a radio. If we split up and go our separate ways, we won't know where anyone is, let alone be able to contact them. The whole idea is absurd."

Before Marc could answer, his radio came alive in the corner and he set his coffee cup down.

"It's early," he muttered, going to the corner of the shed. "This can't be good."

"What are your thoughts on our predicament?" Luc asked Finn, who had been sitting quietly throughout the entire conversation.

"It's not really my place to say, is it?" he asked with a shrug. "I'm being sent to Calais."

"Yes, but you must have an opinion?"

"I think Marc is correct. Right now your best hope for remaining free and undetected by the Nazis is to separate and establish normal lives away from each other." Finn looked at them grimly. "They will be looking for any members of the Allied network. They have already begun in Belgium. They won't tolerate any remnant that could form into a resistance. I think you must shift from thinking of yourselves as working for your government to thinking of yourselves as part of a resistance."

Josephine swallowed and glanced over at Marc in the corner, hunched over his radio with his headset over his ears.

"Then perhaps this *is* the best thing to do. If we separate, we still have a chance."

"And we lose the safety we have with each other's support."

"Better that than lose our freedom and lives," Luc muttered. "And we will find each other again. I have no doubt of that."

"Neither do I," André replied. "My fear is that it will be too late when we do."

"Josephine!" Marc called. "Come."

Josephine turned around in surprise and went over to him. "What is it?"

"A message for you."

"Me?"

"From London."

He took off his headset and handed it to her, getting up. "They are sending it through now."

Josephine set the headset on her head and reached for the pencil and notepad next to the radio. She tore off a piece of paper and bent over it, scribbling down the code as it came through. Marc moved away to give her privacy, but as he joined the others, she was conscious of five sets of eyes watching her. A flash of amusement went through her. They were as bad as children, curious beyond belief.

A few moments later, she removed the headset and set about deciphering the message. When Marc had sent the message yesterday to confirm that Finn was to go to Calais, they hadn't received an answer. Now they were, and then some. The message was a long one, much longer than she was used to from Bill. With the others talking in low voices behind her, Josephine finished going through the message and sat back to read it. After reading it twice, she looked up to find all five pairs of eyes watching her again.

"Finn, you're not going to Calais," she said, getting up. "You're going to Paris."

"Paris!" André exclaimed. "Are they insane? Most of Paris is fleeing the city!"

"He's to join an old friend of mine there." She looked at Finn. "They'll get you out of France."

"Old friend?" Marc asked, raising his eyebrow. "What old friend?"

"The one you met last week. I think your words were, 'She'll do.'"

"She's still in Paris?" Luc asked, surprised.

Josephine shrugged. "I don't know, but these are the instructions."

André was watching her face and his eyes narrowed suddenly. "What else?"

"Pardon?"

"What else is in the instructions?"

Josephine swallowed. "He warns that the Germans are not going to Paris, but are racing for the coast to cut off the Allied troops."

"If that's true, they'll come through Amiens," Mathieu said in alarm. "We can't stay here."

"No," Marc agreed, nodding brusquely. "We will have to move. I think it best if we part ways now. It's not worth the risk of someone remembering us. There are six of us. We are too conspicuous now."

"I'll take Finn to Paris," Josephine said, pulling out a lighter and setting the edge of her paper against the flame. "I'll help them get out of France, and then I will head for Marseilles. I have an old friend there. I can stay with her until I get myself situated."

"Marseilles?" André looked at her with a frown. "How will you get there?"

"I'll find a way." She summoned a smile for him. "Don't worry about me. I'll be there waiting for the rest of you."

"We'll come," Marc said, laying a hand on her arm. "We will finish this."

She met his eyes and nodded, swallowing. "I know."

"When do I have to be in Paris?" Finn asked.

"Tomorrow. Which means we need to leave as soon as possible." Josephine turned for the door. "I'll tell Matilde I'm leaving. André, I'll leave you to tell her about the rest of you. I'm not explaining any of this."

"Josephine?"

"Yes?"

"Leave some guns for us. We'll need them as well."

Chapter Nine

Zürich, Switzerland

Evelyn got out of the taxi and glanced up at the stunningly imposing stone facade before her. Standing over ten stories with ornate stonework adorning the first two floors, the bank made a simple statement of elegance and exclusiveness. She adjusted her gloves and walked towards the impressive doors under a black and gold awning. The building didn't intimidate her. Her own bank in London was just as imposing. Yet what awaited her inside did, and Evelyn's spine stiffened in reaction, her chin edging up in the faintest tilt of resolution.

A doorman opened the door for her, nodding to her respectfully as she approached.

"Mademoiselle," he murmured.

"Merci."

She swept into the lobby of the bank with her purse over her arm and looked around. Spotless marble floors gleamed beneath her heels as she paused, her eyes brushing over the marble counter where patrons could conduct routine transactions before moving to a little gate in a brass fence that separated the lobby from more private rooms. That was where more intricate business was conducted, she knew, and that was most likely where she would need to go.

"Good afternoon, Fraulein. How can I assist you today?"

The question was asked in German, and she turned in some trepidation despite knowing that that language was prominent in Zürich. An older gentleman with graying hair approached her, a deferential smile on his face. He was dressed impeccably in a black suit that was neither ostentatious nor understated, speaking more to his status as a bank manager than an introduction ever could. He was smiling amiably and his head was tilted with the kind of respect that she was used to receiving when she was at home in England. After much debate in her hotel room, Evelyn had decided to dress as she would if she were visiting her own bank in London. Clearly, she had made the correct decision. Her care with her wardrobe had paid off handsomely, speaking more of her stature in society than her name would this far from home.

"Good afternoon. I'd like to discuss an account," she said, also in German.

"Yes, of course. My name is Albert Brunner and I am the manager here."

"I am Evelyn Ainsworth," she said, holding out a gloved hand. "My father was Robert Ainsworth."

Herr Brunner's eyebrows rose and his smile grew as he shook her hand.

"Yes, of course! I remember Herr Ainsworth well. He hasn't been here in quite some time." As he spoke, Herr Brunner led her across the spacious lobby to the little gate. He opened it and waited for her to go through before following. "How is your father?"

Evelyn waited until he'd closed the gate and they had moved away before answering.

"I'm afraid he has passed away."

"Oh, I am sorry to hear that." Brunner paused and looked at her, his face transforming seamlessly from an amiable smile to a study in sympathy. "You have my most sincere condolences."

"Thank you."

"I suppose you must be here to see about the box, and to make arrangements for his accounts." Brunner led her to a corridor on the left. "Just this way, if you please." He motioned her towards a door a few feet away. "When did Herr Ainsworth pass?"

"Last September." Evelyn walked into a large and elegantly appointed office. Furnished with comfortable armchairs and dark, heavy wood, it oozed affluence. A thick, rich, burgundy carpet cushioned her feet as she made her way across the room to one of the armchairs. "It was quite sudden."

"I am sorry to hear that."

Brunner closed the door and moved across the room to seat himself behind a desk gleaming with wood polish. A shining brass desk set reflected her countenance back to her as Evelyn sat down, settling her purse on her lap.

"He was a wonderful man. September, you say? Why, he must have…that is, I believe we last saw him around that time."

"He was in Bern when he died," she offered with a small smile. "So it's very possible."

"Good heavens." Herr Brunner sat back, shaking his head sadly. "How shocking for your family. Did your mother accompany you here to Zürich?"

"No, she's still in England."

He nodded and frowned thoughtfully. "You have a...brother, yes?"

Evelyn raised her eyebrows. "You have a fantastic memory, Herr Brunner," she said with a smile. "Yes, I do."

"As I said, your father was a wonderful man. He and I had many conversations over the years."

"Over the years?" she repeated, surprised. "How long has he had an account with your bank?"

"Oh my, quite a few years now. Let me think." Brunner stroked his chin thoughtfully, pursing his lips. "It must have been '32 or '33 that I first met him. He was on a visit from China. Hong Kong, if my memory serves me correctly."

Despite herself, Evelyn was shaken. She'd had no idea that her father even had a bank account outside of England and France, and she certainly had never heard about him coming to Switzerland while they were in Hong Kong. He had traveled even then, of course, but she had always been under the impression that it was confined to England's interests in Asia.

"I must say that I'm surprised to see you here instead of your brother," he continued. "I would have thought he would be the one taking care of the estate affairs."

"He has taken over management of the family estate, yes. However, he's rather busy with the war effort. He's a pilot, you know." Evelyn smiled apologetically. "I'm afraid I was the only one available to come."

"Ah. Yes. This war is making everything very difficult." Brunner straightened up. "Now, I'll need your identification, of course. And I'm sure your brother sent along a letter releasing the information into your care?"

"No, he didn't." Evelyn opened her eyes very wide and stared at Herr Brunner helplessly. "Goodness, I don't think it even occurred to him. He sent his solicitor to me with the information and requested that I come see to it. He's flying over France at the moment, you see," she added pointedly.

"Oh dear. Well, I suppose given the unique situation, with the proper identification I can arrange something. You *do* have that, don't you?"

"Of course."

Evelyn opened her purse and pulled out her passport and papers, reflecting as she did so how strange it was to see her real name on the documents. It was almost as if her true identity was becoming foreign to her. The thought was a disturbing one, and she shook it off quickly.

"I must confess, Herr Brunner, that I'm not sure of what accounts my father had with your bank. They weren't mentioned in his will, and our family solicitors were unaware of them. The only reason I'm here, to be completely honest, is because he left me a note with a key, and this. I naturally contacted my brother, who contacted our solicitors. It's all very strange."

She passed him the business card with the single account number written across the back. Herr Brunner took the card and glanced at it.

"How unusual. This was all he left you?" he asked, looking up. "How very strange. Your father had three accounts with us, and a safe deposit box." He handed the card back to her and examined her paperwork in silence for a moment before nodding. "Well, this all seems to be in order. There is just one more formality I must check before we can proceed." He stood up and handed her documents back to her. "We require all our depositors to fill out a form with instructions in the event of their death. After the Great War, there was such confusion, you see. If you wouldn't mind waiting a moment?"

"No, of course not."

Evelyn smiled at him and watched as he left the office. As soon as the door closed behind him, she tucked her papers back into her purse and snapped it closed, exhaling. Her mind swirled with confusion. Her father had three accounts here? What on earth for? Why would he keep money in Zürich when he had accounts in both England and France? She frowned and stared blindly at the brass inkwell on the desk. Of course, he had been travelling to Switzerland and Austria, as well as Germany, quite a bit in the years before his death. It would make sense for him to require easy access to funds, but one account would be perfectly sufficient. Why three? And why hadn't anyone known about them?

After a long moment, Evelyn stood up restlessly and walked over to examine a painting on the opposite wall. If he had three accounts, should she close all of them? Was it really her place to do so? Or should she investigate the box and the one account, then alert Robbie to the existence of the others? As soon as the thought occurred to her, Evelyn shook her head. No. How on earth would she explain to Robbie how she'd learned of the bank in Zürich in the first place? Or that she'd actually been here when she was supposed to be safe on English soil, training WAAFs around England?

Turning, she paced back to her chair. Sitting down again, she bit her bottom lip. It didn't seem quite the thing, really, looking at her father's private bank accounts. It almost seemed disrespectful, in a way. This was something the solicitors did, not something she should do. Yet what other choice did she have? She was here, and Robbie was not. Neither were their solicitors.

Oh Dad, what am I to do? What would you want me to do?

The door behind her opened again and Herr Brunner returned with a leather folder in his hands.

"I'm sorry to have kept you waiting, Fraulein Ainsworth," he said, closing the door. "I hope you weren't uncomfortable."

"Not at all."

He went back to sit behind the desk and nodded, undoing the strap around the folder.

"Well then, let's take a look and see what we can do," he said, opening the folder. He pulled a pair of spectacles from his inside pocket and settled them on his nose before examining the letters in the folder.

Evelyn watched him curiously, watching as his forehead creased in concentration. Goodness she hoped her father had had the forethought to allow her access to the safe deposit box! He must have. He had left the key where only she could find it. But what if he hadn't?

"Well, well. I must say that this is most irregular," Brunner murmured, flipping to the next page. "Hm. Mmm."

Evelyn resisted the urge to laugh at the look of pure consternation on the man's face. Heavens, what had her dearly departed father instructed? Bankers were notoriously unflappable, yet Herr Brunner seemed quite taken aback by what he was reading.

When he finally finished, he stacked the letters neatly and closed the folder, removing his glasses. His face had been schooled back into the placid expression he'd had since the beginning.

"Well, Fraulein, we can continue without any hesitation. Your father was very clear in his instructions."

"May I ask what his instructions were?"

"Yes. He leaves sole access, ownership and authority of all his assets in this bank to his daughter, Evelyn Ainsworth. In the event that she is deceased, all rights will pass to his wife, Madeleine Ainsworth." Brunner rubbed his chin with a frown. "It's very irregular. The rights don't pass to his first-born son unless both you and your mother are deceased. I'm sure you understand how unusual that is."

"Yes." Evelyn agreed. "How very strange. Robbie has taken over management of the entire estate. I don't know why Dad would have given those instructions, but it does explain why I received this key and not my brother."

Herr Brunner lowered his hand and his amiable smile was back. "Perhaps this was his nest egg for you," he said gently. "He spoke very highly of you. He was very proud of your ear for languages, and I must say that your German is impeccable."

Evelyn smiled and inclined her head slightly. "Thank you."

"Where would you like to begin, Fraulein? We can begin with the numbered accounts, or perhaps you'd like to examine the box first?"

Evelyn raised her eyes to his. "I think I'll start with the box."

Lvov, Poland

A low, gray ceiling lay over the city as two uniformed guards stood inside the main entrance of the municipal building headquarters. The younger one gazed dutifully out of the glass doors while his superior seemed uninterested in the possibility of any unscheduled visitors. When his subordinate suddenly snapped to attention, he looked at him in surprise before turning his attention outside. An imposing figure strode up the shallow steps of the old building seized by Soviet forces months before. He didn't recognize the man, who was dressed, not in uniform, but in civilian clothes, with a long, steel gray overcoat of thick wool hanging perfectly on his stocky frame. Glancing at the other soldier standing at perfect attention, he frowned and shook his head. There was no reason that he could see for the fuss. It was just another government worker looking for a permit, more than likely. He waited until the man had entered the building before moving to block his path.

"What is your business?" he barked, stepping forward. "Identification!"

There was a moment of silence as the man turned dark eyes upon him. Nothing in the stranger's countenance changed, but the soldier felt a streak of uncertainty go through him at the steely look. The man reached a hand into his inner pocket, pulling out a leather wallet, his eyes never leaving the soldier's face.

"My business is none of your concern, Sergeant," he said coldly, handing him the identification.

The soldier took it and flipped it open. His face paled and he looked up again, startled.

"My apologies, sir. I had no idea—"

"I'm not interested in your apologies, or your excuses." The man cut him off, snatching his identification from suddenly limp fingers and tucking it back into his pocket. "I would advise you to pay attention when your fellow soldier stands to attention. If you did, you would have had an idea. Now let me pass."

"Comrade!" The hapless soldier fell back and stood ramrod straight while the man strode on, beads of sweat forming along his forehead.

"Idiot!" The other guard hissed as soon as the man was out of earshot.

"You could have warned me!" he retorted in just as quiet a tone. "You know who that is?"

"Yes. I saw him a few days ago."

The soldier swallowed and lifted a hand to wipe the moisture from his brow as the man disappeared around the corner and moved out of sight.

"Then it was your duty to tell me!"

The other guard came as close to shrugging as he could without actually doing so. "I didn't have time." He relaxed his stance now that the man was gone. "I'm glad I'm not in your boots, though."

The soldier swallowed again and refused to answer, turning his attention outside. There was no reason to answer. They both knew what could happen. One did not simply treat a senior commanding officer of the People's Commissariat for Internal Affairs with the level of disrespect that he just had and emerge unscathed. There would be repercussions.

The NKVD would demand it.

Vladimir Lyakhov strode down the corridor, stripping off his gloves as he went. The arrogance of the guard could have been dismissed, if not excused, but not the ignorance. Once his compatriot had snapped to attention, he should have been alerted to the fact that someone of some rank was approaching. If that was the level of intelligence the Red Army was producing these days, they were in for a long war indeed.

Of course, it could have been worse. Lyakhov well remembered the days when there was no standard of respect at all in the military.

Into the Iron Shadows

That was in the beginning, after the revolution. At that time, it was believed that a ranking system, and all the power and respect it demanded, was part of the bourgeois customs that every true Bolshevist abhorred. He had been a young man then, just entering the army, and the resulting chaos of those early years was still a sore point with many of his fellow officers now. The period had been characterized by blatant disregard for anything resembling structure, with soldiers voting on which orders they would follow, and which man would command them. The results were, predictably, terrible, and the Kremlin soon rectified the situation by reinstating a ranking system within the army. It was the sharp memory of this time that led to an attitude of zero tolerance among his fellow officers, and Lyakhov was no exception. By morning, that soldier would be on his way back to the motherland to receive a demotion and forced manual labor.

Unlike the majority of his fellow NKVD officers, Vladimir did *not* believe that a minor first offense should necessarily constitute it being the man's last act on this earth. He did, however, believe in repercussions.

He opened a door to stride into a small, utilitarian office. He tossed his hat and gloves onto a chair and unbuttoned his coat, shrugging out of it before draping it carefully over the back of the chair. He looked at his watch and walked around to seat himself behind the desk. He just had time to write out his report and prepare for the briefing in the morning before going back to his apartment for the night. In the morning, he left for Kiev, and then on to Leningrad. His detour into Belgium last week had cost him three days in travel time, but it had been necessary. Now he had much to do to make up those three days.

After unlocking a drawer and pulling out a folder, he got up and went over to a small table in the corner to turn on the radio. Returning to his seat, he picked up a pen and proceeded to get started. The radio program droned in the background while he began to write out his estimation on the facility here in Lvov. While not ideal, it would be sufficient for them to glean operational intelligence from the local population. With any luck, they would be siphoning new information into Moscow within the month.

It was about ten minutes later that the steady movement of his nib across the paper paused. Lifting his head, Vladimir glanced at the radio as the announcer began reading the evening news. When, a few seconds into the segment, he said that the flowers were blooming in the Alps, Vladimir set down his pen and smiled faintly. Getting up, he went over to switch off the radio before returning to open the top drawer of the desk. He pulled out a cigarette and lit it, then crossed over to the small window to gaze outside. So it was done. Lotus had made the arrangements at the hotel in Bern.

He sucked on the cigarette and watched absently as a woman pushed a pram down the street. When he began this quest after Robert Ainsworth died, he had fully expected Ainsworth's daughter to be an acceptable substitute. Upon meeting her last fall, she had exceeded his expectations. Now she was on the road to becoming much more than a simple contact in the West.

Much, much more.

For better or worse, they were now both committed to this relationship. Regardless of what happened on the continent and in the battlefields that covered them, he had an open path of communication with her, and she with him. With that came many risks for them both, not the least of which was certain death should either of them be discovered by his government.

He briefly wondered how she had got out of Brussels in the midst of the German offensive. He had sent her a note on the morning of the invasion, advising her which ways were clear for her to make it to France. He'd received confirmation that his courier had delivered it into her hand in the lobby of the hotel. Even so, he'd had a moments concern when he heard that Brussels was being bombed. Yet she'd made it out, and was able to make her way to Switzerland.

Vladimir stared thoughtfully out of the window. How on earth was she going to get back to England? The German armies were advancing on all fronts, and soon they would be on the northern coast of France, trapping the Allied forces. France was destined to fall quickly, and when it did, there would be no way out. He lifted the cigarette to his lips. It would be interesting to see what happened if she were unable to get back in time. Would she contact him? Or would she continue her work from within France? A faint smile grazed his lips. He had a feeling that she would continue from the depths of Hell if the situation so required.

Turning from the window, Lyakhov went over to put out his cigarette in the ashtray on the desk. Lotus would find her way back to England; he had no doubt of that. When she did, she would be held there until France had settled into some kind of armistice with Germany. MI6 would be incredibly foolish if they did anything else. Of course, he'd known them to be incredibly foolish in the past, but if he knew William Buckley at all, he knew that he wouldn't risk losing his best agent so soon. The man knew that he'd need her later as the war continued.

Into the Iron Shadows

For this war would continue, Vladimir reflected, seating himself. It was just beginning. Hitler was taking France, and then he would take England. And when that happened, Bill would need his best agent alive and able to organize a resistance.

And that was exactly what Vladimir was counting on.

Chapter Ten

Zürich

Evelyn waited until the door closed softly behind Herr Brunner before turning her attention to the medium-sized, steel box he had left on the desk. Opening her purse, she pulled out the key from the house in Blasenflue. After one more glance at the closed office door, she inserted the key into the lock with trembling fingers. There was a faint click and she lifted the lid in some trepidation. Somehow, knowing that her father had left whatever was inside solely to her only increased her nervousness, which in turn thoroughly irritated her. There was no reason for her fingers to be shaking like this, or for her heart to be pounding. It didn't matter that a spy in London had broken into Ainsworth Manor presumably in search of what was inside this box. She was perfectly safe for the moment, locked in Herr Brunner's office. In fact, she couldn't think of a safer place to be than inside a bank. So why were her muscles trembling at the thought of finally discovering what all the fuss was about?

Evelyn flipped the lid of the box back to lay on the desk. Inside was a stack of papers with a sealed envelope laying on top, her name written across it in her father's familiar hand. Swallowing, Evelyn lifted out the envelope and opened it, pulling out a single sheet of paper. It was a letter, and she scanned it quickly, smiling at the familiar phrasing that her father had been wont to use. The smile, however, turned into a frown by the time she got to the end, and Evelyn tucked it back into the envelope with a deep sense of foreboding. What her father asked in the letter seemed fantastically impossible, yet she had no choice. She must do as he asked. He had made that very clear.

She set the letter aside and turned her attention to the stack of papers inside the box. Lifting them out, she went through them slowly, the frown on her face deepening. The first three were covered with hand-drawn diagrams of something that looked like a motor, but it was unlike any motor Evelyn had ever seen. She turned each sheet on its side, and then upside down, trying to make sense of the strange drawings. She shook her head. It was clearly a motor. Her familiarity with the Lagonda's engine had always held her in good stead, and now was no different. She knew a motor when she saw one. She just had absolutely no idea what kind of motor she was looking at.

After studying the three sheets for a few minutes, she finally admitted defeat and set them aside, reaching for the last remaining item in the box. Pulling out a long envelope, she opened it to find four sheets of microfiche. She raised an eyebrow and held them up to the light. They looked like a combination of typewritten pages and photographs, but she couldn't make out what the photographs were, let alone anything typed on the pages. She would need a machine to examine them properly. As she slid them back into the envelope, she frowned once again. Her father's instructions in the letter made that difficult as well.

Evelyn stared into the empty box, her heart fluttering in her chest. This was it. This was where the trail ended. A few sheets of paper, a few sheets of microfiche, and a letter that made absolutely no sense whatsoever, except to instruct her to do something that went against everything she believed in. This was what he'd left her, fully expecting that she would do what had to be done; fully expecting her to *know* what that was.

And she had absolutely no idea what to do.

Exhaling, Evelyn picked up the leather pouch that Herr Brunner had brought along with the box, grateful for his consideration and forethought. She slid everything into the pouch, removed the key from the lock, and closed the box just as a soft knock fell on the office door.

"Yes, come in!" she called, tying the pouch closed with the leather tie.

Herr Brunner entered the office carrying two thick ledgers in one arm, and a briefcase in his other hand.

"I've arranged to have some coffee brought in," he said, walking over to the desk. "I'll take you through the numbered accounts, and you can decide what you would like to do. Of course, I hope that you feel comfortable maintaining the accounts in your father's name, but that is your choice now."

"This is all very surreal," Evelyn said with a smile, seating herself and setting the leather pouch with her purse beside her.

Herr Brunner nodded and laid the ledgers on the desk. He picked up the empty box and moved it to a side table a few feet away.

"I do understand," he said. "It's always difficult when a loved one passes on in the best of circumstances, but it is especially hard when you have to try to sort out affairs that you knew nothing about. I'm sure it's all very overwhelming."

He seated himself behind the desk and smiled at her. "It's my sincere desire to try to make this as easy for you as possible. Before we begin with the numbered accounts, what would you like to do with the safe deposit box? It was paid in full for a term of 15 years. You are, of course, welcome to maintain the box, or we can cancel it and roll over the difference of cost into one of the numbered accounts."

"I'd like to keep it, please."

"Of course. You do, of course, have the option to allow a member of your family to have access to the box. Your brother, perhaps?"

"Not yet," Evelyn said slowly. "For now, I'd like to be the only one with access, at least until I can think better what to do."

"Very well. In that case, I'll leave the box in your father's name, giving you sole access as his beneficiary. I'll have to draw up fresh papers, and you will, of course, have to fill out the same form that your father did with instructions, etc., in the event of your death."

"Yes, I understand."

Herr Brunner nodded, but before he could say anything a soft knock fell on the door. A moment later it opened and a young woman pushed in a trolley with cups, saucers and a coffee pot.

"Ah, here is the coffee. Thank you, Fraulein Brun." Herr Brunner stood and went around the desk to take control of the cart. "That will be all."

The young woman nodded and smiled politely at Evelyn before turning and leaving the office. Herr Brunner poured coffee into two cups and carried one over to hand it to her.

"Thank you," Evelyn said with a smile.

He carried his cup around the desk and sat down, taking a sip. Then he set it down with a clink, and settled his eyeglasses on his nose.

"Well then, shall we get started?"

Hotel Bellevue Palace
May 18

Evelyn stubbed her cigarette out in the crystal ashtray on the writing desk near the window, glancing over her shoulder at the leather briefcase sitting on her bed. It was early afternoon and she had arrived on the train from Zürich an hour before. She had spent the entire trip considering her options. Even now, she wasn't sure of the best way to proceed. Her father, it seemed, had left quite a bit more than a nest egg in the accounts in Zürich, leading her to keep all the accounts open with the exception of one. The account with the lowest balance she closed out, and Herr Brunner had deposited the cash into the leather briefcase. The amount of money in the case was staggering, even by her standards, and Evelyn was loathe to haul it across France. But what else could she do? She was unable to set up a bank account here in Switzerland herself. Herr Brunner had made that abundantly clear. There was, of course, the option of leaving the suitcase with Philip here in the hotel, trusting that he didn't get curious and pick the lock to get it open. But the thought of leaving that amount of money in the hands of a man she'd just met made her feel ill. As far as she could see, the only choice she had was to take it with her. But hauling a briefcase full of cash across France in the midst of an invasion? It was a terrible idea.

Picking up her purse, Evelyn pulled out the key to the briefcase. Crossing to the bed, she unlocked and opened it, staring down at the neat rows of Swiss francs placed inside. Aside from the dilemma of what to do with it, her mind was still spinning with the fact that her father had set up multiple accounts in Switzerland that could only have been for emergency cash while he was traveling. But the very fact that the solicitors knew nothing about it, nor did Robbie, made her question where the money had come from. If it had been part of his estate, the solicitors would have questioned such a large amount of money not being included with the rest when he died. On the other hand, if it had been cash that MI6 had given him for operating costs on the continent, they would certainly want it back. Yet they seemed to know nothing about it either.

It was all rather a tangle, and Evelyn wasn't really sure what to do. Leaving the other two numbered accounts active and transferring access to herself seemed to be the most logical thing to do at the time, but it was still all very strange. She had emptied the last account with the thought that she could stash the money in France for future access, but of course now she realized what a foolish thought that had been. Where on earth would she put it?

Evelyn lifted the leather pouch from the briefcase, turning it over in her hands. And this! This was another tangle altogether.

Before she could continue the thought, a brief knock fell on the door. Dropping the pouch back into the briefcase, she closed and locked it quickly before turning to cross the room. When she opened the door, a hotel porter tipped his hat respectfully, holding out an envelope.

"Good afternoon, mademoiselle," he said. "This telegram arrived for you a few minutes ago."

"Thank you," she said, taking the envelope.

After another bob of his head, the porter turned to leave and Evelyn closed the door. She turned over the telegram and ripped it open, scanning it as she crossed the room towards the writing desk. The message was from London and written in code. She dropped it on the desk and turned to go to her suitcase. After removing her clothes, she lifted the false bottom and pulled out her codebook before going back to the desk. Seating herself, she bent over the telegram and proceeded to decode it quickly on a separate piece of paper.

MEET PLANE AT AIRFIELD 7AM ON 19TH. TIMING CRUCIAL. CANNOT GUARANTEE SAFETY BEYOND THEN. YOU WILL BE FLOWN TO PARIS WHERE YOU WILL MEET CONTACT NAMED FINN. MAKE WAY TO LE HAVRE. CONTACT IS RENE ON RUE POUYER. PRIVATE FISHING BOAT WILL BRING YOU BOTH TO ENGLAND. PROCEED TO LONDON. ACKNOWLEDGE RECEIPT - BARD.

Evelyn sat back in her chair and stared at the message. The fact that Bill had signed with his codename spoke volumes about the state of affairs with the German advance. It was the first time any message she received from London had been signed, and the fact that this one followed the protocol that was to be used once the continent became unsafe was disturbing.

Last night at her hotel in Zürich, Evelyn had read in the newspaper that the German 6th Army had captured Brussels, and it was expected that Antwerp would fall next. With Belgium on the verge of surrender, and German armies moving into France, she could well understand Bill's caution. Shifting her eyes to the briefcase on the bed, she pursed her lips thoughtfully. With Hitler's armies on the move, she would be moving through France with a significant amount of money locked in a leather briefcase. She couldn't think of anything more foolish, yet what choice did she really have?

While that thought was unnerving, she couldn't prevent the smile that twisted her lips. She was worrying about traveling with an excess of cash while, in the false bottom of her suitcase, she was carrying stolen documents from Germany and, soon to join them, hand-drawings and microfiche that her father had smuggled out of Austria. Evelyn lifted her hand to rub her forehead tiredly. It wasn't enough that she would be racing the Nazis across France, but with every passing day she seemed to be gathering more dangerous information to carry with her. Information that, were she to be caught by the Germans, would ensure her arrest and, most likely, execution. She must be insane.

Dropping her hand, she reached for her cigarette case. There was nothing for it but to continue. She would move as much of the cash as she could into the lining of her coat and into the bottom of the suitcase. The leather pouch would be concealed in her suitcase along with the oilskin packet that had come all the way from Stuttgart, and that had already caused some discomfort in her travels. What money she couldn't carry with her, she would be forced to leave in the briefcase. Tonight, when she went down for dinner, she would ask Philip to keep the case until her next visit. It was the best that she could do. She couldn't lug two cases across France. One suitcase was quite enough already. That would have to do, and she would have to trust Philip.

And then she would pray that she and this agent named Finn had no issues making it to Le Havre.

Amiens

"The Germans are moving into Antwerp. They'll have control by the end of the day, if they don't already."

Marc looked up when Luc entered the shed carrying a folded newspaper. He nodded, unsurprised.

"We expected that."

"Yes, but it's still unnerving to see it in black-and-white." Luc dropped the newspaper onto the table next to Marc. "Now that they've lost their major cities, Belgium will surrender. And then Hitler can focus all his might on France. I doubt we'll last a month."

"All the more reason to get moving," Marc said. "Soldiers and Panzers are moving quickly across France, and they're headed straight for us. We need to move."

"Yes, but move where?"

"We'll go southwest and try to swing around them." Marc pointed to a spot on the map that he had been studying. "It's clear that they're heading straight for the coast here," he said, motioning on the map. "If we go this way, we can cut across here and make for Lyons."

"Lyons?" Luc repeated, surprised. "I thought we were going home?"

"Too many people there know what we are doing. With the Germans moving in so quickly, it's not safe. I don't trust anyone anymore. We'll start fresh in Lyons."

Luc stared down at the map thoughtfully, scratching his chin. "There are certainly ample places to hide in Lyons," he said slowly. "The traboules will be particularly useful. Those passages can be used to escape the Gestapo when they come."

"Exactly."

"We can find work in one of the factories. I know several people there who can help, people who have no idea what I've been doing."

Marc nodded. "That's what I'm counting on. We'll find work and wait. When the time is right, we will continue."

"Do you have any idea where André and Mathieu are heading?"

"No. All I know is that they went south."

"André will want to go back to Paris."

"That wouldn't be the worst place they could go. It's a big city, and we will need people there."

Luc shook his head and went over to look out the window on the side of the shed. "I still can't believe that it's come to this."

Marc watched him for a moment then went back to his map, not offering any comment. There was nothing to say. This was not the result that any of them had expected, but it's what they had to face. Silence fell over the small area until finally Marc glanced at his watch and stood up.

"I must contact Metz. Why don't you go tell Matilde that we'll be leaving within the hour, and start loading the car?"

Luc nodded and turned away from the window. Once he had left, Marc turned to his wireless radio and picked up his headset, settling it over his ears. He didn't know how much longer their contact in Metz would be able to transmit, but as long as he still was, Marc could get information on the advancing troops. And Stefan was nothing if not a wealth of information. Josephine always laughed and said that she was convinced he had a crystal ball. The man certainly had a knack for digging out information that no one else could, and he had been invaluable in helping them to avoid the advancing Nazi troops over the past three days.

After turning the knobs on his radio, Marc reached for the paddle to tap out the message. He would give Stefan five minutes to answer, and if he didn't, he was shutting the radio down. They didn't have time to wait; they needed to get on the road as soon as possible.

Into the Iron Shadows

When his headset came alive a few minutes later, Marc reached for his pencil. Good. Stefan was still able to transmit. Either the Germans hadn't taken Metz yet, or they hadn't discovered the radio signal. Either way, Marc would be able to get the latest information on troop movements before he and Luc set off.

When Luc reentered the shed ten minutes later, Marc was staring at his radio, his face pale.

"What is it?" Luc asked quickly. "What's happened? Has Metz fallen?"

"No. It's still safe for now."

"What then?"

"One of Stefan's men intercepted a typed communication bound for one of the SS commanders," Marc said slowly. "Among other things, it appears that our network has somehow become exposed to the Germans."

"How exposed?"

"They have a list of names."

Luc's face paled. "How bad is it?"

Marc lifted his eyes from his radio and turned to look at him. "Josephine's name is on the list."

Luc stared at him for a moment then ran a hand through his hair, letting out a string of curses. "We need to warn her!"

"That's not all."

Luc looked at him apprehensively. "Tell me."

"Finn's name is on there, as well as the young Jens Bernard who stayed with us in Maubeuge. There are several others as well, and they all have one thing in common."

"What?"

"They've all had dealings with the British Secret Service."

"But so have we," Luc pointed out. "Are our names on the list?"

"That's the thing," Marc said grimly. "Stefan thinks that the list is incomplete."

Luc swallowed and ran his hand through his hair once again. This time it was shaking.

"Then we may be exposed as well."

Marc nodded and began to disconnect his radio and secure it in its case.

"Yes. There is no way to know for sure, so we must assume the worst."

"What shall we do?"

"We get on the road to Lyons. When we arrive, we do so as

new men."

"We could stop in Paris," Luc suggested, watching Marc pack up his radio. "They can still provide us with identification papers and a new identity."

Marc was already shaking his head before Luc had finished. "No. We do it ourselves. I know a man outside of Reims. He can help."

"You don't trust our government?"

"Right now, the only people I trust are Josephine, André, Mathieu and you."

"What about Josephine? She needs to be warned."

"There's nothing I can do until she reaches the apartment in Paris. I'll try reaching her then. She should be there by tomorrow."

"And if we can't reach her?"

"Then we pray."

Chapter Eleven

My dearest Evelyn,

If you are reading this then I am no longer with you and you have found the box I left in Blasenflue. I knew you would solve the Chinese puzzle box. I wish I could have explained more at the time, but I'm sure you understand.

The items contained in the safe deposit box came out of Austria at great cost. Two good men risked everything to smuggle them out of Germany and into our hands. I'm sure you'll recognize the drawings. You always did have an interest in motors. This, however, is far different from anything you've ever seen. It could change the face of Europe, if not the world. That is why it is so important to keep it secret. Trust no one. The Nazis know the information was taken out of Vienna and they'll be looking for it. They will stop at nothing to get it back.

There is one man in Switzerland that you can trust. His name is Philip Moreau, and he is a night manager at the Bellevue Palace Hotel in Bern. He's a good man, and trustworthy, but on no account should you leave anything of importance with him, especially these documents. While I would trust him implicitly, he has associates I cannot vouch for. I suggest making friends with him before you leave Switzerland. You may use my name as a reference...

Evelyn stepped out of the lift and went towards the front desk, the briefcase in her hand. There was no sign of Philip, but the young man manning the desk smiled politely as she walked up.

"Good evening, mademoiselle," he greeted her. "How may I be of service?"

"I was hoping to have a word with Monsieur Moreau."

"I apologize, but he's just stepped down to the wine cellar. May I help?"

"I'll wait, thank you. If you could ask him to come see me in the lounge when he returns?"

"Yes of course."

Evelyn nodded and turned to leave. After a few steps, she

turned back. "Actually, if I compose a telegram, can it be sent this evening?"

"Yes, of course. We have the ability to send directly from the hotel."

"Wonderful!" Evelyn gave him her most winning smile. "You'd be amazed how many hotels send them out. Why, I stayed in a hotel in Zürich last night and they had to send it down the street!"

The young man tsked and shook his head. "Rest assured, mademoiselle, that we will transmit it immediately. We take pride in our promptness."

"That is a relief. My uncle is ill, you see."

"I'm sorry to hear that. There are telegrams in the lounge. It's quite comfortable in there, and you won't be disturbed."

"Thank you."

Evelyn turned and walked across the lobby, a small smile playing on her lips. Of course she knew the hotel would send the telegram immediately, but she wanted the young man to believe that her business with his manager was something completely trivial. The last thing either of them needed was undue scrutiny.

The smile faded as she made her way into the lounge. The letter from her father had been very clear about the need for discretion here in Switzerland. Discretion was beginning to become second nature to her, but she realized she still had a lot to learn in that regard. The letter had also made it clear that he was fully aware of her work with MI6, and with Bill, so he had no doubt of her ability to be discreet.

Or of her ability to deceive.

Evelyn seated herself at a desk in the far corner, away from everyone. She pulled a piece of hotel stationery towards her and picked up a complementary fountain pen. After staring thoughtfully at the blank sheet for a moment, she bent her head to write. She would acknowledge Bill's telegram and advise him that she would be at the airport on time the next morning. That was the easy part. The hard part was lying to him about what she'd found in Zürich. In all the time that she had worked for him and for MI6, she had never once found it necessary to lie. She trusted Bill implicitly, but her father had not.

She paused in writing to look up, a frown on her face. That wasn't strictly true, she admitted. He never named William Buckley specifically, or even referred to her direct boss in the letter. All he had said was that she could trust no one in MI6, something that she was beginning to learn herself. After all, someone in London was a spy and had managed to get hold of a lot of information that they shouldn't have had access to. Was the spy active even before her father's death?

Into the Iron Shadows

It seemed the only logical explanation, as it certainly appeared that her father had very definite reasons not to trust the organization that he was working for in London. Why else would he instruct her to keep the contents secret, even from them?

After chewing her bottom lip for a moment, Evelyn decided that brevity was the best course of action. After confirming the early morning flight, she added a single line.

Zürich a dead-end.

Pulling a blank telegraph sheet towards herself, Evelyn glanced around the lounge. There were several other patrons, but none of them were paying her the least amount of attention. She opened her purse and slid her codebook out, partially covering it with the clutch. She then set about encoding the message onto the telegram to send to Bill. She had just finished and was snapping her purse closed again when a shadow fell over the desk.

"Mademoiselle Dufour," Philip said easily. "You wanted to see me?"

Evelyn screwed up the first message in her hand as she looked up with a smile.

"Yes, thank you. I wonder if you might do me a favor?"

"Of course."

"Please sit down," she invited. "It's so tiring to stare up at someone."

Philip glanced around the lounge before pulling a chair over and seating himself next to her.

"I assume this has nothing to do with the telegram you wish to send to your ill uncle?" he asked in some amusement.

"Nothing whatsoever," she said with a light laugh.

"I'm relieved. There's nothing I find more tedious than repeating what the guest already knows."

"Actually, I've run into a bit of a dilemma," Evelyn said slowly. "I find that I'm leaving rather unexpectedly very early tomorrow morning. However, the journey seems as though it will be a bit more complicated, and significantly longer, than I had originally anticipated."

"How disconcerting," he murmured. "I trust everything is all right?"

"Oh yes. It's just that my route will not be quite as direct as I was hoping. Which brings me to my dilemma. I have this briefcase, you see, and it would be quite awkward to try to manage this as well as my luggage. I was rather hoping that perhaps you might hold onto it for me."

Philip glanced down at the briefcase and then raised his eyes back to hers. "Of course. You have two options. I would be more than happy to secure it in the hotel safe until such time as you can return to collect it."

"And the other option?"

He smiled faintly. "Well that all depends on how important the contents of the briefcase are to you. I do have a more secure arrangement that might be of interest to you."

"I'm listening."

"For a small fee, I can conceal the case in a very secure area, hidden behind a wall in our wine cellar. This is a service I only offer to certain clients, you understand. It is, of necessity, not something that I do often. It does entail a bit of risk, you see."

"What kind of risk?"

"Oh, no risk to you or your property, I assure you. Rather the risk is more to me, should anyone else on staff discover the existence of the room."

"Do you mean to tell me that no one knows that it's there?" Evelyn asked incredulously. "How is that possible?"

"The room is very old," Philip told her, lowering his voice. "It dates back to before this building was even a hotel. It's built into the foundation, accessed only by a hidden door in the far corner of the cellar. It's not very large, and so you see my reluctance to offer this option to very many people."

"And yet you are willing to offer it to me?"

Philip smiled disarmingly. "What can I say? I like you. And you remind me very forcibly of someone I once knew," he added, tilting his head to the side. "I feel as if I know you. But if we set all that aside, Shustov is one of my preferred clients. Therefore, I feel it's only fair to extend to you the same courtesy that I extend to him."

Evelyn inclined her head gratefully. "I very much appreciate it," she said. "And you're the only one who knows the existence of this room?"

"Not quite. The sommelier knows as well," he admitted with a shrug. "It is, after all, his domain. But I can assure you that he is a friend. I trust his discretion implicitly. If it sets your mind at ease at all, he pays no attention to what goes in, or comes out, of that room. The only thing he's interested in is the case of Bordeaux that he's had stashed in there for close to five years. You need have no concern on his account."

Evelyn considered him thoughtfully for a long moment, then nodded. "Then I would be very grateful if you would make the arrangements."

Into the Iron Shadows

"As you wish. How long do you expect for the case to remain?"

"Until I can return to retrieve it."

Philip nodded. "Very well. I assure you it will be safe and secure until you have need of it once more."

"Thank you very much," Evelyn said, rising and holding out her hand. "You've been so very helpful over the past few days."

"My dear mademoiselle, that is what I am here for." Philip took her hand with a genuinely warm smile. "I look forward to being of equal service to you in the future."

Evelyn nodded and picked up the briefcase, handing it to him.

"I have a feeling that you will get the opportunity quite often in the coming months," she said with a wry smile. "I'm very relieved that we get along so well. I, too, am looking forward to continuing our association."

Philip took the case and bowed his head politely.

"I wish you a very safe journey tomorrow. It's not a good time to be traveling on the continent. Please take all care of yourself."

Evelyn nodded and watched as he turned to walk, with measured stride, out of the lounge, the briefcase clasped firmly in his hand. She felt rather as if she was watching a close friend walk away for the last time. Shaking her head, she picked up her purse and the telegram. He was right about one thing; it was not a good time to be traveling, especially through France, but she had little choice.

If she was to get back to England, she had to go through hell.

Paris
May 19

Henry finished adjusting his tie and turned to take one final look in the mirror. Satisfied, he turned away and reached for his jacket. As he was pulling it on, a soft knock fell on the door. He called to enter and a very slight man with slicked back hair opened it to move noiselessly into the room.

"Yes? What is it?" Henry asked.

"A telegram for you, sir," the manservant said, holding out an envelope. "It just arrived, and it's marked urgent."

Henry frowned and took the envelope, ripping it open.

WOMAN WHO WENT TO HOUSE WAS IN BERN. LEFT

ON SMALL PLANE THIS MORNING - 7 O'CLOCK. PARIS
MOST LIKELY DESTINATION.

Henry looked at his watch and turned to stride over to the
writing desk. Picking up a lighter, he held the corner of the paper to the
flame, watching as it caught light.

"Have my car brought round," he said, not taking his eyes
from the flames.

"Very good, sir."

The valet turned and left as noiselessly as he had arrived,
closing the door silently behind him. Henry dropped the burning
telegram into an ashtray, watching as the flames curled around the last
bit. So the mystery spy who'd gone to the farmhouse was on their way
to Paris? There was only one airfield near Paris where a small plane
would land, and if he hurried, he might just catch them.

Henry turned from the writing desk and reached for his hat.
He was still awaiting a full report from Berlin on the farmer's family.
He'd also reached out to the same contact in Bern who had sent the
telegram. While he had no doubt that Berlin knew all there was to
know about the dead farmer, his associate in place there would know
the little details about his family that it was impossible to learn as an
outsider. He simply had to be patient and wait for the information to
come through. In the meantime, at least he had this. If he could get a
good look at the spy, that was all he needed. He'd be able to put a face
to the person who stood between him and the package Ainsworth had
stolen.

And then he'd be able to get the package back.

He left the room, his hat in his hand. He would go to the
airfield and see what he could discover. If the plane had left Bern at
seven, then it would be landing soon. Always assuming, of course, that
his contact was correct in his belief that the plane was headed for Paris.
The man had an uncanny way of talking to people and coaxing a world
of information from them that, in most cases, they didn't even know
they possessed. If he believed the airplane was going to Paris, then it
most likely was.

Jogging down the stairs, Henry reflected that it would be a rush
to get to the airfield, and then get back to Paris in time for his meeting
with the ambassador. It would never do to keep that man waiting.
Thankfully, the airfield wasn't far, but it would still be cutting it close.

He nodded to the manservant as he entered the small
entryway.

"Is it here?"

"It just arrived, sir," the man replied, opening the front door for him.

Henry went down the front steps of the narrow house, pulling on his gloves as he went. A black sedan idled at the curb and the driver got out, nodding to him politely.

"Sir."

"Thank you. I won't be needing you. I'll drive myself," Henry said, waving him away.

He got behind the wheel and pulled the door closed, adjusting the mirror. As he pulled away from the sidewalk, his brows drew together in a frown. Something was bothering him about this whole situation, something that kept nagging in the back of his head. It was the most absurd idea, but if Henry had learned anything in the past couple of years, it was that the more absurd ideas usually turned out to be the ones that he should pay attention to. It all stemmed from a very simple question that he'd been asking himself since he learned that someone had gone to the old farmhouse. If the mysterious spy had indeed gone to collect something left behind by the old farmer or Ainsworth himself, they had to be following instructions that were left before either man had been killed.

Who would Robert Ainsworth trust enough to leave that kind of information to?

Chapter Twelve

Evelyn climbed out of the small airplane and turned to reach up for her suitcase. The pilot handed it to her with a nod and a smile, and she held her hand up to shield her eyes from the sun.

"Thank you so much," she said briskly. "Will you continue on to Lyons?"

"No, miss. I'm heading south now, to Spain. I'll just be refueling, and then I'll be off."

"My, you have a busy day!"

The man grinned and scratched his thick head of black curly hair. "That I do, miss. That I do. You take care, now. I think you have someone waiting for you."

Evelyn turned in surprise and looked in the direction he motioned. There, at the edge of the landing strip, was a small gray Renault with a man behind the wheel. A woman was standing beside the car and, as Evelyn turned, she lifted her hand and waved gaily.

"Do you know them, miss?"

"I know the woman, certainly," Evelyn replied with a delighted smile. "She's an old friend." She turned back to hold her hand out to the pilot. "Thank you again. Have a safe flight to Spain."

"Thank you, miss." He shook her hand, gave her a nod, and then ducked back into the plane.

Turning, Evelyn began walking towards the little car in the distance with a strange sense of relief. They had certainly not had an easy trip back from Switzerland. He'd had to divert twice to avoid German airplane formations. One was a squadron of fighters, and the other a group of bombers. Seeing the enemy planes in the air over France had shaken Evelyn, and she had held on to the sides of her seat with a white-knuckled grip, staring at the dark shapes in the distance. Mr. Smith had remained calm, however, and they had avoided the war birds easily enough. Seeing her nervousness, he'd tried to set her mind at ease by telling her that they would hardly shoot down a small unmarked, passenger plane such as theirs, but it hadn't really helped. All she could think was that, while she may be safe enough, Miles was not, and he and Robbie were going up every day in the hopes of meeting them head-on. Seeing the black swarms from the small window as she gazed out helplessly, she'd been struck suddenly by the reality of the situation. Hitler was coming, and when he was finished with France, he would turn towards England.

And then all those shadows would be flying over the Channel to attack *them*.

Evelyn walked towards the car with her suitcase in one hand and her purse strap over her shoulder. Setting the unpleasant thought aside, she focused on Josephine and a wide smile spread over her face.

"Mon amie!" she called as she drew closer. "What are you doing here? I thought you were in Maubeuge!"

"And miss Paris in the spring?" Josephine called back cheerfully. "Never!"

Evelyn laughed and, as she reached her, set down her suitcase to give her a hug, kissing the air beside her cheek.

"How did you know I was coming? Bill?"

"But of course!" Josephine motioned to the Renault. "Your car, my lady!"

Evelyn picked up the suitcase and smiled at the young man who climbed out of the driver's seat to open the back door for her.

"And this is Finn, your temporary chauffeur," Josephine continued with a laugh. "Finn, this is…what *is* your name today?" she asked Evelyn, turning to look at her quizzically.

"Geneviève," Evelyn replied, holding out her hand to Finn. "Geneviève Dufour."

"My pleasure, Mademoiselle Dufour," Finn said with a smile. "I've heard a lot about you."

Evelyn looked at Josephine in surprise, but the woman shook her head.

"Not from me," she said with a shrug. "All I've said was that we were coming to meet you and that you would take him to England."

"I received a message from Bill this morning," Finn explained, taking her suitcase from her. "He said I would be in safe hands. He told me to ask you about the time in Lockerbie when you went fishing."

Evelyn raised an eyebrow and laughed. "Good Lord, he's trying to embarrass me! It was a massive trout, you see, and it had me right over the side of the boat."

"Did it get away?"

"Not at all. I held on and pulled it back into the boat with me." Evelyn smiled and got into the back seat. Peering up at him, she saw his jaw relax and knew that he was satisfied with the code. "And please, call me Geneviève."

Finn nodded and set the suitcase on the floor at her feet before closing the door. She watched as he got behind the wheel again and Josephine went around to get into the passenger seat. So Bill was instituting the safety protocols, was he? It was the first time she'd been asked to pick up, or even meet, a contact who wasn't part of her own mission. Bill obviously wanted Finn to be comfortable in the knowledge that she really was who she was supposed to be. Did he think there was a possibility that she wouldn't have made it back from Switzerland? And that an impostor would have come in her place? The thought sent a chill down her spine and Evelyn felt the skin on her arms prickle in response. What did London know that she didn't?

"I hope you don't mind a small apartment in a modest district," Josephine said, turning in the seat to look at Evelyn. "We'll need to get supplies before we can start out and get you to where you need to go. That will be difficult. We arrived yesterday and most of the shops are already closed, with the owners gone. Everyone is fleeing the city."

"Are the Germans that close?"

"Not yet, but everyone is leaving before they come." Josephine shrugged. "I know someone, though, who may be able to help us get what we need today. We can leave Paris tomorrow if all goes well."

"We?"

"I thought I'd help you as far as I can before I continue south. I'm going to Marseilles."

"And you're not needed there immediately?"

"I'm not needed there at all. Everything is in chaos, and that includes us. Marc thinks it's best for us to separate and stay quiet until…well, until we can figure out a way to resume." Josephine smiled sadly. "We're on our own now."

Evelyn stared at her and saw uncertainty, and sorrow, in her face. Her heart broke for her. She was about to lose her country to the Nazis, along with everything France had ever stood for. Evelyn couldn't even imagine the pain of knowing that her country would no longer be her country, but she nodded briskly. Josephine didn't need pity right now. She needed a friend, an associate.

"I think that's a wise choice," she said. "It's best not to draw attention to yourselves. Wait until things are back to some kind of normal, and then start again. Do you have family in Marseilles?"

Into the Iron Shadows

"No, a friend. We were at school together. She will give me lodging until I find work and can arrange something for myself. Her husband manages a factory of some sort."

Finn glanced in the rear view mirror at her. "Where are we going? I'm hoping you know because I haven't been given a clue."

"Haven't you?" Evelyn asked, surprised. "How strange! We're to go to Le Havre. A private boat there will take us across to England."

"Le Havre!" Josephine exclaimed. "But that's west, not south."

"That's right." Finn and Josephine glanced at each other and Evelyn's eyes narrowed. "What is it? Is there something wrong with going west?"

"Not if you want to go in the same direction as the Germans," Josephine said. "They're racing to the coast, likely to secure the port cities and prevent the retreat of the Allied forces."

Evelyn felt her skin go cold and she pressed her lips together, turning her attention out of the window to the passing countryside. "You're sure?"

"Yes. The last report I heard was this morning. They captured Saint-Quentin yesterday and are still going west. At this rate, they will reach the Channel in a matter of days."

"Then Le Havre is out of the question," Evelyn said decidedly, turning her gaze back to the front of the car. "We'll have to go south."

She stared out of the windshield absently, watching as a black car in the distance came towards them. It was the first car she'd seen since they left the airfield, she realized, and that in itself was strange. She was used to more traffic on the road into Paris, but if what Josephine said was true then all the traffic was on the other side, heading south.

"Do you have a wireless radio at this apartment?" she asked suddenly. "One that I can use?"

"Yes."

"I'll send a message to London as soon as we arrive, alerting them to the fact that we will go south," Evelyn decided. "I'll write it out now so that I can transmit as soon as we get there. They can't have known that the armies were going west when they issued Le Havre as a departure point. They must have thought Paris was the immediate goal."

"They would be forgiven for thinking so. We all assumed they would go straight for Paris." Josephine watched as Evelyn ducked down in the back seat to undo the clasps on her suitcase. "What are you doing?"

"I have to get my pad out of the case," came the muffled reply. The car went over a bump in the road and her head smacked the back of Finn's seat. "Perhaps you could keep it a little more steady?" she asked humorously.

"I'm sorry," Finn said with laugh. "I was trying to move over to give this car more room. He seems to be in a hurry."

"Perhaps he's catching a flight out of France," Josephine said, watching as the black car sped past them in the opposite direction. "I almost wish I could do the same."

Finn glanced at her. "You would leave if you had the opportunity?"

After a moment's thought, she sighed and shook her head. "No, I suppose I wouldn't. There is work to be done, and there will be more once the Nazis arrive. I'm needed here."

He was silent for a long moment, then he nodded slowly. "I would have stayed in Belgium if I had a choice. Unfortunately, it was impossible."

"You came from Belgium?" Evelyn asked in surprise, straightening up in the back seat with a notepad and small book in her hand.

"Yes. I was in Antwerp, but when the Germans invaded, I fled south. Much like the Parisians are doing now."

"Another Belgian," Josephine laughed, glancing at Evelyn. "You must be a magnet for them."

Finn raised his eyebrows. "Oh?"

"I was in Brussels when the invasion began," Evelyn explained. "A young man was kind enough to help get me to France."

"Where is he? I thought he was going to England with you?" Josephine asked.

"He decided to stay in France. He made a fast friend in our associate from Marle."

"Marcel?" It was Josephine's turn to be surprised. "He doesn't usually take in recruits. At least, not that I've ever heard. Well, he's in good hands, at any rate. He will be properly trained and supplied with a solid identity and papers."

"I hope so."

"Do you know where he is?"

"No. He will contact us once he's settled." Evelyn looked at Finn. "Like you, he had little choice in leaving Brussels."

"It's for the best," Finn replied. "Both Brussels and Antwerp have fallen."

"What?!"

Into the Iron Shadows

"Yes. They captured Brussels on Friday, and Antwerp yesterday. Belgium will surrender. They have no choice."

"And now they are in France and going to the Channel," Evelyn said, rubbing her forehead. "They're trapping our armies."

"Yes," Josephine agreed grimly. "There is little hope now. Once Sedan fell, it was over."

Hearing the note of defeat in her voice, Evelyn reached forward and laid a comforting hand on her shoulder.

"No. There is always hope. France may fall, but her people will not. You will continue to fight in any way possible," she said firmly. "The French army is not France. *You* are."

Josephine turned to meet her gaze, smiling tremulously and nodding.

"You're right. No matter what happens, we will resist."

"And you will do so with England behind you."

Henry pulled the car to a stop and got out, watching as a small airplane lifted off at the end of the landing strip. There was no sign of another plane in the vicinity, and he turned to look at the main hangar. After hesitating for a minute, he got back behind the wheel and drove towards the large building in the distance. Someone there would know if the flight from Switzerland had arrived and, if so, where it was.

He'd passed only one other vehicle on the road to the airfield, a small Renault. The driver was a man who looked every inch a Frenchman, and as Henry had passed them, he got a good look at the passenger. She had dark hair and was dressed in a pale blue frock with white around the collar. He dismissed the couple as soon as they passed. If he knew anything about women, it was that they did not travel in day dresses. It could not have been the woman arriving from Switzerland. That woman hadn't been dressed for travel.

Henry had hoped as he sped on towards the airfield that the flight hadn't arrived yet. But, as he pulled up to the open hangar, he had a sinking feeling that the airplane he'd just witnessed taking off was the airplane in question. He switched off the engine and got out, looking towards two mechanics crossing the hangar.

"Pardon!" he called.

They stopped and looked at him. "Yes?"

"I'm looking for an airplane. It was supposed to arrive from Switzerland."

"You just missed it. It came in and refueled, then took off again," one of the men told him, shaking his head.

"Was there a passenger?"

The man looked at his companion. "I didn't see it land. You did. Was there a passenger?"

The other mechanic nodded, wiping his hands on a rag. "Yes. A woman got off. I saw her as I went for a tool. Beautiful woman, with gold hair."

"Gold hair?" Henry repeated. "Are you sure?"

"Yes."

"Did you see where she went?"

"No. I went back to work while she was taking leave of the pilot."

Henry suppressed a curse and nodded. "Thank you."

He turned to leave, then turned back suddenly. "Did you overhear where the airplane was going?"

"No. The pilot never left the plane. Stayed onboard while it refueled," the first man said.

"All right. Thank you."

Henry turned and strode back to his car, his lips pressed together. A blonde woman got off, the pilot refueled and took off again almost immediately, and he had missed it all. At least he was sure of one thing: the car he had passed on the road had most certainly not had a blonde woman inside. But that was the only vehicle on the road to Paris. So where had she gone?

Henry paused at his car and turned to look at the airfield again. Had she got back on the airplane before it took off? Or had she gone in the opposite direction, away from Paris?

"Damn!"

On that muttered exclamation, Henry got behind the wheel and started the engine. He'd missed her. He'd missed his only chance to catch a glimpse of the person he was convinced could lead him to the package Ainsworth had so effectively hidden.

His only hope now was that Berlin, or his man in Bern, would come through with useful information on the farmer's remaining relatives. He knew he had a son. He remembered that much. Had he had a daughter? Or was the son married? Or was the woman altogether unrelated to the deceased owner of the house in Blasenflue?

Henry scowled as he pulled away from the hangar. He hoped that wasn't the case, for if it was, he would never track her down again. And she was the only lead he had to the package.

As he drove towards the road again, Henry didn't notice the

tall figure that moved out of the shadows behind the hangar, a hat pulled low over his brow. Dark eyes watched the black sedan as it drove away before the figure melted back into the shadows, disappearing around the back of the hangar.

Chapter Thirteen

As she got out of the car, Evelyn looked around the Paris street and felt almost befuddled. She'd only been away four days, yet the entire city was different. The usual cheerful bustle that she knew so well was gone. It was like driving through some kind of macabre model of Paris, one that was a mirror image of what it should be, but was not. Gone was the carefree spirit of the City of Lights. In its place was a surreal undercurrent of tension, evident in the hastened movements of what few people were out and about, moving around the city. Shops and cafés were sparsely populated, the amount of vehicles in the wide avenues was half what she was used to, and the pedestrians hurrying along the pavements looked harried and grim as they went on their way. This wasn't the Paris she knew so well. This was a strange shell of a city that was desperately trying to remain calm in the face of the impending invasion.

"It's different, isn't it?" Josephine asked, joining her and seeing the look on her face. "I haven't spent a lot of time in Paris, but even I can see the change."

"Where is everyone?"

"Fleeing south." Josephine hooked her arm through hers and led her across the sidewalk to the door of a tall apartment building. "We went to dinner last night when we arrived and the waiter told us that people have been packing up and leaving in droves since Sedan fell."

Evelyn paused and glanced back at the street as a car drove slowly by, laden with boxes and suitcases that had been strapped to the roof.

"Where do they think they will go?" she wondered, almost to herself. "There is nowhere to go."

"I know." Josephine followed her gaze. "I think they are simply trying to avoid the inevitable for as long as possible." She looked at Evelyn. "Is this how it was in Brussels?"

Evelyn shrugged and followed her through the door. "It was more chaotic. Bombs were falling on the city outskirts, so there was panic. Some people were leaving without anything, and others were trying to take everything they could carry. The entire atmosphere was different."

"Paris doesn't seem to be in a panic. At least, not yet. Right now it seems simply resigned."

"Exactly."

Evelyn followed Josephine up a flight of wooden steps. The apartment building was modest, but seemed clean. The walls were covered in fairly new paper and the steps were swept clean of any dust. While she wasn't familiar with this section of the city, Evelyn was relieved that it appeared respectable and safe. When Josephine had mentioned a modest apartment, she hadn't known quite what to expect.

"Whose apartment is this?" she asked.

"It belongs to a nice lady who is currently in Spain. Somewhere in the south, I believe. She allows me to use it when I'm in Paris, but as I said, I don't come very often."

"Who is she?"

"A friend of my Tante Elizabeth." Josephine stopped outside a door and unlocked it, pushing it open. "She's always been very fond of my father. When she heard that I was traveling quite a bit, she offered it to me."

"Does your Tante Elizabeth know what you do?"

"Goodness, no. She'd never approve. She thinks I'm a student, studying botany."

"Botany!" Evelyn looked at her in amusement and Josephine grinned, motioning her into the apartment.

"Yes. Studying plants takes me all over France."

Evelyn couldn't stop a chuckle. "Well, that would certainly be true. What an ingenious idea! Do you like plants and gardening, then?"

"I do, actually. I used to keep a wonderful garden at my father's house near Lyons, but that was a few years ago now." Josephine closed the door and looked around. "Well, this is it. It's not very large, but it's clean and comfortable. This is the sitting room, and the kitchen is through there. If you come this way, there is a hallway to lead to the bedrooms. There are only two, but I'm in the larger one and there is plenty of room for both of us."

"And Finn?"

"He'll be along when he's parked the car. Are you hungry?"

"No, but I'd love some coffee."

"I'll make some. I bought the last can at the store last night. Here's the bedroom. The washroom is through there. I'm sure you'll want to freshen up after your flight. How was it, by the way?"

"We had to change routes twice to avoid the Luftwaffe. The

first time was a squadron of fighters, and the second was a group of bombers."

"Where?"

Evelyn glanced at her as she set her suitcase down next to the bed. "Over Dijon, and again between there and Paris. The pilot thought they may have been coming from the area of Nancy."

Josephine swallowed and nodded, her face a little pale. "I'm glad you were able to avoid them. I'll go start the coffee."

She left and Evelyn watched her go, a wave of empathy going over her. She'd been taken aback and sobered by the difference in Paris alone, but Josephine was watching it happen all over her country. She couldn't even begin to imagine the pain, anger, and fear that her friend was experiencing. Her government had let her down, and now the Nazis were in France, moving to take complete control.

Turning away from the door, Evelyn looked around the bedroom. As Josephine had said, it was a large room with a double bed, a dresser, and vanity table and stool. She picked up the suitcase and set it on the bed, undoing the straps. There was no point in unpacking, but she would change into something that wasn't travel-creased and brush her hair. Once she'd freshened up a bit, she would feel more like herself and would be able to think clearly. The first order of business was to send a message to London and alert Bill to the fact that the German troops were moving to the coast. She would include what little information she had, such as the bomber and fighter formations, but she didn't imagine it would do much good at this point. Le Havre was out of the question now, and she would tell him as much. Their best option at this point was to go south, along with everyone else leaving Paris.

A frown settled over her brow as she pulled out a pair of wide-legged pants and a blouse. If the roads were clogged with refugees, it would be difficult to make it anywhere in any kind of timely fashion. She would be at the mercy of the traffic, just as they had been in Belgium. Evelyn remembered well the frustration of inching along roads that were packed with pedestrians, vehicles, horses, and carts. If that was to be the case here, she had no idea how long it would take to make her way south. She paused and lifted her head suddenly as a thought occurred to her. She was assuming she would have a car. They couldn't expect Josephine to let them have her car. How on earth was she going to go south without a car?

Evelyn's heart sank as she gathered her clothes and turned to go to the door. As she crossed the hallway to the bathroom, she chewed on her bottom lip. She supposed they might be able to find a couple of bicycles, but it was far from ideal. Still, if it was the only way to make it out of France, they would have to do whatever they could.

She just hoped they would make it. She'd escaped a German invasion twice now. How long would her luck hold? How long could she expect it to hold? And what would happen if she didn't make it out this time?

A tall man climbed behind the wheel of a sedan and sat for a moment, staring across the meadow adjacent to the airfield with a scowl. He'd been on his way back to the car when the black sedan had come racing up the entrance road to the small airfield, drawing his attention. He hadn't intended on staying to see who was in such a hurry to get to the airfield, but that changed when he caught sight of the driver as the car barreled past the outer building where he was standing. It was a face that he knew by sight, if not by name. He'd met him only once, in Berlin before the war, on one of the few occasions that he'd been ordered to attend a formal dinner. He couldn't recall the name at the moment, although he had no doubt that it would come to him, but he never forgot a face. He couldn't afford to. His life and success depended upon it.

And that face was, he knew, the face of their coveted spy in the heart of the British government.

The man knew beyond any shadow of doubt that the spy would never remember him. Few ever did. Even back then, he had worked hard to ensure that nothing stood out or called attention to himself. His entire career had been built on his ability to be invisible. He was Eisenjager, the assassin that was more myth than man. Most had no idea he existed, save for the men and women he dispatched with ruthless efficiency. No. Even if the man in the black sedan had noticed him, he would never be able to identify him. His cover was still intact.

Eisenjager drummed his long fingers on the steering wheel for a moment, staring across the countryside without seeing any of it. He wasn't concerned about his ability to catch up with Jian. He'd done it before. He had a mental note of the registration of the vehicle she was in, and knew he would be able to track her down without too much fuss. No. What concerned him now was the presence of one of Himmler's moles. What was the spy doing here? Why was he looking for Jian, whom Eisenjager himself was under orders to eliminate? And how had he discovered that she was returning to France today? So many questions, and none of them were easily answered.

When the English spy had disappeared from Marle without a trace, Eisenjager had been furious. Not only had he lost his Belgian target, but also the elusive Jian, the woman who had evaded him in Norway weeks ago. His lips tightened as he reached down to turn the ignition key. It was all due to the incompetence of the SD. He couldn't even completely lay the blame for the botched job at Hans Voss' feet, although he would like nothing more, because the Obersturmbannführer had been just as much in the dark as he had been himself. He hadn't known who the woman was until he saw her in person, at the same time that Eisenjager realized who she was. Whether Voss' superiors in the SD had known the identity of their wanted courier was merely an academic question at this point. Because of their ineptitude, Eisenjager had lost not only his immediate target, but the spy he'd been hunting since he last saw her in Namsos.

He pulled out of his spot behind one of the smaller buildings and turned his car towards the road. When Voss had been ordered back to Berlin, Eisenjager had contacted his own handler in Hamburg. After apprising him of the situation, he'd received orders to remain in France and locate both the Belgian and the woman. His orders remained unchanged. They were both targets, and he was expected to eliminate them with all the expediency that he was known for. And so his hunt had begun again.

He'd managed to track them to Paris, but once there, even his skill failed him. It was too large of a city, and he had absolutely nothing to go on. After spending two days searching in Paris, he'd tried the airfield outside the city. He hadn't been expecting to find anything of value. Instead, he'd learned that a small passenger plane carrying a single female had departed for Switzerland just that morning. The description had confirmed that he'd just missed Jian.

Eisenjager was nothing if not a patient man. Knowing that she'd gone to Switzerland, he debated following, but ultimately decided to remain in France. Given the advance of the German troops on all fronts, her departure from the mountain region would have to follow a limited flight plan. She would have to return to England either by way of France, or Spain. If she returned before France fell, she would undoubtedly go through France. It was inherently quicker, and if Jian was on the move, she would want to reach England sooner rather than later. If what everyone said was true, she was carrying several documents that the SD wanted back. She wouldn't risk them falling back into her enemy's hands now.

Into the Iron Shadows

And so he had waited, and watched. He became friendly with several workers at the airfield, and gleaned information from them about the types of aircraft that came through daily. He learned that the small passenger plane that carried her to Switzerland made frequent stops at the airfield, always with different passengers. They believed its home airfield was in England, but no one could be sure. On the rare occasions that the pilots didn't refuel and depart immediately, they never discussed anything other than the airplane itself. And they never stayed more than a few hours. It all amounted to one thing as far as he was concerned: the airplane was transporting men and women into Europe and back again. Only MI6 would have that kind of standing operation, and it further confirmed his belief that Jian would come back into France before making her way to England.

This morning, his patience had been rewarded when he watched her climb out of the passenger plane and accept a suitcase from the pilot. He had watched her leave with the couple in the gray sedan, noting the registration of the vehicle before turning to make his way to his own car. He had recognized the man, at least. He'd been surprised to see him get out of the car and take Jian's suitcase. The last thing he'd heard about him was that he was somewhere in Holland after escaping from the Sudetenland. He was someone the Reich wanted back, and he would be sure to mention him in his next transmission. But what was he doing in France?

The woman was a mystery, but he had no doubt that she was part of the French network. She was a much more likely companion to the English spy than the man. But where was the Belgian? The man called Jens? Eisenjager shook his head and pulled onto the long road that would take him into Paris. The only way to discover that was to find Jian in Paris, and he would have to do it before the German spy did.

The scowl returned to his face. He had no intention of allowing that to happen. The bloody SD had caused enough disruption for him in the past week. They weren't going to get in his way again, even if that meant removing their man from the equation all together.

The Englishwoman wouldn't escape again.

London

Bill reached for the ringing telephone without lifting his eyes from the latest report from France. One of his agents had sent it through this morning and he was just now getting to read it. The news was grim to say the least. Located just outside Metz, the agent was able to describe in detail the assault the German forces were waging on the border.

"Yes?" he answered impatiently.

"Am I interrupting?" Jasper asked dryly.

"Oh! I'm sorry. I'm just reading a report from France."

"That bad?"

"Worse." Bill sat back in his chair and rubbed his eyes. "What can I do for you? I thought you were going to lunch with the prime minister."

"I am. They're bringing the car around. I just heard something I think you should know. It will be in the afternoon brief, but I thought I'd ring you and give you a heads up."

"Oh? More good news?"

"I'm afraid so." Jasper cleared his throat. "It may not be as hopeless as it seems, mind you. Winston still has great hope."

"Winston is getting paid to have great hope, and to ensure that the country keeps the faith accordingly," Bill said tiredly, dropping his hand. "What is it? Let's get it over with."

"Commander General Gort ordered a withdrawal of all troops in Belgium and Northern France to the port cities this morning. They've been completely outflanked, and the latest reports say that Guderian will reach the Channel by tomorrow, at the latest. Communications will be cut off between our forces in the north and the French forces in the south. They've cut us in half."

"Not us, sir. The entire Expeditionary Force is in the north. They've simply cut them off from any reinforcements from the French."

"Quite right."

"I suppose ordering a retreat to the ports is the only course of action now." Bill sat forward and stared at the report on his desk absently. "Where are they concentrating their efforts? Calais?"

"Yes, and Dunkirk." Jasper cleared his throat again. "If you have any agents in the area, you may want to advise them to pull out and go south for now. It won't be pretty there over the next few weeks."

"It's not pretty anywhere. They're aware of what's expected of them. However, this does pose a problem for Jian."

"What? Is she still there? I thought she was on her way back."

"Not yet. She will be, and I was going to extract her from the coast." Bill squeezed his eyes shut, then looked up as soft knock fell on the door. "I'll have to rethink that now. Come in!"

"Where were you thinking?"

"Le Havre."

Jasper clicked his tongue and Bill could almost see him shaking his head. "That won't do at all. Perhaps further south will be best. Ideally, we should fly her out. Is that a possibility?"

"Unfortunately no. Sam is extracting Pietro from Lyons and taking him to Spain. He's been made by the police there and his safety is a concern with the Germans advancing." Bill nodded to his assistant as he entered the office carrying a stack of messages and a leather folder. "Sam sent a message this morning saying that the skies are getting crowded. He had to divert around two separate Luftwaffe formations getting Jian out of Switzerland. It would be suicide to send him back into the heart of France."

"What a bloody mess. Keep me informed, please. She's bringing Oscar back with her?"

"That's the plan."

"Very well. Do your best. If you run into anything I can assist with, do let me know."

"Of course, sir. Enjoy your lunch. Have a whiskey and soda for me."

Bill hung up and held out a hand for the stack of messages from Wesley.

"Was that Montclair?" Wesley asked, nodding to the phone.

"Yes. He's on his way to have lunch with the prime minister." Bill flipped through the messages, pausing when he came to one. He looked up sharply. "When did this come through?"

"Not half an hour ago, sir. Is it from France?"

"Yes." Bill ripped open the sealed message and scanned it. "It's from Jian. She says Le Havre is not possible."

He pushed his chair back and got up, dropping the message on the desk.

"Why? Is there a problem?"

"Yes. The entire British Expeditionary Force will be pulling back to the port cities, and that means the German forces will also be converging there." Bill crossed the office to study the massive map of France hanging on the wall opposite. "We have to come up with a new plan."

"Sir?" Wesley stared at him. "The entire BEF?"

"Yes."

"On the coast of the Channel?"

Bill glanced at him, his brows coming together. "You're not usually slow, Wesley. What's on your mind?"

"Just that...well, where will they go from there?"

"Pardon?"

"I'm not a military strategist, but it seems to me that if the entire BEF pulls back to the coast, they'll be trapped there."

Bill nodded and turned his attention back to the map. "So they will."

"But...then what? Do they have a plan to get them out?"

"I certainly hope so, otherwise England will be in a right pickle, won't we? The BEF is the bulk of the British Army, you know."

"Yes, I do. That's why I'm asking."

Bill stilled and slowly turned to look at the younger man. His lips were pressed together grimly and his face was still pale.

"You've got a brother over there, don't you?" he asked suddenly.

Wesley nodded, swallowing. "Yes, sir. He's in the 63rd Medium Regiment, Royal Artillery."

Bill exhaled and nodded. "I'm sorry. I don't know what the plan is for the troops. I only just found out from Montclair that the order was given to withdraw to Calais and Dunkirk this morning."

"I understand, sir."

"If I learn more, and if I'm able, I'll let you know. But right now, I have to find a way to get Jian and Oscar out of France and back to England before the Nazis roll into Paris and France falls completely."

"Yes, sir." Wesley walked over to stand beside him at the map. "What's your plan for extraction?"

"It will have to be by boat. Sam is on his way to Spain, and the Luftwaffe are taking more control of the air over France every minute."

"Can they go through Spain?"

"It's too far. They're in Paris now, awaiting instructions. They can't stay there. We have to get them moving."

Both men stared at the map for a long moment, then Wesley pointed to La Rochelle.

"Don't we have an agent here?"

"Not anymore." Bill tilted his head and followed a line south. "But we do still have one here, in Bordeaux."

"And they certainly have ports. The Garonne River empties out into the Bay of Biscay."

"More than that, we have cruisers delivering supplies almost daily to Bordeaux." Bill reached over to pull a red pin off of Paris, pushing it into the map at Bordeaux. "If I can get them onto one of those cruisers, that will be a damn sight faster than a fishing trawler."

"And relatively safer," Wesley agreed.

"Take down a message to send back." Bill continued studying the map as Wesley turned and hurried over to the desk to get a pad and pencil. "She'll have to be quick. I've heard that the roads south from Paris are clogged with refugees already. It will take her three times as long to get there, and I don't know how much longer those supply shipments will be going."

"I'm ready, sir."

" 'Le Havre is out. Make for Bordeaux.' " Bill stopped and pursed his lips thoughtfully. " 'Find Leon on Rue Josephine at Café Rosa. Passcode: William told me Leon makes the best Cannelés. Advise when in place.' "

He stopped again and retraced a line back to Paris. After a moment, he glanced over his shoulder. "Add this: 'Proceed with all possible speed. Acknowledge receipt.' Sign it Bard."

Wesley finished writing and laid the pencil down, straightening up. "I'll have this encoded and sent immediately," he said, turning for the door. "Is there anything else, sir?"

"Yes. Are you a praying man, Wesley?"

"Yes, sir."

"Then you'd best offer a few for Jian, our boys, and the entire country of France. They're stuck in it now, and when France falls, there won't be anywhere they can hide."

Chapter Fourteen

Evelyn walked into the kitchen, following the scent of freshly brewed coffee. Josephine looked over her shoulder from where she was standing with her back to the door, busy at the small counter next to the sink.

"Perfect timing. It just finished brewing," she said, filling a cup with coffee. "There's no sugar, I'm afraid."

"That's all right. I'm getting used to it without. Thank you."

Evelyn took the steaming mug and sipped the hot brew thankfully.

"Finn is in the sitting room, monitoring the radio in case London responds to your message. I was trying to get a news report on the wireless, but there's nothing new yet. I wish we knew where the German forces are. It would give us some idea of how much time we have."

"I don't think it would do much good even if we did know." Evelyn turned to follow Josephine out of the kitchen with her coffee. "This is the speed of the Blitzkrieg that we've heard so much about. They're moving faster than the news can report."

"Anything yet?" Josephine asked Finn as they walked into the sitting room. He was seated at a desk in the corner with a radio open in front of him and a headset over his ears. He shook his head and Josephine sighed, looking at Evelyn. "They'll contact you. Bill will want you out of this as soon as possible."

"What about you?" Evelyn sank down onto a settee. "What will you do when you reach Marseilles?"

"I've already contacted my friend and she's expecting me." Josephine sat next to her and crossed her legs carelessly. "She'll help me find work and somewhere to live. I'll settle in and wait, as Marc advises. I just hope and pray that he and Luc are able to do the same."

"Where are they going?"

"I don't know. They wouldn't say. It's best for us not to know, especially if the Germans find out about any of us."

"Is that a possibility?" Evelyn asked, startled.

"Anything is a possibility if they take over France."

130

Into the Iron Shadows

Evelyn was silent for a moment, drinking her coffee. Josephine was right, of course. Once France fell and the Nazis occupied Paris, the entire country would be at the mercy of the Gestapo. When that happened, the risk of neighbors turning against those they used to call friends would be high. She'd heard what happened in Germany and Austria. The fear of the Gestapo was much greater than any loyalty most people had to each other.

"I have something!" Finn said suddenly from the corner. "But it's a code I don't recognize."

"Here come your instructions," Josephine said, smiling at Evelyn. "I told you they'd want to get you moving as soon as possible."

"I don't think this is London," Finn said, looking over to them. "This is something different. I can't make any sense out of it."

Josephine frowned, getting up and going over to him. She took the headset from him and listened for a moment, the frown deepening.

"It's not London," she agreed finally, motioning him out of the chair. "You're right. It's coming from our network here."

Finn moved away from the table as Josephine seated herself and reached for a pencil.

"I don't really understand how these things work," he admitted to Evelyn, sitting next to her. "My wireless training was rudimentary at best."

"What did you do in Belgium?" she asked him, turning slightly to face him.

"Nothing with radios," he replied evasively. "I was in the right place to obtain information, and I passed it back through a small group of people over the border."

"You said you were in Antwerp?"

"Yes. When the Germans came, I moved south."

Evelyn nodded. He clearly was unwilling to tell her anything more, and she was comfortable with that decision. She didn't need to know anything about him. She just needed to get him somewhere south so that they could both get back to England.

"I apologize if I was impolite," Finn said after a long moment of silence. "I'm not used to…well talking about it."

"It's quite all right. I shouldn't have asked." Evelyn smiled at him and finished her coffee. "It doesn't really matter, does it? The only thing that's important is getting out of Paris, and then getting back to England."

"Do you think we will do it? Make it south before the Germans?"

"We have to. It doesn't matter what I think."

131

"How long will it take us? I'm not familiar with the roads or the area."

"It's hard to say. It all depends on where we go. The amount of refugees leaving Paris will make going anywhere more difficult. Under normal circumstances, we could drive all the way to the Mediterranean in less than ten hours. But now? With all the people on the roads? I have no idea." Evelyn leaned her head back. "When I left Brussels on the day the Germans invaded, it took us all day to make it to the border. I've never seen so many cars and people and carts. I imagine it will be the same here."

"I'd forgotten you were in Brussels."

"Yes."

"Then you've done this before."

"What?"

"Escaped an invasion."

Evelyn's lips twisted wryly. "Yes. I've done this before."

She stood up and glanced down at him. "I'm going for another cup of coffee. Would you like one?"

"No, thank you."

She was just turning to leave when she heard Josephine suck in her breath. She glanced over at the corner to find her friend staring at words scrawled on the pad, her face white. Evelyn frowned sharply and changed direction, striding across the room towards her.

"What is it?" she asked, dropping a hand on her shoulder. "What's happened?"

Josephine lifted the headset off with visibly shaking hands.

"That was Marc. Our network has been exposed to the Germans."

Evelyn stared at her, breath catching in her throat. "How badly?"

"They have a list of names." Josephine rubbed her face and reached for a cigarette case on the desk. "One of our contacts in Metz intercepted a typed memo meant for a German commander."

She lit a cigarette and looked up at Evelyn, her lips pressed together. "My name is on it."

"How?" Evelyn demanded, her brows pulled together. "How did they get your name?"

"How did they get any of the names?" Josephine blew smoke out and got up impatiently. "That's not all of it. Finn's name is on it, and so is Jens Bernard."

Evelyn lifted a shaking hand to her cheek and stared at Josephine. An ice-cold shiver went down her spine and she sank into the chair Josephine had just vacated.

"And Marc?"

"No, but they think the list is incomplete." She looked at Finn, sitting silently on the settee, and then back at Evelyn. "Finn isn't even part of our network, and neither was Jens."

"No."

"Then how did they get their names? How did they get any of it?" Josephine strode impatiently to the other side of the room and back again. "If the list is incomplete, Marc and Luc could still be at risk. Marc is working on the assumption that we're all blown. He's contacting Mathieu and André to warn them. Then he and Luc are getting new identification papers and starting over. He thinks I should do the same."

"I agree!" Evelyn said vehemently, looking up and nodding. "It's too dangerous. If the Germans are distributing the list, they're already looking for all of you. As the troops roll in, the Gestapo will be right behind them."

"Or with them." Finn finally broke his silence. "There is a division of the Wehrmacht that is worse than the Gestapo. They're known as—"

"The SS." Evelyn finished for him. "Yes. I know."

He looked at her surprised. "You do?"

She was betrayed into a small smile. "Yes."

"If the Germans are distributing the list, they're giving it to the SS commanders. They have no need to wait for the Gestapo."

"You're as much at risk as I am," Josephine said, looking at him. "I can go to the Deuxième Bureau and get a new identity. What will you do?"

"I have one already," he said with a shrug. "I brought everything with me when I fled Antwerp. Do not concern yourself with me."

Josephine looked at Evelyn. "And Jens? How can we contact him?"

"I don't think we need to worry about him either," she said slowly, forcing herself to think. "When I last spoke with Marcel, he assured me that he would take care of him. He was going to arrange for new papers and a place in the French countryside." Evelyn gasped and looked up. "Was his name on there? Marcel?"

Josephine went over to the desk and picked up the notepad, flipping back a page to where she had written everything Marc said. After scanning over the list, she shook her head.

"No. He's not here. If the list is incomplete, though…"

"He should be warned," Finn said from the couch. "Whoever he is, he needs to know what is happening."

"If I know Marcel, he already does," Josephine said, dropping the notepad back onto the desk. "But you're right. We should warn him. I have no idea where he is, or how to contact him since he left Marle."

"I do," Evelyn said quietly. "I'll take care of it."

Josephine looked at her in surprise. "What? How do you know and I don't?"

She shrugged sheepishly. "He allowed Jens and I to use his Paris flat when we left Marle. I'll send a message there, and if he's still in Paris, he will receive it."

Josephine exhaled in relief. "Well, that's something at least."

"I'll have to go out for a bit."

"We'll go together. I have to go to my controller to get new papers. While I'm doing that, you can send the message to Marcel."

"I don't think using your agency is a good idea," Finn said slowly, shaking his head.

"I agree," Evelyn said.

Josephine looked from one to the other. "They are my employers!"

"They won't be once France falls, and then the Nazis will have all their records," Finn said flatly.

"They'll destroy them before that happens," Josephine scoffed. "They won't let them fall into Nazis hands."

"Are you willing to take that risk?" Evelyn asked quietly. Her eyes met Josephine's. "Marc and Luc aren't coming to Paris for their new papers, are they?"

After a moment's hesitation, Josephine shook her head. "No. He said in the message just now that he doesn't trust anyone after this. The list is too extensive. He won't come to Paris now."

"Do you have any idea where he and Luc will go for new papers?"

Josephine bit her bottom lip, clearly torn about revealing too much to them.

"If it's somewhere you can get to, I think perhaps you should consider that alternative," Evelyn continued when Josephine remained silent. "You can't continue the work if you're dead."

"And that's what will happen if the Nazis get to you," Finn added ruthlessly from his couch.

Evelyn shot him an exasperated look, but Josephine was already nodding in agreement.

Into the Iron Shadows

"No, he is right. This is no time to be stubborn or naive. If I don't want to risk further exposure by using my own agency then I'll have to find another way." Josephine put her cigarette out in the ashtray on the desk. "There's a man just outside of Reims. That's who Marc will use. He's about two hours north of us."

"North?" Finn repeated, staring at her. "That's right in the path of the German troops!"

She shrugged. "There is no one else."

Evelyn pressed her lips together, her heart sinking. If they went north into the path of the advancing troops, they would all be at risk. Yet what other choice did Josephine have?

"Just because the Germans are moving across France towards the Channel doesn't mean that they will pass through Reims," she said, surprised at how steady her voice was. "We'll go and just have to hope for the best."

"Hope for the best?" Finn demanded. "I thought the point was to get away from the Nazis, not go towards them!"

"You don't have to come at all," Josephine pointed out. "I'll go alone and you can start going south. I'll catch up with you."

"No." Evelyn stood up decidedly. "I'm not letting you go alone. They may know your name, but they don't know mine. I can help if you run into trouble. I'm not letting you go alone."

"That's ridiculous, Geneviève. There's no reason for either of you to put yourselves in the path of the Germans. This is my problem. I'll handle it."

"It's all of our problem," she said calmly. "If the Germans catch you and interrogate you, we're all at risk. We need to get you a new identity and make sure you can hide in plain sight before we do anything else."

"And what about going south?"

"We'll go together as soon as you have your new papers. Besides, you're the one with the car," Evelyn added with a grin. "I don't relish the thought of using bicycles, although I will if we have to."

"Geneviève is right," Finn said reluctantly. "Keeping your identity safe will only help us. I wish it wasn't taking us into the path of the German divisions, but so be it. This must be a priority."

Josephine looked from one to the other, her brows furrowed. "You're both out of your minds," she finally said. "Why risk all of us?"

"Because we can help," Evelyn said with a shrug. "And I'm not about to leave you to run straight into the front lines alone. You saved me in Strasbourg, remember? I still need to repay that."

Josephine waved her hand impatiently. "Don't be ridiculous.

You don't owe me a thing. That was a mutual endeavor."

"As is this. We're going to Reims with you, whether you like it or not." Evelyn looked at her watch, then glanced at the radio. "If it's only two hours from Paris, it won't be very much of a delay. Even with the photo processing, it should only mean losing one night."

Josephine looked at her, startled. "How do you know how long…" Her voice trailed off and she shook her head, smiling sheepishly. "Never mind. It's none of my business."

"Once you have your new identity, we will head south."

"If it even *is* south," Finn said. "We won't know for certain until we hear back from London."

"Hopefully that will be soon."

"I'll go back to listening," he said, getting up and moving towards the desk. "You two decide when we're leaving. The sooner we leave, the sooner we can go south."

"Agreed."

Evelyn picked up her forgotten coffee cup and started towards the kitchen. Josephine followed, her lips pressed together grimly.

"Geneviève?"

"Yes?"

"There's something that's bothering me, and I need to get it out into the open before we go anywhere," she said as the two women entered the kitchen.

Evelyn turned to look at her, raising her eyebrows in question. "What is it?"

"Everyone on that list has one thing in common," Josephine said slowly. "They've all had direct dealings with your MI6."

Evelyn swallowed. "Yes."

Josephine stared at her. "Is there something I should know?"

Evelyn met her gaze and saw the confusion and uncertainty in her eyes. She took a deep breath, her mind scrambling to find something to say, something that would not give away the existence of the London spy.

"I don't know how your names got out there, but I know neither Bill nor I had anything to do with it," she heard herself say. "The only thing you need to know is that I'm not leaving France until I know you, Jens, and Marcel are safe. You have my word on that."

Josephine stared hard at her for a long moment, then her mouth relaxed and she nodded.

"All right. As soon as you hear from London, we'll go to Reims. I still think it's pointless for you and Finn to risk it, but I understand why you're both determined to do it."

Into the Iron Shadows

Evelyn smiled. "I'm afraid you won't get rid of us so easily," she said, turning to pick up the coffee pot from the stove. "If I had my way, I'd bring you along with us to England."

"No. My place is here, with my country."

Evelyn looked over her shoulder. "I know. So let's make sure that you can continue to help France."

Chapter Fifteen

RAF Horsham

Miles walked into the lounge and looked around. Spotting Rob and Chris sitting in the corner with their ties undone and cigarettes in their mouths, he started towards them. He'd just returned from a sweep over France and his mood was less than cheerful. Not only had they not seen hide nor hair of the enemy, but his engine had begun acting up on the way back. With each sputter, he became more convinced that he would have to put her down in a field somewhere. Lady Luck was with him, however, and she'd made it back in the end, but barely. When he touched down on the landing strip, the Spit had given one more cough before cutting out altogether. Talk about cutting it close.

"Lacey! Come over and meet our new number five!"

Miles turned, raising an eyebrow as Marcus Hampton, also known as Mother, motioned him over to a long counter on the far wall that doubled as a makeshift bar for the pilots. The flight leader was standing next to a much younger man dressed impeccably in uniform with nary a hair out of place.

"Good Lord, we have another one?" he drawled, walking over to join them.

Mother clapped his hand on the younger man's shoulder. "This is Perry Ainsley. He's joining us fresh from the training school."

"Yes, Mr. Lacey and I have met," Perry said with a hesitant smile. "We met last night as I arrived. You were coming back from Dispersal. Do you remember?"

"Yes, of course." Miles motioned to the porter behind the counter for a pint.

"He's Flying Officer Lacey to you, Ainsley," Mother rebuked. "He's your superior. You're low man on the totem pole here."

Perry flushed and Miles waved a hand carelessly.

"Perry, is it? Well, you can call me Miles. I don't stand on ceremony." He shot Mother an exasperated look. "We're all in it together, after all."

Into the Iron Shadows

"Miles is one of our better fliers in the group," Mother said, lowering his voice. "He bagged himself a 109 over Belgium a few days ago. Watch and learn from him, and me, of course."

"It wouldn't do any harm to learn from any of us," Miles said. "The Yank is an expert in landing without wheels. Ask him about it sometime. How many hours do you have in Spits?"

"Fifteen, sir—Miles."

Miles blinked and looked at Mother. "Imagine that. Fifteen whole hours!"

"Don't listen to him, Perry." Mother shot Miles an admonishing look. "You'll have plenty of flying time before you run into any Jerries."

"Yes, sir."

Miles took the pint the porter set down before him and nodded in thanks, lifting it to his lips.

"Better keep him this side of the Channel, then," he muttered under his breath.

"I'm rather keen to see how it's done," Perry protested. "I'll have to get my feet wet sooner or later."

"Yes, and so you shall," Mother agreed.

"You'll get more than that wet if you're shot down over the drink," Miles said.

"Don't mind Miles. He's obviously had a bit of a day. You'll be just fine."

Perry nodded and visibly brightened when another new pilot walked into the lounge. After murmuring his excuses, he wandered over to his friend, leaving them alone.

"How was the hop over to France?" Mother asked, turning his attention to him.

"We didn't see a dickie bird. You weren't wrong about my day, though. My engine was having trouble on the way back. Didn't think I would make it, to be honest."

"What happened?"

"Dunno. The ground crew are looking at it now. It coughed up and died when I landed."

"That was jolly close."

"Don't I know it." Miles glanced at him. "When did you get back from your flight?"

"About an hour ago. We saw some Dorniers in the distance, but they were gone by the time we got there." Mother leaned against the counter and tilted his head, looking at Miles. "You know, there was a time when you and I only had 15 hours flying time."

"Yes, but that was before Hitler decided to storm through Europe." Miles sipped his beer and glanced at him. "Don't try to tell me that you have all confidence in young Perry. I've known you too long. You can't be happy having a baby in tow."

"Perhaps not, but we'll keep getting them. We need pilots, and the only way to get them up to speed is to throw them up there. As the war goes on, that will mean simply throwing them into the battle."

"I hope you intend to take him up for a few hours before letting him hop across the Channel with us?"

"Already planned, old boy. I'm taking him up at 5 o'clock in the morning, and we won't come down until we're out of fuel."

Miles nodded his approval and picked up his pint, straightening up. "Good man. While you have him up there, you might come at him from the sun. The bastards like to do that, and if you don't know to look for it, you're a sitting duck."

"Duly noted."

"Good." Miles clapped him on his shoulder. "Better you than me. I don't have the patience for nursery games. I'm off to commiserate with Rob and Chris. Care to join us?"

Mother shook his head. "No thanks. I'm off for a shower and shave."

Miles nodded and turned to continue on his way to the corner, pint in hand. As he went, he loosened his tie and unbuttoned his jacket. He was done for the day, and now was the time to relax.

"Well! Look who finally decided to join us," Chris said, lifting his eyes from his newspaper as Miles approached. "Fraternizing with the leadership, were we?"

"Meeting the new pilot fresh from the training school," Miles retorted, dropping into a chair. "Is it just me, or are they getting younger every day?"

"They're not getting younger. We're getting older," Rob said, closing his newspaper and folding it in half.

"Do you know he only has fifteen hours in a Spit?" Miles demanded. "I'm surprised he can land the bloody thing."

"Fifteen?" He looked startled. "Are you sure?"

"He's just told me himself."

"Well, there was a time when we all only had fifteen hours in a Spit," Chris pointed out thoughtfully. "Look at us now."

"The Jerries will have him for breakfast," Rob said, shaking his head. "What's the RAF thinking?"

"They're thinking we need pilots," Chris replied. "And they're right. I overheard Ashmore talking to the ground exec earlier. We have more planes coming, but not enough pilots to fly them. That could be a problem if we're expected to defeat the Luftwaffe."

"More planes?"

"Yes, and they're the new model. They've made some improvements. Apparently we're already flying dinosaurs."

"I can attest to that," Miles muttered. "My engine went on the blink over the Channel. Nearly didn't make it back."

"Oh? Did you run into some Krauts?" Chris asked. "I swear you have all the luck. The only time I see the bastards is when I'm up with you."

"No such luck, I'm afraid. We didn't see a damn thing."

"Then what happened to your engine?" Rob asked.

"Not the faintest, dear boy. It began acting up over the Channel, and got worse over land. I don't mind telling you, there were a few times I was convinced I'd end up in a hedgerow. It held on until I came in to land, then it just gave up. Cut out completely as my wheels touched the grass."

"Well at least it hung on until then," Rob said cheerfully. "All's well, and all that."

"Maybe you'll get one of the new planes," Chris said. "In fact, now that I think about it, we should all sabotage our engines, then we'll all get the new Spit."

"I wonder what the difference is," Rob said.

"I'm sure old Bertie could tell us," Miles said with a grin, glancing across the room to where the intelligence officer was in deep conversation with one of the pilots. "He's the intelligence officer, after all."

"You'd think they'd let us know," Chris said. "After all, we're the poor saps who have to fly them."

"I'm sure we'll have a briefing when they arrive. At least, I hope we have a briefing when they arrive." Rob leaned forward to drop his newspaper on the table between them. "Although, it is the RAF."

"Anything happen today that I should know about?" Miles asked, nodding towards the newspaper.

"You know, for a peer of the realm, you're distressingly uninformed on current events," he drawled. "Don't you read the newspaper?"

"Hard to read a newspaper at 20,000 feet."

"Well Hitler had a banner day," Chris said, tossing his newspaper on top of Rob's. "They've taken over a bunch of French towns that I can't pronounce, and it looks like they've reached the coast. Old Adolf is right over the Channel."

Miles raised an eyebrow and turned his head to look questioningly at Rob.

Rob grinned. "For the benefit of our illiterate American friend, I'll elaborate. German armies captured Amiens, Abbeville, and Noyelles-Sur-Mer." The grin faded. "The BEF has been ordered to retreat to the port cities. It looks like Calais and Dunkirk will be where they're headed."

Miles drained his pint and set the empty glass down on the floor beside his chair.

"So they're surrounded," he stated. "If they've captured Noyelles-Sur-Mer, the Germans have cut off every means of retreat south of Le Touquet."

Rob nodded grimly. "And I'll tell you this much," he said, "they won't stop there. Hitler isn't about to let the entire British Army escape. They'll take Calais next."

Chris looked from one to the other, his eyebrows pulled together. "I know where Calais is," he said, "but I have no clue where the others are. How do the two of you know France so well?"

"I practically grew up there," Rob said with a shrug. "M'mother's French, y'know."

"Anyone who's anyone knows France," Miles added. "My family has a nice little château not far from Pau."

Chris laughed. "Of course you do."

"You mean to tell me your family doesn't have a house somewhere other than wherever you're from?"

"Boston," Chris said with a grin. "How many times do I have to tell you people? I'm from Boston."

"Of course you are," Miles said patronizingly. "And that's somewhere south, right?"

Chris choked, missing the gleam of unholy amusement in Miles' eyes.

"You take the time to learn where every little village in France is, but you don't even know where Boston is. It's a major city!"

"Major to whom?" Rob drawled with a straight face. "Certainly not to us."

Chris stared hard at them both, and then his eyes narrowed suddenly in suspicion.

"You know exactly where Boston is," he exclaimed suddenly. "I thought we'd moved beyond the teasing-the-Colonial stage in our friendship."

"My dear boy, we'll never move beyond it. It's entirely too much fun!" Miles informed him with a grin.

Into the Iron Shadows

"What will happen to your château if the Germans occupy France?" Chris asked after a moment.

"I'd rather not consider it, thank you very much. I rather imagine it will be filled with German officers, or something equally horrid. Perish the thought!"

Chris looked at Rob. "And you?"

"I've no idea. I'm still trying to find out what my aunt and uncle plan to do. I'm hoping they'll come to England. If they do, then I suppose the same fate will befall their homes. They have one in Paris and one in the south of France, near Toulouse."

"For two men contemplating the German occupation of their homes in France, you're both being absurdly pragmatic about it all."

"We've told you before, Yank; there is absolutely no use in getting all worked up and crying over soon-to-be spilled milk," Miles said with a shrug. "When will you learn that we aren't as emotional as you Americans?"

Chris snorted. "Like hell you aren't. I've seen you fight, old boy, and I'll tell you this: you don't back down. Either of you. That takes emotion, and guts. I can't think of anything more American than that."

"Good Lord, did he just call us Americans?" Rob demanded, rolling his eyes over to Miles. "I think he's a bit touched, don't you?"

"I believe he was trying to pay us a compliment," Miles said thoughtfully, his aristocratic nose inching higher into the air. "Although, I'm not sure what our intestines have to do with anything."

Chris burst out laughing. "I was, and they don't. Just nod and smile and thank me."

"Thank you for what?" Rob asked, mystified.

"For seeing past this ridiculous mask you both wear."

"Oh, you're quite wrong there," Miles said, crossing his legs complacently. "These are very much our own faces. After all, just because one is being asked to fight and defend the King and Country, it by no means requires discarding generations of breeding. This is who we are, more's the pity. I'm afraid you've fallen into the company of the British elite, my dear rebel, and we will do whatever it takes to preserve our way of life."

"Especially if it means going toe to toe with Hitler's thugs," Rob agreed. "Or wing to wing, as it were."

"Then God help anyone who tries to invade jolly old England," Chris said. "That's one show I wouldn't want to miss."

"That's just as well," Miles said. "If Hitler tries to invade England, you'll be in it with us, don't worry."

Evelyn lifted her head from the contemplation of the hefty volume in her hands when the sound of footsteps echoed through the empty section of the library. When she'd arrived ten minutes before, she'd been greeted with a mix of astonishment and enthusiasm by the librarian at the front desk. When she asked the woman if the library was still open, she'd been assured that it was. Then, in a hushed whisper that was more from habit than out of respect to patrons, the woman had advised her that they would be closing an hour early. When Evelyn nodded, she'd taken that as a sign of encouragement and added that it was nice to see another person. With the mass exodus of people fleeing the city ahead of the Germans, all the businesses were suffering. It was a dark, sad time. Evelyn had nodded and agreed, then asked for direction to the medieval literature section. The woman had positively beamed, pointed her in the right direction, and then gone back to her work.

Evelyn had felt a heavy feeling of melancholy as she walked through the vacant library. With the exception of a lone elderly gentleman in the corner of the main reading room, she had the entire building to herself. She knew the library well. It was located not far from her aunt and uncle's house, and she and Gisele had been known to spend many a rainy afternoon here when they were younger. The wooden staircases, banisters, and the polished floors, were familiar, and the rows and rows of aged books carried a scent that was as comforting as it was poignant.

Would this be the last time she stepped foot in the old building?

The thought popped into her head as she slid the thick tome back onto the shelf and pulled another down. Opening it, she swallowed. If it was, it seemed fitting that her last visit wouldn't be a visit to the library at all, but a meeting. It seemed that her new job was replacing memories everywhere she went, and libraries were quickly becoming much more than buildings that housed a collection of books. They were becoming clandestine meeting places where she could speak without fear of being overheard. Especially today. There was no one to overhear anything.

"I thought you had returned to England."

The deep voice came from the next aisle and Evelyn smiled faintly, lifting her head. Her eyes encountered a pair of gray ones through a space in the books and she nodded.

"I know," she said, closing the book in her hand.

It was his turn to smile faintly and the man motioned for her to go to the back of her aisle. Evelyn replaced the book on the shelf and turned to walk to the far end of the aisle. She rounded the corner and came face to face with Jean-Pierre.

"And yet here you are, in Paris."

"I did leave," she assured him with a smile. "Circumstances arose, however, that made it necessary for me to return."

"Come. We'll move down a few rows just to be safe. I didn't see anyone on my way up here, but I'd prefer to be careful." He touched her elbow lightly, ushering her along the narrow walkway behind the stacks. "What was so urgent that you had to see me? And more urgent than getting your package back to England safely?"

"The package is safe, don't worry."

"Has it left France?"

"No."

"Then it isn't safe." He stopped at the end of a row and moved into it, releasing her arm. "Especially now. The Germans are advancing and it's inevitable that France will fall. That package can't be here when it does."

"God-willing it won't be."

Jean-Pierre looked down at her for a moment, his gaze pensive. "I hope you know what you're doing, Evelyn. You need to get out of France. You shouldn't be in Paris."

"Rest assured that I am doing everything I can, but right now you have more important things to worry about than me."

He raised an eyebrow. "Oh?"

"I came back to Paris to meet a contact whom I'm supposed to bring to England with me," Evelyn said in a low voice, reaching out and pulling a random book off a shelf. "Josephine was with him. They met me when I arrived."

"How is she?"

"She's fine. Or at least, she was." Evelyn raised her eyes to his. "Marc contacted her this morning. Someone, a member of her network, intercepted a message meant for the advancing German commander near Metz. The Germans have a list of names, all members of the intelligence community here in France."

Jean-Pierre showed now outward sign of emotion to the statement, but he did reach out to pull a book down and open it, pretending to flip through the pages.

"How many names?"

"Several. I didn't read the whole list, but what I saw were at least ten." Evelyn glanced at him under eyelashes. "Marc told Josephine that he thinks the list they intercepted is incomplete. He thinks there are more names than the ones that they have."

"Why would he think that?"

"Josephine didn't say."

Jean-Pierre was silent for a minute, his lips pressed together as he processed that tidbit of information. Then he looked at her.

"Why did you come to tell me this?"

"I wanted to warn you. Your name wasn't on the portion Josephine received, but I thought you should know you may be compromised. And, of course, Jens' name *was* on the list."

"You need have no fear for young Monsieur Bernard. He is no longer. He has a new name and will be settling in as the new clerk in a small firm in Lyons next week."

Evelyn looked at him, her eyebrows soaring into her forehead. "Already?"

Jean-Pierre's lips twisted into smile. "I told you I would take care of him," he reminded her. "I stand by my word."

"Yes, but so quickly!"

"After Sedan fell, there was no time to lose. I was lucky that one of the partners in the firm is an associate of mine, and he lost his clerk to the army. Our young friend will be safe enough with him."

"And if France falls?"

"Don't you mean when? It's inevitable, you know. They're saying the Nazis can be in Paris in a week." He closed his book and moved further down the row, scanning the bindings absently. "When the government leaves Paris, I shall have to go as well. If there is an armistice, my government will push for an unoccupied zone. If we succeed, our friend will be moved there with all haste."

Evelyn shook her head. "It's all a nightmare," she murmured. "What about you? What if the Germans know about you?"

"It's highly unlikely, if not impossible," he replied calmly. "The only name anyone in the field knows is Marcel, and that name doesn't appear anywhere in Paris."

Evelyn blinked in confusion. "Nowhere in Paris? Then who does the Deuxième Bureau think you are?"

"Antoine Dubois," he said with a smile, bowing to her with a flourish. "At your service."

"I don't understand. You said your name was Jean-Pierre."

"And so it is. There are only two men in the Deuxième Bureau who know my true identity. Antoine was created for my position within the Ministry of Foreign Affairs."

"You're a spy within your own government?" she asked in disbelief.

"No, not a spy. My identity is protected for other reasons; reasons I cannot divulge even to you."

"Did you know all this would happen?"

"That Hitler's armies would get through the Maginot? No. But my superior and I wanted to take every precaution. Now I'm very glad that we did."

Evelyn was quiet for a moment, her mind spinning. Then she looked at him, her eyes meeting his.

"What will you do if there is no armistice?"

"There must be. We cannot go on like this. Everyone knows it." He smiled sadly. "And I will continue either way, until I can continue no longer. Just as we all will."

"I wish I could do more than I am," she said suddenly, her voice shaking. "I seem to constantly be running away from the fighting, leaving others, you, to struggle alone."

Jean-Pierre turned to face her, taking both her hands in his.

"*Not* alone," he said fiercely, his eyes capturing hers. "There are others, including yourself. You aren't running away. You're finishing your mission. You have done what you came here to do. The package you carry back to your government will help continue the fight. It must get out of France, and safely out of reach of the Nazis who want it back. That is your job. Staying here and organizing a resistance is mine."

Evelyn stared into his eyes and swallowed, nodding. He was right, of course. But it didn't make it feel any better. She'd left too many people already to their fate. Peder was dead, Anna and Erik were incommunicado in the mountains of Norway, Jens was disappearing into Lyons, Josephine was going to try to create a new identity and life in Marseilles, Marc and Luc were God-knew where doing the same, and now Jean-Pierre would hide in plain sight. All while she went on her merry way back to the relative safety of England.

"You don't believe me." He shook his head and tightened his fingers around hers. "I can see it in your eyes. You blame yourself for leaving. Don't. This is our fight to fight. Yours will come soon enough, but you must be alive to face it."

"Paris is like a second home to me," Evelyn whispered. "To see this happen, to know that I should be here…"

"Being in Paris when the Nazis march in will do no good to anyone," he said bluntly. "You will do more for us by getting that package to London, and then finding a way to help us get information out."

He broke off suddenly, an arrested look taking over his face.

"What? What is it?"

"I've just realized, you're the answer."

Evelyn raised her eyebrows. "Answer to what?"

"To how we can get intelligence out of France."

"Me?"

"Yes. I can set up a resistance network, and gather information in the process, but there is no way to get it out of France. I don't have a direct link to England and MI6, or so I thought."

"You want to pass me any information you gather? Well, I certainly don't mind, but how on earth will we manage that if France is occupied and I can't get here?"

Jean-Pierre smiled slowly. "You'll find a way to get here. That's why you're here now. Your government will need you here, and once you're in, you contact me. We'll make the arrangements then."

Evelyn pulled her hands away from him and rubbed her forehead, shaking her head as if to clear it.

"It's true that there has been talk of France being a semi-permanent theatre of operations for me, but once it falls, I can't guarantee that I will be sent back."

"They'll have to send you back. They have no other way of knowing what's happening, or gaining intelligence to help them win this war. Think about it, Evelyn. It won't just be you; they'll send others as well. You'll be sent to gather intelligence, and I'll have intelligence that needs to be moved on. I'd rather give it to someone I trust."

"Me?" She dropped her hand and stared at him. "Why do you trust me?"

He smiled. "Because you're here now to warn me that I might have been exposed to the Germans on a list being distributed among the advancing commanders."

She shrugged and rolled her eyes. "All right. There's that."

They were silent while she wrestled with the idea of acting as a courier between Jean-Pierre and London. If she was sent back into France after the Germans had taken control, there was no reason not to take information from Jean-Pierre. That wasn't what had her suddenly feeling as if her world was crumbling around her. The problem was the sudden realization that the next time she was here, France would undoubtedly be under Nazi occupation.

And that thought terrified her.

"How will I contact you? How will I find you?"

Into the Iron Shadows

She heard herself ask the questions steadily and was inwardly amazed. She felt as if she was shaking like a leaf, but her voice revealed none of her fear or uncertainty. The smile that curved Jean-Pierre's lips confirmed that he had no idea how petrified she was.

"You can send a message to me at the Ministry of Foreign Affairs. Use the name Claudette. I'll know it's you."

Evelyn exhaled and nodded. "Very well. If I don't come back, I'll arrange something. We'll find a way to get whatever information you gather to MI6."

"I know, but I have every confidence that you will be sent back."

"Why?"

"Because your government would be fools if they didn't. If I didn't know, I would never have believed you weren't a Frenchwoman. Your authenticity will never be questioned by a Frenchman, and if we don't question you, there is no reason for the Germans to think you're anything other than French. You, my dear Evelyn, are the perfect spy."

Chapter Sixteen

Reims, France
May 21

Evelyn went into the small shop and looked around as the door closed behind her. The city of Reims was just as deserted as Paris had been, but it seemed to be a different kind of empty. Where many of the cafés in Paris were closed and locked up, most here still appeared to be open. However, as she and Finn had moved through the quiet streets, it was clear that no one was lingering over their coffee. The city had the same feeling of desolation that pervaded Paris. The difference was that Paris was clearly becoming more and more abandoned by the minute, whereas Reims seemed more as if the entire population was waiting behind closed doors for the worst to happen.

"Yes? How can I help you?"

A large, matronly woman with gray streaking her brown hair turned around behind the wooden counter along the side of the shop. She wiped her hands on her apron while her eyes cursorily swept over Evelyn.

"I'm looking for fruit," Evelyn said, her eyes scanning over the empty wooden crates where fresh produce would once have been stacked. "I can't seem to find any anywhere."

The woman's face softened slightly and she nodded. "The trucks aren't bringing our deliveries. All I have is what I've been able to get from the local farms, but even that is scarce. I do have a few strawberries left in the back."

"Do you?" Evelyn allowed her face to break out into a large smile. "Oh that's wonderful! I'll take them."

The woman nodded and turned to disappear through an open door leading to the back room of the shop. Evelyn looked around again. The shelves and crates were mostly empty, but there were a few potatoes and beans in the corner. She went over to inspect them and was just selecting the best of the lot when the woman emerged again with a small basket of strawberries in her hand.

Into the Iron Shadows

"This is all I have left," she said, setting it on the counter. Seeing her customer examining the potatoes, she came out and crossed the wooden floor. "If you're interested in the potatoes and beans, I have one or two onions in the back. They will make a stew."

"Thank you."

The woman took the potatoes from her and Evelyn gathered up as many beans as she could carry.

"I wish I had more," the woman said, setting the potatoes on the counter. "You're welcome to what I have. If you tell me what you're cooking, I can tell you if I have anything good to have with it."

"I don't have anything specific in mind," Evelyn said, carrying the beans over and laying them with the potatoes. "To be honest, I'm simply gathering what I can before we leave."

The woman nodded. "Ah. Yes. You are in good company. Many have left already, and many more who thought they would stay are now considering leaving. I don't blame anyone. They say the Nazis are coming in this direction. My husband told me they were spotted just a few kilometers east last night. They'll be passing by to the north of us, I expect."

"You don't think they will come here?"

She shrugged. "If they were going to come to Reims, they would have done it by now. This isn't the first German division to pass by us." She stopped and tilted her head. "You didn't know?"

"I don't live here," Evelyn admitted. "I'm here with my husband. We're on our way to join my family just outside Épernay."

"You came from Paris?"

"No. Beauvais."

"And how is it there? Is everyone fleeing?"

"Yes. We…well, we took everything that we could. I don't expect there will be anything left if we can return."

"It's just terrible, isn't it?" The woman shook her head sadly. "We had enough trouble in the last war, but now they've actually broken through the Maginot Line and come into France." She leaned forward and lowered her voice. "I've heard that they're burning farms as they go, and shooting anyone who comes out."

"No!" Evelyn gasped and opened her eyes very wide. "How horrible!"

She nodded soberly. "I pray every morning that our home will be spared, but I admit that I don't think it very likely. The Lord is on the side of Herr Hitler, it would seem."

"I don't believe that for one minute," Evelyn said before she could stop herself.

"No? Then why have they come into France so easily? It's as if they have angels carrying them."

"Demons, more like."

The woman was surprised into a snort of laughter and she turned towards the backroom again.

"I'll get those onions for you. They keep well. I'll see what else I can spare."

"These aren't your own stores, are they?" Evelyn called, alarmed. "I don't want to take your food."

"Mademoiselle, I have more than my small family needs," came the muffled reply from the back. "The money will be of more use to us. We will have to close the shop after today, and then we will decide if we stay or we leave. If we leave, onions will do us no good."

Evelyn looked around the shop again and felt an overwhelming sense of sorrow for the woman and her husband, who were losing everything they had worked for. And for what? It all seemed so pointless.

"I have some carrots here, and two nice beets," the woman said, returning with a larger basket. "Onions and a few more potatoes for you. We'll put it all in this larger basket to make it easier for you to carry."

Evelyn watched as the woman piled all the vegetables into the basket. "I appreciate it very much. Thank you."

"Of course. We must help each other now." The woman glanced up at her. "I wish the government would sign an armistice and get this whole thing over with. Then perhaps we can save our homes."

"An armistice!" Evelyn exclaimed. "But the army is still fighting!"

The woman snorted. "Not very convincingly," she muttered. "If they are still fighting, why are the Nazis tearing up our countryside and fields? I've heard," she lowered her voice again and leaned forward, "that the army at Sedan simply laid down their guns and held up their hands without firing a single shot. Not one single shot!"

"What? No!"

The woman nodded and straightened up again, going back to the vegetables. "Well, if they won't fight then why should we? And if the government signs an armistice, perhaps we will see some light again. Our young men can come back, and the bombing will stop. Do you know Nancy has been bombed repeatedly? There must be nothing left!"

Evelyn stared at her in consternation, trying to understand what she was hearing.

Into the Iron Shadows

"But if we sign an armistice, the Germans will take over France."

"And will we be very worse off? I don't know."

"But…this is France!"

"And there will be nothing left of it if this continues for very much longer. You heard what they did to Rotterdam?"

Evelyn nodded. "Yes. It's terrible."

"I don't want to see Paris destroyed. Do you?"

"No, of course not. I don't want to see anything destroyed."

The woman nodded. "Precisely. An armistice will stop the bleeding."

Evelyn was quiet as the woman calculated what she owed. She wanted to explain to the shopkeeper just how much worse it could be under the Nazi thumb, but she knew she couldn't say anything. As a supposed Frenchwoman, she should be thinking the same way, but she knew better. She knew that when the Nazis came, France would never be the same. How could it?

"Will you be leaving today?" The woman asked as she took the money Evelyn counted out.

"I think so. My husband is in the tobacco store down the street. I believe he said he wanted to be on the road today."

"Be careful how you go. The last I heard, the Germans were moving north of here, going west. If you stay south, you should be all right."

"Thank you very much, for everything." Evelyn smiled and took the basket. "I hope you and your husband remain safe, no matter what you decide."

"We will do what we can. The rest is up to fate." The woman watched as she turned to go to the door. "Don't forget. Stay south."

"We will. Thank you!"

Evelyn left the shop and blinked in the sudden brightness of sunlight cutting through the thick clouds that had hung heavily in the sky all morning.

"Geneviève!" A voice called and she turned to watch as Finn hurried towards her carrying a brown bag in one arm. "I'm here. Did you have any luck?"

"I managed to get a few vegetables and some strawberries, but heaven knows what we can do with them without a pot and a fire," she said with laugh. "And you?"

"We're stocked with cigarettes, and I was able to get some sweets."

"It's not very much, is it?" Evelyn turned to walk with him up the street. "We don't even have any bread."

"I saw a bakery in the next street, but it was closed." Finn looked down at her. "Don't worry. We won't starve. We'll find some, perhaps on our way."

Evelyn thought back to the days of climbing across mountains in Norway without food and pressed her lips together. She had absolutely no desire to ever feel that hungry and tired ever again, but it was beginning to look as though it could happen. If they weren't able to find bread and cheese, at least, then it would be a very long drive south.

"I heard something in the shop that was alarming," Finn said after a moment. "The man remarked on the advancing Germans. Today is the last day he will be open. He's closing and leaving. He said he's going to Lyons."

"What's so alarming about that? Everyone is leaving. They're all panicking and running. I suppose I can't blame them. They're getting absolutely no direction from the government. As far as I can tell, Reynaud hasn't given any real guidance."

"It's not that he was leaving that's alarming. It's what he said to me. He wants an armistice with Hitler!"

Evelyn paused mid-stride to look at him in surprise. "So does the woman who I just spoke with!"

"They seem to think that they will be better off if the government surrenders and stops the fighting." Finn shook his head and continued walking, shifting the bag to his other arm. "If they only knew! They wouldn't think that if they had any idea what the Nazis are capable of."

Something in his voice made Evelyn glance at him from under her eyelashes. He spoke as if he knew firsthand what the Nazis would do, but that couldn't be possible. He'd left Belgium well ahead of the German army.

"The woman I spoke to is afraid Paris will end up like Rotterdam," she said slowly. "I suppose I can see her point, but as you said, if they had any idea what they're asking for, they might not be asking for it."

"I don't know if I've ever seen such a defeatist attitude," he said after a moment, his voice low. "It's as if they've just given up."

"They're tired of war. They just want it to end."

Finn glanced down at her, his jaw set mulishly. "We're all tired of war. Our parents fought in the last one. I remember the struggle finding food when I was a boy, and the men who came back without

154

limbs, or worse, who went mad. None of us want this, but this is what we have. We can't simply give up."

"I agree, but these people obviously do not feel the same." Evelyn pursed her lips thoughtfully and cast her eyes over the city buildings around them. "Reims was damaged in the last war. Perhaps that is still heavy in their memory."

Finn snorted. "So were Antwerp and Brussels."

Evelyn glanced at him and nodded. "I know." She tucked her arm through his comfortingly.

"And yet here I am, willing to do whatever I have to in order to continue the fight."

"And there are those that are willing to fight here," she said, remembering Jean-Pierre's face yesterday. "Not everyone is in favor of an armistice."

Finn was silent for a long moment, then he exhaled loudly.

"You are right. I suppose I was caught off guard. I wasn't expecting it, that is all."

"I understand. Neither was I."

He glanced down at her. "We need to get back to the house. Josephine's papers should be ready by now, and we must get moving. The German army is just north of here. We don't want to risk running into them."

"I was surprised that Yves was able to do everything overnight. We didn't arrive until after eight, and yet this morning he said they were almost ready."

Finn was silent, then he released her arm as they approached where he had parked the car.

"Thank goodness he was," he said, unlocking the passenger door and opening it for her. "I'm not comfortable knowing the Germans are only a few kilometers away."

Evelyn got into the car and he handed her the brown paper bag before closing the door. As he went around to the driver side, she twisted in the seat and set the bag and the basket on the back seat. She wasn't comfortable being this close to the German army either, but so far they had heard nothing to indicate that the enemy was even close. There were no planes overhead, no bombs exploding, and no rifle fire. Only the abandoned city streets told the story of what, exactly, was unfolding in the countryside beyond them. The very silence of the coming storm was more disconcerting than knowing that it was on its way. Unlike Norway and Belgium, where bombs heralded the Germans arrival, Reims seemed to be as it always was.

And Evelyn wasn't sure which was worse.

Eisenjager stood deep in the shadows of an alleyway between two tall buildings and held a small but powerful scope to his eye. He focused on the glass storefront, watching as the Englishwoman stood at the counter talking to the shopkeeper. Her blonde hair gleamed under the lightbulb overhead, a plain hat sitting atop the golden curls. She was dressed neatly but unremarkably in a blue skirt and jacket. He had to appreciate her attention to detail. She didn't want to draw attention to herself, so she was dressing much the same as every other Frenchwoman in the cities. It showed wisdom. It showed that she was aware that someone might come looking for her, and she didn't want to be remembered. It was what he himself did daily.

He lowered the scope and glanced at his watch before returning his gaze to the shop several buildings down. It hadn't been as difficult as he'd expected to find the car from the airfield in Paris. One benefit to the mass exodus taking place was that, while the roads going south out of the city were clogged with pedestrians and vehicles of all types, the reduced number of vehicles inside Paris had made it fairly easy to find the one he wanted. A few well-placed francs and a few discussions with various petrol stations and parking lots had narrowed the possible sections of Paris. Once that was done, it was only a matter of time before he located the car. He'd found it last night, just in time for the man to come and collect it. He'd followed him at a distance and watched as the Englishwoman and her companion loaded suitcases into the back and climbed in.

Eisenjager reached into his jacket pocket for a cigarette. It was still amazing to him that he'd arrived, literally, in time to see them leave. A few more minutes and he would have missed them completely, and she would have disappeared into the cosmos again.

No, he thought, lighting his cigarette. *Not again. I would have found her. I will always find them.*

And that was the truth. He always located his targets. That was why he was the one in such demand in Hamburg and Berlin. He always found his target, and he never failed.

Except with her.

Snapping his lighter closed, Eisenjager lifted his eyes to the store again, watching as the figure moved across the small shop. This woman, this English spy, was his cross to bear. Perhaps she had been placed in his path by the universe to teach him patience. And perseverance. Or perhaps she was simply an extremely lucky woman whose luck had finally run out. Either way, he had her now, and he wasn't going to lose her again. There was no bumbling SD agent to get in his way this time.

What he was going to do with her was another question entirely.

He blew smoke out and shifted his weight, never taking his eyes from the shop down the street. It had been with the greatest reluctance that he'd contacted Hamburg yesterday, requesting instructions. His standing orders were to eliminate her, but the presence of Henry at the airfield yesterday was disturbing. What did he want with her? Had Berlin sent him to intercept and interrogate her? Or was he acting on his own? In almost any other circumstance, Eisenjager would ignore the other spy and continue on his way, completing his mission. But the political climate between the Abwehr and the Sicherheitsdienst was not good. The hatred between Canaris and Himmler was well-known, and nothing one did wrong ever escaped notice from the other. If the SD wanted the woman alive, the worst thing he could do was kill her. Even though his orders were standing, Eisenjager wasn't foolish. He was much better off being safe than sorry. Sorry usually meant dead, and he wasn't about to allow the SD the satisfaction of shooting him. And so he had requested confirmation of the orders.

And was still awaiting it.

His lips tightened. Until he heard back from his handlers, he could only watch the woman, and monitor her movements. He'd already taken detailed notes describing both of her companions, and he would forward them on in his next transmission. He was also making a note of everywhere she went, everyone she spoke to, and even what she wore. If nothing else, he was compiling quite a dossier on the woman known only as Jian.

He straightened up suddenly when the door to the shop opened, lifting the scope back to his eye swiftly. He watched her emerge from the shop with a basket on her arm filled with vegetables. The sun glinted through the clouds as she stepped onto the pavement, catching her hair and making it glow with gold light. He sucked in his breath, the sight bringing to mind the hazy memories of pictures of angels from his childhood. The streak of sunlight disappeared and, in an instant, the memories were gone and he was looking at his target once again. She turned to walk up the street, then paused and turned back when the man came running up behind her. The couple turned to walk together, heading towards him. The man carried a bag and they were talking, oblivious to the possibility that they were being watched.

They were shopping for what supplies they could get, he realized, lowering the scope. They would be moving again.

Eisenjager slid the scope into his pocket and dropped his cigarette onto the ground, putting it out with his shoe. As they passed the alley across the street, he moved out of the shadows and onto the sidewalk, walking on the opposite side of the street and slightly behind them. Neither of them noticed, and he shook his head. She still didn't have the instincts for this. He'd realized it in Oslo, but thought that time would have made her more alert. But it wasn't so. She was still oblivious to her surroundings, and the people in them. She wouldn't last much longer in this war, not without looking over her shoulder.

Especially with him right behind her.

Chapter Seventeen

Evelyn gazed out of the window as they left behind the city proper and headed into the country. The small house where Yves lived and worked was about ten minutes outside the city, set back on a farm accessible only from a lane leading off the main road. While it was close to Reims, it was still isolated in the country. As they drove out of the city, the houses became more infrequent, and when Finn turned onto the main road that would take them to Yves' lane, she sighed.

"I'll miss all of this."

"All of what?" Finn asked, glancing at her. "Trying to find food to take with us as we desperately flee an advancing enemy? Or trying to find our way through strange country roads without running into Nazis?"

"None of that," she said with a laugh. "It's the country I'll miss. Even the countryside has the French charm that I adore. It's not the same as other countries. The attitude here is different. It's a way of life and a way of thinking that sets it apart from the rest of Europe. That's what I'll miss."

"You say that as if you'll never be back. You will, you know. We both will."

"Is that why you're so comfortable going to England? Because you think you will come back?"

"I don't think. I know. They'll want me here, as they will you. You'll see."

Evelyn shifted her gaze out the window again and was silent. She knew that was the plan, why she'd been recruited in the first place. She was the perfect spy, as Jean-Pierre had said, and she knew France well. She'd spent half of her life in Paris and in the south of France. Her uncle's château near Toulouse had been the site of many family summer holidays. She felt as if she knew France almost as well as she knew England. Yet Evelyn still questioned if she would be allowed to come back to France once the Germans took over. It seemed unlikely, despite her skill set and familiarity with the French culture and terrain. She couldn't imagine Bill being willing to take the risk and send her into occupied territory. He was growing more and more like a father-figure every day, and she knew he felt somewhat responsible for her. Sending her into the wolf's den was something she thought he would be unwilling to do when it came right down to it.

"Do you see that?" Finn asked, drawing her attention from the contemplation of the hedges lining the road.

"What?" She peered through the windshield at where he was pointing.

"That cloud. Do you see it?"

Evelyn stared at what appeared to be a grayish cloud in the distance, rising over the fields. After a long moment, she sucked in her breath just as he did the same. A streak of fear snaked down her spine and her heart thumped hard in her chest as she realized just what they were looking at. The cloud was massive, and moving quickly in their direction, crossing through what were probably fields and empty land.

"That's a lot of vehicles," Finn said, his voice unsteady, "and they're moving fast."

"The woman in the shop said the German troops were going to pass by north of here."

"Well, she was wrong. They're closer than that!"

Evelyn nodded, fear making her whole body tremble. "Those are fields. We're on the closest road, aren't we?"

"I think so. Check the map."

Evelyn dug in the pocket of the door for the folded road map that she had stuffed there when they left the house this morning. Spreading it open, she followed the road they were on.

"Well?"

"This is the only main road that runs parallel with where that cloud is coming from," she told him after a minute, lifting her head. "They're heading right for us. But they're on the fields, not the road!"

"The tanks and artillery are on the fields. The smaller vehicles will be on the road." Finn shook his head and glanced at her. "At that speed, the rest of the infantry isn't very far."

"I think we should get off the road," Evelyn said, taking a deep breath and trying to calm her racing heart. "If we pull off into the trees, we can…"

Her voice trailed off suddenly as dark shadows appeared on the horizon directly in front of them.

"Too late!" Finn cried, staring as the shadows rapidly took the shape of trucks.

Into the Iron Shadows

"Pull off the road!" Evelyn directed, her fear making her voice sharp. "Over there. Pull off and we'll get out and go behind the hedges and into the trees. Maybe they won't look twice at the car."

Finn nodded and pulled into the shallow ditch that ran alongside the road. As he did so, Evelyn watched in horror as a smaller vehicle, a car, came into view, pulling past the trucks. There was no doubt in her mind that it was a staff car, and that meant it was a German officer of some importance. They were the only ones who would be traveling in a car with a convoy.

"Geneviève!" Finn said urgently, grabbing her arm and shaking gently as she stared, transfixed, out of the windshield at the oncoming tidal wave of gray and black metal. "Hurry! We must go. Open the door!"

Startled out of her terrified stupor, Evelyn fumbled with the door handle. Finn had stopped on an angle and she half fell out of the car as the door swung open. Catching herself on the frame, Evelyn jumped out and landed on her feet, grateful for the lack of rain that had made the ground hard. If it had been otherwise, she would have lost her fashionable heels in soft earth, and probably fallen flat on her face in the process. As it was, she was able to scramble up the slight incline and head towards the trees at the top of a rise beside the road, Finn right behind her.

"Hurry!" he gasped. "They're almost here!"

Evelyn forced herself to run as quickly as she could in her skirt, battling both the incline and the uneven ground. Grasping her skirt with both hands, she pulled it up above her knees to give her legs more room. Sparing only a brief curse on the skirt and heels that were slowing her down, Evelyn made a beeline for the copse of trees ahead of her. If they could make it to the trees before the troops passed them, they would be safely hidden. They just had to make it to the trees.

Glancing over her shoulder, Evelyn felt her stomach drop as the car pulled past the lead truck and drew ahead, speeding forward. It was impossible for the driver not to see them running up an incline next to a car on the side of the road. She turned her attention back to the trees, willing her legs to run faster as her breath came short and fast.

"Keep going!" Finn cried, looking over his shoulder. "They're stopping!"

Evelyn ran for all she was worth, scrambling up the last few steps of the hill, her heart in her throat. Finn was right beside her, his hand on the small of her back, urging her forward.

"Halt!"

Icy fear shot down her spine and Evelyn gasped, lurching to a stop at the top of the incline, just feet from the protection of the old, twisted trees.

Josephine looked up, closing the book in her hands when a short, stocky man emerged from the kitchen door. She was sitting in the small garden behind his house, leaning against a tree, reading. She was having trouble concentrating on the pages, however, and her mind had been wandering for the past twenty minutes or more.

"They are ready," he announced with a nod. "You may come and look if you like."

Josephine jumped to her feet and walked towards him. Yves Michaud was nothing like what she had been expecting when they set out to come here last night. Marc's friends, the few she'd met over the past year, were young men like himself. Yves Michaud was in his forties if he was a day, and Josephine wondered if he was perhaps even older than that. That he was used to working outside and tending the grape vines in the adjoining field was obvious from his tanned skin and heavily calloused hands. Yet those hands had spent most of the night working on the papers that would bestow on her a whole new identity.

"Fantastic!"

She followed him into the house and through the kitchen to the small room he called his workroom. It was where he'd taken several photographs of her when she arrived. The lights were off now, and the work desk was cleared of the clutter that had been there early this morning. In its place were her new papers.

"You have everything you need here, all the vital records," he said, walking over to the table. "Passport, certificate of birth with both parent's names, certificate of baptism, and I've included a marriage license for your parents."

"Who are my new parents?"

Yves smiled. "They were a couple who really existed. They moved to Morocco, and died there a few years ago during a Typhoid fever outbreak."

"Children?"

"Not until now." He picked up the birth certificate and handed it to her. "My sincere condolences on the loss of your parents."

"Thank you." Josephine took the paper and carried it over to examine it in the light from the window. "Jeannine Renaud?"

Into the Iron Shadows

"I try to keep the initials the same when possible. I've found that most people who come to me have something with their initials on that they don't want to part with. This can create confusion if it is ever found." Yves cleared his throat and looked at her closely. "You understand, of course, what this will entail? You must destroy anything that connects you to your old life. Josephine Rousseau must cease to exist. She is dead. Gone. Jeannine Renaud is who you are now."

"Yes, I understand."

"And you understand that it includes anyone who might know and recognize you as Josephine?"

Josephine paused in her examination of the document and grew still, lifting her head, her eyes widening. He nodded wisely.

"I thought as much. You were going to stay with someone? A family member perhaps?"

"An old friend." Josephine exhaled. "I didn't even think…but of course, you're right. She's expecting Josephine."

"I'd suggest a change in travel itinerary."

"May I see the others?" Josephine asked, motioning to the other documents.

"Of course. You have paid for them. They are yours now." He turned to gather the other documents and hand them to her. "When France falls, the country and government will be in chaos. Records will be lost or inaccessible. That will be to your advantage. These will prove your identity to anyone who needs to know. The Germans will require identification cards, and these will ensure those cards are authentic."

"You think it is inevitable, then?" She glanced up from her study of the passport. "That France will fall?"

"I do, and so do you or you wouldn't be here."

She nodded slowly, her eyes clouding over with sorrow. "That is true."

"If you have any photos or papers with your name on it, I suggest you destroy them as soon as possible. These things have a way of making their way into the open eventually, regardless of how careful you are."

"Yes, I will."

Yves smiled at her gently and reached out to pat her shoulder. "Don't sound so forlorn, Mademoiselle. You have a unique opportunity to reinvent yourself. You can be whoever you choose, and can create for yourself a life that is different from anything you've ever known. That is no bad thing."

"It's no good thing, either." Josephine looked up and was surprised at the compassion and understanding in his weathered face.

"I'm proud of who I am. I have no desire to be anyone different, yet I must. What about my father?"

"He cannot know. Where is he?"

She shrugged and laughed mirthlessly. "Only God Himself knows. The last I heard he was near Bruges, in Belgium, but that was days ago. He could be anywhere now."

"He is with the army?"

"Yes."

"And he will look for you when he returns?"

"Yes, but he won't be surprised when he cannot find me. He understands, you see." She held up the documents. "He will guess this is what happened."

"Then you are very lucky. But don't try to contact him directly. If you must, you may send a message, but no name." Yves shrugged. "I work hard to ensure the legitimacy of the identities I provide. Please do me the honor of maintaining their integrity on your end."

Josephine grinned. "Don't worry, Monsieur. No one will ever suspect that I am not Jeannine Renaud, born in—" She flipped to the birth certificate and scanned it again. "Casablanca."

"It's a port city in Morocco. You were born there, but came back to France at a very young age to attend school. Your parents did not think the education in Morocco was up to their standards."

"I know nothing about this Casablanca," Josephine said with a frown. "How old was I when I left?"

"That is entirely up to you. I'd suggest boarding school at the age of five or six, perhaps? But only you know what you are comfortable with fabricating."

Josephine nodded and grinned. "I've become fairly good at fabricating. I'm sure I'll come up with something."

He nodded and turned towards the door, their business concluded.

"Come. I'll make coffee."

Josephine followed him out of the little room with her new identity in her hands. It seemed strange to think that these documents turned her into a new person, someone the government recognized as a legitimate citizen of France. She would create an entire past that had never happened, and live by that lie from now on. It was almost surreal how easy it had been, but Josephine knew it was far from easy. Yves had been up all night ensuring that these documents would stand up to scrutiny. He had even artificially aged them.

And now it was up to her to make the best use of them.

"Umdrehen!"

The command was given harshly in a voice that carried, not through volume but due to its authority. The officer was a man used to being obeyed, and his tone brooked no argument.

Evelyn swallowed and looked at Finn, her eyes wide. She couldn't let them know she understood the command to turn around, but what else could she do? Looking to him, she saw his lips tighten before he slowly turned around. Following his lead, she turned to see the officer climbing the incline behind them. His gray-green uniform was immaculate, as were his black boots and gloves. Evelyn noted the braided insignia on his shoulder and her mouth went dry. She wasn't as familiar as she should be with the insignias of the Wehrmacht, but she recognized the braid as belonging to an officer of higher rank. A major, perhaps? Her only comfort now was the absence of the strange crooked S-shaped pins on his lapel that she remembered from the men in the mountains in Norway. This man, officer though he may be, was not one of the dreaded SS.

"What are you doing? Why are you running?" The officer spoke in German, looking from one to the other as he grew closer.

Evelyn remained silent, staring at him. She didn't have to pretend to be afraid. Her heart was pounding, her mouth was dry, and her palms had become damp inside her gloves. She was terrified, and she knew her face showed it. What on earth was she going to do? She couldn't let Finn know she spoke German, nor could she let the officer know. That would lead to questions, and questions might lead to him discovering who she really was, and who Finn really was.

"Where are you going?"

Evelyn stole a glance at Finn out of the corner of her eye to find him staring at the officer with a wooden look on his face. Clearly he had no idea what the man was saying. After looking from one to the other again, the officer sighed impatiently and turned his head.

"Leutnant! Get up here and translate. These fools don't understand a word I'm saying!" he yelled back to the two soldiers standing near his car, their rifles trained on Evelyn and Finn. One of them started forward. "And bring Oberfeldwebel Schmidt. I may need him to help restrain the man!"

"Das ist nicht nötig. Ich verstehe dich."

Evelyn sucked in her breath and turned to stare at Finn. He had spoken calmly, his voice even, and his accent perfect. The officer

165

made a motion with his arm, indicating for the soldiers to stand down, and raised his eyebrows as he studied Finn.

"You speak German?"

"Yes."

The officer seemed to relax a bit and he glanced at Evelyn. "And the woman?"

"No."

The officer nodded, seeming to be satisfied with the truth of that statement after a searching glance at her confused face. He turned his attention back to Finn.

"Where are you going? Why are you running?"

"We saw all the trucks and thought it best to get off the road," Finn explained. "We wanted to get out of your way."

"Why leave your vehicle and run to the trees? What's in the trees?"

"Nothing. We just wanted to hide."

The officer stared hard at him, then glanced at Evelyn again. "Are there more of you in those trees? Do I need to have my men search them?"

"What? No. There's no one else."

"And my convoy? Is there a surprise perhaps waiting for us?"

Evelyn almost laughed out at that, but caught herself before making a sound. The man thought they were trying to sabotage the convoy! Didn't he understand that all of France was running away?

"If there is, it has nothing to do with us," Finn said with a shrug. "We are on our way to my wife's family. Her sister is going to have a baby."

The officer looked at Evelyn consideringly. "Your wife?"

"Yes."

"She is very beautiful. You're a lucky man."

"Thank you."

"You speak my language very well. Where were you born?"

"In Brussels. I attended the University of Munich, and worked in Freising for a year."

The officer's face lightened into a grin. "University of Munich? I also was a student there. What was your field of study?"

"History. I came to France to teach."

"Ah. And how did you like Munich?"

"I liked it very much. My studies did prevent me from enjoying the beer as much as I would have liked," Finn said with a short laugh.

The officer laughed. "Munich is famous for its beer halls," he agreed. Then he sobered. "Where is your wife's family?"

Into the Iron Shadows

"Dijon."

"That's southwest, yes?"

"Yes."

"You may continue," the officer said arrogantly, "but I suggest that you stay off the main roads."

"I…yes, of course."

The officer nodded and looked one last time at Evelyn. His eyes slid over her assessingly and he grinned at Finn.

"Very lucky man," he reiterated. "Ah well. Next time, don't run."

"Yes, sir."

The officer turned and scrambled down the incline again, going back to the car. As he did so, the soldiers in the road raised their rifles again, ready to shoot should either Finn or Evelyn attempt to attack their commanding officer. As he reached the road, the officer waved their weapons down and went straight to the car again, saying something to his Lieutenant as he passed. The man saluted and hurried to get behind the wheel again. A moment later, the car was speeding away, the trucks surrounding it once more as the convoy once again continued on its race west.

Evelyn watched them go, barely able to understand all that had just happened. She stood next to Finn on the rise above the road, watching the stream of trucks laden with soldiers and artillery rumble past, and felt her entire body go suddenly weak. She realized she'd been holding herself rigid and now, the threat gone, all of her muscles seemed to want to turn to jelly. That entire encounter could have gone so badly, and yet it hadn't. Finn had talked them out of it. The officer had believed every word, and he needn't have. He could have sent his men to search the trees behind them. He could have brought his staff sergeant up and restrained them, and had them searched. These were things he undoubtedly would have done if Finn hadn't been so convincing.

Shock and terror shot through her at the thought. They would have been searched, and so would their car. In the trunk of the car was her suitcase with the false bottom, holding documents and a stolen package from Stuttgart!

Evelyn's knees suddenly gave out and Finn let out an exclamation, catching her swiftly. He took one look at her white face and wrapped an arm around her waist, leading her over to a patch of grass.

"Come and sit," he said. "You're shaking."

"I'll be all right," she said, shaking her head. "Just give me a minute to collect myself."

He gave her a dubious look but nodded, not removing his supporting arm. Evelyn took a deep breath, trying to calm her racing heart. If they had found that oilskin-wrapped package…a shudder went through her.

"You must sit. Please," Finn urged. "I'm afraid you'll faint."

"I don't make a practice of fainting," she said tartly, drawing a laugh from him. "Besides, we have to get back to Josephine. I just need a moment to collect myself, and then I'll be perfectly all right."

Finn stood silently beside her as she stared over the countryside. The clouds of dust that had first alerted them to the presence of the Germans were receding into the distance, heading west. Were they going to reinforce the armies that had already reached the Channel? Or would they turn south and go towards Paris? Either way, it was clear from the officer's demeanor that he already considered France theirs.

"You speak German?" Evelyn finally asked after a few minutes of silence. Her heart rate had returned to normal and her limbs were no longer trembling. She turned to look at Finn. "Why didn't you say anything before?"

He shrugged. "Why would I? It makes no difference to speak German when you are in France."

"It certainly made a difference just now."

He shrugged again and avoided looking her in her eyes. "I didn't see another way. If he brought other soldiers up here, we would have been restrained and searched. I did what I thought was best to prevent that."

"I appreciate that." She took a few experimental steps and nodded, glancing at him. "I'm all right now. Let's be on our way."

Finn nodded and followed her down the incline towards the road. "I think perhaps we should wait to go south," he said thoughtfully. "Perhaps instead of leaving today, we should go in the morning. I don't want to risk running into anymore divisions."

"We could still run into them tomorrow. We don't know how many more are coming."

"Perhaps, but if there are more, I think they will be close behind them. I wish we had some way of knowing."

Evelyn pursed her lips thoughtfully. "We might. We can see if Yves has a radio. If he does, Josephine might be able to find out where the closest enemy troops are."

They reached the car and Finn hurried to open the door for her. She smiled and climbed in, reflecting that it seemed silly to observe such niceties when they had just narrowly escaped being captured by the Nazis. He closed the door and went around to climb into the driver's side. A moment later, the engine roared to life and he put it in gear.

"Let's hope I can get us out of this ditch," he said, pressing the gas.

"The ground is hard from the lack of rain. You shouldn't have a problem."

Her words proved correct and the car surged back onto the road with only a small fishtail when the back tires hit loose stones. Evelyn exhaled and leaned her head back, staring out the windshield. Her body was a strange mix of taut wariness and exhausted emotion, making her feel very strange. She supposed it was a feeling she would get used to as the months of war dragged on, especially if she ended up working in close proximity with the enemy. She would have to learn how to handle the emotion.

Or become numb to it.

After a few minutes, Finn cleared his throat.

"I'd appreciate it if you wouldn't mention what just happened to Josephine," he said. "The part about my speaking German, I mean. I'd rather no one knew."

Evelyn raised her eyebrows and looked at him in surprise. "Why not?"

He glanced at her, his face inscrutable.

"I imagine for the same reasons that you don't want me to know that *you* speak German."

Chapter Eighteen

RAF Horsham

Miles sipped his beer and loosened his tie, sitting back comfortably. The pub was quiet tonight, and he and Rob had settled into a booth away from the few other locals. After another day in the air, patrolling over Belgium and France, he was thankful for an hour away from the others. His mood had become progressively more sour as the day had worn on, and when Rob suggested they nip down to the pub without the others, he'd jumped at the chance.

"So what has you so crabby this evening?" Rob asked cheerfully, settling across from him.

"I'm not, am I?"

"Certainly seemed so earlier. You almost took Slippy's head off when we were walking back from dispersal."

Miles shrugged. "Just tired, I suppose."

Rob nodded and sipped his beer. "We're all getting a bit on edge, aren't we? Mother and Chris went at it this morning, or so I hear. I'm not especially tired, but I'm restless. Now that France is falling, I'm waiting for the war to come here. I feel like we're back in a holding pattern again. First we were waiting for Hitler to move, now we're waiting for him to come after England."

"He will soon enough. He won't stop with France, not when he's seen how easy it was to take it."

"It won't be so easy to roll into England. He'll have a tough time getting over the Channel for one thing. He can't very well sneak through the Atlantic the way he did the Ardennes." Rob leaned his elbows on the table and stared pensively down into his pint. "They're saying it will come down to us. He'll have to defeat the RAF before he can even attempt a Channel crossing."

"Yes."

Rob glanced up at him, the customary twinkle gone from his eyes. "Miles, tell me something. Do you think we can defeat the Luftwaffe?"

"We'll have to," he said grimly. "If we don't, we'll have the

Nazis goose-stepping up Piccadilly."

"Yes, but do you think we can do it?"

"It doesn't matter what I think. We have to. That's all there is to it."

Rob grunted and both men were silent. Miles swallowed a mouthful of beer and watched as Rob turned his pint slowly in circles on the scarred wood surface of the table. The very fact that they were having this conversation was indicative of their respective states of mind. A few weeks ago, it would never have occurred to either of them to wonder if they'd be able to stop Hitler's war machine. Now, seeing how quickly France was crumbling, Miles realized just how outmatched they really were. The amount of airplanes and pilots they'd already lost in France was telling enough. As far as he could see, while the Germans had also lost planes, they had them to lose. The RAF did not.

"Funny how things change, isn't it?" Rob asked suddenly. "Last month we couldn't wait for the Phony War to end. Now we're facing an end that we didn't imagine."

Miles raised his eyebrows. "Didn't you?"

"Well, did you?"

"I never thought this would be easy once Hitler made up his mind to move, no. This is a different war from the last one. We've known this would be an air war all along."

"Well, yes, but I didn't think they would take France so quickly," Rob muttered. "It's only been eleven days since they attacked Holland and Belgium. Eleven days! Do you realize that?"

"Yes."

"What army only takes eleven days to go through three countries?"

"One that is much better organized, and commanded by younger, brighter leaders who know exactly how to out-think a sixty-eight-year-old general," Miles answered wryly. "Gamelin had no concept of what was coming, and now Weygand is not much better."

Rob was silent for a minute, then he shook his head. "To be fair, apparently neither did we."

Miles grunted and lifted his beer. He wasn't wrong; their leaders had underestimated Adolf Hitler at every turn, right up until his armies tore through the Ardennes.

"Have you had a letter from m'sister, by any chance?" Rob asked after another moment of pensive silence.

"Not recently."

"I've been trying to track her down, and I'm having the devil of a time. I finally got onto someone over at her HQ and they were going to get back to me, but I haven't heard anything yet." He frowned, sipping his beer. "If the RAF can't keep better track of their WAAFs than this, we're in for a bad time of it. They're women, for God's sake! How do you lose 'em?"

"I'm sure they haven't lost her. She was in Dover when she wrote last."

"So I understand, but no one seems to know where. Someone should at least know where she is!"

"Someone, somewhere, does. She moves around quite a bit. I'm sure they'll track down the person who knows where she is at the present moment. As you said, it's the RAF. They haven't lost her." Miles tilted his head and looked at his friend. "What's the matter? Everything all right?"

"What? Oh yes, everything's fine. I just want to talk to her about our French relations."

"Have you heard anything from them since this all started? How are they?"

"They're at the house in Monblanc now. They left Paris as soon as Sedan fell." He rubbed his face and sat back in his chair. "My mother says they're packing up what they can, and then they're coming here to England."

"All of them?"

"I don't know. She said there was some uncertainty about my cousins. Something about Nicolas not wanting to leave, and Gisele refusing to go without him." He shook his head tiredly. "My mother can be vague at times. I was hoping Evelyn knew more. I know she writes to Gisele regularly. It doesn't make much sense for them to stay in France while my aunt and uncle come here, especially if the Germans occupy it, and let's face it, they will."

"Will they stay at Ainsworth Manor?"

"Not a clue. I suppose they will at first, but we have a rather nice-sized hunting lodge in Northumberland that's standing empty at the moment. They might prefer to go there. Or there's the old gatekeepers house, of course." Rob grinned suddenly. "I'm not sure that my Auntie Agatha and Tante Adele would get along very well if this war goes on for any significant amount of time."

"Different personalities?"

"Night and day. And my Uncle Claude won't stand for his wife being upset."

"I really can't wait to meet the infamous Auntie Agatha," Miles said with a grin. "I've heard such good things."

Rob let out a bark of laughter. "You won't have any issues with her. We don't. Evelyn loves her to bits. She's simply her own woman, Auntie Agatha, and she's not afraid to say things as they are. She's rather a sergeant-major, but a lovable old girl. And she dotes on Evie. Always has."

A soft smile crossed Miles' face. "Then I should think we'll get along without a hitch."

Rob made a face. "It's disgusting how true that is. As soon as Auntie Agatha sees how head over heels you are for Evie, she'll take you in. There'll be no escaping then. You'll be stuck with all of us."

"Always assuming that Evelyn is agreeable, of course," Miles replied, lifting his pint and swallowing the last bit of beer.

"Well, from the very beginning I've warned you that she's a fickle thing," Rob pointed out. "Both London and Paris are littered with broken hearts from my sister. But, I can tell you this: I've never seen her this way before. I think you have a better chance than any of the poor sods who came before you. Just be sure that's really what you want *before* you meet Auntie Agatha."

"I don't think that I've ever been more sure of anything in my life," Miles said thoughtfully, setting his empty glass down.

Rob looked at him in surprise. "Are you serious?"

"Yes, I think I am."

Rob stared at him searchingly for a moment, then grinned. He swallowed the last of his beer and reached for Miles' empty glass.

"In that case, I'll buy the next round."

"You'll give your blessing then?"

"Of course!" He stood up with a laugh. "But it's not up to me, old boy. Evie's always followed her own path, y'know. I just hope you know what you're getting yourself into."

"I think I have some idea," Miles said with a grin.

"Then we'll have another round, but don't say I didn't warn you."

"How can I? That's all you've done since I met her."

"Nothing personal, you understand. It's just that it gets a little much always listening to the sorry blighters crying on my shoulder when she inevitably sends them packing."

Miles watched him turn and go to the bar with their glasses and couldn't stop the streak of uncertainty that went through him. He knew that when Evelyn was with him, she felt the same way he did. But what if that changed? They saw each other so rarely, and it would get even worse in the coming months. Now that he was so far from Northolt, their stolen evenings would become few and far between. And then there was that other pilot, Flying Officer Durton. They were very chummy, the two of them.

He shook his head and pulled out his cigarettes. He was letting Rob get into his head. The last time he saw her, Evelyn had shown every indication of being just as committed to this relationship as he was. He would simply have to trust his instincts. They'd never let him down before. But he'd also never met any woman quite like Evelyn before.

And that, of course, was the problem.

Evelyn stared at Finn for a beat, then started laughing.

"Whatever makes you think I speak German?" she demanded, her heart racing again.

"I don't think. I know."

Finn glanced at her and, in that one glance, Evelyn knew that there was no point in keeping up the charade. He obviously knew. The laugh faded from her face and she looked out the window at the passing countryside.

"How do you know?" she finally asked, pleased when her voice was perfectly steady. It belied the trembling in her fingers.

"You haven't asked what was said, for one thing," Finn pointed out. "Anyone else would have been demanding to know what was being said, if not at the time, certainly directly afterwards."

Evelyn couldn't stop a grimace. Of course! He was absolutely right. She should have asked. That was a stupid mistake on her part.

"That's true," she admitted. "I was very shaken by the whole encounter, but nevertheless, I should have played the part better."

"You also almost laughed when he suggested that an ambush might be waiting for them," Finn added with a faint smile. "He may not have noticed, but I certainly did."

Evelyn looked at him thoughtfully. "You seem to notice quite a bit, Monsieur...what *is* your surname?"

His lips tightened briefly and, for a moment, she thought he wouldn't answer, but then he spoke. "Maes. My name is Finn Maes."

"Monsieur Maes, it's a pleasure to be properly introduced."

"Please continue to call me Finn. It's silly to stand on ceremony now."

"You mean after we've shared a run-in with a Wehermacht major? No, I suppose not."

He looked at her, impressed. "You recognized his rank?"

"Yes." She was quiet for a moment, then she sighed. "Now that we're being honest with each other, where did you learn to speak German? And why don't you want anyone to know?"

"I don't see that it's relevant for you to know how or why."

"It is if you want me to keep your secret," Evelyn retorted, her eyes narrowing faintly. "There's no shame in knowing another language. If you want to hide it, that's your affair. But I'd like to know why. If I'm to be responsible for getting you to England, I think I have a right."

Finn was silent, his jaw tight, then he glanced at her and exhaled.

"You're right. If we're to make it to England, we need to trust each other," he agreed reluctantly. "Forgive me. I've been alone so long that I have trouble remembering that sometimes we must have faith in each other."

Evelyn inclined her head. "I understand."

He nodded and seemed to be searching for the words to begin. Finally, after another searching glance, he spoke.

"I'm not Belgian," he told her. "I know you think I am, and I allowed Josephine to believe it as well."

"You're German?" Evelyn asked in surprise, her eyebrows soaring into her forehead.

He shook his head. "No. I'm Czech."

She stared at him, her mind whirling with questions. "Czechoslovakian?"

"Yes." He looked over and his lips twisted in amusement at the look on her face. "Have you never met a Czech before?"

Evelyn swallowed and shook her head. "It's not that," she said hastily. "It's just not what I was expecting. But now that you mention it, I don't actually believe that I have. Where are you from?"

"Originally? I am from a small mining village called Lidice." Finn cleared his throat again, patently uncomfortable speaking about himself. "I was in Prague in March last year when the Germans came. I was excited about the prospect of a new start for my country."

"A new start?"

"Yes. That's how I saw the invasion of the Germans. It's how many of us saw it." His lips tightened briefly, then he laughed sardonically. "We believed that Hitler was a leader who would bring prosperity and stability to our country."

"You believed what he told you."

"Yes. It seems like a lifetime ago. I was proud to join the National Socialist Party, and I went to work for the Germans quite happily."

"What did you do?" Evelyn asked when he showed no inclination to continue.

"I helped process identification papers at first, then I was transferred to another building, where I worked as a clerk." His voice was very tight and Evelyn frowned. "My work there entailed my crossing the border into Germany regularly to carry messages, retrieve packages, and accompany officials when they returned to the Fatherland for meetings and conventions. That was how I came to spend time in Munich."

"They sent you all the way to Munich?"

"Only once. I was there for a week while my superior attended a convention." He shrugged. "Most of the time I was back and forth to Leipzig and Dresden."

"I'm surprised they allowed you to travel so freely."

"I was always accompanied by an official or officer."

Evelyn studied him, her head tilted. "What aren't you saying?" she asked. "What did you do, exactly?"

He was silent for a moment, then he shook his head. "It wasn't what I did," he said slowly. "I was nothing but a glorified secretary. It was who I did it for."

"Well?"

"I worked for the Sicherheitsdienst."

Evelyn couldn't stop her gasp. "The SS!"

He nodded and looked at her. "You see now why I don't wish it to become known?"

She nodded, gripping her hands in her lap to stop the trembling.

"How did you come to be in Belgium?" she whispered.

"It wasn't long before I saw what they were doing in my country. It was nothing like what I imagined it would be. We weren't people to them, and certainly not considered Germans. They were taking our production, our factories, and dismantling them, only to move them into Greater Germany and reassemble them there. Our people were left without work, and without any means of making a living. If there were protests, the Nazis retaliated. They were brutal and merciless. I couldn't continue to do nothing." Finn paused and took a deep breath. He turned into the narrow lane that would take them to the house and pulled to the side of the road, stopping the car. He turned to face her. "You must understand that after only six months, I'd seen what they do to anyone who is not one of them. I could no longer pretend that I was part of something good. I had become part of

176

something unspeakably evil."

"How did you leave?"

"I had been contacted once by the resistance shortly after I went to work as a clerk, but I refused to help them. Once I realized how things really were, I reached out to them. Because of my papers and identification, I was able to move freely into Germany. I began working to move funds through Germany and into Holland."

"Funds?" Evelyn stared at him. "As in money?"

"Yes. Oh, it wasn't currency. It was jewels, mainly. Jewels and gold, which were then sold in Amsterdam and converted into currency."

"And this was to fund the resistance?"

"Yes, among other things." He hesitated, then sighed. Clearly realizing that he was already committed to telling her everything, he leaned his head back against the seat and squeezed the bridge of his nose. "Some of the items were from Jews trapped in Czechoslovakia. They were not allowed to work, or travel. The Nazis have very strong opinions about the Jews. The Germans were rounding them up and taking everything they had. The funds were to be there for them if they managed to get out and make it to Holland."

"They let you do this? Take their jewels and sell them?"

"It wasn't a question of letting us. They *asked* us to do it for them." He lowered his hand and looked at her. "You have to realize that they had no choice. Either we took them and guaranteed that they'd have something if they were able to find a way out, or the Nazis took them. If their possessions remained in Czechoslovakia, they were going to lose everything. At least by giving them to us, they had a chance."

Evelyn swallowed painfully. "Did any of them escape?"

"A few, but not nearly as many as we hoped. Now it is too late. They've been put into ghettos and there is no hope for them to get out."

"And you?"

"In January, I was in Leipzig, preparing to return to Prague, when I made the decision to leave. My contact in the resistance had been urging me to remain in Holland in order to begin building a resistance there. He believed it would only be a matter of time before Hitler went west, and he knew I had become familiar with the Dutch. I had nothing with me but what I was carrying. I took several different trains, handing over different papers each time I was asked, and I created a trail that was impossible to follow. When I reached Holland, I went to Amsterdam and began to organize a network there. That's when your Bill found me."

"When did you learn French?"

"At the same time I learned German. I attended the University of Prague. I studied history, and learned both German and French. It is one of the reasons the Nazis wanted me to work for them. I could understand and be understood."

"Is that why Bill recruited you?"

Finn smiled and shook his head. "No. He was more interested in…well, my other skills."

Evelyn was silent for a few minutes, absorbing what she'd learned. "When did you move to Antwerp?"

"At the end of March. By then I'd managed to organize communication between the resistance groups in Austria and Czechoslovakia, as well as begin a fledgling network in Holland. I went to Antwerp to do the same. My intention was to get the networks started in both countries, and then travel between the two to build them."

"And then Hitler moved west."

"Yes. I was cut off from contact with both London and Prague. I moved south with no idea where to go. I had a contact near Mons, so I went there. That's where Josephine's friends found me. They told me they had been asked by Bill to bring me out of Belgium."

"And now here you are."

"Yes."

Evelyn took a deep breath and rubbed her neck. "Well, I must say that I never expected any of that when I asked how you spoke German," she said after a moment with a short laugh. "And yes, I can quite understand why you wouldn't want any of that to be public knowledge. If the Germans ever find out even part of that…"

"Exactly." He looked at her. "I'm trusting you, Geneviève."

She nodded. "I'll keep your secrets," she assured him. "Never fear."

"And you? How do you come to speak German?"

Evelyn laughed ruefully. "It's not quite as dramatic as your story, I'm afraid. I'm something of a linguist. I speak several languages fluently."

"Is that why Bill found you?"

"It's certainly part of the reason I'm here, yes, but I won't pretend to be anything other than a glorified courier with a very good ear for language." She smiled and shrugged. "I certainly haven't had the experience that you have, and I haven't been of such service."

His lips twisted humorlessly. "It's inevitable that that will change, and change quickly. Unfortunately, once the Germans move in, everything moves much faster than you can ever imagine. You're already gaining experience, and your service will be invaluable."

"I seem to be spending more time running away from the Germans than I do gaining experience or doing anything useful."

"That is the wise thing to do at the moment." He was quiet for a moment. "You said you are a glorified courier. You also said you were in Brussels."

Evelyn swallowed, her mouth suddenly dry. "Yes."

"If you're who I think you are, then what you're carrying is far more important than gaining experience right now," he told her soberly. "You must get to England safely."

"I have no idea what you're talking about."

"Of course not." He smiled and started the engine again. "But don't feel that what you're doing is not important. I assure you, it is. Several good men died getting that packet out of Germany. Two of them I had come to consider my friends. You have been entrusted to carry on their efforts, Geneviève. I can think of no greater service."

Evelyn was silent as he pulled back onto the narrow lane. It certainly hadn't taken him any time at all to put two and two together and come up with four. There were no flies on him, that much was certain. There was much, much more to Finn than any of them knew, and she could understand why Bill wanted him safe in England. He'd been in Germany, and he'd worked directly with the SS! That alone made him a fountain of information. Add to it his work with the resistance groups and no wonder Bill was desperate to get him to London.

Why on earth had he entrusted that task to her?

Chapter Nineteen

Evelyn set the large basket of produce down on the counter in the small kitchen.

"This was all I could get," she told Josephine. "There wasn't a bakery open that I could locate, and of the few grocers that I found, only one had anything left."

"The city is half shuttered," Finn added. "I was able to buy cigarettes and some boiled sweets, but that was all."

"Half the city has fled south," Yves said behind them as he walked into the kitchen, "and the other half is trying to stock their homes so that they can survive a siege."

"It wasn't even this bad in Paris," Josephine said, looking through the basket.

"It will be." Yves scratched his head and looked at them. "What will you do for food? Most of that will be useless to you unless you can build a fire."

"We'll do what we can, and hope that we come across something as we move south," Evelyn said briskly. "That's all we can do."

He didn't say anything, but went instead to the pantry. "I'm making soup for supper," he called over his shoulder. "You're welcome to share it with me. There is bread and I have cheese. At least I can send you off with full stomachs."

"We should leave," Josephine said. "It's getting late, and we need to be on our way."

"I was thinking about that on our way back," Evelyn said slowly, sinking down into a chair at the table. She glanced at Finn, then back at Josephine. "I think perhaps we should wait until the German divisions have passed before we get onto the road."

Josephine stared at her. "Wait? Why? Every second we stay here is another second that they get closer."

"They're already close," Finn said. "We ran into them on the road."

"What?!" Josephine exclaimed, drawing Yves back out of the pantry.

"What's wrong?" he demanded, a brown pottery jug in one hand.

"They say they ran into German troops on the road!"

"Well that's not surprising. They were bound to pass by this way. They were only a few kilometers away early this morning." Yves set the jug down on the counter and turned to go back to the pantry. "They passed by a little further north yesterday."

He disappeared after that statement and Evelyn felt a chuckle pulling at her lips. The older man's prosaic calm in the face of an invasion was something she didn't think she would ever forget. He almost looked as though he was discussing the bus routes rather than an invasion force.

"What happened? Where did you see them?"

"On the road leaving Reims. They were going west." Finn pulled out the chair across from Evelyn and sat down. "We had to get off the road."

"How many were there?" Josephine looked from one to the other. "Did they stop?"

"I didn't take the time to count," Evelyn said dryly. "And I couldn't see the tanks. They were in the fields. All we could see was the dust they were causing."

Josephine blinked and leaned against the counter, her face pale. "Tanks? There were Panzers?"

Finn got up and went over to take her arm, guiding her to his vacant chair. "Yes. Please sit. You look as though you'll fall down."

"It's simply unbelievable," she stammered, sinking into the offered chair. "It's one thing to know they're here, but another to know that you actually saw them. Did they see you?"

"Yes, but they didn't stop," Evelyn said calmly. "It was disconcerting, though. It makes me wonder if perhaps it would be best to try to avoid running into more of them. I don't think it's an experience I'd like to repeat."

"Surely they're gone, though?" Josephine looked up at Finn. "You said they were going west? They must be going to reinforce the troops that have reached the coast."

"Yes, but what if there are more?"

"Do you think there are?"

"I don't know."

"I can answer that question," Yves said, emerging from the pantry again, this time with an armful of root vegetables. "There are at least two more coming through before tomorrow."

"How do you know?" Josephine asked.

"I have a radio transmitter. I listened this morning to the reports from Maubeuge."

"You have a radio?" Evelyn asked, surprised.

Yves smiled. "It is only a receiver. I can listen, but I cannot talk."

"Where did you get it?" Josephine asked.

"It was left here as payment from another such as yourself," he said with a shrug. "I have no idea who I'm listening to, but they've been correct so far. They forecast every division that has passed Reims."

"And they said two more are coming?"

He nodded. "Three throughout the day. I believe the one you saw was the first."

The trio at the table looked at each other, then Josephine shook her head.

"Even if we do wait until morning to leave, where will we stay?"

"Here, of course," Yves said over his shoulder as he pulled a large knife out of a block and prepared to begin chopping vegetables. "I don't mind having you for another night."

"We can't impose on you, Monsieur Michaud," Evelyn protested. "You've already been more than kind."

"And I don't mind continuing," he said, turning around with the knife in his hand. "It's your decision, of course, but I'm happy to have you another night."

Josephine and Evelyn looked at each other, then at Finn. He shrugged.

"I'd rather wait until morning. Being on the road with them today wasn't pleasant. I'll do whatever you decide, though."

"I don't know which is better," Josephine said slowly. "If we leave, we may run into them on the road, yes. But if we stay, we may run the risk of them stopping and taking control of Reims, which would be worse."

"If you're worried that the Germans will raid the house, you can sleep in the barn," Yves offered. "There's an old wine cellar below it where I store, well, things that I wouldn't want the police to find. If they come here, you can take refuge there until they're gone. Although, I hardly think it likely that will be necessary. The Germans are too intent on reaching the coast and cutting off the troops and supplies. There's nothing of interest here yet. We're hardly in a strategic position."

Evelyn met Josephine's gaze. "Well?"

"What do you think?"

Into the Iron Shadows

"As much as I want to get moving, I think it would be foolish to risk it today," Evelyn said slowly. "If Monsieur Michaud is willing to allow us to remain for one more night, and we truly aren't being an imposition…"

"Of course not!" Yves said, waving a hand impatiently. "I wouldn't have offered if you were. I welcome the company."

"Very well," Josephine agreed. "We'll stay here for today and leave at dawn."

Evelyn let out a silent exhale and, as Josephine got up to help Yves with the soup preparation, she met Finn's eyes across the kitchen. He looked relieved and gave her a small smile. She smiled back and stood up to pick up their basket of vegetables.

"I'll carry this outside so that it's out of the way," she murmured, turning towards the back door.

"If you put it in the barn, the rabbits won't get at your vegetables," Yves said. "It's clean and cool. I keep my winter stores there."

"Thank you. I will."

Evelyn went out of the door and started across the small kitchen garden towards the stone path that led to an old stone structure behind the house. Finn was happy to avoid another encounter with the Germans, and so was she. Her lips tightened. As it turned out, he was in just as much danger, if captured, as she was herself. He had just as much to lose, if not more. If the SS had any inkling of what he had been doing when he escaped to Holland, he would be considered a traitor and killed…or worse.

And yet he was still willing to continue to England with her, and continue the fight.

She shook her head, going through the little gate at the end of the garden and towards the barn. They were in a house with a man who created new papers and new identities for people. Finn could recreate himself and melt into the French countryside without looking back, yet he wasn't considering it. He was coming with her to England, where he would presumably continue to work towards defeating the Nazis.

Evelyn took a deep breath, marveling at the bravery of the people around her. Jean-Pierre was going to continue from within the annals of the government for as long as he could, committed to building a resistance. Jens had refused to come to England with her, choosing instead to stay and help the French people. Josephine was remaining in France in order to continue the fight while the Germans were pouring into her country, knowing that she was already exposed as an intelligence agent. Her mind inevitably went to Norway, to Anna

183

and Erik, who stayed behind to fight for their country even though the Germans had taken control. And then there was Peder, who had died so that she could live.

How could she ever live up to what they all had done, and were continuing to do every day?

Paris

Henry entered his hotel and went towards the front desk. The lobby was empty and only a single porter stood near the door. Paris was far from the bustling City of Lights these days. It was rapidly becoming a ghost town as panicked citizens fled in the face of the German advance. He supposed he should be grateful that London was arranging all his transportation home. The roads were clogged, the trains were running non-stop and were packed to capacity, and even getting a taxi was becoming near impossible. His meeting had been cut short this morning, and it was becoming evident, even to the French government, that they might have to leave Paris. It was something that they had refused to consider, but now he didn't see how they could continue to ignore the facts.

"Are there any messages?" he asked the uniformed man behind the counter.

"Yes, Monsieur. It came an hour ago." The man turned to retrieve a telegram, handing it to him a moment later.

"Thank you."

Henry turned away and continued towards the lift. Once the BEF was cut off from reinforcements, there would be nowhere for them to go. The cream of the British army would be trapped on the coast of France. Once their allies were taken prisoner, France would be forced to surrender. It was only a matter of time.

And then the Führer would control Europe to the Channel.

Henry stepped into the lift, nodding to the attendant. There was a time when he would have scoffed at the idea of Germany taking over so many countries in so short a time, but those days were long in the past. He had seen the power of the German armies, and the might of its air force. The Führer had brought Germany back into the forefront of global power. He had proven that the Third Reich was a force that could not be opposed. France was only another link in the chain; England was the next.

Into the Iron Shadows

Once the opposition was quelled, Henry could then take his place in Berlin with the victors.

The lift came to a stop and the attendant opened the doors with a nod. Henry stepped out, turning down the corridor towards his room. In the meantime, however, he still had work to do both here in Paris and in London. He couldn't celebrate yet. This war was far from over, and he still had to do his part.

A moment later, Henry was closing his door and unbuttoning his overcoat. He reached into his pocket to pull out the telegram, ripping it open as he crossed the room to the writing desk near the window. It was the message from Berlin that he'd been waiting for.

FARMER HAD TWO CHILDREN. SON OWNS A FARM WEST OF LUCERNE. DAUGHTER'S WHEREABOUTS UNKNOWN. BELIEVED TO HAVE LEFT SWITZERLAND.

Henry dropped the telegram on the desk and turned to remove his coat. So the old man had a daughter. That had to have been the woman who visited the house, but why? Her father had been dead for over a year. Why return to an empty house, if not to look for something?

He draped his coat over the foot of the bed and pulled out a cigarette case. Taking one out, he tapped it on the case thoughtfully. Why hadn't he known about the daughter before? His lips tightened suddenly and he made an impatient sound in his throat. Because she was a woman. The people in Berlin had obviously not considered that a man would confide in a daughter over a son.

"And so she is invisible," he murmured to himself, lifting the cigarette to his lips with one hand while he fished in his pockets for his lighter. "It really is intolerable."

He lit his cigarette and turned to go back to the desk, staring down at the telegram. Believed to have left Switzerland, but when? This week? Last month? Last year? Could they be any more vague?

His gaze shifted to the window and he went to stand beside it, staring down into the street below. He supposed she could have gone to the house to look around and revisit memories. Women were known to be emotional creatures. Yet he found it to be too much of a coincidence that she'd gone back to the house when she did. Smoking his cigarette slowly, Henry gazed pensively out the window. What did she know? Had the old man told her something about Ainsworth? Had he told her where to look if something happened to him?

Henry turned away from the window impatiently. They had searched the house. It was empty. But what if it wasn't? What if they'd missed something? And what if she knew what it was? And had it now?

185

So many questions, and he was running out of time to find the answers. Soon he would be forced to remain in London as the German army swept through France. And once France surrendered, he would lose access to Paris. If the daughter was here in France, and he now believed that she was the one who got off the airplane, then this was his only opportunity to find her, and to find out what she knew.

Stubbing the cigarette out in the ashtray, Henry sat down at the table and pulled a clean telegram sheet towards him. He would send an urgent message to his man in Bern. If anyone could dig up information on the children, he would be the one to do it. He may even know himself. He'd lived in the area for most of his life, and knew everyone worth knowing.

Composing the coded message, Henry felt some of the tension leave his shoulders. While he may only have a limited amount of time left in France, he knew that it would be enough if his contact came through with information quickly. He had at least another week before the situation became critical in France and he would be forced to leave. Plenty of time to find the daughter, and find out what she knew.

Henry didn't know why he was so sure that it had something to do with Ainsworth, but he was convinced that it did. There was no one else the old man was close with. Oh, he'd had contact with other spies and so-called intelligence officers, but Ainsworth was the big fish. He was the one who mattered. All the others were small fry, and had been rolled up one by one before they finally made it to the old man. No. If she knew anything at all, Henry was positive it was about Ainsworth. It could lead him to the missing package, or at least point him in the right direction.

His pen paused and he looked up, staring at the window, lost in thought. Once he had the package back, he could focus all his energy on locating the mysterious Jian. Berlin wanted what Ainsworth had stolen back, but they wanted the English spy more. He didn't know why, nor did he care. All he knew was that if he was able to hand both over to his handler, his place in Berlin would be assured. He would not only be the only spy left in England, but he would have the distinction of doing what the SS could not: locating the spy called Jian and leading them to her.

A cold smile twisted his lips and he returned his attention to the message before him. But first, the daughter must be found.

Chapter Twenty

Evelyn looked up as Josephine came out of the house, a sweater thrown around her shoulders. The day was coming to a close and a cool breeze was blowing across the small garden. Seeing the sweater, Evelyn realized that she was chilly and shivering. She had come outside for some fresh air over an hour before, settling on the soft ground beneath a tree, and had been lost in her own thoughts ever since.

"Aren't you cold?" Josephine called.

"I wasn't until I saw your sweater," Evelyn replied with a laugh, preparing to get up. "Now I am."

"Wait. I'll get you something."

Josephine turned and disappeared back into the house, reappearing a moment later with a man's sweater.

"Yves said to use this. He keeps it near the back door for running out to the barn," she said, crossing the garden and holding out the maroon cardigan.

"That's very kind of him." Evelyn took the sweater, pulling it around her shoulders as Josephine settled down beside her. "He's going out of his way to help us."

"He's a good man. Once we got the soup cooking, he said he would make us some bread to take with us. He said it would give us more than some strawberries and beans to eat."

Evelyn blinked. "He makes his own bread?"

"Yes. He seems to do everything. He told me when his wife was alive, he enjoyed helping her in the kitchen. Now that she's gone, he prefers to cook for himself." Josephine leaned back against the tree, her head on the side of the wide trunk. She stretched her legs out, facing diagonally from Evelyn, and exhaled contentedly. "He's really an interesting character. Did you know that he has a small vineyard? He sells the grapes to a winemaker on the other side of Reims."

"I saw it on the other side of the barn, but I didn't know that was his."

"Yes. He said the drought this year has been terrible for him." Josephine paused then chuckled. "But then he said that the war is helping by making his other job lucrative."

Evelyn grinned. "At least he has another form of income." Then she sobered. "What will he do if…when the Germans occupy the area?"

"I didn't ask, and he didn't say. He's too old to be sent to work in a factory. I suppose he'll stay here and try to make a living with his grapes."

They were both silent, sobered by the thought of the hardships ahead for the man who was doing so much for them.

"The papers he gave me are perfect," Josephine said after a few moments, lowering her voice. "I wouldn't know they weren't real. He even aged the birth certificate. I have no idea how he did it, but it genuinely looks old. I don't know why he isn't working for the government."

"What is your new name?"

"Jeannine Renaud."

"It's a pleasure to meet you, Mademoiselle Renaud."

"I must destroy everything with my name on it. I thought I'd wait until after dinner and burn them in the fireplace. I don't want to risk drawing attention with a fire outside." Josephine paused for a moment, then cleared her throat. "He brought up a valid point when he gave them to me. I can't go anywhere that anyone knows me for who I really am."

Evelyn glanced at her. "Like Marseilles?"

"Yes. I was going to stay with an old friend of mine, and her husband was going to try to find me work in his factory. I can't do that now."

"What will you do?"

"I have absolutely no idea. I don't have the funds to go where there's no work. I just don't know where to go."

Evelyn frowned and thought for a moment. "What about Lyon?"

"Yves believes that that is where Marc and Luc are heading. If I end up there as well, it would defeat the purpose of us splitting up."

"That's true." They were both silent again and then Evelyn looked at her consideringly. "You could always come all the way to Bordeaux and stay there. It's a port city. I'm sure there must be work there."

Josephine was silent for a moment, thinking. "I stayed there once with my parents for a holiday. Well, not in the city, but outside it.

Into the Iron Shadows

I was only a girl at the time. We stayed with friends of my mother in the country. I remember I loved it. The weather was warm and mild. It was near Saint-Émilion, I believe. What *was* the name of it?"

She fell silent, thinking, and Evelyn watched as a large hawk circled high above the house, looking for dinner. The bird of prey was completely unaware of the turmoil affecting its hunting ground below. Suddenly she envied the wildlife. They had no idea what was happening and were continuing their daily existence in complete ignorance of the war raging across their land.

"Castillon-sur-Dordogne!" Josephine exclaimed suddenly a few moments later, startling Evelyn out of her reverie. "That was it!"

"I've never heard of it."

"It's named after the river. I remember my father telling me when we went fishing during a picnic one day."

"Do you think that's a possibility?"

"It's as good as any," Josephine replied with a shrug. "If you cross the bridge, you're in the country. I may be able to find a boarding house or someone with a room to let. It's a large town, if I remember correctly."

"Well, it's a starting point, at any rate," Evelyn said. "What kind of work will you get?"

"Any that I can find. I won't be choosy. I can't afford to be. I have enough francs to get there and find a room, but that's it."

"I can give you some money to help you get yourself settled," Evelyn offered, thinking of the stacks of cash hidden in the bottom of her suitcase. "It will be enough to get started."

"I can't take your money," Josephine said, shaking her head. "No. I will be fine."

"What if you can't find work right away?" Evelyn turned to face her with a frown. "Don't be ridiculous. After paying for your new papers, you can't have very much left. Let me help you. If you must, consider it a loan."

"Then what will you do if you can't get back to England before the Germans come? I can't leave you short."

"Let me worry about that. Please. I'd like to help. You've done so much for me. Allow me to repay you."

Josephine looked at her for a moment. "I've not done much at all," she finally said. "No more than anyone else would have done."

"Rubbish. You've been a friend, and helped me when I needed food, sleep, and a guide. And that's not taking into account the little matter of your saving me from the Gestapo in Strasbourg."

"Rubbish? Be careful. Your English is showing," Josephine said with a grin. Then she sighed. "All those things I did precisely because I *do* consider you a friend. Well, perhaps not Strasbourg. But certainly everything afterwards. There is nothing to repay."

"Then allow me to return the favor. Every time I see you, I'm in need of assistance. Now I can be of help to you."

The two women stared at each other for a moment, then Josephine relented. "Very well."

Evelyn smiled and stood up, brushing off her skirt and reaching out a hand to help Josephine up.

"Thank you. Now let's go help Monsieur Michaud with the bread."

Josephine stood up and hooked her arm through Evelyn's as they walked towards the house.

"I'm so glad you decided to join the cause after Strasbourg," she said with a smile. "You're like the sister I never had."

Evelyn laughed and squeezed her arm. "As are you. Promise me you'll take care of yourself."

"Of course! I'm like a cat. I always land on my feet."

Eisenjager climbed out of the car and stretched, closing the door quietly. He had parked it behind a hedge along the lane leading to the house where Jian and her companions were staying. The sun had gone down over an hour before and he was surrounded by the kind of inky darkness that could only be found in the countryside away from a city. It reminded him of his home before he joined the military. His family had lived on a farm in the country. The economic crisis had hit them hard. When Hitler promised food and work, both he and his father had leapt at the chance. His father was able to revive his farm, and Eisenjager was able to make a career for himself in the newly formed Sicherheitsdienst des Reichsführers. Making his way through the darkness, he reflected on how very different things were now.

Yet the darkness was the same.

Holding a thin flashlight pointed to the ground, Eisenjager made his way across a fallow field in the direction of the house. They had come here the night before, and they hadn't left yet. Just to be sure, though, he was going to look himself. After losing her in Marle, he wasn't about to take the chance of the Englishwoman having slipped past him again.

Into the Iron Shadows

His lips tightened as his foot slipped in a divot in the ground, sending him stumbling forward. He regained his balance easily, but turned his eyes back to the uneven terrain. When she and the man had been caught on the road with the advancing troops, Eisenjager had been well behind them. He came along the road to find them standing on a hill, confronted by a German officer, while his division waited in the road. He shook his head. He had felt a moment of enraged panic at the prospect of losing his target once again, but the emotion had faded as the officer turned to leave them. Whatever had been said, it had convinced him that they were no threat. For once, Eisenjager was not amused at the foolishness of others, but grateful that the commanding officer was unaware of the woman's identity. If it had been one of the SS divisions, it could have ended very differently, and he would have lost the spy once again.

And then his controller in Hamburg would have been angry.

Through the darkness, a light flickered, drawing his attention up and away from the ground. The house was ahead of him, on the other side of a low, stone wall. He switched off the flashlight and slowly made his way forward in pitch blackness.

He had received a message from his handler this morning. His orders were to hold for now. They wanted to know why the spy from London was interested in Jian before confirming the order to terminate her. For that matter, Eisenjager wanted to know what his interest was as well. But he knew the Abwehr wouldn't share that information with him. They would simply confirm or pull his standing order. For now, his instructions were to continue to watch her and monitor who she saw and where she went. He was to contact them again on the 27th, or if he thought she was about to leave France. On no account was he to allow anything to happen to the spy.

Easier said than done in the middle of an invasion.

Reaching the low wall, Eisenjager went over it and crept forward to crouch in the night under a tree. The house wasn't big, but the front windows were large and light poured from them. The curtains hadn't been closed and he could see right into the front room. It was empty now, but he waited patiently. Electricity was expensive. If the light had been left on, it was because someone was coming back into the room. All he needed to see was whether or not the spy was still there. If she was, he could return to his car and wait until morning. The only way back to the road was to pass him. He would be able to ensure they didn't sneak away.

A moment later, an older man walked into the room carrying a glass in his hand. Right behind him was the man who had been with

Jian this morning in the city. Eisenjager continued to watch. The two men settled down in chairs and the younger one lit a cigarette. There was no sign of the women.

Pursing his lips, Eisenjager waited another minute, then turned and went around the side of the house, keeping to the shadows. Perhaps they were in the kitchen, washing up.

He passed the car they had been driving this morning, but didn't lend it any more than a cursory glance. The car meant nothing. It could belong to the man, and Jian could have snuck away on foot. She had done so in Marle. There was not saying she hadn't once again. If she was still there now, however, the chances were high that she would remain for the night. In Marle, she knew she'd been seen. Of course she ran. But now, she had no idea he'd found her again; she thought she was safe.

Reaching a small garden behind the house, he moved along the edge, careful not to step into the light cast from the kitchen window. Peering out of the darkness, he felt a surge of satisfaction at the sight of both women standing near the window. They were busy with their hands, washing dishes no doubt. As he watched, the Englishwoman laughed at something the other said and he pressed his lips together. She really was a beautiful woman.

What was she doing here? She should be home with a husband and small children, not gallivanting across Europe in the middle of a war. But here she was, and there was nothing he could do about her fate, whatever it might be. Her life was in his hands, and his hands were bound by the Abwehr. If they gave the order, he would shoot her without thinking twice. If they didn't, she would live to see another day. It was the way of it.

Turning, he retraced his steps to return to the car. At least he knew she was still there. That was all he needed to see to be able to rest easy. He hadn't lost her again. She was right where she should be.

And when she left, he would be right there to follow her.

Evelyn made herself as comfortable as possible on the back seat of the Renault. She was surrounded by food. Her suitcase had been stowed in the storage compartment at the back, along with Josephine's and Finn's, in order to make room for the provisions around her. In addition to the basket of vegetables that she'd purchased the day before, there was an old wine crate filled with two loaves of bread, fresh out of the oven just before they left, three bottles of wine, and two large jugs filled with water. Yves had insisted on all of it, telling them that he didn't want to think of them on their journey without the basic necessities. When Finn had laughingly questioned the wine as a necessity, he was met with exclamations of outrage. Evelyn smiled now, glancing at the wine. As the sun was just breaking over the horizon, turning the sky from black to gray, Finn had learned to never question a Frenchman's wine.

"Are you comfortable?" Finn asked, glancing back at her. "There isn't much room, is there?"

"I'm perfectly all right," she assured him with a smile. "I wish Yves would have taken more for all of this. He would only allow me to pay him for the petrol."

"I'm still wondering why he has a store of it in his cellar," Josephine said. "It's ridiculously expensive, and getting more and more scarce. Farmers don't have it for their tractors, yet he has a cellar full of it."

"He's a smart man, Monsieur Michaud," Finn said, turning his eyes back to the road in front of him. "He can sell it, as he did to us, or use it to bargain with for food and supplies."

"I hadn't thought of that," Josephine said. "How horrible that it's come to that!"

"Finn, when you get tired, I can drive for a while," Evelyn said, shifting in her seat.

"You can drive?" he asked, surprised.

"Yes. I enjoy it."

"Then I will be happy to share the driving with you." He glanced at Josephine. "I know you can, but don't like to."

"No. I hate it, and I'm not very good. I'll leave it to both of you," she said cheerfully. "I'm a much better navigator. I'll take charge of the map!"

Evelyn watched rolling fields speed by the window as Finn skirted around the city of Reims on his way to the road that would take them south. Before leaving Yves' house, they had listened to the wireless receiver, trying to determine where the advancing troops were, and where they were going. By all accounts, the Germans were still heading west. They were converging on Calais, no doubt with an aim to make it impossible for Allied soldiers to move south. While that was bad news for the BEF, it was good news for them. It meant that once they were going towards Paris, they should be out of the range of any more German divisions. At least, for the time being.

"When you reach Bordeaux, what then?" Josephine asked, breaking the silence some time later. "Will there be a boat waiting for you?"

"I don't think so." Evelyn shifted her attention from the passing countryside. "I'm to go to a café and ask for a man there. Then I'm to contact London."

"How?"

"I have absolutely no idea. I presume the man I'm to make contact with will have a way. If not, I can send an encoded telegram." Evelyn shifted in her seat. "He didn't give a time frame, so I assume transport will be sent when he receives word that we've arrived."

"Is it always so vague?"

Evelyn chuckled. "No. I usually have my transportation waiting for me."

"I suppose this isn't the usual situation," Josephine mused. "If you're meeting a contact, I think I'll leave you before you enter Bordeaux, if you don't mind. I don't want the risk of anyone involved seeing me with you. I hope it's not offending you, but I will need to start a new life without any ties."

"Of course I understand," Evelyn assured her. "You need to be discreet now."

Finn looked at Josephine. "You are not going to Marseilles?"

"No. I've decided Bordeaux will be better," she said with a shrug. "It's best to go where no one knows me as me, now that I am someone else."

"Ah, of course." Finn's brow cleared in sudden understanding. "I understand."

"It will be exciting," Evelyn said after a minute. "You can start fresh. You have an open, blank page before you."

"Yes, if we ever get there," Josephine murmured, staring ahead.

Evelyn raised her eyebrow and leaned forward to look through the windshield. She stared at the traffic ahead of them. Cars, trucks, carts, bicycles: if it could move, it seemed as if it was on the road.

"What on earth?" she breathed. "Already? I thought we'd at least make it past Paris before we ran into this!"

"It looks like everyone and their mother is going south," Finn said, slowing his speed as they approached the much slower-moving traffic. "This is worse than it was in Belgium!"

Evelyn sat back in her seat, suppressing a sigh. Finn was right. It looked as if most of northern France was on the road going south.

It was going to be a long drive.

Chapter Twenty-One

Henry was eating dinner alone in the hotel restaurant when the maître d' approached his table, an envelope in his gloved hand.

"I'm sorry to intrude, sir. A telegram for you," he said, bowing apologetically and holding out the envelope.

"Thank you."

Henry took the telegram and laid it next to his plate while he continued eating. Once the man had disappeared back to his post at the front of the restaurant, he laid down his knife and fork. He had left instructions at the front desk for them to bring any telegrams to the restaurant immediately. They had done as asked, and he was conscious of a sense of relief as he tore it open. He'd received a message from London this morning, instructing him to return the following day. Once he was back in England, it would be more difficult for his contact in Bern to reach him. Thankfully, he'd responded before that became necessary.

FARMER DID HAVE DAUGHTER. NAME ISABELLE. MARRIED FRENCHMAN. MOVED TO FRANCE TWO YEARS AGO. LIVES IN BORDEAUX.

He folded the message and tucked it into the inside pocket of his dinner jacket before picking up his utensils once more. She lived here in France. That settled it, then. It had to have been the daughter that got off the plane that morning. He'd missed her, but it didn't matter now. He knew where she had gone.

A surge of satisfaction mixed with excitement went through him as he cut into his fish. All he had to do was go to Bordeaux and find her. He could pose as an old friend of her father's. He had no doubt that he would learn everything he needed to know. He could be very charming and persuasive when he wanted to be.

A frown marred his forehead. He was supposed to leave for London in the morning, but that would have to be put off. He couldn't use his work in Paris as an excuse; that was finished as of today. He also couldn't use social engagements as an excuse, for those were scarce in Paris now. It would have to be something else. Something they wouldn't question.

He had almost finished his dinner and was sipping his wine when the answer came to him. It was so simple, it was almost laughable that he hadn't thought of it immediately. He would request a few days to spend in France before the Germans made travel impossible. He only needed a week, at most, to find the woman in Bordeaux and question her. It would take much longer than that for the German troops to turn their attention to Paris. They were too busy with the coast at the moment. There was no reason for London to deny him a few days to say goodbye to France. It was no secret that he had spent many summers here, or that he had family here. No, it wouldn't be questioned. He would wire them as soon as he'd finished his dessert.

And in the morning he would set about locating the farmer's daughter.

Somewhere over Calais

Miles looked to his right as Mother led them across the Channel towards Calais. The entire squadron was up today, flying support over the port city after German bombers had repeatedly dropped loads on them over the course of a couple of days. Miles had yet to see any of the blighters over the French coast, but today it was expected to be different. Two Spitfires from another squadron had been shot down this morning, and the presence of both 109s and Stukas had increased over the city. Ashmore, their CO, had informed them tersely in their briefing that there were English troops trapped in Calais. The Germans had them under heavy fire, and the fighters and Stukas had been called in by the Germans for air support. With the Luftwaffe wreaking havoc on the men below, they were bound to see some scraps at last. They had taken off from their forward base in the south of England in order to give them as much fuel over the target as possible, but even so they wouldn't have very long. They had to try to get as many Jerries as they could in the short time they would have, and then hightail it home before they exhausted their fuel. As Ashmore had said, make every shot count.

"Blue Leader to Command. Approaching Vector 2-1-0."

Mother's voice came over his headset and he glanced to his left at his flight leader. They were flying in formation and Miles pressed his lips together, glancing back at the tail-end Charlie. It was the new pilot officer, Perry. He shook his head and turned his attention forward again. He was too far away. He had to get closer to the rest of them. Right now, he was ripe for the picking for some Jerry pilot. The tail-end Charlie, or last in line in formation, was the pilot most exposed and at risk for a surprise attack from above and behind. It didn't matter if it was a new pilot or a veteran, it was the worst place to be in formation. There was no one to protect your flank, so unless you had eyes in the back of your head, your first hint that a fighter was behind you was when you were shot.

"Command to Blue Leader. Received. And good luck."

The male officer replying from HQ sounded both very young and very eager. Miles shook his head again. He supposed he must have been like that once, but he honestly didn't remember it.

"You heard the man, lads," Mother said cheerfully. "We're approaching vector, so keep your eyes peeled. Blue 5, close up, for God's sake! You're too far away!"

Miles looked back again and watched as Perry pulled closer to Chris. At least now he was closer to the formation, and not such a blatantly easy target. He turned his eyes to the skies above them, scanning constantly. If the 109s were there, they would be up in the sun. He'd learned that fast enough. The Messerschmitt fighters liked to dive down with the light behind them, making them almost invisible until it was too late.

"Tally ho!" Rob sang out. "There they are! Seven o'clock!"

Miles looked down and spotted a swarm of Junker 87s below them. Stukas. The small, deadly dive bombers that were causing such havoc on their troops were approaching the ports and preparing to begin their diving runs.

"Right. I see them. Let's stop them before the—"

"Fighters!" Chris cried, cutting off Mother. "Coming in fast!"

Miles whipped his head around and broke formation, banking right and arching up to engage the one closest to him. Within seconds, he and Chris were in the middle of a swarm of 109s while the rest of their formation scattered to engage the rest of the fighters. Only Mother and Rob continued for the now-diving Stukas.

"Go get 'em, boys!" Chris called out, drawing a grin from Miles despite the mess they were in. "We'll keep these bastards off you!"

"You'll have to get the one off your tail first," Slippy said, his voice sounding breathless.

Conversation ended as the dogfight shifted into a twisting, writhing battle of wills. Miles had just got away from one, looping around behind it to get into firing range, when another shot into his peripheral vision and dodged behind him. With a grunt, Miles abandoned his target and banked left, leading the 109 into a tight upward spiral. A few seconds later, he was able to spin out of it and dive below the little fighter. Swinging around, he blinked against the glare of the sun and focused on the thick black cross painted on the gray underwing. He pressed the button on his control column and felt his aircraft shudder as bullets streamed out of the .303 Browning machine guns. His bullets soared past the fighter and he released the button, breaking away with a low curse. The fighter twisted around and Miles was forced to take evasive action, diving down to avoid a stream of return fire.

"Perry! On your tail!" Slippy called out, breaking the radio silence.

Miles glanced over to see two 109s behind the new pilot. Cursing again, he rolled to the left to avoid another stream of bullets from the fighter behind him, keeping one eye on Perry. If he could just get away from this bastard, he was in a perfect position to pick off that second fighter behind him!

Another stream of bullets went by his canopy and Miles sucked in his breath. That was too close! He twisted his head to find his opponent and saw that two were now behind him.

"Miles! You've got two!" Chris called.

"Never mind me, Yank. Help Perry!"

With those words, he led his two opponents into a steep climb, opening the throttle. As soon as they committed to the ascent, he broke right and dove, out-maneuvering them to come up behind them. This time when he held the button on his column, he had the satisfaction of watching his bullets tear into the wing of the one closest to him. He banked left as the wing came apart and the small aircraft spun out of control.

"Got you, you bastard."

Turning, he dove down to try to help Perry. The fight had moved further away, the writhing bevy of fighters below and to the right of him. Chris was on the tail of the second fighter behind Perry, leaving only one for him to contend with, but the new pilot was no match for the German behind him. Miles watched helplessly as smoke began pouring from Perry's Spit. The 109 broke away as Perry went into a dive, thick black clouds pouring out around the airplane.

"Bail out, you idiot," Miles whispered, watching as the plane continued to plummet towards the Channel. Then, in a blast of black and orange, the Spitfire exploded.

Miles squeezed his eyes shut for a second, then turned his

198

attention to the fighter who was responsible. He scowled. The fighter was gone. Twisting his head behind him, his scowl grew. The one behind him had disappeared as well.

"They're all gone!" Slippy gasped.

And he was right. The swarm of German fighters had disappeared just as quickly as they had arrived.

"They're out of fuel!" Miles exclaimed.

"And so am I," Chris announced breathlessly. "Or I will be. Where are the others?"

Miles looked around but could see no sign of the Stukas, Mother, or Rob. Their fighting had moved them away from Calais and over the water.

"On their way home if they're looking at their gauges," Slippy said. "Miles?"

"I don't see them. Let's head home while we still have the fuel." He looked at his gauges and turned his nose for England. "They'll make it back."

The other two fell into formation next to him and they opened their throttles, heading back over the Channel. Ten minutes later, the white cliffs came into view before them, rising up out of the choppy water in a long, pale and welcoming beacon. Relief mixed with sorrow went through Miles, and he lifted a hand to wipe sweat off his face. He was coming home, but young Perry would never see this beautiful sight again. He had flown his last hour in a Spitfire.

"God that's a pretty sight," Chris said as they approached.

"Yes, it is," Miles replied, his chest tight. "It's home."

Evelyn rubbed her face and leaned forward to stare out of the windshield at the chaos around them. They had been able to make some progress south, but not much. The slower moving, horse-drawn carts and pedestrians tended to stay close to the sides of the roads, allowing room for them to pass, but they were still hampered by the never-ending line before them.

"I've never seen anything like this," Josephine said, shaking her head. "Look at that truck! How is it even moving?"

She motioned to an old truck with a flatbed piled high with furniture. Balancing precariously atop the mound of chairs, tables, and what looked like a dresser, were huge bundles. They looked like sheets that had been filled with clothes and tied shut with rope. Staring at it,

Evelyn shook her head. The pile was much higher than where the driver sat, and it swayed with each bump in the road.

"How is it staying upright?" she replied. "It's top-heavy!"

"I'm going to try to get around it," Finn said. "When that topples, I don't want to be behind it."

"How are you going to go around? There's nowhere to go!" Josephine exclaimed. "There's nothing but vehicles, carts, and people in front of it."

"I can pull off the road and go along the grass, then pull back in further up."

"You can't do that! That's cheating!"

Evelyn looked at Josephine and bit back a laugh. "Cheating?" she repeated. "Is there a Rules for Refugees manual I'm unaware of?"

Finn chuckled and Josephine glared at both of them.

"No, of course not. But we're where we are in line, and we should stay here," she said stubbornly. "What if someone came up from behind and then pulled in front of you? What would you think?"

"I'd think that now they'd be the ones to get hit with pieces of furniture when that disaster falls over," Finn replied.

Evelyn did laugh at that. "He does have a point," she said, grinning. "When that thing goes, it will make a huge mess."

"Then let it get a little ahead of you," Josephine said. "We're not moving fast enough for it to do any real damage. The driver will probably stop as soon as it starts to go."

Evelyn sat back and looked around. Spotting a break in the trees and shrubs lining the road ahead, she sat forward again.

"Why don't we pull off up there and stretch our legs?" she suggested. "We've been in the car for hours."

"And we're getting grumpy," Josephine agreed. "The fresh air will do us good. We can have a drink and something to eat."

Finn nodded and maneuvered the car to the right to make it easier to pull off. "It will also get us out from behind this truck."

A few minutes later, Finn was pulling through the trees and onto a stretch of meadow. He shut off the engine and they all climbed out stiffly. A brisk breeze pulled at Evelyn's hair and she tilted her head back to the sky, closing her eyes and breathing deeply. The sun was warm on her face and, if it weren't for the road packed with refugees behind her, she could almost believe it was just another lovely May day.

"Where are we?" she asked, opening her eyes and turning to look at Josephine. "Have we made any progress at all?"

"We've just passed Paris," she answered before bending over to touch her feet, stretching.

Into the Iron Shadows

Evelyn looked at her watch and her heart sank. "We're only to Paris? We've been driving for six hours! At this rate it will take us weeks to reach Bordeaux!"

"I'll look at the map and see if we can get off this road somewhere and try a different one," Josephine said, straightening. "I'm not sure that it will be any better, but I suppose it's worth a try."

"Let's take half an hour to relax first," Finn said, looking around. "Why don't we stretch our legs and eat something, then we'll look at the map and decide? I think if I look at one now, I'll tear it up."

Josephine nodded. "I agree. I want to walk and clear my head."

Evelyn yawned and stretched, then turned towards her. "I'll come with you."

"Wait!" Finn said, holding up his hand, a frown on his face. "What's that noise?"

Evelyn stopped and was quiet listening. "I don't hear anything," she said after a moment.

"There. It's getting louder. You don't hear that?" Finn turned around, looking up. "It sounds like—"

"Bombers," Evelyn finished grimly, catching the low sound that Finn had heard. It was a low drone that she'd heard several times on her flight from Brussels to France. It was a sound she didn't think she'd ever forget.

"There they are!" Josephine said, covering her eyes as she stared into the sky on the horizon. "My God, look at them all!"

Evelyn and Finn followed her gaze, and Evelyn swallowed hard. A black swarm covered the horizon. The traffic on the road came to a stop as everyone turned to watch the waves of German bombers fly towards them.

"They must be going to the coast," Finn said. "They're going west."

Josephine made a strangled noise in her throat and looked at Evelyn, her face pale and her eyes wide.

"I don't feel like walking anymore," she said hoarsely.

Evelyn nodded mutely, watching as the waves of bombers grew closer. They were flying at such a high altitude that she couldn't tell exactly what kind of bomber they were, but she supposed it didn't matter. Heavy bomber or light bomber, they all did the same thing: destroyed everything below them.

"How did it come to this?" she whispered.

She didn't expect an answer, nor did she get one. The trio stood silent in the meadow, their heads turned to the sky, staring silently as the machines of war droned overhead, passing over them.

Evelyn didn't know how long they stood there watching, but when the bombers were disappearing into the distance and she finally lowered her gaze, her neck was sore and her eyes hurt from staring into the bright and sunny sky.

"Let's eat," Finn said finally, turning back to the car. "Then we'll look at the map and get moving again."

Josephine and Evelyn nodded and followed him. As they approached the car again, Josephine suddenly veered to the right, hurrying towards something caught against a tree. Evelyn watched her curiously.

"What is it?" she called when Josephine bent down to pick it up.

"A newspaper," she called back, turning to come back towards them with her head bent over the paper. "It's last night's Paris edition."

As she drew closer, Evelyn saw her frown. "What's wrong?" she asked apprehensively. "What does it say?"

Josephine looked up. "I think I know where those bombers were going," she said, holding out the newspaper.

Evelyn took it and Finn peered over her shoulder as she focused on the headline splashed across the front page.

GERMANS SURROUND CALAIS. CITY UNDER SIEGE.

Chapter Twenty-Two

London
May 25th

Bill nodded in greeting to the guard at the top of the stairs and waited while he examined his credentials.

"Thank you, sir," the man said finally, lifting his head and handing the identification back to him.

Bill moved past him and went down the corridor to the office at the far end. Jasper had called him an hour before to ask him to come see him, but this was the first Bill had been able to get away from his office. The messages from France were coming in fast and furious, each one more critical than the last. The Germans were advancing everywhere, Belgium was close to surrendering, and many of their agents were being forced to flee south along with thousands of other refugees. The continent was a shambles, and the only ones who seemed to have any clear idea of what was happening were the Germans themselves. They, unfortunately, were completely unaffected by the chaos engulfing Belgium and France.

He knocked on the last door and opened it when he heard the command to enter.

"Ah, there you are," Jasper greeted him, glancing up from the reports spread out over his desk. "About time."

"My apologies," Bill said, closing the door. "I've had messages coming in from Belgium and France all morning. It's taken all my time to decode them and make sense of what our people are seeing."

"And? What's the picture look like?" Jasper asked, waving him to a seat.

"Chaotic, at best." Bill sat down and crossed his legs. "What agents we have left in Belgium are trying to get to France. I don't know how much longer we'll have communication with them. The ones in France are reporting from all over the country, and many of them are also trying to go south to escape the Germans."

"And the Germans themselves?"

"Still moving west by all accounts. So far, none have made the

203

turn towards Paris."

Jasper nodded and sat back in his chair.

"No. They're trying to secure the beaches along the Channel and cut off our troops from any escape. Calais is virtually surrounded now."

"Yes, I know."

"Boulogne has fallen. The Germans won that battle today." He removed his glasses and rubbed his eyes tiredly. "Did you hear the king's speech yesterday?"

"Not all of it, I'm afraid. I was in the middle of coordinating with Percy to try to get two of his agents into Spain."

"He didn't pull any punches. He pressed the point home that if we fail in stopping Hitler, it won't merely be territory that is lost, but our empire itself. It was quite blunt, actually. He made mention of the cruelty of which the Nazis have already proven themselves capable."

"He's not wrong. If Hitler takes England, he'll try for the world. We really are the last stand, I'm afraid, and we're on our heels."

"I know." Jasper replaced his glasses and leaned forward, picking up one of the sheets of paper on his desk. "Calais is being defended, but the units are trapped there. They can't hold out for much longer. The Germans are close to victory. They keep sending demands to surrender, but the Brigadier is holding and refuses."

"Can they evacuate?"

"They were going to, but the French commander of the Channel ports has forbidden an evacuation. Our troops have no choice but to comply. It's a bloody mess, that's all. They're running out of ammunition and supplies. I'll be surprised if they hold it for more than a couple of days."

"And the rest of our divisions?"

"Everyone who can is withdrawing to Dunkirk." Jasper looked up from the paper in his hand. "What's interesting is that General Rundstedt has suddenly stopped advancing towards Dunkirk. The Panzer divisions have halted some twenty miles away."

"One of the messages I received this morning said as much," Bill said, nodding. "I've been waiting for confirmation before sending the information on."

"It's been confirmed by both reconnaissance and reports from Dunkirk. The Germans have halted." Jasper laid the paper down and looked at him. "I can't imagine for the life of me why they would, but I shan't complain. It's giving our boys time to fill the gap and evacuate all the troops to Dunkirk."

"All except the ones trapped in Calais," Bill said grimly.

Into the Iron Shadows

Jasper nodded solemnly. "Quite. I understand there's some debate over the Admiralty sending some ships over anyway, but even if they are allowed to evacuate, I'm not sure it would make much difference now. The Germans have already surrounded them. The battle for Calais is doing something, though."

"What's that?"

"It's delaying more German divisions from proceeding to Dunkirk. That's key, I'm told."

"Well, of course, but why?"

"Because Churchill is going to attempt an evacuation of all the troops trapped in Dunkirk," he said calmly.

Bill stared at him, stunned. "What?!"

"Seems incredible, doesn't it? Yet preparations are underway. He's calling it Operation Dynamo."

"How many troops are there?"

"The BEF, most of it anyway, and more French and Belgians coming every day. Estimations vary too much for any kind of accurate count, but the last number I heard was over three hundred thousand all together."

"Three hundred..." Bill sputtered. "How the devil are we going to pull that many men from the very teeth of the tiger?"

Something like a wry smile crossed Jasper's face.

"Winston *was* the First Lord of the Admiralty," he said. "He's calling on every vessel that can hold water to go."

"It will take weeks!"

"We don't have weeks. Once the Germans realize what's happening, they'll close in fast. Our troops aren't equipped to hold them off for much more than a week, at most. And then, of course, there's the Luftwaffe. They'll be all over the skies, bombing the hell out of them." Jasper exhaled and sat back in his chair, looking very tired. "Winston is hoping to save around fifty or seventy-five thousand, but even he admits that that's being extremely optimistic. Most of those boys will be lost."

Bill swallowed and they were silent for a long moment, then Jasper met his gaze across the desk.

"I need any information at all that you're able to get from France regarding the German troop movements. We need to buy all the time we can to get as many of those men off that beach as possible. Even a few hours will help. If we know where the German armies will go and can delay them, a few more men can be evacuated. The French will hold a perimeter, along with our men of course, but they'll only be able to hold it for so long."

"I understand. I'll get on to what agents I have left in the north and see what I can pass on."

"Good. The RAF will be sending Fighter Command over to support the evacuation, but they've warned that the fighters will only have a limited amount of time over the target due to fuel. This will be an all-hands-on-deck operation, and the prime minister expects all of us to do our part."

"Of course."

"Where do we stand with Jian and Oscar?" Jasper asked, sitting back in his chair.

"They're on their way to Bordeaux. They'll contact me once they arrive."

"It's terrible timing. I don't know if I can guarantee a ship to bring them home. They'll all be ferrying troops. Do you have any idea when they'll reach Bordeaux?"

"No. Refugees are pouring south, clogging the roads. They're in there somewhere with them." Bill pinched the bridge of his nose, closing his eyes for a moment. The headache that had been nagging him all morning was growing steadily worse, and this added news wasn't helping. "If we can't get a cruiser to Bordeaux, I'll try to arrange for a fishing boat. It will take longer, of course."

"Let me know as soon as you hear something and I'll see what I can manage, but the way it looks now, there won't be anything afloat that's not at Dunkirk. I've heard they're even requisitioning civilian vessels."

"I understand."

Jasper nodded and leaned forward again, picking up a pen. "I know you do, and we'll do what we can."

Bill stood up and turned towards the door, the interview over. He was just reaching for the handle when Jasper spoke again, glancing up.

"You might say a prayer for our men over there. We'll need a miracle to get them home."

Bill thought of Evelyn, caught in the midst of yet another invasion. She'd made it out of Norway, and made it out of Belgium. In both cases, if he'd listened to the intelligence reports and looked at the sheer numbers against her, she should never have succeeded and escaped. His lips twisted into a small smile.

"It's funny how those miracles can happen, sir."

Into the Iron Shadows

Miles climbed out of the cockpit onto the wing, taking a deep breath of fresh air before jumping down and nodding to the ground crew sergeant.

"Refuel and rearm, sergeant," he said, stripping off his gloves.

"Yes, sir. Happy hunting?" the man asked hopefully.

Miles glanced at him and shook his head. "We ran into Stukas and Dorniers, but no hits, I'm afraid."

"Ah, well, never mind, sir. I'm sure you'll get another soon enough. Still plenty o' time."

Miles grinned despite himself and turned to watch Chris taxi to a stop a few yards away. The ground crew were taking an inordinate amount of pride in the fact that their pilots were beginning to notch up kills. Miles had heard rumors that there was a pool going on which of the pilots would end with the most confirmed enemy kills. He had no idea what the pool was up to, or what the time frame was, but he knew that he and Chris were leading the pack, with Rob holding a very close third. Considering that he only had two confirmed himself, it wasn't saying very much. But as the good sergeant had pointed out, there was still plenty of time.

He pulled his cigarettes from his inside pocket and lit one, waiting while Chris shut down his engine and climbed out of the cockpit.

"Are you waiting for me?" Chris called, jumping down.

"Well I'm not standing here for my health, Yank," Miles called back. "Hurry up. I'm hungry."

Chris unzipped his leather flight jacket as he strode towards him. "You're not waiting for the others?"

"Whatever for?" Miles turned and began walking across the grass, away from the landing strip.

"I don't know. To make sure they all make it back?" Chris fell into step beside him and Miles looked at him in amusement.

"And do what if they don't? Don't be wet. I'm going for my lunch."

"We didn't get any of the bombers," Chris said, pulling out a cigarette and shoving it in the side of his mouth. It hung there, bouncing with each step they took, while he fished in his pocket for his lighter. "I keep thinking about the poor bastards trapped in Calais dealing with those dive bombers."

"Don't," Miles advised, glancing at him. "That way leads to

207

madness."

"It doesn't bother you?" Chris pulled out his lighter and paused mid-stride to light the cigarette. "They got through. Isn't that our job? To stop them from getting through?"

"They didn't get. They were already there. Our job is to get the ones we can and live to do it again the next time. That's it."

Chris grunted. "I guess I'll get used to it," he muttered, "but right now I feel responsible for every bomb that falls on Calais."

Miles threw away his cigarette butt and looked up at the cloudless sky, exhaling. He knew what Chris meant. He felt the same.

"Do you think they'll make it out?"

"Who?"

"The guys stuck in Calais!"

Miles shook his head. "They're completely surrounded. If they do, it will be a miracle."

"Yeah. That's what I thought."

They fell silent again. Then Chris blew his cheeks out and threw his head back, taking a deep breath.

"So when Calais falls, that just leaves Dunkirk. What about all those troops?"

Miles shrugged. "I don't know. I know they're cut off from both reinforcements and retreat. The only way out is the Channel."

"Think they'll evacuate them?"

"I don't see how we can. It would take weeks."

"This is a real mess, huh?"

"Your talent for understatement never ceases to amaze me," Miles said with a short laugh. "Yes. It's a real mess. Or, in my vernacular, a complete cock-up."

"Yeah, we have a vernacular for that too. It's called FUBAR."

"Pardon?"

"If we're ever in it ourselves, something like that, I'll explain it to you."

"Why not simply tell me now?"

"I think you'd be terribly offended, old chap," Chris said with a grin, mimicking an English accent. Then he sobered. "But seriously, how did it all come to this? How did the Germans even get the resources to do any of this?"

Miles' lips tightened. "We gave them to Hitler," he said grimly. "France, Poland, Italy, your country. Everyone wanted to keep him happy and avoid another war. We enabled this. We *caused* it. Our leaders refused to acknowledge a threat, and now we have to mop up their mess."

Into the Iron Shadows

"Yeah, and watch Perry explode in the process," Chris muttered. "How many have died in France so far?"

"Not as many as will have before this is all over."

"Exactly. And for what?"

"To stop the disease from spreading," Miles said promptly. "You've seen the news reels. If we don't do this, the Nazis will be goose-stepping down Whitehall."

Chris was silent for a moment, then he turned his head to look at Miles.

"You know what really gets me?" he demanded. "Back home, they're all saying that it's not our problem and we should stay out of it. What do they think will happen if the Nazis take over all of Europe? Do they think Hitler will just shake hands with Roosevelt and agree to leave the United States alone?"

"I never really got the impression that you Americans thought much at all," Miles said with a grin.

"I'm beginning to wonder myself," Chris said morosely. "What the hell is going on, Miles? When did the world go insane?"

"I don't know, Yank. I suspect it always was to some extent."

"Yeah, but not like this. I heard that German fighters are strafing civilians. Refugees. They're just flying over and shooting them."

Miles felt his chest tighten. He'd heard the same thing from one of the pilots who had just come back from France. He claimed to have witnessed it himself, first in Belgium and then in France.

"So I understand."

"They really are shits, aren't they? The Luftwaffe pilots?"

"So it would seem. And that, my dear boy, is why we need to stop them."

Chapter Twenty-Three

Evelyn knelt beside the stream and cupped her hands in the water, scooping it up and splashing it over her face. The cold water felt wonderful and she quickly repeated the motion, closing her eyes in pleasure.

"How is it? Cold?" Josephine asked, kneeling beside her and handing her a cloth to dry her face.

"It's lovely," Evelyn replied, taking the cloth and mopping the water off her face.

"After two days in the car, I think anything would be lovely." Josephine leaned down and scooped up water, splashing it over her face. "Oh! That *is* wonderful!"

Evelyn laughed and shoved her arms into the stream, washing her hands and forearms with the cool water. They had passed Bourges that morning, placing them about halfway to their destination. No matter what route they tried, they met the same columns of refugees, all fleeing south to escape the German divisions. While they were clogging the roads, Allied troops were trying to go north to aid in the fight at the ports. The streams of refugees made it slow going for everyone, and Evelyn was resigned to the fact that they would be inching their way to Bordeaux. The only comfort she had was that the newspapers were filled with reports and photographs of lines of people pouring south. Bill had to be aware of the situation, and she was sure he was arranging transportation accordingly.

At least, she hoped he was.

"Oh, I needed that!" Josephine exclaimed, wiping off her face and arms. "I felt like I was covered in a film of dirt."

"So did I. Thankfully we don't look like it." Evelyn picked up one of the pottery jugs they'd brought with them and leaned forward to immerse it in the stream, filling it. "I hope this will be enough water to last us."

"We'll come to another stream soon enough. We're in the middle of the country. Water is the least of our concerns." Josephine picked up the second jug. "When we go back to the car, I'll tell Finn to come and rinse off. It will do him a world of good. He's getting more and more bad-tempered with every kilometer."

"He's worried that we won't reach Bordeaux in time."

"Aren't you?"

"I'm sure they realize the situation," Evelyn said, setting her pitcher on the grass and sitting back on her heels. "It's in all the newspapers, and I know Bill is getting regular reports every day. He must know that it will take some time to get there."

Josephine finished filling her jug and took a deep breath, looking around. The stream ran through a small clearing surrounded by centuries-old trees. It was some distance from the road, offering a false sense of seclusion and safety from the reality around them.

"I could sit here all day," she breathed. "Isn't it beautiful?"

Evelyn smiled and closed her eyes, allowing the sun to bathe her face in warmth. "Mmm."

"Perhaps we can talk Finn into staying long enough to eat lunch. We could sit here for an hour, drink some wine, and pretend that we're on a picnic."

Evelyn opened her eyes. "I think it would take a lot to convince him to stop that long," she said with a sigh. "He's determined to keep moving."

"He acts as though he has the Devil himself behind him." Josephine pursed her lips and then shook her head. "I suppose we do."

"At least we're putting some distance between us, for now, at least."

"It's only a matter of time before they turn towards Paris."

Evelyn looked at Josephine sharply, catching the note of sadness in her voice. Her friend was staring across the stream and into the trees, a strange look on her face.

"You know, I never really believed that this would happen," she said slowly, her eyes transfixed on something unseen. "When the war began, I thought it was all a grand adventure. I was able to leave home and go to different places, living a life that I'd only ever dreamt of, full of excitement and new experiences. Of course I knew the danger. How could I not? I heard stories from contacts who came over the border from Germany. They warned of what was coming. They told us of the evil that had taken hold of their country. But I never truly thought that it would come to France."

"You thought it would remain in Germany."

"Yes."

"I think we all hoped it would remain there," Evelyn said in a low voice. "I know I did. I've said all along that we needed to be ready if the war came, but I think deep down I didn't believe that it would happen."

"And now it has." Josephine turned her head and Evelyn saw the anguish in her gray eyes. "Will France ever be the same again? Even if we're able to stop them now, today, look at what has already been lost. And our government is doing nothing. They give us no direction. They fill their broadcasts with empty words of hope when we can clearly see that there is none. Our generals have failed us! Our government has failed us."

A deep hollow ache filled Evelyn as she nodded in agreement. Everything Josephine said was true. After spending two days on a road crowded with women, children, old men and infants, all displaced and left with nowhere to go, she was coming to the realization that this wasn't just a war of territory. It was a war of power. The Germans wanted power over every man, woman, and child, and would destroy them to get it. She'd gazed into the eyes of the old French men and women on the road, and had seen their resignation. They had lived through one war, only to be thrown into the middle of another one. Everything they owned was with them, and they had nowhere to go. They were on the road and moving south for only one reason: hope.

"Hope." Evelyn's voice came out stronger than she expected.

"Pardon?"

"Hope. That's what you must hold on to. It's why all these people are on the road. They're clinging to the hope that they can build a new life away from their homes, away from everything they've known. It's that hope that will pull France through this. She may not be the same, but she will still be France."

Josephine was silent for a long time, then she slowly nodded.

"This will be our legacy," she said in a low voice. "This is why I'm now Jeannine Renaud. I will continue to stand and fight, and oppose the Nazi tyranny when it comes, so that France *can* be France once more."

"*Aux armes, citoyens; Formez vos bataillons; Marchons, marchons!*" Evelyn quoted soberly.

Josephine looked at her, startled, then a shining smile broke over her face. "La Marseillaise. Vive la France!"

Evelyn was just opening her mouth to repeat the phrase when the air was suddenly filled with a low sound that grew rapidly in both pitch and volume. Her heart stopped, then thudded heavily against her ribs as fear shot through her. She looked at Josephine to find her eyes widening and the color draining from her face. They turned as one to look up behind them.

Into the Iron Shadows

"What are they?" Josephine asked, staring at black specks diving out of the sky.

"Stukas!" Evelyn cried, jumping to her feet and grabbing her jug. "Quick! The trees!"

The awful noise got louder, sounding just like an air raid siren as the small, deadly dive bombers descended, aiming for the road clogged with people and vehicles. Evelyn looked up as they reached the cover of the old trees just as the first one dropped its bombs before pulling out of his dive, leveling out just above tree level. She squeezed her eyes shut, dropping down to a crouch and leaning against a thick trunk. Branches thick with leaves hid the sight of the bombers, leaving only the ability to listen. The bomb exploded, echoing through the countryside and causing the ground to shake. Evelyn gasped, her heart pounding and her breath coming fast. Opening her eyes, she looked at Josephine beside her in terror. They stared at each other, listening to another explosion as another bomb hit the road. The branches above them trembled, and then, they heard something even worse.

Ratta-tatta-ratta-tatta!

Evelyn sucked in her breath, dropping the jug and covering her mouth to hold in her scream. They weren't just bombing the road crowded with refugees. They were shooting it!

RAF Horsham

"Come on, Yank! We don't have all bloody night, y'know," Slippy exclaimed. "It's your go!"

Miles sipped his beer and watched as Chris finished lighting his cigarette before ambling over to take the three darts Slippy was holding out. Most of the squadron was gathered in the officer's recreation room and, because they were English and drinking, a game of darts had been started. Chris, as the only one who hadn't been throwing darts since he was in short pants, was taking his fair share of ribbing in stride.

"Try to actually hit the board," Mother drawled, lifting his pint.

Chris stood at the line, his cigarette hanging out of his mouth and his tie half undone, peering at the board.

"Where am I aiming?" he asked, drawing a few guffaws.

"In the middle!"

"Good Lord, we're finished," Rob mourned, glancing at Miles. "You were right to sit this one out, Miles. Tell me again why I took the

Yank?"

Miles didn't answer as Chris lined up his shot and then released his first dart. His eyebrows soared into his forehead and he looked at Rob with a grin.

"You were saying?" he asked.

"Bloody hell!" Slippy cried. "He's hit a bulls-eye!"

"Beginners luck," Chris announced, taking his cigarette out of his mouth and blowing out smoke. He turned to set it in an ashtray before going back to the line. "I won't do it again."

"Do it as many times as you like, old boy!" Rob said.

His next dart landed in the black a few inches from center and Miles chuckled.

"Never played in your life? Bollocks!" Mother said, shaking his head.

"No, I really never have," Chris protested. "But I can shoot a running jack rabbit at fifty yards."

"Rabbits? What've they got to do with darts?" Slippy demanded.

"It means he has a good eye," Mother retorted. "Get your head out of your arse."

Chris' third dart landed a double, drawing a loud groan from Mother and whoop from Rob.

"Never doubted you, Yank," he chortled. "Not for a moment."

"You really should have known better," Miles told him. "There's a reason he's got two confirmed Me 109s."

"So do you."

"And you refuse to play against me in darts."

"Lacey!" A voice called from the doorway.

Miles turned around and looked at their CO in surprise. "Yes, sir?"

"I'd like a word, please. Sorry to interrupt."

"Oh, that's all right, sir." Miles gulped down the last few sips of his beer and set the empty pint down. "I'm not playing."

He walked across the room to join Squadron Leader Boyd Ashmore, their CO, at the door. Ashmore was a stocky man of medium height who looked more suited to boxing than flying. He had been a star boxer at Oxford, but when he discovered flying, that was the end of the fighting. He was one of the best pilots Miles had ever seen, and one of the best commanding officers, and Miles had immense respect for him.

"Is everything all right, sir?" he asked.

Into the Iron Shadows

"Tickety-boo. I just want a quick word."

Ashmore led him out of the recreation room and across the hallway to the door leading outside. Once they'd stepped out into the fresh, night air, he threw his shoulders back and inhaled.

"Gorgeous night." He looked around and shook his head. "Wouldn't know there was a war on, would you?"

"No, sir."

"I understand there's a pool on with the ground crews on who will end up with the most confirmed enemy kills," Ashmore said, turning and beginning to walk along the gravel road.

"So I've been told."

"You and the American are leading. Did you know?"

"I believe it's been mentioned once or twice," Miles said dryly. "Every time I come back, my ground sergeant asks for an update."

Ashmore chuckled. "If it keeps them in good spirits, it's all to the good. I want to make it clear, however, that I don't want you hunting out the bastards just to keep your numbers up."

Miles frowned. "Of course not, sir."

Ashmore glanced at him and sighed. "I don't for a moment think that you would be so careless, but the wing commander got wind of it and asked me to have this conversation with both of you. He's worried about losing pilots. We have precious few as it is."

"I understand, sir. You don't need to worry about me, and I don't think you need to worry about Chris, either. He's not as much of a cowboy as Mother would lead you to believe."

Ashmore waved his hand impatiently. "I'm aware of that. He's a fantastic flier. I'm lucky to have him. And you."

Miles raised his eyebrows in surprise. "Thank you, sir."

"There's something I want to discuss with you, Miles. I've already spoken to Mother, and the rest of the squadron will be briefed first thing in the morning, but I want to talk to you personally." He clasped his hands behind his back and looked up at the sky as they walked. "The prime minister has hatched a scheme to evacuate as many of the soldiers trapped at Dunkirk as possible. It's damn near impossible to get them all, but he's determined to try. He's calling it Operation Dynamo, and he's sending over anything that can float to get them. It's going to be hell. The Germans know they're there, and once they realize what's happening, they'll send in the Luftwaffe to stop it."

Miles was silent, waiting for him continue. He should have guessed that Churchill wouldn't leave thousands of men trapped in France. But a full evacuation? It would take weeks!

"In truth, it would take weeks to get that many soldiers out of France," Ashmore continued, unconsciously echoing his thoughts. "But we don't have weeks. So Churchill is ordering that they get as many as possible in the few days we *do* have. They're sending everything. I wasn't joking when I said anything that can float is being sent over. They're even requisitioning private vessels. Fighter Command will be giving full air support to the evacuation."

"When?"

"We start tomorrow."

Miles inhaled sharply, a strange mix of exhilaration and nervous excitement rushing through him.

"I'm telling you all this because we're bound to run into heavy opposition. The last thing Jerry wants is for us to rescue even a portion of our Expeditionary Force. Right now, if France falls, we won't have an army to speak of that can oppose him. If we manage to pull this off, we'll live to fight another day, and I can assure you that Hitler does not want that." Ashmore glanced at him and cleared his throat. "This next bit will *not* be in the briefing tomorrow, so I'm trusting that you'll keep it to yourself."

Miles raised his eyebrows in surprise. "Of course, sir."

"We're dreadfully outnumbered. There is no hope of matching the Jerries fighter for fighter. They outnumber us three to one in fighters alone. We'll be flying multiple sorties a day just to try to keep pace. The plan is to try to have two squadrons over Dunkirk at all times, but even so, it'll be a hell of a scrap."

"Yes, I know the numbers, sir."

Ashmore looked at him in surprise. "You do?"

He nodded, shrugging sheepishly. "Things like that get around, sir. We all know what we're up against."

"Yes, well, there you are, then." Ashmore shook his head. "We're going to lose pilots. It's inevitable. Fighter Command is hoping the losses won't be substantial, but given the amount of planes and pilots we've lost over France so far…"

"I understand, sir."

"I know Perry's loss was a blow to the others. According to Chris' account of the battle, you tried to get over to help."

"I did, but I was tied up with a couple of 109s," Miles said soberly. "I wasn't in time."

"You did the right thing. Always take care of your own kite first. The other pilots aren't your responsibility, you know."

"Yes, sir."

"Good. The point is that the others look up to you. You're a natural leader. I've been asked to forward a list to HQ of pilots whom I deem capable to take over in the event of losses. More specifically, the loss of flight and squadron leaders. I've given your name."

"Sir?" Miles stopped and stared at him. "I don't understand. Mother is the flight leader."

"Yes, and now you're next in line." Ashmore shrugged and gave him a twisted smile. "The realities of war, my boy. Everyone must have a successor. You've been bumped to the top of the ladder."

"I don't know what to say to that," Miles admitted, rubbing the back of his neck. "I suppose I should say thank you, but I'm not sure that would be appropriate."

Ashmore let out a laugh. "It wouldn't be inappropriate. No one's dead yet."

Miles grinned sheepishly. "I suppose not. Then, thank you."

"No need to thank me. You're a terrific pilot and a strong leader. The others like you and, more importantly, they respect you. They'll follow you anywhere. That's the sign of a good leader."

"If you don't mind my asking, how long was the list that you sent to HQ?"

"Three names in the entire squadron. If we lose more than that in quick succession, then I'm afraid 66 Squadron is in real trouble. God willing we won't lose any."

"Yes, sir."

"Do me a favor, will you?"

"What's that, sir?"

"Don't get yourself killed over Dunkirk."

Miles nodded, his lips curving into a wry smile. "I'll do my best not to."

Chapter Twenty-Four

Evelyn and Josephine huddled against the trunk of the ancient oak tree, listening to the seemingly endless screams of the deadly dive bombers, followed by explosions and machine gun fire. Screams filtered through the trees from the road, and Evelyn shook uncontrollably, pressing her fists against her mouth. With every wail from a diving Stuka, she waited for a bomb to fall through the trees and find them. They were so close! The ground trembled with each explosion, and her ears rang with the hideous sounds as she squeezed her eyes shut, willing it to end. Next to her, Josephine wrapped her arms around her legs and stared straight ahead, her bottom lip caught between her teeth to prevent a sound from escaping.

After what seemed like forever, but was, in reality, only a few minutes, the machine guns went silent and the noise of the engines drew away. As the airplanes receded into the distance, Evelyn slowly lowered her hands and unclenched her fists.

"They're leaving," she whispered. She looked at Josephine and reached out to touch her shoulder. "They're gone."

Josephine nodded, letting go of her knees and turning to look at her. They stared at each other in shock for a moment, then Evelyn forced herself to move.

"Come. We must find Finn."

The mention of Finn seemed to rouse Josephine from her stupor and her eyes widened.

"My God! He's with the car! What if…" her voice trailed off on a sob and she struggled to her feet. "You're right. We must find him."

Evelyn held on to the tree to support her shaking legs as she stood, reaching for the jug of water at her feet. Through her distraction, she noticed that it had, amazingly, landed upright when she dropped it. She turned to look at Josephine's jug, laying on its side.

"Your jug," she murmured, staring at it. "It's empty now."

Josephine swiped it up in one hand and grabbed Evelyn's arm with the other.

"Forget about the water," she said briskly. "Come on. Let's

218

move."

Evelyn shook her head, trying to focus, and allowed the other woman to pull her forward. Once her legs began moving, the fog began to clear and she shook her head again. She had to pull herself together.

And then they heard the cries.

The sounds filtered through the trees from the direction of the road, disjointed and sporadic at first before multiplying into a chaotic symphony of pain. Crying, wailing, screams of agony, they all mixed together to form a cacophony of terrible noise that made Evelyn's blood run cold. She and Josephine looked at each other, and Josephine visibly swallowed. Their steps faltered briefly, then she squared her shoulders.

"Come. We must face it," she said firmly.

Evelyn nodded and the two women walked resolutely towards the edge of the copse of trees. Evelyn gulped and forced herself to continue walking. Whatever greeted them, it had to be faced, as Josephine said. They had to find Finn, and the car, and then they had to continue on to Bordeaux. A shudder went through her. No matter what confronted them when they came out of the trees, they had to continue.

It was far worse than she could have ever imagined.

Stepping out from the shady protection of the trees, Evelyn stared at the road in horror. Carts were overturned, horses lay dead on their sides, and vehicles had been abandoned in the road, the doors left open as the occupants ran for their lives. Huge craters had decimated several parts of the road where the bombs had fallen, destroying whatever had been there and sending debris, stone, dirt and body parts in every direction. Those who had been caught in the hailstorm of bullets lay dead, scattered about like so many dolls, blood pouring out around them. They were the ones who were silent. The ones screaming with pain were the ones who had survived.

"Mon Dieu," Josephine breathed beside her, staring.

Evelyn couldn't bring herself to utter even a sound. A woman stumbled out from behind an overturned cart, blood pouring down the side of her face, screaming for Pierre, while a few feet away a man lay face down and still in the road. She ran to fall over him, screaming and sobbing. Her cries mingled with those of countless others as, slowly, people began to move and try to recover. The screams of the wounded became one with the cries of the bereft, and Evelyn gazed around them helplessly. The number of dead was overwhelming and she felt a lump form in her throat as her eyes filled with tears.

People who had taken cover in the ditches lining either side of the road seemed to have fared better. They crawled out, shaken and stunned, to survey the damage around them. Slowly, they began to move among the debris and bodies in the road, looking for loved ones and trying to help those that were still living.

"They're just civilians," Josephine whispered hoarsely. "Refugees. They aren't soldiers. These are just innocent people."

Evelyn tore her eyes away from a child, no more than six, laying prone next to a horse. Tears blurred her vision as she raised a hand to her forehead, not knowing what to do. She didn't know how to move, or how to help. All she could do was stare in shock at the nightmare around them.

"Geneviève! Thank God!"

She spun around to see Finn running along the grass next to the ditch towards them, and grabbed Josephine's arm.

"He's all right!" she cried. "It's Finn! He's alive!"

Josephine let out a relieved sob. "Oh thank God!"

Finn reached them and threw his arms around Evelyn, half laughing in relief.

"I'm so glad you're safe," he exclaimed, releasing her and turning to Josephine. "I couldn't do anything but dive behind the car and pray that you were safe."

"We went under the trees," she told him, smiling tearfully. "And the car? It escaped damage?"

"Yes. After you left, I pulled it off the road and behind some bushes. I thought it would give us privacy to eat something before continuing. The bushes protected it, and me, from the shrapnel." He ran a hand through his hair and looked around at the carnage around them. "Come. We must leave before they come back."

"Come back?" Josephine stared at him. "Why would they come back? They've already done their damage."

The look on Finn's face made Evelyn shudder.

"There are still people here," he said grimly. "They will be back."

"Why? To what purpose?" Evelyn demanded. "We're not soldiers. We're civilians. Women and children. Why?"

"To spread fear," he said, gently guiding them both back the way he had come. "It's what they do. A frightened person is easily controlled. A terrified nation is easily subdued."

Evelyn swallowed and allowed herself to be led along the road, a strange numbness stealing over her. What kind of person was capable of shooting unarmed civilians who were no threat to anyone? Who were only trying to move to safety? More than that, what kind of government allowed, or even worse, ordered their people to do it? Her lips tightened. She already knew the answer to that one. She'd seen it all too clearly.

"Wait," Josephine said, shaking her head and stopping. "We can't just leave."

"We must!" Finn said.

But Josephine was shaking her head violently now. "No! We must help those that we can. We can't just leave them like this. They *need* help!"

"There are others who can help. We don't have time to stop and spend another half of the day without getting any further ahead," Finn argued, his voice low. "Geneviève and I must get to Bordeaux. It's already taken too much time."

"But all these wounded people!" Josephine protested, looking around. "They need assistance. And the dead need to be moved. We can't just walk away!"

"We can, and we must!"

Evelyn looked from Finn to Josephine and noted the stubborn set of her jaw. She was beginning to look decidedly mulish.

"Finn, look around," she said softly, putting her hand on his arm. "We can't go anywhere until the road is cleared. No one can. We can't get through, and we can't go around with all these people moving the…dead…off the road. If we help, it will be cleared that much faster and we can be on our way."

"We should have already been in Bordeaux," he replied stubbornly, his dark eyes boring into hers. "We cannot run the risk of getting trapped in France. You know that."

"Yes, I know. But the state of the roads is all over the newspapers, and I'm sure they're aware of it in London. They will be expecting the delays."

Finn exhaled and ran a hand through his hair, leaving it standing up at the back of his head.

"Will we be able to leave?" he asked bluntly, staring at her. "You know your people. Will they get us out?"

"Yes." She nodded, her voice firm with conviction. "I don't pretend to know how, but I know that Bill will do everything in his power to get us out, no matter when we arrive."

Finn stared at her for another moment, then looked at the debris and destruction surrounding them. His eyes went to the road and the overturned carts and dead horses blocking the way and his gaze wavered.

"All right," he finally relented. "I'll gather some men and start moving the largest obstacles out of the road. Both of you can help with the wounded. We'll stay and help, but as soon as there is room to pull around, we continue on. I don't want to be caught again when the Stukas come back. We may not be as lucky next time."

Evelyn finished cleaning the gravel out of a deep, jagged wound slashing across a young woman's upper thigh. Shaking her head, she reached for some clean strips of cotton linen. Someone had presented a pile of sheets to cut up for bandages, and she had a stack of the strips beside her on the edge of the road. The young woman next to her held an infant girl in her arms, soothing her softly as Evelyn worked to clean and bandage her leg. Bullets from the Stuka's high-powered machine guns had hit the road with such force that chunks of pavement had been thrown up into the air, and into the leg of the woman beside her.

"How old is your baby?" Evelyn asked, glancing up as she folded a piece of linen to press against the wound.

"Five months."

"And her name?"

"Josephine."

Evelyn smiled and placed the folded bandage on the wound. "That's a beautiful name. A dear friend of mine is called Josephine. Do you think you can manage to hold this in place?"

The young woman nodded and shifted the infant to her shoulder where she could hold her with one arm while she pressed the bandage on her leg with the other hand.

"Is your husband fighting?" Evelyn asked, sorting through the strips of linen until she found one long enough to wrap around the leg.

"Yes. I'm on my way to stay with his family in Pau. He thought it would be safer for me, if the Germans came, to go south," she said, her voice breaking.

Evelyn nodded and began wrapping a bandage around her leg. "Are you traveling alone?"

"No. I am with my friends. They're over there, trying to help move that automobile."

She nodded to the other side of the road where a group of people were trying to push a car off the road. Bullets had torn through the engine housing, rendering it useless for travel. No one seemed to know where the owner was, and it had been assumed that the person was one of the dead lining the road. Evelyn glanced at the group and then back at the young woman.

"You're very lucky," she told her, tying off the bandage. "The wound is deep, but you will be all right. I cleaned out the rock and gravel as best that I could, but you must try to keep it clean. Perhaps wash it again this evening, if you can."

The woman nodded. "Thank you. I will." She watched as Evelyn prepared to stand, gathering her stack of bandages and water jug. "Are you a nurse?"

"No. I'm afraid I don't have the temperament."

"You've been wonderful with me. Thank you."

Evelyn smiled and stood, looking down at her. "I only wish I could do more."

The woman shrugged. "What more can any of us do?"

Evelyn nodded and turned away, looking for Josephine. She was some distance up the road, kneeling next to an old man, wrapping linen around his arm. She started towards her, averting her eyes resolutely from the growing line of bodies in the ditch next to the road. As the bodies were moved from the road, they were placed in the ditch and their faces covered in a feeble attempt at preserving the dignity of the departed. However, in shifting her gaze from one gruesome sight, she inadvertently found herself staring at another. A group of five men were struggling to move a dead horse to the ditch. Bullets had ripped through the animal's head, and her chest tightened as sorrow and anger rolled over her. Her only comfort was that the poor animal had had no idea what hit it, nor did many of the dead lining the road.

"Please! Somebody help me!"

Evelyn turned, looking for the source of the plea, and found an old man standing in the middle of the road, looking around helplessly. He saw her and took a few shaky steps towards her, reaching out a blood soaked hand.

"Please? Will you help me?" he implored.

Evelyn went forward, scanning him for the source of the blood.

"Of course," she said, reaching him and taking his arm gently. "What is it? Where are you injured?"

He shook his head, his weathered face lined with age and sorrow. "Not me. It's my wife."

"Where is she?"

"Over there."

He turned and motioned to an overturned cart. The two donkeys that had been pulling it were now untied and next to the road, alternating between chewing on the grass and watching the chaos taking place around them. Evelyn swallowed and nodded, walking beside him towards the cart. It was a heavy, older wooden conveyance with a bench that had room for the driver and one passenger to sit. Bags of clothing, some wooden boxes, and a few pieces of furniture had been thrown to the ground when the cart went over. Large holes, perfectly spaced apart, were in a row along the side where bullets had torn through the wood. The man led her around the backside of the cart and pointed with a visibly shaking hand.

"I know there's nothing you can do to help her. She's gone," he said, tears welling up in his eyes. "I want to move the cart to get her out, but I'm not strong enough."

Evelyn felt her throat close and her chest tighten once more as she gazed at the lifeless eyes gazing at nothing from an aged and lined face. The cart had trapped the woman beneath it, but the cause of death was quite clearly the bullet hole in the center of her chest.

"I don't suppose you will be strong enough, either," the man said sadly, staring down at his wife helplessly.

Evelyn forced back her tears and turned to look at him. She rested a hand on his shoulder.

"I'll find someone," she whispered. "Wait here with your wife. We'll get her out."

The look of gratitude on his face was almost her undoing and she set down her jug of water and bandages quickly, taking a deep, steadying breath. This was no time for an emotional outburst. This grieving old man didn't need tears from her, he needed assistance. Turning, she went around the cart, intent on calling on some men to help.

"Ooof!"

She grunted as she walked into something tall and solid. Hands gripped her arms, steadying her, and Evelyn looked up into a lean face towering over her.

"Oh! I'm so sorry!" she exclaimed. "I didn't know anyone was here!"

"Are you all right, mademoiselle?" The man had a deep, rich voice with a hint of an accent that she couldn't place. "I heard the man ask for help. Is there anything I can do?"

He released her and Evelyn nodded eagerly.

"Yes! His wife is trapped under this cart. She's dead, but he can't move the cart himself."

The man nodded and followed her around the corner of the cart to where the man was crouching next to his wife. He looked up as they approached and struggled to his feet, almost losing his balance. Evelyn rushed to his side, giving him her arm to help him up.

"Thank you," he said. "I lost my cane."

"We'll see if we can find it once we've got the cart righted," she promised. Then she looked at the tall man examining the cart. "Do you think we need a third? I'm strong, but perhaps you think another man would be better?"

The man turned to look at her consideringly, then shook his head.

"I think we can manage it between us," he said. "It's solid, but it's laying at an angle. Let's try it ourselves."

Evelyn nodded and led the elderly man over to the donkeys. She smiled at him gently.

"You wait here and we'll see what we can do," she said.

The old man nodded and she turned back to the cart to find the other man examining the back end. As she approached, he turned and nodded to the front end.

"If you get on that side, we should be able to angle it up enough for me to get under it and lift," he told her.

"It's not too heavy to do that?" she asked, moving to the spot he indicated.

"No. With some leverage, we should be able to get it back upright. The wheels, miraculously, appear to be intact. Are you ready?"

"Yes, I think so."

Evelyn bent her knees and gripped the bottom edge, trying to avoid looking at the woman laying between her and the man.

"On my count," the man called, hunched over his end. "One, two, three!"

Evelyn took a deep breath and heaved with all her strength. At first she didn't think the heavy cart was budging, but then she realized that it was rising slowly. Gritting her teeth and squeezing her eyes shut, she used her legs to help her lift, grunting with the exertion.

"Good! Keep going!" The man called from his end. "It's going!"

Evelyn redoubled her efforts, ignoring the wood cutting into her palms. Her arms began shaking with the effort, but the cart was rising and the higher the side got, the easier it was to lift. Her arms stopped shaking when they were perpendicular to the road, and then she bent her knees and got under the side, using her legs and shoulders to push from underneath. Breathing heavily, she looked to her right and saw the tall man doing the same on his end. A moment later, the weight shifted and was suddenly gone as the cart fell away from them, settling on its wheels.

Evelyn gasped and bent over with her hands on her knees, breathing heavily as her arms went wobbly on her. Sweat had gathered on her forehead and upper lip, and she lifted a hand to wipe it away only to find her palms cut and covered with blood and dirt. Turning her hand, she wiped her forehead with the back of her hand, straightening up.

"How are you? Are you all right?" The tall man was at her side, looking at her hands in concern. "You've hurt your hands."

"It's nothing," she said. "It's from the side of the cart. I have some water in my jug. I'll rinse them off and wrap some linen around them."

"You did it," he said, smiling at her. "You're right. You are strong. It was heavier than I thought it would be."

Evelyn laughed tiredly. "Aren't they always?"

They turned as the old man rushed forward and fell to his knees beside his dead wife, sobbing softly as he smoothed the matted hair off of her face.

"It's gone, my love. I can move you now. I'll take you under the trees and you'll be at peace. You always loved the trees," he said, tears streaming down his face.

Evelyn swallowed painfully and took a deep breath. "I'll help him move her," she said, looking up at the man beside her. "Thank you for helping with the cart."

He waved her thanks aside and strode forward, crouching on the other side of the woman.

"If you'll allow me, I'd be honored to carry her for you," he told the old man. "She is old and has lived a full life. She should not be dragged."

The old man nodded tearfully and Evelyn watched as the tall man very gently lifted the woman's body into his arms and stood, turning towards the ditch. The old man touched his arm.

"Please. Not in there. I want to bury her," he said. "I have a shovel here. It was in the cart."

The man looked down at him for a moment, then nodded. He carried the woman past the donkeys and to the meadow beyond, the old man walking beside him. Evelyn felt hot tears rolling down her face and she sucked in her breath, brushing them away impatiently. It was too much. After everything she'd seen, the little old man who'd just lost his lifelong companion was too much for her. Yet she couldn't give in now. She must be strong. Tears would do nothing to help any of these people who had lost so much.

Into the Iron Shadows

She went over to where she'd left her water jug and picked it up, splashing her hands with water to wash away the dirt so she could examine the cuts on her palms. They weren't deep and, after picking out some splinters, she wrapped first one hand and then the other with two strips of linen. When she was finished, she looked up across the meadow to find the tall man digging a hole under a tree while the old man knelt next to his wife. The sight filled her with both sorrow and a strange feeling of solidarity.

Evelyn turned and looked around her. Everywhere, people were helping each other. Men were helping clear the road while women were helping the wounded, and gathering belongings that had been scattered everywhere. The crying and wailing had stopped, the shock was past, and now the feeling was one of resignation and determination. Tears filled her eyes again and she swallowed hard.

The Germans were trying to break them, and perhaps they would succeed. But for right now, in this moment, the people of France on this small section of road in the middle of the country were joining together to help carry each other.

And it was that very determination to survive, and to help others survive, that just might be what would help save her beloved France.

Chapter Twenty-Five

27th May, 1940

Dear Evelyn,

I hope this letter finds you safe and well. Has Rob reached you yet? He was trying to contact you the other day to discuss the fun side of your family. I hope you were able to set his mind at ease. He's been rather worried about them.

We've been patrolling over France several times a day. I can't tell you anything more, but we've been seeing more and more of the Luftwaffe every day. I've shot down three 109s so far. I've been trying for a Stuka, but I haven't managed one yet. The Yank is doing well. He's got three to his credit as well. We both bagged our third today. We're all rather chuffed over it. The ground crew have a pool going on who will end with the most confirmed kills. I've heard that yours truly is at the top of the betting. It's strange having blokes put money down on you. I think perhaps they'd be better off spending it at the pub, but I have no say in what they do.

We've been seeing quite a bit of action now. We lost our first pilot. His name was Perry, and he was brand new. I met him briefly when he first arrived. He only had fifteen hours in a Spit when he came to us. I don't think he made it past twenty hours before he bought it. He was the tail-end Charlie. Chris refuses to fly that position. He says it's where you go to die. Perry was new, but he was a fair pilot. It took two of the bastards to bring him down. I was trying to get there to help, but I had a pair on my tail as well. I can't help thinking I should have been able to do more, but the CO says that's nonsense.

They're bloody fast, the Messerschmitts. But so is the Spitfire, so please don't worry about us. We can outmaneuver them fairly easily. Their main danger is that they like to jump a bloke from the sun where we can't see them coming.

I had a letter from old Barnaby yesterday. You remember him, don't you? You met him briefly at the pub when you came in with all the pilots from your station. He joined the

Into the Iron Shadows

RAF in the bombers. It turns out he finally went on his first mission a few weeks ago. He was very excited about the whole thing. He remembered you and asked after you. Told me to send his regards. Consider them sent.

We're off again early in the morning, so I need to turn out the light. We're flying several times a day and start at an ungodly hour. Today it was four-thirty in the morning. Indecent hour no matter which way you look at it.

One last bit of news is that I'm moving stations again. We're relocating on the 29ᵗʰ. I had a feeling we wouldn't be here long. So just as we're settling in, we're off again.

I think of you every day, and pray that you're well. Please take care of yourself and write when you can. I look forward to your letters.

Always yours,

FO Miles Lacey

London

Bill dropped the folded newspaper on his desk before stripping off his gloves and unbuttoning his overcoat. He stared at the headline as he removed the coat.

BELGIUM SURRENDERS.

So it had happened at last. He'd been waiting for it since Rotterdam, but the Belgians had held on as long as they could. Now they'd obviously reached the end.

He turned to hang his coat on the rack near the door. With Belgium out of it, and France rapidly losing ground against the overwhelming assault of the Nazi troops, England was fast becoming Hitler's final opponent. They would soon be the last country able and willing to stand against him.

Bill turned to go back to his desk, suddenly very tired despite the early hour. Winston had mobilized the navy and every vessel that could still hold water, as well as some that couldn't by some accounts, across to Dunkirk to begin evacuating the troops from the beach. The operation had begun the day before with the RAF flying air cover above while boats and ships of all sizes, from paddle boats to navy

229

destroyers, began ferrying Allied soldiers across the Channel to the relative safety of England. No one thought they would succeed in rescuing all the soldiers in Dunkirk. There were too many of them, and the Battle for Dunkirk was raging around the perimeter as German forces tried to breach the town before the evacuation could be completed.

Sinking into his chair, Bill rubbed his eyes and then picked up the newspaper, unfolding it to scan the article. With Belgium's surrender, the northern flank was now gone. There was nowhere else to run. The evacuation had to work, or England would lose over two hundred thousand of her best troops, almost the entire British Expeditionary Force, along with over one hundred thousand other Allied troops. How would they resist Hitler and his Nazi thugs then? With the Home Guard? He dropped the paper and sat back in his chair. They were made up of old-timers from the last war and young men with medical conditions that precluded them serving in this one. The navy and air force were their last hope if Operation Dynamo failed.

Despite the overwhelming response from civilians who had heard what was happening, and had begun to join the convoys across the Channel, they were still short on boats. Several were making multiple trips, if they survived the first one. The response was tremendous, but no one knew if it would be enough. Hell, if Montclair would let him, he'd take his own yacht across the Channel to try to get the boys home.

Bill chuckled despite his grim mood. He could only imagine Jasper's face if he suggested it. He would be appalled. The chuckle faded and Bill tapped his chin thoughtfully. He couldn't take the *Daydream* himself, but someone else certainly could. He had any number of experienced sailors working for him. One of them would probably be more than willing to join the effort.

He was just reaching for the telephone when Wesley knocked briefly before entering, carrying a tray with a stack of folders and a pot of tea.

"Good morning, sir," he said cheerfully. "I've brought the morning briefings. How was your evening last night? Did you enjoy the theatre?"

"I didn't go," Bill said, dialing. "Just set that over there, will you? Hello, Ethan? Ethan, is that you? Yes. Will you track down Larry Whitmore and have him give me a ring? Yes. Right. Thanks!"

He hung up and watched as Wesley carried the stack of folders over to place them on the desk.

"Did Mrs. Buckley change her mind, then?"

"What? Oh, right. The theatre. Yes, we decided to have a late dinner instead. I'm afraid I was late leaving here again." Bill reached for the top folder. "I'm very blessed to have an understanding wife. Wesley, if you ever decide you want to settle down, make sure it's to a woman who understands the demands of government life. Her worth is far above anything you could imagine."

"Yes, sir." Wesley glanced at the newspaper on the desk. "I see you've seen the news."

"Yes."

Wesley hesitated, as if he wanted to say something more, but then turned to leave. Bill glanced up when he was halfway to the door.

"What's on your mind, Wesley?"

The young assistant paused, then turned back, his face troubled.

"I'm worried about my brother, sir. The last we heard they were in Belgium, near Ghent. Now that Belgium has surrendered, if he hasn't withdrawn to France and Dunkirk…" His voice trailed off and he shrugged. "I'm not sure which would be worse. For him to be stuck as a prisoner of war, or to be stuck on a beach being bombed by the Germans."

Bill sat back in his chair. "He was near Ghent, you say?"

Wesley nodded.

"I'll see if I can find out where they are. They would have pulled back when the order was given, but I know some of our troops are still in Belgium. I'll try to track down his outfit for you."

"I do appreciate that, sir. It's my mother more than me. She's beside herself."

"I understand. If it offers you comfort, I heard that we pulled over seven thousand men out of Dunkirk yesterday. If he is there, he may have been one of them. Keep your chin up and carry on. It's all we can do."

"Yes, sir."

He turned to leave and Bill sat forward again. After he'd closed the door, Bill lifted his eyes from the brief before him and considered the closed door thoughtfully. Wesley had never wavered in his duties, and he was a bright young man. He had become invaluable over the past months.

Bill reached for the phone. The least he could do was set his mind at rest, regardless of what the news would be.

Eisenjager lit a cigarette and shifted in his seat, stifling a yawn. He'd managed to sleep a few hours when the gray Renault pulled off the road and stayed put for the night. It was the first time they had stopped for more than an hour, and at first he wondered how the man was driving constantly without rest. Then he realized that he wasn't. He was sharing the driving with the Englishwoman. While one drove, the other rested. Eisenjager didn't have that luxury. Thankfully, he had a tube of Pervitin in his arsenal. The little pills were amazing things; they gave you energy for days. He rarely found the need to use them, but they had been invaluable over the past week. Even so, he had been beginning to feel the strain of not sleeping when the Renault ahead had finally stopped for the night. They must have both been exhausted after the destruction caused by the Stukas.

He rolled down his window and blew smoke out, his eyes on the car several meters in front of him. The Stukas had been an unexpected and unpleasant surprise. He had seen them coming while he was relieving his bladder. They were unmistakable, even from a distance, to any Wehrmacht soldier. His car was already off the road, so all he had to do was take cover and wait it out. His primary concern in those tense minutes behind a row of hedges was that the Luftwaffe would rob him of his target. And so it had been with as close to relief as he was capable of feeling that he'd seen Jian and her companions alive and moving among the wounded.

Approaching her had been reckless, he admitted now. He considered the events in the road with a complete lack of self-recrimination or embarrassment, but rather with a detached sense of interest. It was uncharacteristic of him to do something so foolish. It was never a good idea to let your target see you, let alone talk to them. His job was to be effective and invisible. He'd built his entire reputation around the fact that he had learned to become invisible, even when standing right before a person. He was a legend. A myth. All because his targets never saw him coming, and no one else ever remembered seeing him at all. He was a ghost, and had worked hard to become one.

Why, then, had he felt compelled to meet the English spy? To talk to her? To help her help an old man?

He shook his head and sucked on his cigarette, inching along with the column of vehicles past the slower moving carts and people on foot. He had no explanation. He'd seen an opportunity to learn more about his mark, and he'd taken it without thinking. Now he simply had to hope that she, too, would forget all about him as hundreds of others had.

Jian had been a surprise to him. He knew everything his handlers in Hamburg had been able to find out about her, and had observed her from a distance in Oslo. He'd followed her across Norway, learning how resourceful she could be. She had slipped away from him in Marle without a trace. He knew she was slippery, intelligent, and not afraid to take risks. That should have been enough for him. Yet, he had felt compelled to learn more about this adversary of his, and what he'd learned was more than he'd been expecting.

That she was a new agent had been evident from the beginning. The mistakes she made were cringe-worthy to a seasoned veteran such as himself. And yet, she was learning very quickly. In the past week he'd seen many improvements since those days in Norway. She was more confident now, and much more cautious; both things she had no doubt learned through experience. The fact that she had learned them so quickly was alarming. With each passing day that she remained in the field, she became more difficult to pin down, and more of a threat.

His lips tightened briefly, then he lifted the cigarette to his mouth again. He had been told to stand down for now, and it had given him the opportunity to actually speak to her and learn that she was flawless in her accent. No small feat, that. He had studied French under a master, then had been sent to live in Metz for a year. Even so, he knew he still had an accent. It was why he used Switzerland as his country of origin in almost all of his aliases. If circumstances made Zürich unwise or dangerous, he claimed to be from Liechtenstein. Yet Jian had no accent. He knew she was from England, but she sounded as though she had been born and raised in Paris. It was amazing to him. No wonder Hans Voss had been duped in Strasbourg. Eisenjager wasn't confident that he would not have been fooled himself.

More than the accent, though, he had been most impressed with her strength in assisting the men and women after the Stukas attacked. While others were in shock and crying over the blood, she had quietly gone about helping where needed. Even when her hands were cut open by the old man's cart, she had simply wrapped them and continued on. It was the kind of strength that could not be taught in any classroom or on any training ground. It was the kind of thing you either had, or you didn't. He'd seen enough men crumble in the brutal face of battle to know that no amount of training could prepare anyone for the stink of death.

And that made her a most formidable foe indeed, for she would not bend to pressure. He had seen it in her blue eyes yesterday. The sorrow had quickly turned to anger and determination, and that was the most dangerous reaction of all. There was no controlling that. Once she was fully comfortable and seasoned in her position with the intelligence underworld, she would be nearly impossible to find, especially with that accent. He had no doubt that she could adopt the accent of any region of France. She would blend in, and disappear. And it wasn't only France. Their information said she also spoke German. If her German was as good as her French, they were in serious trouble indeed.

He had to eliminate her now, while they still had the opportunity.

Eisenjager threw his cigarette away and reached for the canteen laying on the seat beside him. Perhaps it would have been better if she *had* perished in the attack yesterday. Then it would have been done, and he wouldn't have broken his orders.

At the thought of the attack, he frowned, unscrewing the lid of the canteen and raising it to his lips. He had seen death before. He was an instrument of death himself. But the sight of women, children, men, and animals, all mowed down in the matter of a few minutes had been jarring.

Once it was clear that Jian and her companions were helping others, he'd had no choice but to do so as well. To have sat in his car and done nothing would have drawn more attention. But by helping move dead horses and corpses out of the road, he had been reminded of darker days when he was still in the Sicherheitsdienst. Death was never pretty or dignified, but yesterday it had also seemed so meaningless. There was no tactical reason to attack civilians, except to spread fear. He understood the theory behind it all too well. He employed it himself when necessary, but that didn't mean he necessarily agreed with it.

He replaced the cap and set the steel bottle down again, pursing his lips thoughtfully. He didn't disagree with it, either. He just found it a waste of resources. There were far better ways to command the attention and fear of a population without killing masses indiscriminately. But the Führer was more interested in expediency, and yesterday had been nothing if not expedient. The refugee columns had come to a halt and many of them had changed directions as soon as they were able. Knowing how his high command operated, Eisenjager was willing to bet that the new flow of refugees would interfere with the troop movements of the remaining French forces. More clogged roads meant divisions would wait longer for reinforcements and supplies.

He thought of the old man and the grave he'd dug for his wife. He didn't know why he'd done that. Something about the stoic grief in the old man had reminded him of something long forgotten. It had drawn him away from the Englishwoman, whom he was already regretting meeting face to face, and from the carnage left on the road. The manual labor had felt good after sitting in a car for days, and the old man had been very grateful. Eisenjager glanced at his wrist, and the watch that the old man had insisted he take as payment. He had a perfectly good watch. He didn't know why he was wearing it, except that it had made the old man feel as if he wasn't completely useless in the face of his wife's death.

Eisenjager pressed his lips together and turned his attention back to the gray car, still inching forward ahead of him. None of that was relevant to the problem facing him in that vehicle. She would have to be dealt with before she became an insurmountable threat. He had contacted Hamburg yesterday from his wireless radio, as instructed, but had been told to continue as he was until she reached her destination. They wanted to know where she was going, but what did it matter? She was a threat. She was a threat that they had recognized must be dealt with, so why the sudden delay? What was the spy from London up to?

What was Hamburg waiting for?

RAF Horsham

Miles glanced up from his plate at the startled exclamation from Rob. He raised an eyebrow questioningly.

"Bad news?" he asked, his eyes dropping to the letter in Rob's hand.

"What? Oh, no. Well, yes. They're out of their minds, completely out of their minds."

Rob tossed the letter down next to his plate and picked up his knife and fork. They had spent most of the day in the air over Dunkirk, and were both hungry and tired. It wasn't the best time to be bothered with letters bringing less than joyful tidings. Miles watched him cut into his food for a moment, then went back to his own dinner.

"Whom?" he asked.

"My cousins. The ones in France. You remember, I told you

about them."

"The fun ones?"

He let out a short laugh. "Those are the ones."

Miles glanced up after a moment when he didn't continue. "Is the letter from them?"

"No. It's from my mother. Remember I told you that I thought my aunt and uncle were coming to England?"

"Yes. Has that changed?"

"Yes. Well, no. That is, they're still coming, but apparently my cousins aren't," Rob said. "They want to stay in France."

Miles cocked an eyebrow. "They do realize the Germans will be in Paris within a month?"

"Well they should. My uncle certainly does. He and my aunt are leaving tomorrow. They expect to be in London in a few days. They're coming over on a private yacht with some friends of theirs." He laid down his knife and fork and reached for his glass. "My mother writes that they will stay in our house in London for a few days while my uncle arranges his affairs. Then they'll join her at Ainsworth."

"Without their children?"

Rob nodded, his face creased in a scowl. "Apparently so. They will remain in France."

Miles was silent, going back to his dinner. There really wasn't much to say. They certainly had every right to remain, regardless of any potential danger. He wondered if Evelyn knew. She was close to her cousins. She was bound to be upset when she heard that they had refused the opportunity to leave and come to England.

"Any idea why they're staying?" he finally asked.

"Not the faintest. If I had to lay a wager on it, I'd say they have something up their sleeves. They usually do."

"Such as?"

"Oh, God only knows! They were always getting into trouble, and they haven't changed as they've got older. No sense of caution at all with those two." Rob looked up with a sudden grin. "They used to drag Evelyn right along with them until she grew more sense."

Miles smiled faintly. "That surprises me."

"That Evelyn used to get into trouble?"

"No. That she grew some sense."

That drew a bark of laughter from Rob. "There's a reason we call them the fun ones. Several reasons, in fact. They've settled down over the past few years, I admit, but they both still look for trouble."

Miles tilted his head thoughtfully. "And you think that's why they've chosen to remain in France?"

"Well I can't think of any other reason to stay. They're both reckless, but they're not stupid. They know France will fall. My guess is that they've decided to stay and do whatever they can to disrupt the Germans."

"You're talking about resistance."

"Yes."

"But that's tantamount to suicide!"

He nodded glumly. "I've told you, they've always had a penchant for getting themselves into trouble. Usually Evelyn was the one to pull them out again, but she won't be there this time."

Miles finished his dinner quietly. He didn't know what words he could offer to set Rob's mind at ease. When France fell, and it would fall, the Nazis would take complete control. Nowhere would be safe, especially for anyone whom the Germans suspected of organizing any form of resistance. As Rob had said, his cousins were clearly out of their minds.

"Of course, I could have it all wrong," Rob said a few minutes later, pushing away his empty plate. "They may still come yet. My uncle has extensive assets and properties in the south of France. Perhaps they're staying behind to try to arrange things before the Germans come and seize them. They may follow later."

"Your mother gives no indication of why they aren't coming?"

"No. She does seem dreadfully upset over it though."

"I imagine she would be."

"She writes that she and Auntie Agatha are going to London so they can be there to meet them when they arrive. She's having dinner with the Buckleys while she's there." Rob sat back, wiping his mouth with a napkin. "You remember them, I'm sure. They stayed with us at Christmas."

"Yes, of course. Sir William is friendly with my father. Same club, I believe."

"Marguerite, his wife, always cheers Mummy up. She's also from France, you know. She'll understand more than anyone, I expect." Rob threw his napkin on the table and exhaled loudly. "I just can't imagine what they're thinking."

"Have you got hold of your sister? What does she say?"

He made a face and pulled out his cigarettes. "I haven't spoken to her. I never did manage to get a firm answer on where she is. I've written a letter to her at Northolt, but had no reply yet."

"Well, I wouldn't worry too much. She does seem to move around quite a bit, but that's her job. She never stays in the same place for long, but she always ends up back at Northolt." Miles pushed his chair back and stood. "Come on," he said. "Let's go have a pint before I go to bed. I'm completely knackered."

"Then why are we going to have a pint?" Rob asked, standing.

"I'm never too tired for a beer."

Chapter Twenty-Six

May 29th
5am

"'Tally ho! Four o'clock!'"

Miles pulled his gaze from the cloud cover above him and looked down to his right. There, far below them, was a group of Dornier 17s. After one more searching glance for their escort, he broke right and dove down with the others to attack the light bombers. They had arrived over Dunkirk only moments before, armed with the knowledge that there had already been several reports of bombing in and around Dunkirk overnight and into this morning. Their briefing before leaving England had been short and clear: stop the bastards any way possible.

As he dove down towards the group of bombers, Miles glanced up behind him again. Where there were bombers, there were fighters. Yet he hadn't seen any.

"Does anyone see their escort?" he asked into his radio.

"Not a thing," Rob answered cheerfully. "Take aim!"

"Watch for them," Mother warned. "They're here somewhere."

Miles picked out a bomber on the end and pressed the firing button on his steering column as he zoomed towards it. He released the button and cut to the right as the gunners returned fire, coming around to approach from behind.

"Got one!" Chris cried as one of the bombers fell out of formation, smoke pouring from the right engine. "It's easier than shooting pigeons at Coney Island!"

Miles' grin at the excitement in his voice was short lived. As he flew up behind his target, the gunners returned fire again and he rolled into a dive to avoid it. Coming up beneath the tail, he blinked and refocused on the left fuselage. It wouldn't get any more picture perfect than that. He was in perfect position to take out the engine, and he pressed the button on the column. His aircraft shuddered as the guns in his wings let loose, and he watched in confusion as the bullets streamed past the engine, missing completely.

"Damn!"

He broke away and arched up to come around again, scowling. That was a perfect shot! The engine was right in the center of his sight mounted on the dash. How the hell had he missed?

As Miles looped around to take another crack it, the answer hit him like a gut punch. He'd been too close to the bomber. His guns were calibrated for 450 yards. He'd been much, much closer. He grit his teeth and repositioned himself further away, avoiding the return fire easily. Trying to shoot from that distance was ridiculous, but he swung in and tried to get the bomber positioned in his cross-hairs once again.

"Miles! Three o'clock!" Rob suddenly cried, just as Miles pressed the button on his column.

At the same time that his bullets tore into the right side engine of the Dornier, Miles felt his Spitfire jerk violently to the left, and the airplane shuddered, sending painful vibrations up his arms from the control stick. Black smoke began pouring out of his nose and Miles automatically pulled left, breaking away from the bombers.

"I'm hit," he announced, surprised at how calm his voice sounded. "All gauges are functioning. I'm making for home."

"Save me some tea," Chris said.

"Red Three, escort him back," Mother commanded. "Keep the bastards off of him."

"Roger that, Red One," Rob said, appearing off Miles' right wing a moment later. Miles looked over to find him examining his plane as they flew towards the Channel. "You're hit near your fuel tank," he told him, "and in the wing."

Miles looked at his fuel gauge and let out a low curse. "I'm losing fuel," he said grimly. "Rudder is working, but the coolant needle is rising. He must have hit the radiator as well. Damn!"

Miles checked his other gauges and a dull feeling of shock went through him. It had really happened. He'd been hit, and his Spitfire wasn't going to get him back to England. He began taking stock of all the instruments, noting how long he had before he was out of fuel or the engine overheated.

"I won't make it back. I'm losing fuel too quickly. I'll take her down and see if I can set her in the water," he said, looking over at Rob. Then he stiffened at the sight of two 109s diving towards them. "Fighters! One o'clock!"

"I'll take care of them," Rob said, breaking right. "Get your kite down. Do try not to die, won't you? I'd hate to explain it to Evie."

Miles choked on a laugh as he pushed his stick forward. "I'll do my best, Rob. Thanks!"

He looked up in time to see Rob disappear into the clouds above, drawing the two fighters away from him. Taking a deep breath, Miles turned his attention back to his instruments. He should be over water by now. He could try to do as he'd said and land in the drink without killing himself, or he could turn back inland and try to put her down on a beach. He was losing fuel rapidly, but he thought he should have enough to make it to land.

He came out of the low clouds and blinked at the sudden glare of early morning sunlight glistening off the waves of the Channel. To his right, he saw the coast. Taking another look at the choppy waves below, Miles swallowed. He was a good pilot, but he didn't know if he was that good. If he tried to land on the water, and he dipped a wing one way or another, he ran the risk of the airplane breaking up before he could get out of the cockpit. A sudden image of Evelyn flashed across his mind and Miles clenched his jaw, turning his nose towards the shoreline. He would take his chances over land.

As he came over the coast and turned north, looking for a stretch of beach where he could put it down, Miles glanced at his instruments again. Shaking his head, his gut clenched. Needles were in the red, both for fuel and engine temperature, and the whole airplane was shaking violently now, the engine sputtering. Struggling to keep the wings up and steady, Miles felt his hands begin to tremble. It was taking all his arm strength to keep the Spitfire level, and he knew he didn't have much time. He had to get it down.

Spotting a clear, straight stretch of sand, he steered towards it, sweat beading on his forehead. As he descended, the sun beat into the cockpit, briefly blinding him. Miles squeezed his eyes shut and opened them again, trying to focus on the white strip below. Suddenly, there was a violent jerk and his propellers sputtered, then began missing rotation until, with a less violent shudder, they stopped altogether.

Miles worked the rudders, trying to keep the nose up and the wings level as his airplane coasted towards the beach. The sudden silence was the loudest and most terrifying sound he'd ever heard, and as he lowered the landing gear, Miles realized that he was completely alone. There was no ground crew below to rush out with the fire hoses, nor any fellow pilots to help him out of the stricken airplane. His survival depended entirely on him.

Sweat poured down his face, and his heart was pounding as he watched the sand getting closer. He was going too fast, but had no way to control it without his engine. All he could do was keep her as steady and level as possible.

And pray.

There was no thought for anything except fighting to keep the wings even as the ground rushed up to meet the Spitfire. There was no thought of Evelyn, or his parents, or even the rest of the squadron still battling above. There was no thought for anything except to land, and to survive.

The impact came all at once, stopping his rapid descent with a bone-jarring crash. His wheels hit the wet sand near the water and stuck, the forward momentum sending the nose of the plane into the sand. Miles felt the air get sucked out of his lungs as his body flew forward, driving against his restraints. He saw his instrument panel, and then a flash of blinding light.

And everything went black.

Outside Saint-Émilion, France

Evelyn sipped her water and stared out over the river. The sky had lightened and the sun was just beginning to cast streaks across the rippling waves. They had arrived in Saint-Émilion late last night. After skirting the city, Finn had stopped near the river, too tired to continue. Josephine had suggested they stay there for the night, and in the morning get breakfast in the city. After some discussion, he'd agreed.

Evelyn glanced back at the car. He was still asleep in the driver's seat, his head resting on his folded up jacket against the window.

"He's still sleeping?" Josephine asked, joining her.

Evelyn nodded. "Yes."

Josephine stretched and looked over the water. "We'll be in Bordeaux by late morning," she said, pulling out a cigarette. "There shouldn't be any delays between here and there. Once we turned towards Saint-Émilion, we left most of the refugees behind. I think everyone is going as far away as they can."

"Thank goodness for that." Evelyn finished drinking her water and shook the remaining drops out of the earthenware mug. "I'm looking forward to a coffee and something other than cold potatoes."

Josephine chuckled. "I agree. We're far enough away from the fighting now; the cafés will be open. I don't know what they'll think of us, with our rumpled clothing, but I don't really care, do you?"

"Not a bit."

They were quiet for a moment, watching the waves and

enjoying the soft morning breeze, then Josephine sighed.

"It's surreal to think that further north buildings are being ripped apart by bombs, and all hell is breaking loose," she said. "Look at how quiet and peaceful it is! No bomber formations flying overhead. Nothing to interrupt the dawn, or the start of a perfect day."

Evelyn was silent, thinking of the news headlines they had seen yesterday when they left the crowded road and went through a small village. Belgium had surrendered. France and England were on their own now, and the Germans were driving them all to the beaches. There would be nowhere for the troops to go. All those men, trapped on the beaches in northern France, with no escape. She could only imagine the horror and chaos as the German troops bombarded them.

"How long will France hold on now that Belgium has surrendered?" she murmured. "Soon it will not be so peaceful, even here."

"I know. They will take Paris, and then it will be over. And then the real war will begin for us."

Evelyn glanced at her. "The real war?"

"Yes. Not the one between armies, but the one between soldiers and civilians."

A shudder went through her and Evelyn turned her gaze back to the calm waves of the Dordogne River. Once again, she was preparing to leave while her friend was preparing to remain behind and fight. How many times would she have to do this? Say goodbye to friends, knowing that they were about to enter hell?

"Will you come into Bordeaux with us?" she asked after a moment.

"I will take you into the city, but then I will leave you. It's best that no one remembers seeing us together. We'll find the café, and I'll leave you within walking distance."

"If you'd rather leave us outside the city, we can find our way," Evelyn said. "You don't have to take us all the way in."

Josephine smiled and shook her head. "No. I said I would see you to Bordeaux, not to just outside. Besides, I don't think anyone will look twice at a woman dropping off two people in the middle of the city. It's only if I stay with you that it will become dangerous for me."

"What will you do?"

"I'll find somewhere to stay for the night, have a hot bath, and sleep," Josephine said promptly. "And then, tomorrow, I will decide where to look for work. I may come back here," she added, looking around. "I prefer to be outside of the cities. I find I can breathe easier."

"I pray you find work and a place to live quickly," Evelyn said, linking her arm through Josephine's and squeezing. "I will forever be grateful for your company and help this past week."

"I will forever be grateful that you did the driving so that I only had to read the map," Josephine replied with a grin.

Evelyn laughed and turned to look at the car. "We should wake Finn. It's getting late."

Josephine nodded and the two women started walking back to the car.

"I will miss you, Evelyn," she said suddenly. "Do you know, I don't think I've called you by your name since Strasbourg? Each time we meet, you're using a different one!"

"I appreciate your discretion," Evelyn said with a laugh.

"I wonder who you will be the next time I see you? Giselle, perhaps?"

"Perhaps." Evelyn's smile faded. They were speaking as if they would definitely see each other again, and yet they were both aware that they may not. "I will miss you too, Josephine."

"Ah, don't forget, it's Jeannine now!" Josephine said with a wink. Then she sobered and stopped, turning to face her. "Promise me that you will get back to England," she said, her voice low and urgent. "Promise me that you will continue to fight for us, even when we can no longer fight for ourselves."

Evelyn met her gaze and saw her own fear and uncertainty reflected in the gray eyes staring back at her. They had no idea what was in their future, or if they even had a future. The attack on the road had driven home the realization that it only took a minute for everything to end. If one of them failed, the other would continue for as long as they could. And, hopefully, one day they would see an end to the iron storm consuming Europe. Until then, all they could do was fight.

"I promise."

Henry walked through the train station towards the entrance to the street. Before leaving Paris, he'd learned everything he could about the old farmer's daughter. After contacting an associate in the French Ministry of Foreign Affairs, he'd been able to determine that the woman's name was Isabelle Decoux. It had been three more days before his associate had been able to provide a current address.

As he'd expected, his office in London had approved a few days for him to say goodbye to France. Their only stipulation was that he had to be back in London by the beginning of June. He had plenty of time. Even waiting three days for an address hadn't dampened his mood. Henry was on the trail of someone who might lead to the package Ainsworth had smuggled out of Austria. He would be able to deliver on his promise to Berlin at last.

Stepping out onto the street, he looked around and turned to walk up the pavement. He would find a café, order a coffee, and see if there was someone who could point him in the right direction. The sun was shining, the breeze was gentle, and it was going to be a good morning. Women hurried along the pavement with him, doing their morning shopping, and cars moved along the road as if it were a normal Wednesday on any normal week. He marveled at the difference between this city and the one he'd just left. The only traffic in the streets of Paris these days were cars and trucks piled high with cases, boxes, and furniture, leaving the city. There was the occasional taxi, but even those had dwindled over the past three days. The city was virtually deserted now, until you reached the train station. Then it seemed as if all the remaining residents of Paris were crammed onto the platforms, waiting for another train to carry them away. The trains were constantly running at full capacity as citizens continued to flee the capital.

Of course, it was bound to happen. Once the Germans broke through at Sedan, the panic had begun. The people of Paris knew that the Nazis were coming, despite their government's assurances that they would win the battle for France. Henry shook his head. The citizens of Paris had more sense than their government. What they didn't realize was that there was nowhere they could go. The German armies would win the battle, and take Paris, and then take France. No matter where all these refugees landed, in the end, they would be under German control. It was inevitable.

Spying a café across the road, Henry went to the corner and waited for the light to change. Once he'd had a coffee and perhaps a pastry, he would find Isabelle Decoux. He'd already decided that he would present himself as an old associate of her father's. He knew enough about the farmer to be able to converse believably about him, and perhaps gain her trust as an old friend of the family. It shouldn't be too difficult to get her talking about the old homestead. And, of course, then he would soon learn why she had gone back, and what, if anything, she'd brought away.

In a few hours, he would know if Ainsworth had left anything behind in Blasenflue.

Chapter Twenty-Seven

Miles became aware of the smell first. It was a smell he recognized, but caught in the throes of a hazy state of semi-consciousness, he couldn't quite remember why. Where did he remember it from? Was it at Oxford? On the farm in York, perhaps? No. This smell had nothing to do with the country. It was from somewhere else. Somewhere busy and crowded. What *was* it?

The haziness was dissipating now, and he slowly became aware of something dripping down his face. He lifted his arm to wipe it away, frowning when his arm wouldn't move.

All at once, the darkness disappeared as a shock went through his body. He saw the beach again, coming towards him much too fast. His propellers sputtered and then stopped.

Good Lord, he had crashed!

His heart started pounding and his skin went hot, then cold, with the recollection. Pain flooded his body with the memory, throbbing in every muscle and making him inhale sharply. Miles forced his eyes open, squinting against the blinding sunlight. He was still in the cockpit, buckled into his seat. His head had fallen forward and hit the instrument panel, trapping one arm between his body and the door. His other arm seemed to be hanging at an odd angle and Miles frowned, lifting his head. Blood was smeared across the instrument panel, but that wasn't what made him suck in his breath again. It was the excruciating pain shooting down his arm and, as he sat up, he realized that it was hanging at an odd angle because he couldn't move it at all. The muscles weren't working; they were screaming with pain instead. Lifting his left arm, he gingerly felt his right wrist, then started working his way up the arm. He must have broken it in the crash. *Well, if I walk away from this with no more than a broken arm, I'll call that a perfect landing.*

He reached his shoulder and squeezed his eyes shut, gritting his teeth as fire shot through his shoulder and neck. His arm wasn't broken. His shoulder was dislocated. Gasping in pain, he reached for the buckles to unstrap himself with his left hand. He had to try to get his shoulder back in, but he had no idea how. The only other time this had happened, he'd been fourteen and playing rugby at Eaton. One of the coaches had done it on the sideline and he'd gone back into the game. He was a long way from Eaton now.

Miles had just finished unbuckling himself when he suddenly recognized the smell that had been filling his nostrils since he woke up. His eyes flew to the right wing, a wave of fear crashing over him. Gasoline! The smell was burning gasoline! Smoke was still pouring out of the engine and he looked at his gauges. They were all in the red, and the temperature needle had buried itself.

"Bugger!"

Miles fumbled with the canopy, trying to get it open with only one hand. As he did, the smell in the cockpit suddenly changed, turning almost acrid. Flames appeared on the wing, and Miles swore, pushing on the canopy with all his strength, his eyes on the orange flames licking around the wing and towards the cockpit.

Sheer panic gave him strength and the cracked canopy suddenly gave way, sliding back. A rush of salt air and heavy smoke surged into the cockpit, making his eyes burn and water. The smoke filled his lungs, making him choke and cough, but Miles ignored it and opened the half door next to him, standing to climb out. His limp arm hung useless as he scrambled onto the wing just as the flames reached the other side of the cockpit.

He leapt off the wing to land in the sand heavily, stumbling as he did so. Behind him, he heard a loud pop and then an ungodly creak that sounded as if the entire Spitfire was breaking in half. Miles spun around to see that the flames had already engulfed the entire cockpit, spreading faster than he would have ever dreamt possible.

Holding his useless arm against his stomach with his good one, Miles turned and ran, willing his flying boots to not get stuck in the sand. Hearing a small explosion behind him, he forced himself to go faster, putting as much distance between himself and the burning airplane as possible. Suddenly, a deafening explosion caused him to stumble forward. Turning, he watched as a ball of flame shot towards the sky before settling back to consume the entire aircraft.

He stared at the burning wreckage of his Spitfire through streaming eyes, his heart thumping against his chest and his blood pounding in his ears. Numbness stole over him and Miles couldn't tear his eyes away from the sight. He had just barely got out. Another few seconds, and he would be charred along with his plane. A few precious seconds was all that had saved his life.

"Hallo!! Hallo!! Jij daar!"

The sound of yelling made it through the noise of the roaring fire and Miles turned around in confusion to see two soldiers running towards him, their rifles pointed at him. He held up his good arm, his bad one hanging at an impossible angle at his side. He recognized the language as Dutch, but he had no idea what they were yelling as they ran towards him.

"I'm English," he called in French, hoping they could understand him. "Do you speak French?"

"Oui," one of them said, drawing up before him, panting. "We speak French."

"I'm an English pilot," Miles said, eyeing the rifles, then the uniforms. They were Belgian soldiers. "I just crashed on the beach."

"We saw you come down," the other soldier said, lowering his weapon. "Are you hurt?"

"My shoulder. I think it's dislocated."

The soldier nodded and slung his rifle over his shoulder. "Come. I can put it back in."

"What?" Miles stared at him in apprehension. "How?"

The other man laughed at the look on his face. "It is all right. He is a medic. But let's get away from the fire and off the beach. I do not trust the Germans. That will draw their attention."

He turned to lead them across the sand to the dunes.

"Germans? There are troops nearby?" Miles asked in alarm, following. He looked at the medic walking beside him. "Where are we?"

"This is Saint-Idesbald. You are south of Ostend," he said. "There are German troops everywhere, but what my friend meant is that they are bombing everywhere. If they see the burning, they will come and bomb here. We must move away from it." He frowned. "Your head is also hurt, not just your shoulder."

Miles lifted his hand to touch the blood on his face. "I'd forgotten. I hit my head when I landed."

"I will do what I can, but my supplies are limited. My name is Antoine."

"Miles." Miles held out his good hand to have it gripped in a surprisingly firm shake.

"That is Raf," Antoine added, nodding to the man ahead of them.

Raf waved a hand in acknowledgement, never turning his head.

"There is a port in Ostend, isn't there?" Miles asked as they made their way over the dune. "How long will it take to get there?"

"To Ostend?" Antoine stared at him. "No. You do not want to go to Ostend. The Germans have overrun the city. You don't want to go that way."

Into the Iron Shadows

"South," Raf said over his shoulder. "You want to go south."

They reached the top of the dune and Miles saw a road below. He grit his teeth in pain, holding his arm as they half slid, half jogged down the side of the dune until they reached the solid ground.

"What's south?" he asked, short of breath from the pain.

"France," came the dry answer. "You are about seven kilometers from the border. If you go to France, you can try for Dunkirk."

Miles couldn't stop himself from letting out a laugh.

"This is funny?"

"I was flying over Dunkirk when I was shot," he explained. "We're trying to keep the bombers and fighters away from the beach."

Both soldiers nodded knowingly.

"Then you already know that is your only chance of getting back to your squadron," Raf said, stopping and turning to look at him. "Belgium is lost, and France will fall soon as well. That is your only hope."

Miles nodded and looked down the road. "This way?" he asked, pointing.

Raf nodded. "This road goes along the coast to the border. Once there, just follow the other soldiers."

"But first, let me fix your shoulder," Antoine said. "And I will clean the gash on your head."

"Be quick," Raf warned. "We must catch up with the others."

Antoine nodded, waving away the warning. "Yes, yes. I will be quick."

Miles swallowed and allowed the man to ease his Mae West over his head, gritting his teeth as his shoulder was jarred in the process.

"Thank you. I do appreciate this."

"We must take your flight jacket off. Here. I will help. It will hurt."

Antoine helped ease the heavy leather coat off Miles' shoulders. He was as careful as possible, but Miles sucked in his breath and felt dizzy with the pain just the same.

"Bloody hell," he muttered, drawing a short laugh from the medic.

"You're doing much better than the last man I had with a dislocation. He was screaming bloody murder and fainted dead away," he informed him, laying the jacket over the Mae West on the ground. He eyed Miles' uniform jacket and shook his head. "That has to go as well. Do you need a minute, or shall we continue?"

Miles grit his teeth and shook his head. "Let's get it over with."

Antoine helped him off with his uniform jacket, then nodded.

"I can do it now. You are very lucky these are your only injuries," Antoine said, moving in front of him and lifting his forearm until it was parallel to the ground. "Try to relax."

Despite his gentle touch, pain was already streaking down Miles' arm when the medic rotated his forearm away from his body. Keeping one hand on his arm, Antoine moved his other to his bicep and began to rotate his upper arm away from his torso. Without warning, the joint popped back into place. Miles let out an exclamation before clamping his teeth shut just in time to stop from screaming in pain.

"There. It is done. That was not so bad, right?" Antoine moved in front of him again and produced a cloth from his pouch at his side. He began dabbing at Miles' forehead while Miles sucked in his breath, pain still throbbing through his arm and shoulder. "This looks worse than it is. It's not deep. I will clean it. I have no more bandages, but perhaps we can use your tie?"

"My tie?" Miles repeated, appalled. "I'd rather bleed to death, thank you very much."

Antoine shrugged, undisturbed. "You're not likely to bleed to death. Have it your way."

He pulled out a small bottle and doused the cloth with the liquid, then cleaned the gash. The alcohol burned like the devil, but next to the pain in his shoulder, Miles barely felt it. When Antoine was finished, he put away his bottle and handed Miles the cloth.

"You can use that to staunch the bleeding until it stops," he said. "I'll help you back on with your jackets, if you like."

"Thank you."

Antoine held the uniform jacket and Miles gingerly angled his bad arm into the sleeve before sliding his other arm in and settling it over his shoulders. His shoulder still hurt like hell, but at least his arm was moving now. The flight jacket was heavier and more awkward, but it went on much easier than he had been expecting.

"Thank you again. I appreciate all your help."

"You're welcome. Now you go to Dunkirk." Antoine held out his hand. "God speed, my friend. I pray you get back in the air soon."

Miles shook his hand and nodded. "And you? Where are you going?"

"We are going to surrender," Antoine said, smiling sadly. "We have our orders."

Into the Iron Shadows

Miles swallowed and looked from one to the other. Both men seemed resigned. He knew there was nothing he could say. It was no use asking them to come to Dunkirk with him. Orders were orders, and they would be offended if he suggested anything otherwise.

"I wish you the best of luck," he said, holding out his hand to Raf.

He took it with a nod of acknowledgement. "Thank you. God speed to you."

Miles nodded and picked up his Mae West, turning to start walking. A moment later, he glanced over his shoulder to see the two men crossing into the trees on the other side of the road. They were going to rejoin their unit, and then to surrender to the German army. They would spend the rest of the war in a prisoner of war camp. He turned his eyes forward along the road, a heavy sense of sadness rolling over him. While he had a chance at escaping back to England, they were out of chances.

Miles lifted the cloth to his forehead when he felt wetness start to roll alongside his eye again. He had about seven kilometers until he reached France. He was going to have to walk faster than this if he was to have any chance at making it off that beach.

He lifted the Mae West and settled it over his shoulders again, wincing at the pain. Realizing that he had used his arm without thinking, Miles moved his right arm again, testing it gingerly. It hurt like hell, but he had the use of his arm back.

If only he still had his airplane!

London

Bill finished pouring himself a fresh cup of tea and picked two biscuits off the plate, setting them in the saucer. He picked up the cup and saucer, turning to carry it over to his desk with a stifled yawn. It was mid-morning and he'd already been to two meetings, one of which was with Jasper. He was waiting for Wesley to bring him the second batch of messages from the radio room, hoping that today would be the day that brought word that Evelyn had finally reached Bordeaux. He was beginning to get worried about the amount of time it had been since he last heard from her.

He carefully set his tea down and then sank into the chair

behind his desk. He'd heard reports of Luftwaffe pilots strafing the lines of refugees on the roads in France. He couldn't imagine a world where military pilots were permitted to fire on innocent civilians, yet by all accounts, that was exactly what was happening in France. He prayed Evelyn hadn't been caught in such an attack. It was one thing to contemplate losing her in the execution of her duty, but quite another to consider that she might be shot with other civilians simply moving from one place to another.

He was just lifting his cup of tea to his lips when the telephone on his desk rang shrilly. With a sigh, he set the cup down and reached for the handset. It never failed. Just as he was about to enjoy a nice cuppa, the phone always rang.

"Yes?"

"Sir William?"

"Yes?"

"This is Martin from the radio room, sir. I've just sent Wesley up with a few messages that came through. You asked to be notified as soon as one came in from Bordeaux."

"Yes. Has it?"

"Yes, sir. Wesley has it now."

"Thank you, Martin. Please stand by. I'll be sending one back."

"Of course, sir. I'll notify them to expect a transmission."

"Thank you."

Bill hung up and rubbed his hands together. Good! She'd arrived safely. Now he just had to figure out how to get her home. He reached for his tea again. Every available boat, ship, sloop, trawler, launch, and bloody pontoon had been commandeered for the evacuation effort. Everything short of kayaks had been sent over to France, leaving nothing for him to send to pick up Jian and Oscar. Unless something became available, which was highly unlikely, they were going to have to stay in Bordeaux, at least until Operation Dynamo was complete.

Sipping his tea, he shook head. There was nothing else he could do. Sam was the only pilot crazy enough to fly into France right now, but he was unable to fly until his airplane was serviced. It had developed mechanical issues on his way to Spain, resulting in a forced landing just over the border. The repairs were expected to take at least a week, maybe longer. No. Jian and Oscar would have to remain in Bordeaux until he could send a boat.

A light knock fell on his door and then Wesley entered, carrying a handful of messages from the radio room.

"There's a message, sir, from—"

Into the Iron Shadows

"Bordeaux," Bill finished with a smile, setting his cup down and holding out his hand. "Yes. Martin rang up to tell me."

Wesley grinned and fished the message in question out from the stack, handing it to him. He laid the rest on the desk next to the teacup.

"Shall I wait, sir?"

"Yes. I'll be sending a reply."

Bill opened the message and scanned it. His smile turned to a frown, then he sighed.

"It's not what I was hoping for," he said, laying the paper down.

"It's not from Leon?"

"It is, but Jian hasn't arrived yet. This is to tell me that Romeo is out of action."

Wesley frowned. "Romeo, sir?"

"Our agent in Rouen."

"Ah. And what does that mean, out of action?"

Bill glanced up at him. "It means he's either dead or captured. We're losing them at an alarming rate, and we didn't have many to begin with." He pinched the bridge of his nose and shook his head, exhaling. "Since we have Leon waiting, I will send a message. Just give me a moment to write it out."

"Of course, sir."

Wesley moved to stand a little further away, his hands clasped behind his back. Bill glanced at him as he pulled a sheet of paper towards himself.

"By the way, I found out some news about your brother," he said, picking up a pencil. "His unit was ordered to pull back to the port cities when General Gort gave the order. By all accounts, they should be part of the lot at Dunkirk. So, keep your chin up, boy. He may just make it back yet."

The beaming look of relief on Wesley's face made Bill smile.

"Thank you, sir. That's a relief!"

"Yes, I suppose it is."

Bill turned his attention to the blank piece of paper before him. After thinking for a moment, he wrote out a message to send back to Bordeaux. It was longer than he liked, but it couldn't be helped. There was a lot of information to include, and none of it was familiar to Leon. When he was finished, he folded the paper and tucked it into an envelope, sealing it.

"Have Martin encode and send it immediately, and then tell him to continue to monitor the messages for any from Bordeaux," he said, holding the envelope out to his assistant. "She still may arrive today. I want to know as soon as she does. The rest of these can wait until you return."

"Yes, sir."

Wesley took the message and left the office, closing the door softly. Bill reached for his tea again. His meeting with Jasper that morning had been to receive approval to recruit two new agents in France. At first, Montclair had thought he was insane. The Germans were advancing, they were losing people all over France, leading them to believe that the Germans had discovered the new agents' identities, and he wanted to add two more? Bill chuckled, remembering the acid comment that had been thrown his way at his proposal.

That was before Jasper found out their identities.

Bill sat back in his chair, cradling his teacup in his hands thoughtfully as he stared across the office. When he and Marguerite went to dinner last night with Madeleine Ainsworth, he had been expecting a light evening filled with the kind of trivial niceties that allowed him to forget his work, forget the agents disappearing and dying on the continent, forget the whole bloody war, if only for an hour or so. Instead, Madeleine had unknowingly handed him the perfect pair of spies.

He'd met Gisele and Nicolas in Paris many times. He'd watched them grow from mischievous and reckless teenagers into lively and fun-loving young adults. He'd laughed at Nicolas' caricatures of political figures, and watched as Gisele had cut a swath through Paris society with her cousin Evelyn at her side. They were popular, loved by everyone, invited to all the best houses and parties, and undisputed leaders of society. They were the perfect spies.

And they had chosen to remain in France rather than come to England with their parents.

As soon as Madeleine had told them, he had lost interest in the rest of the conversation and been distracted for the rest of the evening. His wife had laughingly teased him for not paying attention, then explained to Madeleine and Agatha that he was constantly working now. Thankfully, Madeleine was such an old friend that no offense was taken, and he had been allowed to retreat into his thoughts for the rest of their dinner.

That morning, he had gone into Jasper's office with a daring proposition, and one that Montclair had reluctantly approved. If Zell and Nicki were staying in France anyway, it would be foolish of him not to approach them. With their money and connections, they would be welcomed as part of the elite when the Germans came. They were everything the German High Command aspired to be: rich, well-bred, well-educated, and they came from a long and impeccable lineage. They would be invited to every dinner, welcomed into association with the German officers, and befriended by their wives. They would be in a position unlike anyone MI6 currently had in France.

And Leon was the only agent in the south of France. He was the only one who might be able to reach them.

If they agreed, there was a risk involved, but not just for them. There would be a large risk involved for Jian. Gisele and Nicolas could never know Evelyn was working in France, or for MI6. While Bill had every confidence in their ability to rub shoulders with the German High Command and not give themselves away, he was not as sure that they would not reveal Evelyn's identity under pressure. And the Germans were very good at applying pressure.

No. The two could never know that their cousin was also an agent.

Just as Evelyn could never know that her beloved cousins were working for him as well.

Chapter Twenty-Eight

Miles looked up at the deep drone of engines, holding a hand over his eyes as he peered up into the morning sky. The sun was getting brighter with each passing minute, and he squinted, scanning the horizon for the source of the noise. He finally spotted it: a formation of airplanes moving southeast, towards the northern coast of France.

Frustration rolled through him as he dropped his hand and lowered his gaze. Bombers on their way to Dunkirk, and here he was, walking along the side of a deserted road in Belgium. He should be up there helping the rest of Fighter Command to fend them off. He kicked a rock at the side of the road, the first act of frustration since he'd felt the bullets rip into the side of his Spitfire. As soon as he'd done it, Miles felt like a fool. Throwing a tantrum and kicking things wasn't going to get him back with his squadron. All it would do is expend energy that he needed to conserve.

He'd been walking for almost an hour, and the Mae West around his neck was getting hot and uncomfortable. He debated removing it, then shook his head. Knowing his luck, he'd need it if he did. He may be on land now, but if he succeeded in reaching Dunkirk, he had a chance to make it onto a boat. He'd be glad of his flotation device then.

If he made it to Dunkirk.

Miles wiped moisture off his forehead. The bleeding from the gash had stopped some time ago, but now sweat was taking its place, rolling down his forehead. The sun was warming up the earth, and dressed as he was in his uniform, flight jacket and Mae West, it was getting bloody uncomfortable. How far was it now? He had no way of knowing. Seven kilometers is what Raf had said. That was about four miles, but he had no idea how far he'd come. He did know one thing: this hike was taking far too long. His mouth was dry, his feet were getting tired, and the dull ache in his shoulder was making him feel more and more weary with every step he took. He supposed he should be happy to be alive, and he was, but he was getting knackered.

Into the Iron Shadows

Miles looked at his watch. It was just past eight and he hadn't even reached the border yet. Once he did, he knew Dunkirk wasn't far, but how long it would take him to get there was anyone's guess. He lifted his eyes and sighed. That was if he could even get there at all. The Germans were knocking on Dunkirk's door. For all he knew, it may be surrounded already, and he might be walking into German troops. The thought was a sobering one and he tightened his lips. All he could do was keep going, and pray that he made it to the beach. He would worry about getting off it once he was there. One thing at a time. Right now, he had to make it to France. He couldn't risk getting trapped in Belgium, not after their surrender. He had absolutely no desire to spend the rest of this bloody war as a prisoner. He wasn't built that way.

Something up ahead caught his attention. He'd been walking past abandoned military vehicles for the better part of an hour, most of them burned out shells. There had been other debris left behind by the retreating army as well, but whatever was ahead between the trees was something different. He squinted, peering ahead. As he drew closer, Miles blinked and raised his eyebrows in astonishment. It was a bicycle, leaning against a tree for all the world as if someone had just got off it to go into a shop. Yet he hadn't seen another soul on this deserted road the entire time he'd been walking.

The sight of the bicycle was incongruous amidst the discarded rubble and broken, abandoned instruments of war. It was a picture of civilian innocence in the center of the jaded, battle-hardened machinery of soldiers.

And Miles had never been so happy to see anything in his life.

He broke into a jog. He didn't know how it had ended up there, or who had abandoned it, but if it had a chain and the tires were good, he had every intention of taking advantage of it. And even if the tires weren't good, he knew he'd still take it. It was faster than walking, and right now, time was his worst enemy.

Reaching the bicycle, he bent to examine it. It was old, and the frame was rusting and had seen much better days, but the chain was solid and the tires were filled with air. The back one was a little soft, but it would do. Grabbing the handles, Miles walked it out of the trees and onto the road. Climbing on, he pedaled a few feet, testing it. It squeaked, a testimony to how long it had been abandoned under the trees, but the brakes worked and, more importantly, it moved. It would do.

Miles couldn't believe his luck and, as he pedaled on his way, he felt a wave of exhilaration go through him. This was much, much better. For the first time in over an hour, he felt as if he had a legitimate shot at making the border and getting to Dunkirk. He tried not to consider what would happen if he ran into German soldiers along the way. He would simply handle each challenge as it presented itself. He had his standard issue, RAF sidearm if he ran into any real trouble. While it would be useless against a rifle or machine gun, it was something.

Enough to take at least one of the bastards with him.

But he wouldn't worry about what could happen until it did happen. Right now, it was enough that he was pedaling along the road, past the remnants of a defeated and retreating army, towards the one place that was the reason he was here in Belgium at all.

Dunkirk.

Evelyn looked up as Finn approached, a folded newspaper in his hand. She was sitting on a bench, enjoying a very picturesque view of the Garonne River, in the heart of Bordeaux. Her suitcase and Finn's large knapsack were at her feet. Any self-consciousness that she might have felt at sitting in the middle of a city with a suitcase had been discarded when she had taken a good look around her. The city was flooded with refugees, some carrying suitcases like herself, and others pushing carts piled high with cases and boxes. She was just another refugee, nameless and faceless, joining the hundreds that had converged on the busy port city.

"I bought today's paper," Finn said, sitting beside her and handing it to her. "I also spoke to the shop keeper. He said that Rue Josephine is only about a ten-minute walk from here. He gave me directions."

Evelyn took the newspaper and opened it, scanning the front page. There was more about Belgium's surrender, and the advances being made by the Germans in northern France. Then a small headline in the bottom corner caught her attention.

ALLIED TROOPS CONVERGE ON DUNKIRK.

Finn watched as she tilted the newspaper to see the bottom corner better. "Yes, I thought you'd go to that," he said. "The English are sending ships to try to evacuate them."

"They have to do something," Evelyn murmured, reading the short article. "It says the British are abandoning France. Well, that's a fine thing to say. They've been trapped into a corner because of Gamelin and Weygand's terrible handling of the front!"

Into the Iron Shadows

"Shh," Finn hissed with a frown. "Do you want to broadcast that you're English?"

Evelyn glanced up, then looked around.

"No one is paying us any attention," she retorted, lowering her voice nonetheless. "But really, it does make me angry. Those soldiers are the only trained army England has. If they're captured, we don't have another one to take their place. We'll be left with reservists and untrained recruits."

"That's undoubtedly what the Germans are counting on. Do you think they can do it?"

"Evacuate the troops? I have no idea. I do know that if there is any possibility at all of getting just a handful off, they'll try. Aside from wanting to save the men's lives, Churchill knows how important that army is to the defense of England, not to mention the morale of the country."

"I can't imagine how they'll do it. The Luftwaffe will bomb anything that tries to move near the coast."

Evelyn pressed her lips together, a pair of sparkling green eyes coming into her mind's eye. Her chest tightened, but she resolutely pushed the sudden feeling of anxiety aside.

"The RAF will send their fighters," she said in a low voice. "The French coast is within their range. They'll take on the Luftwaffe in the air while the navy tries to extract the troops."

Finn glanced at her. "And do you think the RAF is a match for the Luftwaffe?"

She swallowed, her mouth dry. "I certainly hope so. It's the best defense England's got at the moment."

"Then, for all of our sakes, I hope they are," he said grimly. He looked at his watch. "It's just past eight. We should be on our way."

Evelyn folded the paper and nodded, standing. "Yes. Let's go and find Café Rosa. If nothing else, I'm looking forward to a coffee and a pastry."

Finn stood and picked up his bag, swinging it over his shoulder. He reached for her suitcase but she waved his hand away.

"I'm perfectly capable of carrying my own bag," she said with a smile. "Thank you, but I can manage."

He shook his head. "It's that attitude that will get you caught by the Germans," he informed her as they started up the street. "They don't like women who are independent."

"I'll remember that if I ever find myself in their company," she retorted.

"God willing, you never will."

Henry pressed the bell once more, then stepped back on the front step to look up at the house. It was in the center of a row of attached homes in a modest neighborhood. It looked deserted, but so did many of the houses. This was a working neighborhood. Mid-morning in the middle of the week meant that most inhabitants were at work. He'd rung the bell several times and had waited more than a few minutes. Clearly there was no one home. Turning away, he stepped off the stoop. He would have to try back again later this evening. Perhaps he would have better luck then.

He was just turning to walk up the sidewalk when he felt someone watching him. Turning his head sharply, he caught sight of a face peering through the curtains of the window next door. Changing his direction, he waved and motioned to the door. The woman hesitated, then nodded before the curtain swung back into place. Henry walked towards the neighbor's door, arriving just as it opened to reveal an older woman wearing an apron over a well-worn day dress.

"Yes?"

"Pardon my intrusion. I wonder if you could tell me who lives next door?" Henry asked, smiling his most charming smile and removing his hat. "I've tried ringing the bell, but there's no answer."

"Well that's because no one lives there," the woman said with a shrug. "There was a couple, but the husband went away with the army last September when the war started."

"Do you remember his name?"

"Oh yes. It was Decoux. Pierre Decoux. He was a very nice young man, and his wife was very sweet. She used to come and help me with my ironing."

"Used to? Did she go to stay with family when her husband went away?"

The woman shook her head. "Oh no. She stayed here. She worked as a nurse, you see, at the hospital."

"Ah, of course."

"What business do you have with them?" she asked, tilting her head. "You don't look like a tradesman."

"No, I'm not. I represent her father's estate. In Switzerland."

"Oh! I see!" The woman's face cleared. "Yes, you look like a banker."

Henry raised an eyebrow, momentarily at a loss for words. He could honestly say that he had never been told that he resembled a banker.

"Do you know where I can find Madame Decoux?" he asked, finding his voice again.

"Well, you can't."

"Pardon?"

"You can't find her. She's dead."

Henry stared at her. "Dead?"

"Yes. She caught pneumonia. I'm afraid she wasn't in very good health to begin with, the poor woman. Once her husband left, she simply refused to eat very much." The woman shook her head sadly. "It was very sad. She just faded away, and then when she fell ill, well…" She shrugged. "It was too much for her."

He swallowed, his mouth suddenly dry. "When was this?"

"Oh, about six months ago now."

Henry inclined his head slightly. "Thank you. I had no idea."

"I wish I could have given you better news."

"It's quite all right. Thank you for your time."

Henry turned away and went down the steps as the door closed behind him. His mind was spinning and, as he turned to walk up the street, his hand clenched. Isabelle Decoux had died six months ago?

Then who the bloody hell had gone to the house in Blasenflue? And what did they do there?

Miles got off his bicycle and stared around him. He had crossed the border with little difficulty and had followed the signs until he came upon a group of French soldiers. They had directed him the rest of the way, telling him to follow the road straight into Dunkirk and to take cover if any airplanes came along. As he rode away from them, he heard one remark that it was a miracle he'd got through at all on a bicycle.

He'd had a few scary moments, it was true. All around him, not half a mile from the road, he could hear the sounds of big guns firing. The battle waged along the perimeter that both the French and English soldiers had established, and they were fighting fiercely to keep the Germans beyond that perimeter while the evacuation effort was underway on the shore. He had come through near the coast, and the German artillery hadn't been able to advance that far, thank God. Yet, hearing the remark, Miles realized just how lucky he had been. If he had landed south of the beach rather than north, it could have been an entirely different experience. And he may not have made it at all.

At first, the dull, muffled sound of mortar fire was terrifying. Followed with machine gun fire, and then periods of silence, the boom of the guns startled him each time they thudded from the distance. The enemy was so close, and yet he couldn't see them. He could only hear them. Miles wondered what was worse, then quickly decided that seeing them would be much, much worse. He had no rifle, no ammunition. Nothing to use to defend himself, or the town towards which he cycled, aside from his pistol. He could only pray that the troops manning the perimeter would be able to hold them at bay.

When he approached the town, he was shocked at the rubble lining the roads. The Luftwaffe had done their part, and many of the outer buildings leading into the town were reduced to huge mounds of brick and stone. Coupled with the charred remains of military vehicles and downed power lines, huge black plumes of smoke rose in thick columns from the town. Dunkirk was burning, and Miles had the unholy feeling that he was riding into Hell.

And then, suddenly, he was in Hell. Inside the town, some streets were destroyed, and others were intact. Soldiers were posted at the outer corners with artillery, taking cover behind protective sandbag walls, crumbling stone garden walls, wooden houses, and anything else they could find. In the narrow streets, the smell of death hung on the air heavily and Miles tightened his lips. Wounded soldiers were making their way through the town towards a building that had been turned into a military hospital, but others had not been as fortunate.

Miles tore his gaze away from the body of a French soldier, half covered by a mound of rubble. Leaning the bicycle up against a low wall, he turned and followed a group of soldiers through the street towards the beach. As they drew closer to the shore, Miles began to get whiffs of salt air, and a breeze made its way into the street, pushing the stench of war behind him.

They went down a narrow road between two rows of what were once brightly colored houses, now covered with soot and grime, emerging onto a road running parallel with the coast. Miles stopped and stared, a mix of relief and astonishment washing over him. There, on the other side of the road, dunes rose and fell until they met the flat sand that stretched some distance until it met the English Channel. It was a large beach, but what held him transfixed were the rows upon rows of soldiers lining the length and breadth of the sand. Thousands of men stood in orderly columns, snaking down to the edge of the water, waiting for a miracle. Behind them, in the dunes, thousands more were sitting in groups, exhausted and waiting for their turn. There were soldiers everywhere, packing into the dunes and onto the beach, with more joining them every minute. He didn't think he'd ever seen so many men in uniform in one place, and they were all exhausted and battle-weary. How they had made it here was immaterial. They were here now and, as one, they were waiting for the chance to leave these shores.

Taking a deep breath, Miles fought down an onslaught of emotion that he didn't recognize, nor could even put a name to. His hands began to shake, but he ignored it, crossing the road and stepping onto the sand. He made his way through the dunes, drawing only an occasional curious look. These men were too tired to notice a downed pilot walking among them, if they noticed him at all.

Reaching the beach, he went forward, wondering where on earth he should go or what he should do. All the columns were so neatly organized that there was clearly a system in place, but he had no idea what that system might be.

"Watch yourself, mate!"

A surprisingly British voice called behind him and Miles turned to see four English infantrymen coming towards him bearing a stretcher. The man lying on the stretcher had a bloody bandage wrapped around his head and another one wrapped around a bloody stump where his arm used to be. Miles moved out of their way, nodding to them as they passed. The man on the stretcher looked at him and Miles felt a shock go through him at the realization that he was awake and completely lucid.

The party passed on, heading towards a column of soldiers waiting on the beach, and Miles swallowed, looking around again. Suddenly, he felt very alone, and very uncertain. He felt as though he didn't belong here. These men had been in the worst of battle, fighting the Germans face to face. They were the real soldiers. He felt like an imposter.

"You there!" A voice called. "Ho! You there!"

Miles turned to his right and found a tall officer staring at him from several yards away. He looked behind him quickly, but the man yelled again.

"Yes, I mean you!"

Miles walked towards him, squinting in the sunlight. He was a Major in the British Expeditionary Forces according to his uniform coat, and he was motioning Miles to hurry.

"You look lost, son," he said without ceremony as Miles drew closer. "Where did you come from?"

Miles choked back a laugh and pointed up. The Major chuckled.

"I'm Major Runnemede. Where did you come down?"

"In Belgium. Saint-Idesbald. I'm Flying Officer Miles Lacey, of 66 Squadron." Miles introduced himself. "I was attacking a formation of Dorniers when I was shot."

"Lacey…Lacey…you're not old Edward Lacey's boy, are you?"

Miles stared at him, stunned. "Why, yes, sir. But how do you know?"

"Good Lord, your father told me his son had taken up flying," Major Runnemede exclaimed, holding out his hand. "Never imagined I'd have cause to run into you like this! Pleasure to meet you, my boy. Your father and I were at school together, you know. We're members of the same club in London. Fancy running into you on this god-forsaken stretch of hell."

Miles shook his head, a tired grin crossing his face as he shook his hand. "I'm very glad to meet you, sir. If I make it home, I'll be sure to send my father your regards."

"Please do! Feels like years since I've seen him. Well, so they shot you down, did they?" The Major shook his head. "The bastards have been making passes all morning. They're responsible for that mess over there," he added, nodding behind Miles.

Miles turned to look and sucked in his breath. Soldiers were piling bodies along the edge of what looked like a large trench dug into the sand.

"Not a pretty sight, is it?" The Major asked, watching Miles' face.

"No, sir."

"I hope you got one of the bastards before you went down."

"I did, actually."

"Good! Glad to hear it. I suppose you're trying to get back to your squadron." Major Runnemede turned and started walking along the sand, motioning for Miles to join him. "How did you find us?"

"Two Belgian soldiers helped me. They came along as my kite exploded, as a matter of fact."

"Good Lord, it actually exploded?"

"Yes, sir. I climbed out just in time. They fixed me up and pointed me in the right direction." Miles scratched his neck. "I'm glad they found me. I would have gone north to Ostend."

"You wouldn't have had an easy time of it there. The Germans have taken Ostend."

Into the Iron Shadows

"So they told me."

"This place will be overrun soon enough," the Major said, shaking his head. "You're lucky you got here when you did. I don't know how long we can hold them, if the truth were known. Long enough to get all these boys out, I hope."

Miles turned his head, distracted by the sound of a truck motor. Seeing him look, the Major followed his gaze and chuckled.

"Ah. That's our morale builder. He's been at it for the past hour or more."

Miles watched, transfixed, as an army truck rumbled along the sand. What looked like cartons of cigarettes were being tossed out to the soldiers waiting in the columns on the beach.

"Are those—"

"Cigarettes? Yes. Craven A, to be precise. I had a few packs off him myself. Not my brand, you understand, but I'll take what I can get."

"Where on earth did he get them?"

"God only knows! He seems to have an endless supply of the things." Major Runnemede paused to watch the truck for a moment. "He's keeping the men's spirits up. That's all I care about."

Over the sound of the waves and the engine, Miles heard a disconcertingly cheerful voice yelling out of the window as the cartons went flying into waiting hands.

"Here we are lads! All free and with the complements of NAAFI!"

Miles burst out laughing and waved to the truck. "Bloody marvelous!" he called, still laughing.

The man driving saw him and beeped his horn before tossing a carton towards them. Major Runnemede watched as Miles ran forward to pick up the cigarettes. He waited while Miles tore it open, pulling out a pack of cigarettes, before throwing the carton towards the nearest group of soldiers in the dunes. A soldier jumped up to grab it, his curly hair in disarray as the ocean breeze whipped at it. Miles watched him turn to his unit, a huge grin on his face, before he started passing the cigarettes out.

"Good Lord, he doesn't look old enough to be out of school," he said, turning back to the Major. "Did you see him?"

"Aye. You'd be surprised how young some of these lads are."

Miles thought of young Perry and shook his head, a heavy feeling settling onto his chest.

"We had a young pilot come through the squadron. He died over Calais." He looked at the columns of soldiers on the beach, then back at the dunes. "I have to get back to my squadron so I can get back up there," he said grimly. "All of these men are sitting targets out here."

The major glanced at him. "Yes. Well, get in a line and hopefully you'll be on your way soon."

"What line?"

"If I were you, I'd go to that far pier. They're loading onto destroyers there. These other columns are being picked up by smaller craft that can come in to get them, or wading out to meet the larger ones. The waters are too shallow for the ships, you see." Major Runnemede paused and looked out over the beach. "They're carrying them out to those larger ships out there." He pointed on the horizon. "The bloody Stukas are taking aim at those smaller boats, as well as the cruisers. One of the destroyers will be faster than those small ones, and it has bigger guns. Make your way over there and join the line. One should be coming along any time now."

Miles nodded. "What happens when it's filled?"

"It leaves and another one comes." Major Runnemede pulled out a pair of binoculars and held them to his eyes. "Yes. That's *The Grafton* there. She's just begun boarding." He lowered the binoculars. "If you hurry, you might make this run. If not, wait for the next one."

Miles saluted him. "Thank you, sir."

Major Runnemede returned the salute, then held out his hand. "Get back to your squadron, Lacey, and then come back over here and give 'em hell."

Miles grinned and nodded. "Yes, sir!"

Chapter Twenty-Nine

Café Rosa was located on a corner of Rue Josephine and a narrow lane. Its entrance curved across the corner of the old stone building with glass windows on either side, giving an almost panoramic view of the world outside. Evelyn inhaled deeply as they stepped through the door, basking in the familiar smell of freshly baked pastries mixed with the heavy aroma of fresh-brewed coffee.

"Doesn't that smell wonderful?" she asked Finn.

"Indeed."

They walked to the counter where a man stood wearing an apron over his trousers and collared shirt. He wasn't a tall man, and was very lean with dark hair and a mustache that he kept neatly trimmed. What he lacked in stature, however, he more than made up for in charisma.

"Welcome to Café Rosa," he said cheerfully, eyeing their cases. "I see you've just arrived in Bordeaux. Welcome!"

"Thank you," Finn murmured, taken aback at the man's outgoing greeting.

"What would you like, sir? Café? Croissant? Perhaps a plate of financiers and macaroons?"

Finn looked at Evelyn and she almost laughed out at the startled look in his eyes.

"Bonjour!" she said, taking pity on the uncomfortable Czech. "All of that sounds wonderful. We will have two coffees, certainly, and if we could have a moment to decide?"

"Of course, mademoiselle! Take all the time you need."

"Thank you." Evelyn gave him her most winning smile. "I wonder if Leon is here? We were told to look for him while we were in Bordeaux."

"You've found him, mademoiselle. I am Leon."

"Oh how wonderful! A dear friend of mine in Paris, William, told me that I really must search out Café Rosa while I was here. He said that you make the best cannelés in the city."

Leon nodded, his wide smile never faltering. "William is too kind, but he is also correct. You won't find any better. I will bring them

267

to you with your coffee."

Evelyn smiled and she and Finn turned to survey the café. Only two tables were occupied at this time of the morning and, as they turned, the occupants of both quickly lowered their gazes. Finn led her to a table on the opposite side, tucked near the back.

Evelyn sank into a seat while he settled himself facing the door. She looked at his face and smiled.

"They're locals," she said in a low voice. "Relax. There is no need to be so suspicious."

"They were watching and listening to every word that was said," he replied in an equally low voice.

"Yes. They probably come here every day and are curious." Evelyn opened her purse and pulled out a small compact, opening it to examine her appearance. "This is not Leipzig. It is France." She patted her hair, tucking a stray strand back into the twist at the back of her head. "There are no Gestapo spies in Bordeaux. At least, not yet."

Finn grunted and shifted in his seat. "I am still not comfortable."

"I know." She adjusted her hat and closed her compact, putting it away. She smiled at him. "That is why you have me to help you."

"Here they are," Leon sang out, heading towards their table with a tray in his hands. "The best cannelés in Bordeaux."

He expertly balanced the tray with one hand and set a plate in front of each of them.

"When you leave, go around to the back," he said in a low voice while he set their cups of coffee down. "I will speak to you then."

"Thank you." Evelyn nodded. "They look delicious," she added in a slightly louder voice.

"Enjoy, mademoiselle. Monsieur." Leon bowed slightly and turned to go back to the counter.

Finn watched him go, then turned his attention to the small, round cake on the plate.

"What is this?"

"It is a specialty of Bordeaux, made with vanilla and rum, and it's very good." Evelyn picked up the small fork on her plate and cut into the pastry. "I had it once a long time ago when—" She stopped herself abruptly. "Well, a long time ago."

Finn picked up his fork. "I don't care very much for sweets, but it must be better than cold potatoes," he murmured. "I am glad you stopped yourself," he added, glancing up from his plate. "The less we know of each other, the better."

Into the Iron Shadows

Evelyn nodded, chewing thoughtfully. He was right, but it was still strange to be forced to censor herself. After all, they'd lived through a Stuka attack together, and he'd confided his past and his journey to her. It seemed as though they had known each other much longer than the week that they had. They had spent days in the car together, discussing inane topics along the way, and they were still strangers. It was a strange existence, this life of theirs.

And she could only imagine that it would get stranger as the war went on.

Miles moved forward with the line of soldiers standing two abreast, walking towards the pier that stretched out over the surf to the waiting gray destroyer. They had loaded the wounded first, and now the line was moving slowly, but steadily, as men boarded the ship. He hadn't even reached the pier yet and, judging by the number of soldiers before him, he didn't think he would reach the ship before it had reached capacity. He looked at his watch tiredly. It was after midday and the sun was high in the sky, beating down on them without mercy. Perfect weather for the Luftwaffe to inflict their damage. Their fighters would be having a heyday with theirs up there, using the sun to full advantage. He knew that, beyond the town and where he couldn't see them, the RAF was battling just as hard as the soldiers down here. Shaking his head, he swallowed painfully. His mouth and throat were dry, he was hot and tired, and yet he wanted nothing more than to be up in his Spitfire with them. But his kite was a charred out shell now, and he was standing here instead, wishing he had a canteen of water. He was so thirsty!

"'ere mate, have you got a light?"

Miles turned to look at a soldier holding a crooked cigarette behind him. He nodded and felt in his uniform pocket for his lighter. Locating it, he pulled it out and handed it to the man.

"Cheers." He lit his cigarette and handed the lighter back to him. "I lost mine somewhere."

Miles nodded, tucking the lighter back into his pocket. The man stared at him for a minute, smoking.

"How did you get 'ere then?" he finally asked.

"Courtesy of a Messerschmitt 109."

The man nodded slowly. "Where did you run into the bastard?"

269

Miles pointed up and the man choked. "Up there? *Here* up there?"

"That's right."

"So you blokes are around after all," he said, shaking his head. "A bunch of the lads said the RAF wasn't here."

"Oh, we're here," Miles said, his voice hoarse. "We're up there."

"We haven't seen any of you from down 'ere. All we see are the bloody Germans, right before they drop their bombs and start shooting."

"We're above the clouds. Trust me. We're there."

The man studied him for a minute, his crooked cigarette hanging out of his mouth, then he shoved his hand out.

"Private Bernard Taylor, 91st Field Regiment."

"Flying Officer Miles Lacey, 66 Squadron."

"What's your machine? Hurricane?"

"Spitfire."

Bernard's face brightened. "Spitfire! Bloody brilliant, they are! I saw one fly outside London once."

Miles couldn't stop his smile. "Yes. They're fantastic kites."

"Where did you come down?"

"Just over the border, in Belgium, early this morning."

Bernard clucked his tongue and shook his head. "And you made it here? You must have someone watching over you. I came from Ploegsteert, and it was hell getting out of there. Lost m' captain and my lance corporal before we made it from one side o' the street to the other. Ended up adrift with two others, separated from my unit."

Miles made a sympathetic noise in the back of his throat, not having any idea where the place was that Bernard was talking about. He was about to ask if he'd eventually found the rest of his regiment when a low noise caught his attention. It was a low drone, growing louder, and he looked up, lifting a hand to shade his eyes against the sun. He sucked in his breath when he saw the shadows coming towards them. He recognized the shape immediately and lowered his hand.

"Stukas!" he breathed hoarsely.

"What's that?" Bernard leaned forward. "You know, I can barely understand you. Something's wrong with your throat."

The low drone turned into a high pitched wail.

"Stukas!!" Miles yelled, his voice booming out in his panic. "Everybody down!!"

Bernard gaped at him, then turned to stare as the first ones dove towards the beach. Miles grabbed him, throwing him to the sand

and following him down. All around them, soldiers dove to the ground, covering their ears against the ghastly wail of the dive bombers as they streaked towards the beach. Miles lifted his head, watching as column by column, the soldiers exposed on the beach fell to the sand in a desperate and hopeless attempt to save themselves from the deadly fighter bombers.

The deafening sound of the first bomb exploding forced Miles' head down and he lay there in the sand, his heart pounding in his chest. Pure, unadulterated terror streaked through him as he listened to the MG 17 machine guns fire rounds over him. He turned his head and watched sand fly in the air a mere foot away as the bullets thudded into the beach. He watched long enough to see the perfect rows streak along the ground, hitting soldiers stretched out in their path. Miles squeezed his eyes shut, but not before seeing several men jerk uncontrollably as the bullets tore through them.

The high pitched wailing seemed to go on forever, heralding the arrival of more and more Stukas, followed by the explosions of bombs and ungodly sound of gun fire, until suddenly it stopped as the last ones flew over the beach, unloading their 7.92 caliber ammunition as they went. The whole thing, while seeming like an eternity, was over within minutes.

Miles lay prone in the sand, not daring to move for fear of what he'd find when he did. The last of the Stukas were flying off into the distance, their mission finished, before he finally lifted his head slowly, taking mental stock of his body. Nothing hurt any more than anything else, and the only real discomfort was emanating from his shoulder, which had been violently jarred when he threw his arm around Bernard to get him down.

Miles pushed himself up, turning to look at Private Taylor. He was still lying face down in the sand, not moving.

"Private Taylor!" Miles leaned over to touch his shoulder, his hand shaking. "Are you all right? Bernard!"

A groan came from the prone figure and he rolled over, staring up at Miles with a grimace.

"Are the shits gone?"

Miles stared at him for a beat, then laughed, his body going limp with relief. "Yes. They're gone."

"Bloody bastards."

He struggled to sit up, then fell back again. Miles got to his knees, leaning over him.

"What is it? Are you hit?"

"It's my back. I took some shrapnel a few days ago. It gets stiff

271

on me." Bernard tried again and Miles hooked his arm around him, helping him up. After a moment of struggle, he managed to get to his feet, panting. "It'll be awright now. Doc said the muscles wouldn't work right for a while. When we get back home, I expect they'll do something about it."

"You gave me a scare," Miles said, releasing him. "I thought you'd bought it."

They turned and looked out over the beach. As soldiers struggled to their feet again, the amount that remained unmoving on the sand became clear. Miles sucked in his breath, staring over the expansive coastline. Hundreds of slain soldiers littered the beach, strewn at angles around the deep craters left by the bombs. In the long columns snaking into the water, dozens more were floating with the tide, unmoving. It wasn't enough for the Stukas to have dropped their bombs, but they'd also used their guns to mow down as many as they could. Shouts for medics and stretchers echoed all along the beach as men rushed to try to help the ones who were wounded and still breathing.

"Bastards," he breathed in horror.

"Do me a favor, mate," Bernard said, staring at all the bodies. "Remember what happened 'ere today. When you get back in your Spitfire, you take as many of those shits out as you possibly can. Send 'em to 'ell where they belong."

"Private Taylor, it will be my absolute pleasure."

The tiny courtyard behind the café was paved with old cobblestones and surrounded by a stone wall with a wooden gate for access. Closing the gate behind them, Evelyn and Finn walked across the small space towards the back door of the café. As they approached, it swung open and Leon stood in the opening, watching them.

"Come inside," he said, standing aside and motioning them forward. "We will go upstairs to my apartment where we can talk."

Evelyn stepped into a bright kitchen, lined on one side with long wooden counters. Two ovens stood on another wall, along with a large, strange contraption that looked rather like a vat. Leon closed the door behind them and ushered them to the right, moving them quickly out of the kitchen and along a short, narrow corridor to a flight of stairs.

Into the Iron Shadows

"I've been expecting you for a week," he said over his shoulder as he led them up the steps. "Did you run into trouble?"

"We ran into refugees," Evelyn replied dryly. "The roads are clogged everywhere."

"Ah. Of course! I should have realized. The newspapers have been saying that Paris is emptying. Everyone is trying to escape the Nazis." Leon opened a door at the top of the stairs and led them into a comfortably furnished sitting room. "Welcome to my home. It isn't very much, but it's comfortable. Please sit."

He waved them towards the short couch and turned to walk over to the window, pulling the curtains aside to let in the sunlight. Turning, he clasped his hands together and studied them.

"You look exhausted," he announced, "but you are here now. Let me properly introduce myself. I am Leon Petron. You are Oscar and Jian, no?"

"Yes." Evelyn glanced at Finn. "At least, I am Jian."

"I am Oscar," he said with a nod.

"Good! Then we can begin." Leon went over to a tall wooden armoire and opened the door. He pulled out a square case and carried it over to a table, setting it down. "I will contact London and tell them you have arrived."

"Is there somewhere I can wash my face and hands?" Evelyn asked, watching as he opened the case to reveal a wireless radio. It was the same model that she had had a crash course on before leaving for Belgium. "You trained in London?" she asked, surprised.

He looked up with a twinkle in his eyes. "But yes! What did you think? That SIS sent me a manual?"

She got up and went over to look at the radio unit. "SIS? How long have you worked for them?"

"Since before war was declared," he said, pulling out a chair and sitting down before the radio. "I know the name is now MI6, but I prefer the old one."

Evelyn smiled. "Many do."

"If you go down the hallway there, the bathroom is on your left," he said, pointing to the short hallway on the other side of the room.

"Thank you."

She turned and went across the room, picking up her purse as she passed the couch. She smiled at Finn, then continued to the hallway. A few minutes later she was rinsing her hands and face in a small basin sink. Raising her face to look in the mirror, she saw the dark rings under her eyes and the strained look around her mouth. She was tired, and the long days in Belgium and France were taking their toll.

Pressing her lips together, she dried her face and opened her purse to pull out her lipstick, wondering if Josephine had found somewhere to stay. She had left her with enough money to keep her going for a few weeks, ignoring her repeated protests that it was far too much. It would have ensured that she could find a good, clean hotel to sleep and regroup. Evelyn's lips twisted wryly. What she wouldn't give for a nice bed in a hotel room right now!

She capped her lipstick and put it back in the purse, staring at herself in the mirror.

What are you doing, Evie?

Why was she here, in Bordeaux, in a small apartment over a café? Who was she trying to pretend to be? Finn had worked for the SS. He had started an underground movement in Holland, and had built upon it in Belgium. He had lived under Nazi occupation, had traveled with Nazi commanders, and knew everything there was to know about this world. He was an agent.

She felt like a tourist.

Evelyn exhaled and turned towards the door. Except she wasn't a tourist. She had documents in her suitcase that had been smuggled out of Germany, and drawings of some kind of motor that her father had thought was important enough to hide in a bank in Zürich. Finn's abilities lay in organizing and setting up a network of resistance against the Nazis. Hers lay in gathering the information that would help defeat them.

She knew what Bill would say if he were in front of her; he would say that one wasn't better than the other. That they both had an important part to play. But as Evelyn opened the door and went back down the hallway to the little sitting room, she didn't feel like an equal. She felt extremely unqualified to be the one responsible for escorting Finn to England. In fact, she felt extremely unqualified to be doing any of the things she'd been doing for the past month.

How on earth was she going to make it through the war?

Chapter Thirty

E isenjager opened the door to the café and walked in, his dark eyes sweeping over the interior dispassionately. A few tables were occupied, mainly with women having their mid-morning coffee before returning to their daily errands. A young man stood behind the counter in an apron and, as Eisenjager approached, he looked up from the cup he was polishing and nodded.

"Good morning," he said, setting the cup down.

"Good morning." Eisenjager looked at the array of pastries available for a moment. "One coffee, and perhaps a macaroon."

"Of course. If you'd have a seat, I will bring it to you."

Eisenjager nodded and turned to walk to the table in front of the windows facing the corner. Seating himself, he looked outside. He had a panoramic view of the corner and intersection. When the Englishwoman and the man left, he would see them.

He had watched them enter the café, then had waited across the street on a bench with a newspaper until they left. Instead of continuing on their way, they went around the corner and into the back courtyard of the building. They were obviously meeting someone there, but he had no way of knowing who. The gate had been closed behind them and when he tried to open it a few minutes later, he found it locked. It made no difference. He knew where they were, and he would follow them when they left again.

Last night, when they had stopped for the night, he had contacted Hamburg to alert them to the fact that they were moving towards Bordeaux. He gave his opinion that Jian would be leaving France by way of the Garonne River to the sea beyond. It was what he would do if he were her. She had come south for a reason, and had gone straight to a port city. The fighting hadn't reached this far south yet, and with the German armies concentrated on Dunkirk and the surrounding ports in the north, this was her safest bet for getting back to England. They had cut off every other avenue.

Eisenjager looked up as the young man set his coffee and macaroon down on the table before him.

"Thank you," he murmured.

The man nodded and turned to go back to the counter. Eisenjager was thankful that he wasn't a chatty server. He wasn't in the mood to make pleasantries. He only wanted to enjoy his coffee for the few minutes that he could do nothing else.

After sending his message to his handler, he had waited for an answer, dozing in the car with the headset on. After almost an hour, he'd been startled awake by the sound of the reply. They had determined that the spy called Henry had no business with the target. He was cleared to proceed.

Sipping the strong coffee, Eisenjager looked out of the window, watching the morning traffic along the Rue Josephine absently. He never did catch a name for the man with her, but he supposed it didn't matter. Whoever he was, he was none of Eisenjager's concern. His only interest was in the English spy. The man was simply collateral damage. Now if it had been Jens Bernard, that would have been a different story entirely. His lips tightened ever so slightly as his eyes narrowed. That was another one he would have to look for when he was finished here in Bordeaux. But first, Jian.

He felt a strange mix of both relief and melancholy at the prospect of completing his assignment with her. She had the potential to become an incredibly dangerous foe, and it was better to prevent that from happening rather than wait and have a much larger task on their hands. On the other hand, she was also a fascinating nemesis, and one that he would have enjoyed matching wits with over time. Alas, he was a practical man. A threat was a threat, and it must be dealt with.

Jian must be dealt with.

"Here it comes."

Evelyn turned from the window at Leon's words, a cigarette in her hand. She watched as he listened intently and began scribbling on a pad of paper. Finn stretched his arms over his head, yawning widely. They had been waiting for over half an hour for a reply to the message Leon had sent to London, and now they exchanged relieved looks with each other. Soon, they would be on their way to England.

Evelyn walked across the room to put out her cigarette in an ashtray on the table. Leon had his head down and his shoulders hunched over the paper, and she turned to cross back to the window, pacing restlessly. She glanced at him a moment later, frowning. It was a long message. He was still listening and writing, his forehead creased in concentration. She resumed pacing.

"You've been pacing back and forth since we arrived," Finn said with another yawn. "You'll wear a path in the rug."

"I'm restless."

"I can see that." He got up and went over to glance out of the window, then turned to look at her. "We will be on our way soon," he said, unconsciously echoing her own thoughts.

"Not quite that soon," Leon said, looking up from his pad and removing his headset. He tore off the paper and held it out to Evelyn. "There's a problem."

Evelyn went forward quickly and took the message from him, scanning it.

"It says he can't send transport for us," she said in dismay. "They're all tied up in Dunkirk. We have to wait until something becomes free."

"What?" Finn scowled. "For how long?"

"It doesn't say." Evelyn looked up, meeting his gaze. "We're to stay in Bordeaux and wait."

"I can recommend a clean, modest boarding house not far from here," Leon said, sitting back in his chair. "The woman who runs it is a particular friend of mine."

"But we cannot wait," Finn exclaimed. "We must leave France!"

Evelyn stared at him, her eyes narrowing at the vehemence in his voice.

"I agree, but we can't do that without transportation, which is not forthcoming," she said logically. "We don't have any choice but to wait."

"There must be another way." Finn looked at Leon. "There must be some way to get to England."

"Do you dislike Bordeaux so much?" he asked, raising his eyebrows. "Why are you in such a rush? The German armies are far from here at the moment. There's no need for panic."

"The German armies may be, but someone has been following us since we left Reims," Finn said grimly. "I'm not willing to risk that they might not be the enemy."

"What?!" Evelyn gasped, staring at him. "What do you mean? I have seen no one!"

"He has been behind us all the way. He is driving a black sedan. He's a tall man, but I was never able to get a good look at his face." Finn ran a hand through his hair. "I didn't want to say anything because I didn't want to alarm you, and I thought we would be leaving soon enough anyway. But now you must know."

"How do you know he is following you? You were on a road crowded with people fleeing Paris. He could be just another one, going in the same direction," Leon pointed out practically.

Evelyn shook her head slowly, her eyes on Finn's face.

"No. We changed routes several times, trying to find one that was less crowded. If he was just another refugee, he would not have been likely to take all the same routes as we did. That is too much of a coincidence. You say he's been there since Reims?"

"Yes. I noticed him shortly after we left. He has kept his distance, and appears to simply be following us, but I don't like it."

Evelyn took a deep breath, her mind spinning. How had she not noticed a black car following them for days? Then she shook her head. Because they were on crowded roads packed with every type of vehicle imaginable, and that included several black sedans. Even if she had noticed, she wouldn't have thought anything of it. Why, then, had Finn?

"Why did he get your attention?" she asked, looking at him. "What made you notice him?"

His eyes met hers. "I don't know," he said, shaking his head. "Something just felt…off."

"Well," Leon said, pulling out a cigarette and lighting it. "This changes things. If you are being watched, you must leave Bordeaux as soon as possible. And I must take care myself, for whoever it is now knows that I am an associate."

Finn looked at him, startled. "My God, you're right. I should have thought of that before coming here. My sincere apologies."

Leon waved his apology away. "It will be fine. I will think of a perfectly reasonable excuse to have had such a long visit with you. But we must think! You cannot stay and wait for Bill to send transportation. We don't know who this person is, or what they want. They may be dangerous."

"If he was, wouldn't he have done something on the road?" Evelyn asked.

"Not necessarily," Finn said. "He may have been waiting to see where we were going, and who we were meeting."

"And now that you're here, he may make his move," Leon finished. "Yes. You must leave Bordeaux with all possible speed."

"Yes, but how?" Evelyn looked from one man to the other. "We don't have a boat."

Leon looked up at that. "What did you say?"

"That we don't have a boat," she repeated. "Why? What are

you thinking?"

"That we may have something after all," he said slowly. "There is a man, a captain of a large fishing trawler, who might be persuaded to help. He has been in port for over a week now. Provided that he hasn't left again, he may be willing to take you to England."

"Who is he?" Finn asked.

"Oh, he's someone of very questionable character," Leon said cheerfully. "His family has been smuggling for generations. There isn't much he doesn't know about how to get things in and out of France undetected."

"A smuggler!"

Leon nodded. "Yes. Are you shocked? You really shouldn't be. It is a very lucrative and exciting means of making a living."

"Can he be trusted?" Finn demanded.

"Of course he can, for a price. He is a good man, but he won't do anything for free."

Finn and Evelyn looked at each other, then Evelyn slowly nodded.

"Try to reach him," she said. "If he can get us to England, I'll pay him whatever he asks."

"I told you another would be along shortly."

Miles looked at Bernard and managed a tired smile. After the Stukas had disappeared into the horizon, *HMS Grafton* had cast off. Miles had watched her go with a sense of forlorn helplessness until his new friend had cheerfully told him that another ship would come. It was how it had been all morning. And he had been correct. Not long after the *Grafton* had headed into the channel, another destroyer sailed up.

"So you did," he murmured now, moving along the pier as the ship began loading the column of soldiers.

"We just might make it away before more Jerries come," Bernard said, glancing up into the sky as he shuffled alongside Miles. "I know you said your boys are up there, but where were your mates when those Stukas came diving down?"

Miles glanced at him. "Probably keeping fifty more away," he said shortly.

Bernard caught the edge in his voice and peered at him for a minute, then wisely dropped the subject. Miles looked at the destroyer just ahead of them, watching as the soldiers were loaded on and directed along the deck. It was afternoon now, and he was starving. The worst of his thirst had been appeased by Bernard and his canteen, which he offered willingly when he realized Miles didn't have anything, but there was nothing he could do about the hunger gnawing at his insides. Yet neither the rumbling of his stomach nor his pure exhaustion could dampen his joy at realizing that in a few minutes, he would be aboard a destroyer in His Majesty's Royal Navy, going home to rejoin his squadron. As much as this would never rate as one of his better days, Miles was acutely aware of just how lucky he was to be yards away from going home.

"If I don't see you again, best of luck to you," he said suddenly, turning to hold his hand out to Bernard as they reached the gang plank. "Thank you."

"For what?" Bernard asked, shaking his hand.

"For the water, and the conversation."

Bernard grinned. "Aw, that was nothing. You saved me life by getting me down in the sand, so that makes us even."

Miles smiled tiredly and turned to go up the gangway to the ship. At the end, an officer was waiting with a clipboard in his hand, a nurse by his side. Seeing his uniform and wings, the man motioned to him.

"Officers are in the ward room," he said. "What's your name?"

"Flying Officer Miles Lacey, 66 Squadron, RAF Horsham. Well, I suppose it's Coltishall now. We're moving today."

He wrote on his sheet and nodded, looking up. "Shot down, were you?"

"Yes. Early this morning."

"Well, welcome aboard, Flying Officer. We'll send a signal to Fighter Command and let them know you're aboard. Don't worry. We'll get you back to your squadron." He motioned to a different direction from where they were sending all the non-officers. "Go along that way and someone will direct you."

"Thank you."

Miles went along the narrow deck, suddenly feeling almost weepy. The sway of the ship on the water was comforting, and he allowed himself the luxury of knowing that he would be on his way back to England soon. He'd survived getting shot and crashing, and then had survived a bloody Stuka attack. He was lucky to be alive, and even luckier to have made it not only to Dunkirk, but off the beach as well.

Into the Iron Shadows

A petty officer stood ahead, watching him come along the deck. When he reached him, the young man directed him down a narrow flight of metal steps, telling him to turn left at the bottom. Miles did as he was told, the sun disappearing as he descended below decks. A few minutes later, after another sailor's directions and several more turns, he ended up being shown into the ship's wardroom.

It was a large room already partially filled with several army officers. The tables had been moved to make room for more seating and, as Miles entered, all the officers already present looked up to see who the newcomer was. At the sight of his uniform, the room fell silent, and Miles was conscious of several stony looks of dislike.

He cleared his throat and moved through the room to a place in the corner, feeling their eyes on him as he went. The silence was thick and Miles suddenly wished he were back on deck, away from the hostile looks he was receiving now. You wouldn't even know they were all on the same side, he reflected, seating himself. As he settled onto a chair, his feet and legs throbbed in relief. He'd been standing in line for over six hours in flight boots that were not made for it, and he couldn't stop the silent exhale of relief.

"Looks like the RAF finally decided to show up," someone said, breaking the silence. "Nice of them to join us."

Miles felt his mouth tighten, but chose to ignore the remark and instead reached into his jacket pocket, feeling for his cigarette case.

"Where the bloody hell have they been? That's what I want to know," another voice said.

"Having tea," quipped another.

"That's enough of that, lads." An older man barked from the opposite corner. He was sitting with two others, and Miles heard the authority in his voice. He was obviously the ranking officer in the room. "We've had enough fighting as it is. Give the lad a break."

There was an unintelligible mumble, but the comments stopped and the low-voiced conversations that had been happening when he first walked in continued.

Pulling out his cigarettes, Miles was suddenly and irrevocably exhausted. He couldn't even begin to imagine what kind of image he presented with his bloody forehead, dirt-streaked uniform, and the bloody Mae West still hanging around his neck. Yet he was too tired to even care. The moment he sat down, it was as if his body had given up carrying him and was checking out for the day. Any adrenaline that had kept him going was long gone. He was weary, hungry, thirsty, and now he was irritated by the attitude in the room.

They thought the RAF weren't doing anything to protect them, but how the bloody hell did they think he ended up in here with them? Did they think he was out for a pleasure flight?

Miles suddenly wished he was in the recreation room back at Horsham, sitting with Chris and Rob. Amusement went through him at the thought and, as he lit his cigarette, Miles reflected on just what the Yank would have said a moment ago if he'd been on hand to hear the comments. Good Lord, a second Revolutionary War would have commenced right here on a royal ship, and Miles wasn't sure that Chris wouldn't have won that particular fight.

The amusement faded just as quickly as it had come and he blew smoke out, wondering if Rob, Chris and the others had made it through the day. Were they back up there now? They had been flying multiple sorties over the patrol line the past two days, trying to keep the bombers away from Dunkirk. He looked at his watch. This was about the time that his flight would have been back over the Channel. Had anyone else been hit? He thought of Rob, disappearing into the clouds with two 109s on his tail. Had he got either of them? Or had they got him?

Had 66 Squadron done anything at all today to help protect the columns of troops on that beach? Suddenly, Miles wasn't so sure that any of it was worth it. They were so desperately outnumbered up there, by nearly four to one at his calculation, and the blokes on the ground obviously thought they weren't doing enough. Perhaps they weren't, but they were bloody well doing the best they could.

He just hoped it would be enough.

Chapter Thirty-One

Evelyn lay awkwardly on her side in the backseat of Leon's Citroen, wondering what on earth Miles would say if he could see her. She had never been so exceedingly glad that the likelihood of running into him was nonexistent. Finn was behind her, laying in the opposite direction, doing his best to give her enough room on the narrow seat to be respectable. It was a losing battle, however, and as the car went around the corner, he grabbed her around her waist to keep her from tumbling onto the floor.

"Is this all really necessary?" she asked in exasperation. "We must be away from the café by now!"

"Yes, but there are three black sedans behind us," Leon said from the driver's seat. "Without knowing if one of them is your friend, it's best for you to stay hidden."

"Ooof!" Finn grunted as they went over a bump in the road.

"Almost there. Just one more turn," Leon assured them cheerfully.

The turn nearly sent Evelyn flying again and Finn hauled her back with an arm around her waist.

"I'm sorry," he muttered. "I assure you this is just as awkward for me."

Evelyn was betrayed in a laugh. "At least there are only the two of us. Imagine if Josephine was here as well!"

"She wouldn't fit."

"Ah! Here we are!" Leon announced a few minutes later before coming to a stop. "Stay down another minute while I ensure all black sedans have passed."

He got out of the car and Evelyn lifted her head to look at Finn. He shrugged.

"He's conscientious," he said. "I'll give him that."

A moment later Leon tapped on the glass of the back window, grinning. He motioned them out and Evelyn sat up thankfully, straightening her jacket and smoothing her skirt back down over her knees. Leon opened the door for her and she accepted his offered hand to help her climb out.

"We are quite safe from curious eyes," he told her. "There is only one way back here and I have closed the gate."

They were in a large enclosed area that looked as if it may have once been the courtyard of an inn. A stone building ran along two sides of the square, and on the third was what looked to be a stable that had been converted into parking for automobiles.

"Where are we?" Finn asked, climbing out behind her and looking around. "Is this an inn?"

"It used to be, many years ago. Now it is a restaurant, among other things." Leon turned and led them across the pavement to a door a few feet away. "This is the back entrance. We will go through the kitchens, but you will not mind, no?"

"Not at all," Evelyn said, adjusting her hat. "Is the Captain here already?"

"Oh yes. He's always here. He rents a room when he's in port."

Leon opened the door and they went into a large and bustling kitchen. It wasn't yet time for the evening rush and the kitchen was fairly empty. The few cooks that were there paid no attention as they went through their domain. They were obviously used to strangers coming and going through the back door, which made Evelyn wonder just what kind of establishment they were in.

She followed Leon into the restaurant with some apprehension, but relaxed when it turned out to be a perfectly respectable dining room. The only occupants were at the corner table, and Leon led them towards it, breaking into a large smile as he went.

"Jacques!" he cried. "How good to see you, my friend!"

Three men were seated at the table with bread, cheese, and wine in front of them, but it was evident that they weren't there to eat. They hadn't touched the food, but the bottle of wine on the table was nearly empty. As they approached, all three stood up, staring at Evelyn.

"It is always a pleasure, Leon!"

The man in the corner wiped his mouth with his napkin and nodded to Leon, a congenial smile on his face. Evelyn studied him, pleasantly surprised. He didn't look like a smuggler. He was dressed fashionably and, while his hair was a little too long for respectable circles, his mustache was neatly trimmed and his chin was smooth. In fact, he looked like the type of man one would find at the theatre with a woman on each arm.

"Mademoiselle Dufour, may I present Captain Beaulieu," Leon said with a flourish. "Captain, Mademoiselle Dufour and her companion, Monsieur Maes."

Into the Iron Shadows

Captain Beaulieu came around the table and took the hand she offered, bowing over it gallantly in true French fashion.

"Mademoiselle," he murmured, straightening up and smiling easily. "Monsieur," he added, turning to shake Finn's hand. "I understand from Leon that you'd like to hire my boat."

Evelyn glanced at Leon, who smiled and shrugged.

"Yes, but we were hoping you would captain it," she said, turning her gaze back to the Captain.

He smiled enigmatically. "But of course! It goes nowhere without me. Where do you wish to go?"

Evelyn hesitated and he made a tsk-ing noise with his mouth, a comically chagrined look on his face.

"But my apologies, Mademoiselle! Leon told me it was a delicate matter, and I was so distracted by your beauty that I failed to remember. Please forgive me. We will go into another room where we can speak privately." He turned to look at Finn and Leon. "Please have a seat, gentlemen, and some wine. Our business will take but a moment! Pedro, open another bottle of wine!"

Finn looked at Evelyn sharply. "Geneviève?"

She smiled reassuringly. "It's quite all right, Finn. I'll be back in a moment."

He frowned, but nodded. Evelyn smiled at the captain and he held out his arm, motioning for her to accompany him. They walked across the restaurant to a door behind a well-placed screen, and he stood aside for her to enter.

She walked into a small room that was both office and storage closet, and looked around. A desk was positioned on one side with two chairs before it, and cases of wine and cigarettes were stacked along the wall on the other side. She turned to look at the captain as he closed the door. A feeling of uneasiness went through her, but she pushed it aside. If this man could get her out of France, she could spend a few minutes alone with him.

"Now then, that's better, no?" he asked, turning to her with a smile. "Please sit down! This is my office when I am in Bordeaux."

"Your office?" she asked, raising her eyebrows. "Do you own the restaurant?"

"I do," came the unexpected answer. "Of course, I have a manager who takes care of the business for me. It's difficult to run a restaurant from a boat, after all."

"Yes, I imagine it would be." Evelyn sat down in one of the chairs as he went around to seat himself behind the desk.

"Cigarette?" he offered.

"No thank you."

"To business, then! Where would you like me to take you and Monsieur Maes?" he asked, sitting back and folding his hands over his stomach. "Please don't say Corsica. I've just returned, and I'm afraid I was forced to leave in a hurry. It wouldn't be wise for me to go back so soon."

Evelyn choked back a laugh. "No, it's not Corsica. I was hoping you would take us to England."

"Ah! Yes, that's much better." His brown eyes studied her for a moment and she had the uncomfortable sense that he saw much more than was apparent. "What is in England?"

"The king," she said pertly.

He burst out laughing and sat forward, his eyes still dancing. "So you will not tell me, eh? That's your business, of course, but I like to know what I'm sailing into. There won't be a jealous husband standing in port with a blunderbuss, for example?"

It was Evelyn's turn to laugh. "No. I assure you, there is no jealous husband or blunderbuss in your immediate future."

"What a pity. It's been some time since I saw some real excitement," he said with a wink. "Very well, then. I can convey you and your companion to Plymouth. Leon did tell you there would be a fee?"

"Yes, of course. How much?"

He considered her for a moment. "Twelve thousand francs. Not a penny less."

Evelyn raised her eyebrow. "I can take an airplane for that amount."

He smiled and shrugged. "But you are not taking an airplane. You are asking to take a boat. My boat. That is my price."

"That's robbery."

"That, mademoiselle, is good business. You have a demand; I have the supply."

Evelyn exhaled and stood, nodding. "Very well. I will give you half now and half when we arrive safely in Plymouth."

She opened her purse and counted out six thousand francs, laying them on the desk. He watched her and, when she was closing her purse, he gathered up the notes and opened the top desk drawer, placing them inside. Pulling a key from his pocket, he locked the drawer and stood up, coming around the side of the desk.

"And what's to stop me from taking the rest of the money now?" he asked, stopping in front of her and blocking her exit to the door.

Into the Iron Shadows

Evelyn looked into his face, inches away, and smiled faintly, setting her purse on the desk.

"I wouldn't advise it."

He crooked an eyebrow. "Oh? Why?"

Evelyn swept her foot forward, knocking one of his ankles to the side at the same time that her left hand shot in an arc towards his neck, slicing down to land solidly in the crevice between his collarbone and base of the neck. A moment later, his head was pressed down on his desk, face down, and his arms were bent at an awkward angle behind his back.

"This is me being a lady," she said calmly. "If you try to rob me, I will no longer be a lady. Do we understand each other?"

Captain nodded and she released him. He straightened up slowly, touching his neck gingerly, and turned to face her. Instead of looking wary or angry, he was grinning widely. A gold tooth sparkled in the light from a lamp on the desk.

"I think we will get along very well together, mademoiselle," he announced cheerfully, turning for the door. "I will take you to Plymouth. We will leave immediately. I've already had my boat made ready."

"You have?" she asked, picking up her purse and following him.

"But of course! I had a premonition we would come to an agreement, and so we have." He opened the door and gave her a half-bow, still grinning. "It will be a pleasure to have such a fascinating lady aboard."

Miles was dozing, his head tilted to the side and resting on the Mae West, when he was almost thrown from his chair as the ship listed suddenly to the side. He looked around in alarm to find all the officers in the wardroom in the same state of startled confusion.

"What the bloody hell was that?" someone demanded.

They had left Dunkirk just ten minutes before after the last of the soldiers had been loaded on. As they pulled away, there was a collective sigh of relief throughout the wardroom. Now they were all staring at each other in alarmed apprehension, some jolted out of their naps like Miles, and others out of their low-voiced conversation. The ship listed again to the opposite side, and Miles grabbed the side of his chair with one hand and planted the other on the wall to keep his balance.

Then they heard the sound of the destroyer's guns firing above them.

"It's the bloody Luftwaffe!" the same voice exclaimed in disgust. "They're bombing the ship!"

Miles sucked in his breath as they listed again. He tried to listen for the sound of bombs, but all he could hear were the ships own guns. How many were there? Were they Dornier 17s? Stukas? Were there fighters as well? The questions clamored in his head as he grit his teeth, watching an officer slip off his seat, falling to the floor as the ship lurched violently.

The door to the wardroom swung open suddenly and a lieutenant gripped the sides of the frame to keep his balance while he looked inside.

"Flying Officer Lacey?" he called.

Miles looked up in surprise. "Yes?"

"Will you come with me, please? The Captain would like a word."

Miles nodded and stood up, bracing his legs as the ship lurched again. As he made his way to the door and the waiting officer, he felt some relief to be getting away from the side-long stares and outright hostile looks that he'd been ignoring for the better part of an hour. That he was getting the chance to go above deck and get some air was even better. The smell of sweat, dirt and cigarettes was overwhelming in the wardroom and, while he was perfectly prepared to ignore it, he certainly wouldn't turn down the opportunity to get away from it.

The officer waited for him to go through the door, then he closed it firmly and led the way down the narrow corridor to metal steps. Miles followed, keeping his balance fairly well now that he was on his feet and moving.

"We're being attacked?" he asked, climbing the steps.

"Yes. They've been attacking the ships all morning," the lieutenant said over his shoulder. "The *Grafton's* gone down. The Captain will help pick up the survivors but we have to make it through this first."

Miles swallowed, his blood running cold. If he'd reached the beach just half an hour earlier, he might have been on the *Grafton* now.

"Down as in sunk?" he heard himself asking.

"That's the only down I know of."

They reached an upper deck and the officer opened a metal door. Fresh air and saltwater met them as they stepped onto the outer deck and Miles took a deep breath. It caught in his throat as he stared out over the railing. Both Stukas and Dornier 17s were swarming in the sky above, raining bombs around the destroyer. As he stared, frozen in shock, one such bomb hit the water next to where they were, sending spray over the side of the railing and causing the ship to lurch again.

"This way!" The lieutenant yelled over the cacophony of noise. Bombs, airplanes and the ships own guns made it almost impossible to hear anything, and Miles had to bend his head forward and strain to hear him. "Stay away from the side!"

He nodded and followed him along the wall until they reached the bridge. The officer opened the door and they ducked inside just as another bomb fell into the water near the bow.

"Officer Lacey, sir!" The lieutenant announced.

A tall imposing man turned from the panoramic window to look at Miles. He waved him forward, lowering the binoculars he was holding.

"Officer Lacey!" He greeted him with a nod, waving him forward. "I understand you're a pilot?"

"Yes, sir. With 66 Squadron," Miles said, walking forward to join the Captain.

"I'm Captain Dennings." The Captain introduced himself briefly and turned to look back out the window. "Do you know what those are?"

"Yes, sir. Dornier 17s and Stuka dive bombers."

"And the ones over there?" he asked, pointing. "You can use these if you need to," he added, holding out the binoculars.

Miles shook his head. "No need, sir. Those are Me 109s. They're escorting the Dorniers. The ones coming from over there: they're Hurricanes. They're going for the Stukas."

The Captain nodded and motioned to the lieutenant who was still standing near the door.

"Good. I wonder if you would mind going up and giving our gunners a hand?" he asked, looking at Miles fully for the first time. "They can't tell the difference between ours and theirs. They don't know which ones to shoot. It was pretty straight-forward until the fighters showed up, but now they need some help with identification. I'm afraid they haven't had to tell them apart yet."

Miles nodded. "Of course, sir."

"I have to advise you that if those fighters get close enough, they'll aim for the guns. It's dangerous up there. Are you still willing?"

"It's no more dangerous than anything else I've done today," Miles said with a grin.

The Captain broke into a smile. "Good show. What do you

fly?"

"Spitfire, sir."

"Well, I'll do my best to get you back up in one. We need all the help we can get."

"Yes, sir."

The Captain nodded and saluted. "Good luck, lad. And thank you. Lieutenant Brown will show you to the gunners."

Miles saluted smartly and turned to leave. As he stepped out of the bridge, a high-pitched wail sent a bolt of fear shooting through him. Images of bodies jerking on the beach flashed into his mind, and he sucked in his breath. Forcing the memory away, he looked up to find one of the Stukas in a steep dive, aiming for their ship. He was in perfect position to hit midship. Miles stared in horrified fascination as the deadly machine drew closer, the wailing scream heard over the sound of the guns. Before he could get his bombs away, a Hurricane shot into view, firing directly into the exposed belly of the bomber. The Stuka came apart in a fire ball, and the Hurricane spun upwards to go after another one.

"Huzzah!" Lieutenant Brown cheered, turning to grab Miles' hand in his excitement. "I thought we were done for," he exclaimed, pumping his hand in his enthusiasm. "Thank God for the RAF! Was that one of yours?"

"No, but I'd buy him a pint if I knew who it was," Miles replied, relief making his legs weak.

"Come on. Let's get you to the guns before we shoot one of our own!"

Miles nodded, following him back down the deck. His shoulder throbbed from the excited handshake he'd just received, but he barely noticed the pain. Relief was still mixing with adrenaline, making him feel both shaky and invincible at the same time. Along with it came a feeling of immense pride. Fighter Command was up there, and they'd just saved this destroyer and thousands of men onboard from a sure hit from a Stuka. Despite what the army thought, they *were* making a difference.

And he couldn't wait to get back up there with them.

Evelyn walked next to Finn along the pier, eyeing Captain Beaulieu's boat. It was the only one at the end of the dock and, as Leon had said, it was a large fishing trawler. She suspected that the nets hanging at the sides had never been used, but that was none of her concern. It looked to be a solid vessel, and it would take her and Finn to Plymouth. That was all that mattered.

"Please let Pedro carry your case," Captain Beaulieu pleaded. "I don't feel comfortable with a lady, and guest, carrying her own luggage."

"Thank you, but it is quite light, and I like to keep it with me," she said with a smile.

He shook his head and threw his hands up in the age-old male expression of hopelessness.

"As you wish, mademoiselle."

Finn looked around the pier as they walked. "Yours is the only boat docked," he said.

"Yes. I prefer to keep my boat separate from the others. I pay for the use of the entire pier," the Captain said, glancing at Evelyn. "Nothing is too expensive if it ensures my own comfort."

"Touché," she murmured with a chuckle.

"How long will it take to cast off?" Finn asked, and the captain shrugged.

"No more than fifteen minutes. Ten if we hurry."

"Shall we say ten minutes?" Evelyn asked after a glance at Finn's face.

"For you, mademoiselle? The world!"

Evelyn smiled. Despite everything, she was suddenly enjoying herself immensely. The Captain was amusing, the sun was warm and bright, and she was on her way home after almost a month away. She had been sent to Belgium with the instructions to be quick in case Hitler moved at last. Now Belgium, Holland, and Luxembourg had fallen, and France was all but lost. The smile faded. Once again, she had been caught in the German's path. At this rate, she would begin to think that she brought the Nazis with her!

"Tell me, Captain Beaulieu," she said, looking up at him. "What will you do if the Germans come to Bordeaux?"

He glanced at her and the charming smile that had been on his face since she met him an hour ago disappeared.

"I will do what my family has done for generations," he said promptly.

"And what is that?"

"I will make the best of a bad situation."

Evelyn was just opening her mouth to respond when she heard a sharp intake of breath beside her. She turned her head to look at Finn just as he threw himself into her, throwing her to the ground.

It happened so quickly that she didn't even have time to take a breath. One minute she was walking between the captain and Finn, and the very next minute she was hitting the wooden planks, her suitcase flying from her hand. Evelyn grabbed for it, her heart in her throat as it skidded towards the edge of the pier. Just before it went over the edge, the captain grabbed it. She sucked in her breath in relief only to have it knocked right back out when Finn landed on top of her.

"Uunh!"

She grunted and winced as her head hit the pier with the force of his body impacting hers. Through the ringing in her ears, she heard Captain Beaulieu yell and boots pounded along the pier, causing the wooden planks to vibrate.

"Finn!" she gasped. "I can't breathe! Get off of me!"

Finn rolled off her, clutching his shoulder. "Apologies," he gasped, his face pale. "It was all I could think to do."

"All you could think—" Evelyn began angrily, pushing herself up onto her arm. She stopped suddenly and her eyes widened as Finn's slid closed. "Finn? Finn!"

Evelyn leaned over him, patting his face. She looked down and saw blood covering his chest and the gasp turned to a cry of alarm.

"Captain!" she cried, twisting around to look for him. "He's bleeding!"

"I know," he said, his back to her.

Evelyn suddenly realized she and Finn were surrounded with the captain's crew and that every one of them was holding a gun. The weapons, however, weren't pointed at her or Finn, but were facing outside the circle.

"What's happening?!"

"Someone tried to shoot you. Pedro, get her to the boat! George!" A massive man turned in response. "Carry the monsieur aboard and take him to Philip. Richard, you come with me. Everyone else, make sure nothing happens to either of them until I return!"

Evelyn listened to the calm orders and shook her head as if to clear it. Her mind was spinning and she looked down at Finn in a daze. He was covered in blood, his eyes closed and his body still. She had no idea what was happening, but when Pedro bent to help her up, she allowed him to gently pull her to her feet. As soon as she was out of the way, George bent down and picked up Finn's motionless figure. He tossed him over his shoulder like a bag of grain and Evelyn gasped, wincing. Finn didn't stir. And then she was being rushed along the pier in the center of a group of men, unable to do anything but hurry along with them.

"My case!" she cried suddenly. Without a word, Pedro held up the suitcase and she exhaled in relief. "Thank you," she said automatically, not expecting a reply. She didn't even know if the man had heard her, moving as fast as they were.

She looked at Finn's head, bouncing against the giant's back. His dark hair was hanging down, swaying with the movement of his head, and she bit her lip, her gut tightening. Was he alive? She didn't know. All she knew was that he had just saved her life.

But from whom?

Chapter Thirty-Two

Miles stared out of the window and watched as the platform began moving, appearing to slide backwards as the train pulled out of the station. Darkness had fallen, and once they left the station, all he saw in the window was his own reflection. His hair hung over his ears and forehead in disarray, and his face was streaked with dried blood, dirt and something that looked suspiciously like oil. He looked as if he'd been through Hell, and he turned his face away tiredly. He had.

"Are you expecting to drown on the train?"

Miles looked at the navy lieutenant sitting opposite him. He was staring at him in some amusement and, when Miles frowned in confusion, he motioned to the Mae West still hanging around Miles' neck.

"Good Lord," he said tiredly, lifting it off. "I'd forgotten it was there."

The lieutenant chuckled and leaned forward to help when Miles' right arm refused to cooperate.

"Been through a day, have you?" he asked, pulling the life vest over his head. "There. That's better."

Miles took the Mae West and dropped it onto the seat next to him. "You could say that. Thanks."

The sailor watched him for a moment, then held out his hand. "Lieutenant Willis."

"Flying Officer Lacey," Miles said, shaking his hand.

"So what happened?"

"I went down over Belgium. I've just come from Dunkirk."

Lieutenant Willis nodded, not surprised. "So did I. I'm to London for the night, then back again in the morning."

"Well, on behalf of the poor blokes on the beach, thank you," Miles said.

Lieutenant Willis nodded. "And on behalf of the blokes on the ships, thank *you*."

Miles grimaced tiredly. "It doesn't seem like we're making much of a difference."

Into the Iron Shadows

"A Spitfire made all the difference today to us. It took out a Dornier that was about to drop a load of bombs on our boat."

Despite his exhaustion, Miles felt a surge of pride. "That's my kite," he murmured, leaning his head back. "It's what I fly."

His eyes began to close and he heard the lieutenant get up. A second later, a light blanket was draped over him. He forced his eyes open in time to see the sailor settle back onto his seat. Catching him looking at him, the lieutenant smiled.

"You're worn out. Get some rest. It's a long ride to London."

Miles thought he thanked him, but he wasn't positive. He couldn't keep his eyes open any longer. They slid closed of their own accord and he sighed. The rocking motion of the train relaxed him and, as he drifted off to sleep, a pair of blue eyes smiled at him.

Evie. I made it. I made it back from Hell. I can't wait to see you again...

Evelyn stood at the railing, watching France grow smaller in the distance. The breeze from the water snatched at her hair and she lifted her hands to pull her hat from her head. As soon as she removed it, the wind whipped at her hair, pulling it free from the pins that secured it in a twist behind her head. She inhaled deeply, relishing the brisk salt air and the feel of the boat swaying beneath her feet.

"I've left everything behind," Finn said, joining her at the rail. "My home, my country, my family. And now I'm leaving the continent altogether." He stared at the coastline of France in the distance. "Am I doing the right thing?"

Evelyn looked at him thoughtfully. "Only you can answer that."

He was silent, staring at the horizon. Evelyn looked back at France, then turned and leaned back against the railing.

"How are you feeling?"

"Like I've been shot."

"You gave me quite a scare. I was trying to decide how I was going to tell Bill that I lost you."

Finn looked down at her with a flash of a grin. "And what did you come up with?"

"That you got into a quarrel with a butcher over a pig," she said promptly.

Finn laughed, then winced in pain. "Don't make me laugh," he begged. "I don't know where Captain Beaulieu found his doctor, but I think he's more suited to pulling bullets out of corpses."

"I'm glad he wasn't," Evelyn said fervently. "Thank God it was only lodged in your shoulder. You shouldn't be standing out here. Let's get you below deck where you can rest."

"No. I need the fresh air. It's nothing. Just a flesh wound."

"At least come and sit down, then," she said, nodding to a few piles of rope a few feet away.

He made a face but followed her over to the rope, sitting down. She sat next to him and they were quiet for a moment, watching as France became a sliver in the distance.

"You saved my life." Evelyn finally broke the silence. "I can't begin to express my gratefulness, but thank you."

Finn glanced at her, a faint smile on his lips. "Don't thank me. I fully expect you to repay the favor one day."

She chuckled. "If I ever can, I will."

"What's it like in England?" he asked after a moment of silence. "Will I like it?"

"I think so," she said slowly. "London is much like any other city, but if you get into the country, well," she shrugged, "it's beautiful."

"I wonder if I will ever see my home again. I feel as though I won't."

Evelyn looked at him sharply. "Why do you say that?"

"I don't know. It's just a feeling I have." He shook his head and glanced at her, obviously forcing a smile. "Perhaps my brush with death has made me pessimistic."

"I thought you said it was just a flesh wound."

"Yes, but it could have been worse."

"Everything can always be worse. Stop being dramatic."

"You're not very sympathetic. You wouldn't make a very good nurse."

"I know. That's why I joined MI6."

Finn chuckled and they watched France completely disappear in companionable silence.

"It will never be the same," she murmured sadly. "I fear that the France I love is about to disappear forever."

He was quiet for a moment, then he reached out and squeezed her hand gently.

"Perhaps. And perhaps something stronger will come from the rubble. You must have faith. We will win. Such evil cannot triumph forever."

Evelyn was silent for a long time, then she nodded slowly. "I believe you're right. But what will we have to endure until that day?"

Into the Iron Shadows

"Tears. Pain. Anger." He looked at her. "But also laughter. Joy. Hope. These are the things you will hold on to. They are what will give you purpose."

"How have you done it?" she asked. "How have you continued in the face of such…such…"

"Hopelessness?"

She nodded.

"Because even hopelessness must have hope. You cannot have an absence of something that doesn't exist."

Evelyn absorbed that silently, then sighed. "I feel as if you're years older than me, and yet you can't be."

"I have seen much more than you." Finn shrugged. "I pray that you will never see the things that I have. But I have not seen everything, and I do not know everything. I can only share with you what I have learned so far."

"And I thank you for that."

A sudden wind whipped around them, causing her to shiver, and Evelyn stood up.

"I'm going below. Will you come?"

"I'll stay here for a little while. The fresh air is good for me."

She nodded and began to turn away, then hesitated and turned back.

"How did you know that someone was going to shoot at me?"

Finn looked up at her for a moment, then he sighed almost imperceptibly.

"I was looking behind us at the road," he said slowly. "I was looking for the sedan that had been following us. I didn't see it, but I saw *him*. The sunlight gave him away. He was standing in shadows, but he moved and the sun just lit his face. Once I saw him, I saw the gun."

Evelyn nodded and began to turn away again only to turn back once more.

"How did you know it was him?"

"Because I recognized him. You would have too. It was the man who helped you with the cart in the road after the Stukas attacked."

Evelyn stared at him, her skin growing colder. "What?"

He nodded.

"And I can tell you positively that he is not a refugee. He's a German assassin, and he was clearly there for you."

Chapter Thirty-Three

RAF Coltishall
May 30

Miles knocked on the door, opening it on the command to enter. He stepped into a small office dominated by a desk in front of a window. Half unpacked boxes were stacked on the desk and chairs and, as he entered, Ashmore looked up, lifting a stack of folders out of one of them.

"Ah Miles! You found us all right?" he asked, setting the stack down on the desk.

"Yes, sir. I remembered last night when I got into London. Lucky thing or I would have gone on to Horsham."

"One hell of a day to move stations, wasn't it?" Ashmore moved a box off a chair and motioned from Miles to have a seat. "You had quite a day. I received the message from HQ that you'd been picked up at Dunkirk last night when we got back from a sortie. I was jolly glad to hear it."

He went around and sat down behind the desk, moving another box onto the floor so that he could see Miles. He studied him for a minute, then sat back.

"You've been to see the doctor?"

"Yes, sir. I'm grounded today. He wants me to rest and he will look me over again in the morning."

"Injuries?"

"A bump on the head and a dislocated shoulder, nothing more," Miles said with a smile. "I was fortunate enough to run into a Belgian medic. He took care of my shoulder at the side of the road and I went on my way."

"Bertie showed me the report. You landed south of Ostend?"

"Yes, on the beach at Saint-Idesbald."

"Ainsworth said you were hit in your fuel tank."

"That's right. I decided to try my luck over land rather than go into the drink. The engine went as I was coming over the beach, but I put her down right enough. It must have been then that I hit my head.

The next thing I remember, the wing was on fire. I just made it out in time."

"There was nothing left for the Germans to find?" Ashmore asked.

"No, sir. It exploded right enough. There would have been nothing left."

"Good." He shook his head. "You're one lucky blighter. We were glad to hear you'd made it. Ainsworth was rather put out, I believe, until we got the news. He seemed to think he should have stayed with you."

"He had two 109s on him, sir. He led them away from me. I couldn't do a bloody thing about them."

"So I understand." Ashmore exhaled and rubbed his face. "The rest of the squadron is up now, and I'll be going up with the next flight. I wanted to talk to you before they return. There's no easy way to say it, so I'll just say it. Mother's gone."

"What?" Miles stared at him, an empty feeling of shock rolling through him.

"He went down yesterday afternoon. No chute."

Miles was silent, taking a deep breath. Ashmore gave him a moment, then cleared his throat.

"Bad luck all around yesterday, I'm afraid," he said. "But with Mother out of it, you know what that means."

"Yes, sir." Miles swallowed. "I'm the new Flight Leader."

"That's right. I completed the paperwork last night after we heard you were on your way back. It's going to HQ today." Ashmore sat forward. "Once you're cleared to fly tomorrow, you'll take over A flight. Try not to get shot down again, will you?"

Miles choked on a short laugh. "I'll do my best, sir."

"Your new kite is waiting for you. It's one of the new Spits. Why don't you go out and get familiar with it? Have the ground sergeant run you through the differences?"

"Yes, sir." Miles stood and turned towards the door, still feeling numb.

"Lacey?"

He paused and turned back. "Yes, sir?"

"Welcome home."

Miles looked up from the evening newspaper as Rob and Chris

strode into the officer's lounge. It was smaller than the recreational room at Horsham, but the arm chairs were comfortable, and Miles had been ensconced in one for over an hour, waiting for A flight to return.

"Where the hell have you been?" Chris demanded cheerfully, spotting him in the corner. "Taking a tour of France?"

"Belgium *and* France," Miles drawled, folding the paper. "If a thing's worth doing, it's worth doing thoroughly."

"It's bloody good to see you," Rob announced, striding forward. "I went back over the Channel to try to find where you ditched, but there was no sign."

"That's because I wasn't in the drink. I decided to take my chances over land."

"Where did you set down?" Chris asked, sitting in a chair and loosening his tie.

"On a beach in Belgium, just south of Ostend."

Rob paused in the act of pulling out his cigarette case, lifting his eyes. "Ostend? The Germans have taken Ostend!"

"So I was informed," Miles drawled. "I met two rather wonderful Belgian soldiers who were kind enough to warn me off making for Ostend. They pointed me in the direction of France and sent me on my way."

"Jolly obliging of them." Rob leaned forward, offering Miles a cigarette. "They didn't go with you?"

"No. They were on their way to join their unit and surrender, of all the bloody things." Miles took a cigarette and reached in his pocket for his lighter. "There was no point in talking them out of it."

"Why would they surrender if they weren't caught?" Chris demanded with a frown.

"Because they were given orders to."

"I think I would have disregarded those particular orders," Rob murmured.

"I know I would," Chris agreed.

They were silent for a moment, reflecting on that, then Chris tilted his head, staring at Miles.

"When did you get back?"

"This morning. I had to take three different trains from Dover. Slept in the station in London, waiting for the last one." Miles sat back in his chair. "I saw the doctor when I got in. He grounded me today. He'll reevaluate in the morning."

"What's wrong with you?" Rob asked, eyeing him. "You look fine to me."

"I bumped my head when I landed, and dislocated my

shoulder. The shoulder is all right, but he's concerned about the head."

"Did you tell him you have a thick skull?" Rob asked with a grin.

"I told him some think I do. He wasn't impressed."

"How *did* you land?" Chris asked. "Rob said you were hit in the fuel tank."

"Without an engine," Miles said with a shrug. "It went out over the beach."

"Damn lucky you made it that far," Rob said, shaking his head. "How did you get to France?"

"Walked part of the way, then came across a bicycle and rode that the rest of the way. I'll tell you what, though. I'm bloody happy that we're up in the air and not on the ground. I discovered that I am *not* a fan of being bombed."

Chris and Rob were silent for a minute, then Chris looked up. "Was it bad?"

"It wasn't much of a picnic, no."

"Mother's dead," Rob said suddenly. "Went into the drink after a 109 got behind him."

"Ashmore told me." Miles shook his head. "I can't believe it. It doesn't seem real."

"Oh, it was real enough," Chris muttered. "The Kraut bastard shot straight into the cockpit."

Miles blanched at that. "You saw it happen?"

"Yeah. We were attacking a formation of Stukas." Chris looked up suddenly. "And the damnedest thing happened. I had one dead to rights in his dive, and I overshot him!"

Miles raised his eyebrows and sat forward. "That's what happened to me right before I got popped," he said. "I had a perfect shot at a Dornier. It couldn't get any better. I think it's because the guns are calibrated for 450 yards."

"That's too far!" Rob exclaimed. "You can't hit anything at that range! Not with fighters buzzing around all over us."

"I made the acquaintance of my new kite this afternoon, and I told the sergeant to re-calibrate the guns for 200 yards," Miles said, lowering his voice. "If I were you, I'd do the same."

"Can we do that?" Chris asked, intrigued. "I thought the RAF set the standard."

"The people who came up with 450 yards aren't the ones up there trying to shoot the bastards," Miles retorted. "I don't care if we can do it or not, my ground sergeant is doing it. I'm not risking my neck just to miss the buggers because I'm too close."

Rob nodded slowly and stood up. "You're right. I'm off to talk to Jones right now." He turned to leave, cigarette in hand, then turned back. "I'm glad you're back, by the way. I wasn't looking forward to telling Evie you'd gone in the drink."

Miles nodded, his eyes meeting Rob's. He saw the relief and smiled.

"Not this time, anyway," he said. "You know, I never thought I'd be this happy to see your ugly face."

Rob grinned and turned to continue to the door. Chris looked at Miles and shook his head.

"I guess you've earned your battle scars," he said. "What's it feel like?"

"Like I want a beer," Miles said, standing. "Care to join me?"

Chris nodded and stood up. "I thought you'd never suggest it."

As they reached the door, Miles paused and turned to look around the new officer's lounge. It wasn't the view he'd imagined on the ship in Dunkirk, but it would do. He was welcome here, and among friends who had become family.

He was home.

Epilogue

30th May, 1940
Dear Evelyn,
I hope you're having a better week than we are here.
It's been rather nonstop, and I'm exhausted. The war has
finally arrived, and we're right in the middle of it. I know I've
been complaining about not seeing Jerries, and now I realize just
how silly that was. All we see now are the enemy, and they are
much faster and more numerous than we ever dreamt.

We lost two pilots this week. One was another new
pilot officer, and the other was my flight leader. It doesn't seem to
matter if you're an experienced pilot or not up there. I'm
beginning to wonder if it's all just a matter of luck. It certainly
seems that way. At least, it was for me.

I was shot down yesterday. An Me 109 hit me in my
fuel tank. I was lucky enough to walk away with only a bump
on the head and dislocated shoulder. My luck continued and I
was able to catch a ride home with His Majesty's Royal Navy.
They dropped me in Kent and I took a few trains to get back to
my squadron. I've never been so happy to see the inside of a
London train station in all my life.

While I was on the grand tour, my squadron moved
stations again. I returned to a new airfield, a new Spitfire, and a
new position. It's now Flight Leader Lacey, at your service. It
seems that war is good for advancement, if nothing else. I think
I'd rather have Mother back, but since that's not an option, I'll
do my best to lead these ragamuffin pilots. I've no idea how I'll
do that, but I suppose I'll muddle my way through. If the doc
clears me to fly, I'll be back up tomorrow. I don't mind saying
that I'll be going back up with a rather large chip on my
shoulder. There's nothing quite like being shot down to put an
even larger fire in your belly.

CW Browning

There's so much I want to say, but it's late and I'm tired. I'll dream of you and pray that you're safe and well.

Always yours,

Flight Leader Miles Lacey

Author's Notes

1. **Pervitin.** In 1939, the pharmaceutical company Temmler in Berlin introduced a new drug. Briefly available to purchase over the counter, it was marketed to increase alertness and combat depression. It came to the attention of a German military doctor, who began testing it on students. He became convinced that the drug could ensure German victory in war. Soldiers who used Pervitin were capable of remaining awake for days while fighting and marching continuously. What was this miracle drug? It was methamphetamine, now commonly known as crystal meth, in tablet form. The German military quickly took Pervitin and ran with it, issuing it huge amounts to the soldiers and pilots of the German forces to keep them awake and alert. In April, 1940, over 35 million tables of Pervitin were sent to the front lines to fuel the Nazi's Blitzkrieg through the Ardennes and across France. The use of the drug continued throughout the war, issued alongside cigarettes and candy to Hitler's military forces. Known as 'tank chocolate' by the soldiers, and 'pilot's salt' by the pilots, the drug not only kept the men awake and alert for hours or days, it also induced a euphoric state in which the horrors of war had no effect on them. As such, it really did create 'super soldiers.' The use of Pervitin continued beyond the way, despite the obvious side effects. In fact, it continued to be included in the medical arsenal of the German armies of both East and West Germany up until the late 1970s. (The Atlantic: https://www.theatlantic.com/technology/archive/2013/05/pilots-salt-the-third-reich-kept-its-soldiers-alert-with-meth/276429/) (History.com: https://www.history.com/news/inside-the-drug-use-that-fueled-nazi-germany)

2. **Luftwaffe Attacks on Civilians**. This is a matter of continual debate. Did the Luftwaffe pilots attack the columns of refugees on the roads from Paris in 1940? The answer is yes, but it isn't as clear as it seems. The speed of the German advance had thrown Allied troops into chaos, and retreat. As many divisions were retreating, and others were moving up from the south to reinforce those pulling back to

protect Paris and the port cities, all the troops were using the same roads as the refugees. The sheer number of refugees hampered troop movements. This is a well-documented fact. Therefore, the argument can be made that the Luftwaffe pilots were targeting soldiers, not civilians. That being said, there are any number of eye-witness accounts from both civilians and allied military personnel that confirm that at least some of the attacks were made on areas of roads where no allied troops were present. One such account was documented by an RAF fighter pilot, who famously went back to his squadron and said, "They really are shits." * He was speaking of the German pilots who carried out the orders to attack the roads and trains used by civilians. The pilots themselves were acting under orders from their high command to attack the roads and railway lines used by civilians. Their secondary objective was to disrupt movement of the allied troops and prevent them from reaching the front. Unfortunately, this often translated into hundreds of French refugees being slaughtered on their trek to safety. * (Fighter Aces of the RAF in the Battle of Britain, Philip Kaplan)

3. **Battle of Calais.** May 23-26, 1940. On May 22, a battle that would affect the outcome of Operation Dynamo, the evacuation of over 300,000 troops from Dunkirk, began. Boulogne and Calais were the main ports south of Dunkirk, and German Panzer divisions had been ordered to take both. Knowing the ports had to be defended, on May 22, the first waves of Calais Force, the troops who would defend Calais, arrived from England. They were joined by more troops on May 23. They arrived without knowing just how close the German Panzer divisions were, and were under orders to secure Calais and open supply lines with Dunkirk. By mid-morning on May 23, columns of German tanks from the 1st Panzer division were approaching from the southwest. The actual task of taking Calais was given to the 10th Panzer Division, but 1st Panzer Division was ordered to try to take Calais as they passed on their way to Dunkirk. After a skirmish in which they met fierce resistance from three English squadrons of tanks, the 1st Panzer Division continued on to Dunkirk, leaving Calais to the 10th Division. On May 24th, the battle for Calais began in earnest. Fighting ensued around the entire perimeter of the port city and, by 6pm, the Germans had broken through the outer perimeter. On May 25th, the Germans began a systematic attack on the inner perimeter. By mid-afternoon, Brigadier Nicholson, the commander of the Allied forces, was forced to move to the Citadel, where he would make his last stand. By On the same day, Boulogne fell to the south, leaving Calais as the

last remaining port city before Dunkirk. Winston Churchill, along with his war cabinet, realized that the troops defending Dunkirk needed more time to establish a perimeter that could withstand the Panzer Divisions, giving the British Expeditionary Force time to reach Dunkirk. Calais was successfully delaying an entire division from joining the battle for Dunkirk, and giving the troops time that they desperately needed to bridge the gap, set up a perimeter around Dunkirk, and reach the beaches. By the evening of the 25th, with the fall of Calais imminent, Churchill and two ranking members of the war cabinet were forced to make a decision. They decided not to evacuate the troops at Calais in order to give the troops at Dunkirk more time. Shortly before midnight, Nicholson received a telegram from the War Office in London: "Every hour you continue to exist is of the greatest help to the B.E.F. Government has therefore decided you must continue to fight. Have greatest possible admiration for your splendid stand. Evacuation will not (repeat not) take place…" It is not certain that Nicholson ever received the communication, but his troops did indeed continue to fight. They held the Citadel until 5pm the following day, when Nicholson was captured, and then continued to fight in the streets of the harbor, where they held on until 9pm.

- Brigadier Nicholson commanded the British troops along with 800 French soldiers, for a total of around 4,000 troops. The 10th Panzer Division, the German division given the task of taking Calais, contained over 15,000 men and at least 300 tanks. The battle raged for 3 days, involving Luftwaffe and RAF battles as well.
- After making the decision not to evacuate Calais, Churchill recorded feeling physically sick after making the first of many heartbreakingly hard decisions.
- The 3-day battle delayed the 10th Panzer Division long enough that Allied troops were able to secure a perimeter around Dunkirk, and hundreds of thousands of troops were able to reach the beaches in time for evacuation.

(The Second World War, Martin Gilbert, pp 75-76) (History of War: http://www.historyofwar.org/articles/siege_calais_1940.html) (HistoryNet.com: https://www.historynet.com/world-war-ii-defending-calais.htm)

4. **HMS Grafton**. *HMS Grafton* was a G-class destroyer that was part of Operation Dynamo. On May 29, 1940, she had just picked up 800 troops from Dunkirk when another destroyer, HMS Wakefield, was hit

by a torpedo from the German Schnellboot *S-30* (Zimmerman). *HMS Grafton* joined other vessels in searching for survivors, unaware that the German submarine, U-62, was nearby. At 2:50am, U-62 fired a torpedo into the wardroom of *HMS Grafton*, killing 35 officers. A second hit followed. In total, 16 crew members were killed, including the Captain, in addition to the 35 army officers. The remaining 750 troops rescued from Dunkirk and 130 crew members were successfully rescued by a ferry, *Malines*, before *HMS Ivanhoe* successfully scuttled what remained of the Grafton.

- The real attack on *HMS Grafton* took place at 2:50am. I changed the timing, and therefore the manner, of the sinking for the purposes of dramatic representation in this book. By moving it to mid-afternoon, I had to remove the threat of U-boats, as at that point in the war, they operated primarily under cover of darkness.
- On May 29th, the Royal navy lost 3 of her modern destroyers in Operation Dynamo: *HMS Grafton, HMS Grenade*, and *HMS Wakeful*. It also lost *HMS Waverly*, a paddle steamer that was converted into a mine sweeper. The total casualties from these 4 ships were over 1,000 men. However, the total number of troops evacuated from Dunkirk that day totaled 47,310.
- Following the losses on May 29th, the British Admiralty ordered all modern destroyers out of the evacuation. They left 18 older destroyers to continue the operation.

(The Second World War, Martin Gilbert, pp 78-81) (U-boat.net: https://uboat.net/allies/merchants/ship/328.html) (Dunkirk1940.org: http://dunkirk1940.org/index.php?&p=1_249; http://dunkirk1940.org/index.php?p=1_306) (naval-history.net: https://www.naval-history.net/xGM-Chrono-10DD-25G-HMS_Grafton.htm)

5. **Cigarette Dispenser at Dunkirk**. While hundreds of thousands of troops were converging on the beach at Dunkirk, forming orderly columns in the sand and wading out into the Channel, waiting for the opportunity to evacuate, there was one bright spot. Some enterprising soldier had somehow secured an unlimited supply of Craven A cigarettes from an unknown source. On the 29th of May, he was careening up and down the beach and the lines of troops in a truck, tossing cartons of cigarettes out to the waiting troops. According to the first-hand account of an RAF fighter pilot on the beach at the time, he

was yelling out, "Here we are lads! All free and with the compliments of NAAFI. Take your pick!" While spirit of the "Tommy" was severely dampened by the defeat in France, this one incident proved that it was not dead. I couldn't resist including the incident in this book because it's one of those amazing details that I feel demands to be shared. It shows that these were men, just ordinary men, who were called to extraordinary things, and yet who were determined to help each other's spirits even in the face of the impossible. (Fighter Aces of the RAF in the Battle of Britain, Philip Kaplan, p. 18)

6. **Evacuation of Dunkirk by the Numbers**. On May 26, 1940, Winston Churchill authorized Operation Dynamo – the evacuation of the Allied troops from Dunkirk. On that day, he and his war cabinet expected that they would have a maximum of 2 days to carry out the evacuation before the German forces broke through, and estimated that they would be able to save 45,000 troops in that time. In fact, the resolve and bravery of the troops defending the outer perimeter of Dunkirk allowed what has become known as The Miracle at Dunkirk.

- # of days: 9
- # of ships involved: Over 930, 850 of which were privately-owned vessels.
- # of ships sunk: 226. Of these, 6 British and 3 French destroyers were lost. Of the 226, 170 were privately-owned vessels.
- # of RAF Fighter Command planes lost: 106
- # of RAF Pilots lost: 87
- # of troops killed/captured: Over 62,000 (Estimate. Actual number will never be known)
- # of troops evacuated: 338,226

(The Second World War, Martin Gilbert, pp 75-84) (RAFBF.org: https://www.rafbf.org/news-and-blogs/rafs-hard-battle-support-evacuation-troops-dunkirk) (RAFMuseum.org: https://www.rafmuseum.org.uk/blog/the-rafs-role-in-the-evacuation-of-dunkirk/) (Wikipedia: https://en.wikipedia.org/wiki/Dunkirk_evacuation)

7. **RAF Over Dunkirk.** During and after the war, there was a common misconception among the army that the RAF had done

nothing to aid in the evacuation at Dunkirk. While the idea seems ridiculous, the fact is that the men on the beaches and in the town couldn't see the fighter planes above. Apart from two days, low clouds obscured the view of the men on the ground. In addition, when the skies were clear, many of the battles in the air took place away from the actual beaches as the Luftwaffe were intercepted on their way *to* the beach. This was because Fighter Command flew their patrols along two patrol lines, one from Gravelines to Furnes, and the other further inland from Dunkirk to St Omer and Furnes St Omer. These deeper patrol lines were not visible from the beaches or the town. And so the misconception was that they were not there at all. However, they most certainly were. Over the 9 days of the evacuation, the RAF flew 2,739 fighter sorties, 651 bombing raids, and 171 reconnaissance flights. They lost 177 aircraft, 106 of which were fighters. 432 combined Hurricanes and Spitfires took part for a total of 4,822 hours of flying time. German aircraft losses totaled an estimated 402 planes. When looked at in this light, the RAF played a huge part in enabling 338,000 troops to be evacuated from Dunkirk.

- Dunkirk brought the total of fighter lost in the whole Battle of France to 250 fighters. This reduced the strength of Fighter Command to 570 operational fighters: 280 Spitfires and 290 Hurricanes. This meant that when Operation Dynamo ended on June 4, the RAF was looking forward to the Battle of Britain with only 570 fighter planes. The German Luftwaffe had over 1,000. While the men on the ground may have thought the RAF was not taking part, they were, in fact, losing precious planes and pilots that they could not afford to lose in their effort to lend air support to the evacuation.

(The Battle of Britain, Richard Hough and Denis Richards, pp 98-104) (RAFBF.org: https://www.rafbf.org/news-and-blogs/rafs-hard-battle-support-evacuation-troops-dunkirk) (RAFMuseum.org: https://www.rafmuseum.org.uk/blog/the-rafs-role-in-the-evacuation-of-dunkirk/) (airuniversity.af.edu: https://www.airuniversity.af.edu/AUPress/Book-Reviews/Display/Article/1994949/air-battle-for-dunkirk-26-may3-june-1940/) (The National Archives: https://blog.nationalarchives.gov.uk/miracles-and-myths-the-dunkirk-evacuation-part-1-where-was-the-raf/)

8. **Letters in Wartime**. As we progress further along in the war, I

think it's only right to address the issue of letters in wartime England. Throughout the books in this series, and moving forward, the use of letters between Miles and Evelyn is my literary way of portraying how their relationship is maintained, and how it will grow through the very difficult years ahead. This was a writing decision I made before ever beginning the series. However, as the information that is discussed grows more and more classified in nature as the war continues, it's worth noting that most of it would never have made it past the censors. All letters written by the military were opened, photocopied, and then redacted before being sent on to their intended recipients. The originals were, presumably, destroyed. This was done by the military personnel. The armed forces also did not use the regular postal service in Britain, but had their own delivery service. Civilian mail was also heavily censored. As a result, anything that could give away military positions, names, or strategy would have been redacted and/or destroyed. Photos were often removed and destroyed if they had something in them that could be considered useful in aiding the enemy. And so, as we move along in Evelyn and Miles' adventures, please keep in mind that the letters are intended to be more of an embellishment, rather than an accurate representation of just what their letters would have been.

Other Titles in the Shadows of War Series by CW Browning:

The Courier

The Oslo Affair

Night Falls in Norway

The Iron Storm

When Wolves Gather

Other Titles by CW Browning:

Next Exit, Three Miles (Exit Series #1)

Next Exit, Pay Toll (Exit Series #2)

Next Exit, Dead Ahead (Exit Series #3)

Next Exit, Quarter Mile (Exit Series #4)

Next Exit, Use Caution (Exit Series #5)

Next Exit, One Way (Exit Series #6)

Next Exit, No Outlet (Exit Series #7)

The Cuban (After the Exit #1)

Games of Deceit (Kai Corbyn Series #1)

Close Target (Kai Corbyn Series #2)

About the Author

CW Browning was writing before she could spell. Making up stories with her childhood best friend in the backyard in Olathe, Kansas, imagination ran wild from the very beginning. At the age of eight, she printed out her first full-length novel on a dot-matrix printer. All eighteen chapters of it. Through the years, the writing took a backseat to the mechanics of life as she pursued other avenues of interest. Those mechanics, however, have a great way of underlining what truly lifts a spirt and makes the soul sing. After attending Rutgers University and studying History, her love for writing was rekindled. It became apparent where her heart lay. Picking up an old manuscript, she dusted it off and went back to what made her whole. CW still makes up stories in her backyard, but now she crafts them for her readers to enjoy. She makes her home in Southern New Jersey, where she loves to grill steak and sip red wine on the patio.

Visit her at: www.cwbrowning.com
Also find her on Facebook, Instagram and Twitter!